FROM BURNING ASHES

THE COLLECTOR SERIES BOOK 4

STACEY MARIE BROWN

ALSO BY STACEY MARIE BROWN

Dedicated to my amazing readers:
Sorry about all the cliff-hangers and emotional turmoil
I put you through.
Hahaha.

No, I'm not!
I'm evil and enjoy every moment!
Thank you for putting up with me.

Love you awesome nerds.

TABLE OF CONTENTS

PROLOGUE

He was going to kill me. It was exactly what I asked him to do, but I was no longer willing to go. Instinct to survive was ingrained deep, and when it came down to the moment, I fought. For myself. For him. For Lexie, Sprig, Croygen, Daniel... for the girl who was still trapped in Duc's warehouse being used as an escort. For all the lives Rapava was destroying or would.

A heaviness gripped my brain, tugging sleepiness into my mind. My sight drifted down a dark ravine into blackness. I didn't want to go out this way. If I were going to die, I wanted to be far away from DMG, where I knew my loved ones would be safe. Anger punched my abdomen. All Ryker and I had been through, the love we finally found and let in and this was how our story would end?

It felt life was mocking me again. Daniel's death had been horrible, but this was vindictive and cruel. Memories of Ryker and me flashed in my head, our bodies intertwined, discovering each other. The moment by the creek in Peru where he told me about his past, when I realized I was falling for him. The night he curled up behind me because I had a bad dream. When he kissed me in the rain... the night he snuck into the closet while Amara was across the hall. Putting a birthday candle in the loaf of bread for me. Every moment played out in my head with the man I fell for.

I held no blame or anger at Ryker as I felt my life slip from me. This was my doing. The only fury I could feel was at myself, for forcing him to do this, something he would have to live with.

I think we all wish for that epic ending, where everything is resolved and our death would have meaning. This was not the case. A tear slipped down my face. A sorrow for what could have been. The loss of hope and happiness.

And because my love wasn't strong enough. This time we couldn't fight and win.

I had lost.

Everything.

Not something I was good at.

I heard a strange pop as my life slipped across the divide into nothingness.

ONE

I could feel it the moment it happened—the instant my lungs gave up the struggle, burning with a blistering fire, clinging to the last bits of oxygen. In usual Zoey style, I didn't slip peacefully into the quiet darkness.

No. Of course not. Far too easy.

Electrical charges burst through my muscles, sizzling in my veins, and inflicted excruciating agony down every tendon. I had experienced a lot of pain in my time, but this felt as if my soul were being seared and torn from my body.

Death was a bitch.

My ears filled with bellows of pain, sounding more like a lion's roar. *Am I doing that? Can someone dead make those sounds?* The aching grew more intense. Penetrating and cruel. I wished for it to end.

The inferno moved through me, torching out the last trace of life. Death finally claimed me, wrapped me up in its arms and took me away, leaving my shell behind.

Finally.

Peace.

But even in my demise, I didn't do things like normal people.

The quiet blackness only lasted a moment before the electricity clustered together in a huddle, striking lightning at my lifeless heart. Agony reached up and plucked me from oblivion and shoved me back in my body. My lids and mouth opened and I gasped, sucking in a mass of air, which scorched my lungs. The torment stayed locked in my throat, but the anguish filled my mind and soul with a shattering scream.

Then with a pop, it released, my muscles going limp. It took me a few moments to comprehend objects around me. My brain started out simple: Ceiling. Floor. Me.

Movement tugged at the corner of my eye, pulling my attention to the two massive bodies sliding across the floor, slamming into a wall.

I watched them. Every breath was painful, spurring a coughing fit. But air felt good rushing back in, filling my lungs, returning my senses.

The figures moved violently around me, my ears full of the loud grunts and exhales. A stunning, dark-haired man moved into my view. He had almond-shaped eyes, high cheekbones, and a lean, built body. A trickle of blood dribbled down his cut lip as he leaped at another figure.

Croygen! My brain registered the man, his fist slamming into the other huge guy below. I struggled to sit up. My throat ached as coughs and breath fought to get in and out.

A growl erupted from the man under Croygen, and it was like someone flicked on the light, pouring memories back into my head.

Ryker.

Oath.

My brain scrambled to try and make sense of what happened. How did Croygen get in here? Where was my sister? Why didn't he just run for it like I asked? Why did he come back?

Slowly, I pushed myself up and stood, the room spinning. I gritted my teeth, trying to stay upright. The space echoed with the sounds of skin and bone crashing into each other as Ryker and Croygen rolled and punched one another.

Ryker grunted, his white eyes unfocused, confused, and glowing bright. He pushed Croygen off and struggled to his feet, his arms up in defense. Or offense. It was hard to tell. His shoulders expanded, filling the room with the threat of an impending attack, but then he retreated from us.

"Zoey, get back!" Croygen shouted, jumping between us. "Listen to me, Wanderer. You make one move toward her and I will destroy you. Because if you kill her, you kill me, and I like myself far too much for that."

Without the power of the oath controlling Ryker, he would never hurt me. I had forced him into the vow. At the time I thought there might be a chance I was dying, and if he didn't kill me himself, he most definitely would have died. I also knew the oath would connect us. He would be able to find me. This all happened before I knew where I was going and the danger of him coming after me.

But Ryker *had* killed me. I *had* died. It remained the one thing I was sure about. Deep in my soul I felt the bond connecting us had been severed.

"You are stronger than this." Croygen moved and blocked Ryker's direct line to me. "Believe me, you are the most stubborn ass. You can fight it."

Ryker's eyes locked on Croygen with wildness. He looked around confused and scared. His bare shoulders rose up and down with his staggered breaths. He wore only gray scrub pants, his powerful torso heaving in and out, drawing my attention.

I stared at the wounds, at what used to be gashes. The deep cuts I had created across his stomach and chest, only hours before, were no longer oozing. They had closed and looked like day-old wounds.

It was all the confirmation I needed.

"Ryker?" My scratchy voice wavered, my hand still protectively around my neck. He froze at my voice, but his eyes stayed on Croygen.

"What are you doing?" Croygen hissed at me.

"Trust me." I swallowed and inched closer to the Wanderer. "Ryker, look at me."

Ryker's chin twitched, but he didn't glance over.

"Zoey…?" Croygen tried to move in front of me, but I sidestepped him, letting Ryker see me.

"Look at me, Viking," I tried to demand, but my voice barely formed the words.

"Zoey, no." The pirate reached for me.

"He's okay. The oath is broken."

"What? How?" Croygen sputtered.

"Because he killed me."

"No. I saved you." Croygen shook his head. "I felt it."

"Not before I died," I responded but kept my gaze on Ryker.

"You look pretty good for a dead girl."

"I don't know how it all works. Maybe it was long enough to break the curse. He has his magic back." I motioned to his healing wounds. There should have been an emptiness inside me, though, a giant hole where his powers used to be, but I sensed no change, even though I knew they must be gone. "I felt his powers leave me." I took a timid step closer to Ryker, holding up my hand. He growled like a cornered animal. "You're okay. We're not going to hurt you. We're your friends."

Ryker shifted his weight, his gaze finally roaming over me, fastening on mine. His eyes dropped down to my neck, then back to my face. A grunt rolled from his gut, and he blinked a few times. The vague clouds dissolved in his eyes, filling with recognition. The tension crowding the room deflated along with the muscles curling his neck. He licked his lips.

"Zoey?" he muttered.

"Viking." I took another stride toward him.

"Don't." He jerked back with a growl. "It's still there."

"What?" I stopped so suddenly I rocked back on my feet.

"I can feel it." He pushed himself against the wall. "Less now but still there."

"I... no. It broke. I felt it," I exclaimed.

"I have a plan." Croygen held up his palm. "How about we get out of here first? *Then* we can get drunk and converse about all our crazy, hysterical theories."

Croygen was right. All this could wait. Now wasn't the time.

"Where are my sister and Sprig?" I twisted toward Croygen.

Croygen motioned through the window. Sprig sat on top of a blanket wrapped around my unconscious sister. Sprig held his tail, stroking it nervously.

"We have to go."

"Like I said." He rolled his eyes.

"My axe." Ryker's voice sounded deep and unemotional.

"Good luck finding it." Croygen headed for the door.

"My axe," Ryker rumbled, pushing off the wall, following us. "I'm not leaving without it."

"Viking!" Sprig's voice squeaked as Ryker stepped into the outer room. He ran up to Ryker's feet. The Wanderer didn't say anything but leaned down and picked him up, giving his head a rub before putting him on his shoulder. "I know you've missed me." Sprig snuggled into Ryker, happiness widening his smile.

7

"I actually did," Ryker mumbled and shot me a look again. The instant his eyes settled on me, his pupils flickered with a cold, angry expression. His chest puffed, and he turned his head away. He sucked in a strangled breath, putting more distance between us. A battle waged inside him.

"Keep her away from me," Ryker growled at Croygen.

"No." I stepped to him, causing him to backpedal.

"Stay back, Zoey!" He held up his hand. "The oath is still there."

"Zoey." Croygen motioned me over to him. "Get behind me."

"No!" I exclaimed. "I am not afraid of you, Ryker."

"I still might *kill* you, Zoey."

"No. You won't." I shook my head.

"How are you so sure?" he seethed.

"Because you already did." My eyes narrowed.

Ryker turned away from me. "Escape while you can. I'll cause a distraction."

"What? No!" I cried. Sprig straightened, his smile dropping.

"No way. We didn't come all the way down here to leave you." Croygen shook his head.

"I don't give a shit. I am not safe. It's better if I stay locked up here."

"Are you pooping out your brain again, Viking?" Sprig peered into the Wanderer's ear. "Did it turn to mush in there?"

"Absolutely not, Ryker." Croygen and I spoke at the same time. There was no way I would leave without him again.

"Oh, mush... with sugar and honey."

"I don't trust myself. What I've already done..." Ryker rubbed at his head.

"Or honey with a little mush on top?" Sprig chattered.

Croygen glanced over at me. I could feel his questioning stare, but my focus locked on Ryker's back.

"Fuck you," I spat. Ryker jerked his head over his shoulder.

"Excuse me?"

"Fuck. You."

He turned to fully face me.

"You think you're being noble? That sacrificing yourself for me is the right thing?"

Irritation and confusion flickered over Ryker's face. "I am not going to fight about this with you. You're going."

Fury slammed into me, pushing my legs forward until I stood in front of him. "You selfish bastard. If you think you are taking the high road here, let me tell you... You. Are. Not."

Ryker's bewilderment only deepened, his eyes pinching in the corners. He glanced over at Croygen for help who only offered a shrug in return.

I shoved at his chest, bringing his attention back to me. "You are not going to do this to me. Not after what we've done to get you."

Ryker's face flushed scarlet. "*To* you? I am doing this *for* you."

"No, you're not!" I clenched my palms into fists.

"What the hell? I'm trying to save your life, Zoey." He gritted his teeth.

"Well, stop."

"Okay, human. You are not making any sense." He leaned in, getting into my face. "I still feel the oath. It's not as strong, but it's there. I could hurt you again. Do you realize that?"

"Yes."

"Do you want to die?"

"No."

He threw back his head, his arms flailing at his side. "Then why are you arguing with me?"

"Because..." I shifted awkwardly. I took a deep breath and looked into his face. "We are survivors. We fight. We live. No matter what it takes, it's who we are. We don't let things beat us: DMG, an oath, Vadik. You and I are a team, and we will fight against whatever comes our way. Good or bad, we claw, bite, and battle our way out." I moved to him, and he went rigid. "And don't assume I will be so easy to kill, Viking. I came back this last time. Remember I'm the Avenging Angel," I whispered hoarsely. "Okay?"

He waited a beat before nodding. He remained distant, keeping a wall between us, but at least he agreed.

"Wow. This is better than a Spanish soap opera." Sprig peered down from Ryker's shoulder. "Does this make anyone else hungry for a snack?"

Ryker actually snorted. "Some things never change."

"Can we get out of here now?" Croygen started toward my sister. "Seriously, we've wasted too much time."

"Still need to find my axe."

"Really? I think getting out of here is the first priority."

"I agree. We have no idea where they put it." I reached for Sprig. He leaped to my shoulder, crawling under my hair.

"I can feel it call to me." Ryker grabbed the blood-coated scrub shirt on the table, slipping it on. "Just need to be close enough to know its exact location."

"Come on." Croygen bent over and lifted Lexie into his arms, pressing her to his chest.

"You need to be silent, okay?" I whispered to Sprig. He nodded in agreement, holding on to chunks of my loose strands.

10

Ryker and I followed Croygen out. Nerves flittered all over me.

"Okay. Let's do this." Croygen winked at me. Ahead of us lay the impossible, and we had no choice but to bulldoze straight into it.

Sink or swim.

Into a tank full of sharks and other deadly predators.

TWO

The hallway was quiet other than the chirping of computer noises and a low hum of electricity. It had only been fifteen minutes since I came down this hall for Ryker, but it felt like hours. The stillness unnerved me more than if a wall of men awaited us.

Rapava had always been a step ahead. Even when Croygen and I snuck down here the first time, I somehow sensed that he'd missed none of my movements. I shoved down my anxiety as we slunk through the passage, the elevator in sight. We were only halfway when a chill latched on to my ankle and walked itself up to my neck, plopping itself down next to Sprig.

I twisted to look behind me. No one except for Ryker and Croygen in the shadows. Apprehension wrapped itself around my throat like a scarf, strangling me till my skin prickled. Then a crackling sound came overhead. My insides ran icy with terror.

"Oh, Zoey. You have disappointed me greatly. Although I can't say I'm surprised." Rapava's accented voice filtered down from a speaker in the ceiling, stopping all of us in our tracks. "I am impressed with how far you have gotten on your own. Daniel taught you well."

My heart bucked against my ribs as I whirled around,

my gaze searching. He could see me. Where was he? Finally my eyes landed on the camera by the elevator. It pointed straight at me, a tiny red light on below it.

Oh hell. The cameras did work—when he wanted them to. At the time we came down here it had not been on, but it was operating now. How many times did I pass one with no knowledge that it was on? Watching. Spying.

"You are my test case for security. Every move you make only renders this place more of a fortress."

His words made me feel dirty. Used. What if this whole time he let me get away crawling in the rafters and vents only to point out their weaknesses?

All I could do was fight fire with fire. Fearful he could hear as well as see me, I kept my voice to a whisper. "Sprig, I need you to do your thing."

"Put the camera to sleep?" He stroked my earlobe like he was soothing it into slumber.

"Permanently," I murmured. "Stick to the darkness and move slowly. Rapava will be looking for you. Take the key card from my hip and have the elevator ready. And please be careful."

His arms stretched around my neck and hugged me before he used my ponytail to descend my back like a rock climber. He hit my waist, the plastic card scratching against my skin as he tugged it out, then he dropped to the ground.

"You are only harming your sister, Zoey," Rapava crooned. "She needs me. Needs to be here so she can continue to get better. And you are only inflicting more pain and torture for your accomplices." He kept talking. I focused my eyes on the camera but watched Sprig in my peripheral. He stayed against the wall trying to stay undetected, traveling slow as the darkness moved around him. He was so good a few times I lost sight of him. Right when he reached the base of the elevator, it dinged.

Oh. Hell. We had visitors.

The doors peeled apart.

Liam, Hugo, and Marv stood there, guns pointed at us. My old Collector family coming to capture their enemy. Me.

"Put your hands up." Liam took the lead, stepping out of the lift and heading for us.

"Kind of hard for me to do that," Croygen appeared from the shadows and replied derisively, tucking Lexie firmer against him.

"Put the girl down." Liam motioned with his gun to the ground.

Croygen hesitated, but with three guns pointed right at us, *fae* guns no less, he bent over, setting her on the corner of the intersection of hallways, her back propped against the wall.

"Take them to their new and much-improved holding cells," Rapava ordered over the speakers. "But if they cause any trouble, including Zoey, kill them."

My entire body tensed rigidly. The moment he locked us up in these new digs, we were done. There would be no chance of escape.

Ryker's skin moved over his flexing muscles, his eyes narrowing on Liam.

"Oh please, give me a reason to shoot you." Liam directed his gun at Ryker. "I only need one."

Something showed in Liam's crimped expression I had never seen before. Fear. Ryker was stronger, bigger, faster, and a better fighter than Liam could ever wish to be. Liam had always been insecure around Daniel, but with Ryker he was petrified.

Marv and Hugo kept their weapons aimed at us,

scouring us with hostile frowns. At one time their disgusted, hateful looks would have upset me. Not anymore.

"Now, let's be good little fae and head back to the room." Liam pressed his barrel into the Wanderer. A deep threat ebbed out of Ryker's throat. Liam clicked back the hammer, his chin shoving up high, trying to look tough. "Last warning, asshole. Now move!"

With one quick stride, Marv grabbed my bicep and twisted me toward another hallway. I glanced over my shoulder to see Sprig crawl under the lens of the camera. His tiny, deft fingers clutched at the wires and pulled. A spark zapped the air. The camera's light blinked out. With another shove the camera toppled to the tile with a crack.

Everyone swung around. It was our only opportunity. Big Brother was no longer watching.

My boys did not need any prompting. Croygen and Ryker struck out at their captors.

My elbow went back into Marv's ribs before my ankle curled around his and yanked. As he stumbled, I swung around, my fist meeting his ear when he twisted away. His hand dove into my gut. Biting back the pain, I gripped his wrist and rotated my body till he stood behind me, his arm bent the wrong way. I flipped him over on his back and kicked the gun out of his hand. It hit the floor and glided far down the hallway, skating over the tile, out of his reach, but out of mine too.

Shit.

"Zoey!" Croygen yelled. I spun, instantly following his voice. Even though the three Collectors lay on the ground, they were already scrambling back to their feet, reaching for their guns. Ryker, Croygen, and I just made it back to the hallway where we had left Lexie, diving behind the wall, when the gunshots rang out.

15

The elevator was so close, but it was like walking a bridge with no cover. We might as well have been wearing shirts with huge neon targets on the backs. And they had guns. Ryker only managed to get the dart gun from Liam.

"You are a fool. You just sealed your fate, bitch," Liam snarled from around the corner.

I ignored his taunts, my attention on Ryker. He stared across the gulf to where the hallway continued its path.

"My axe... it's down there." He took a step, his bare feet set firmly, like nothing in the world could stop him.

"Ryker." I grabbed for him just as a bullet zigged past him, nicking a hole in his scrubs. I shrieked, yanking him back. "What are you doing?"

"Getting it." He jerked away.

I tried to grab him again, but he shoved me to the side.

"The axe is down here. I can feel it calling me." He clenched his jaw, moving again. "I'm not leaving it here."

"Don't be an idiot." Croygen stepped around me and rammed him back against the wall. "You want to risk your life? Fine. But you know Zoey won't leave here without you. Believe me, I've tried to get her to. No matter how much of an asshole you are, don't risk her life, too. Not for an axe." He rammed Ryker again.

The clips of soles heading in our direction echoed down the hall. "We have to go now." Croygen reached down for Lexie. For one second I saw her lids lift, a tiny smile ghosting on her features, before they fluttered closed.

"You don't understand. You don't have a connection to your sword."

Croygen glared at him. "I understand being connected to things more than you know."

The elevator dinged, and the doors opened. Sprig twittered excitedly for us, wiggling the key card in his hand.

16

We only had a short way to go before we would reach the lift. Our only way out.

"Get that little freak," Liam called to Marv and Hugo.

A tranquilizer dart shot down the hall and burrowed into Sprig's chest. He made a squeak and looked down at the object digging into his skin. "Whoa... that feels like I just stepped into a tub of warm honey. My butt tingles. So do my nuts..." He tipped over, crumpling onto the ground, the card falling out of his hands.

"No!" I lurched forward, but hands grabbed me, holding me in place. I turned to see Ryker; his eyes closed as if he struggled being this close to me. He quickly let go at the sound of boots shuffling toward us.

"You guys run for the elevator. I'll cover you." He gripped the dart gun. As they came around the corner for us, Ryker stepped out, elbowing Hugo in the face with a crack. Hugo's body flew back into Marv, knocking them both down. Marv untangled himself and came barreling for Ryker.

My shoe hit his face with a resounding crunch, and he fell back onto the ground.

"Go!" Ryker ordered as his finger pulled back the trigger. It shot toward its intended. Liam roared with fury, tugging the dart quickly out of his arm. It gave us just enough time to run.

With Lexie in his arms, Croygen took off for the elevator. I bolted for Sprig, scooping him up in my hands, tugging out the dart. His mouth opened, soft snores sluggishly coming from him.

"Hurry!" Croygen pounded a finger into the door's close button.

I looked up to see Ryker standing in the middle of the hallway, staring down the path.

"Ryker, come on!" I screamed.

17

Torment flashed across his face as he looked at me then the men blocking his way. The agony of leaving his axe tore at him. It was as much part of him as his arm, but I'd rather have him armless than dead.

Bullets zipped past him as Hugo got back on his feet. It would only take one.

"Ryker!" My soul slashed up out of my throat.

He hesitated one more moment, blurted an anguished cry, and then turned, running for me. He slipped next to Croygen in the elevator.

The doors shifted closed.

I grabbed the key card, shoved it in my hip pocket, and bounded for them.

I took one second too long.

A form slammed into my back. In my forward lurch, Sprig flew from my grasp, his body rolling into the corner of the lift. I fell face-first halfway into the elevator, cracking my chin on the floor. Ryker quickly seized under my arms and slid me forward as Liam grabbed my boot, wrapping his hands around my leg. He yanked on my heel, pulling my leg out of the shutting doors.

I normally would have kicked it off, leaving him with my shoe, like Cinderella, slipping away into the night with my faithful mice and hound. But I couldn't. This boot was no ordinary glass slipper. It held the power of the world and destruction and death in it. I wouldn't let it slide off my foot and let the Stone of Destiny fall into Rapava's hands.

I grunted, flipping over, and kicked at Liam's fingers. Ryker kept tugging me, pulling me backward. The motion parting me with my shoe.

"Let go." I wiggled out of Ryker's grasp. The doors banged against my knees, trying to seal. I shuffled forward and pushed my foot deeper into the boot. Liam's lids were

18

half-mast, the drug kicking in, but he held on with all he had left. I crossed my other leg over and slammed the heel of my boot into his face. Blood burst from his nose, and he loosened his grip on me. I yanked my foot back, scrambling back into the wall. The doors slid shut.

During a moment of quiet, only our breaths could be heard.

"You really like those shoes." Croygen broke the silence, his eyebrows lifted in amusement, adjusting Lexie in his arms.

"Yeah. They're my favorite pair." I shrugged and got to my feet, snatching Sprig on the way up. "They are also my only ones."

Croygen and Ryker knew perfectly well why I fought so hard. The Lia Fáil, the extremely powerful, mythological Stone of Destiny, lay unceremoniously in the heel of my boot.

So many enemies had come after us for the gray rock, and they'd stop at nothing to get it. Especially Vadik. Ryker had put it there when we were in Peru, knowing if he were caught, they would search him. It had a chance to stay undiscovered with me.

Vadik, that evil son-of-a-bitch demon, was Ryker's father. It turned out Ryker was part demon. Only twenty minutes earlier he had told me this while trying to kill me. My mind still struggled to accept this news. I couldn't fathom how Ryker was taking it.

Focus, Zoey. You can think about that later.

The elevator shot up, passing each floor. *Almost there. Almost there.* I bobbed on my feet nervously. I should have known it was too easy.

The elevator dinged, alerting us we were arriving at level two, when an intense grinding sound clanged above us. The box came to a sudden rattling halt.

"That's probably not a good thing, huh?" Croygen glanced at Ryker and me.

I swallowed and set Sprig on Lexie's chest. My free hands investigated every elevator button, searching for any kind of override switch. Of course Rapava would have complete control of the elevator system, just in case a situation like this presented itself. "We need to get out now. The stairs out to street level don't go below level two."

"But there are six more levels down." Croygen secured Lexie higher in his arms, rustling Sprig.

"I don't know where those stairs are. Did you ever see any on the floor they kept us on?"

"No." A hint of panic coated Croygen tone. "I didn't."

"The top two levels of DMG are for the hunters, offices, and government-approved testing labs. Everything below those floors is hidden from the world, probably even from parts of the government itself. He doesn't want to make it easy for anything locked up below those levels to escape." I ran my hands along every panel, desperate for anything to help us. I knew what was coming, and it didn't take long before my fears were confirmed.

The elevator gave an abrupt jerk, my stomach slipping down to my feet. *Shit!* Ryker and I both flew for the doors, digging our fingers in the space to pry them apart.

Frantic terror ripped through my body as the doors fought against us, stealing the last seconds we had to get free. Finally with a grunt from Ryker, the doors gave, opening to another pair of doors, a number two painted on them. Instantly, Ryker and I began to tear into them, separating them enough to fit through.

The elevator jolted again, this time lurching us down, dragging us back to the depths of hell.

"Croygen, go!" I screamed.

Croygen tossed Lexie into Ryker's arms and took a running start, the second-level opening starting to shrink. He got through and spun, motioning for Lexie. "Hand her to me!"

Ryker offered Lexie and Sprig to Croygen in a blink of an eye. The opening thinned, collapsing with every second. I could barely breathe. Croygen was not gentle as he yanked Lexie and Sprig, her head scraping the top of the elevator as we continued to plunge.

I didn't even have time to feel relief as her body slipped through the tiny gap before Ryker turned to me. He grabbed my legs, lifting me to the ceiling.

"There should be some kind of emergency exit. It's probably locked, but you can break it open!" His hold on me tightened as he shoved me higher up. With his momentum and my adrenaline, it took me only two hits to pop open the lock and shove off the cover. I pulled myself up on top of the box.

"Go. Use the cables attached to the elevator and climb up." He pointed at the pulley running the elevator up and down.

"What about you?" I looked back down on him.

"Don't worry." His eyes darkened and his pupils became vacant. "I'm coming for you, human." He leaped up, his hands gripping the edge of the opening, starting to pull himself up.

I knew that look. From the guy who wanted to kill me. *Shit!*

Climbing a rope was one of the training exercises I hated most. I would have rather sparred or done pretty much anything else. Because of that, Daniel made me do it all the time. I caught on quick. Right then I had to admit to being glad he forced me do it so often.

21

Every Collector in this place, along with an enraged Viking, was up my ass. His eyes were set on me with determination as he tugged himself through the opening and latched on to the pulley.

"When I get my hands around your neck this time, no one will be around to save you."

Sweat trickled down my face, my arms shaking as I heaved myself higher. The second-level opening still remained over a floor away.

My smaller frame gave me speed, but Ryker's arm strength outperformed me. He rapidly gained on me, rage radiating from his eyes and coiled muscles.

"Come here, little human." His fingers wrapped around my ankle, tugging me down.

"Ryker, stop." My arms trembled violently, trying to pull myself away from him.

"I'll stop when you're dead." He yanked at my leg again. I squirmed to free myself from his grasp, but he held on. I bit down on my lip and did the only thing I knew to do. It had worked with Liam. With as much energy as I could muster, I slammed my heel into his forehead. A burst of energy exploded inside me and down my leg.

Wanderer. The stone's voice sounded like a harsh shove. Ryker's neck snapped back, his body sliding a few feet down the rope. *She is mine.*

Ryker's white-blue eyes blinked, and within them I saw the man I knew. He swore, turning his head away with guilt.

Wow. The stone wanted to protect me. That was interesting.

"Come on. We don't have time for awkward apologies." I continued up the rope, and the second floor came into view. Croygen was gone. Hopefully hiding or well on his way out.

Ryker moved quickly behind me, swinging the rope till

I got close enough to jump. The edge of the floor crushed into my ribs as my fingers scrabbled on the tile for purchase. I grunted, forcing my knees up enough to push myself to my feet.

Ryker leaped and moaned in pain when his legs bashed into the ledge.

"Serves you right." I leaned down to grab his arms.

"Don't." He hissed through his teeth. "Don't touch me."

The quick stab of rejection stung, but I swung around searching for signs of Croygen.

"They're on level two! Near the north elevator," a man's voice barked from the maze of hallways. "Orders are shoot to kill. Except her. The doctor wants to keep her alive."

I'd rather they just kill me.

Ryker tapped my arm and ran down the corridor. Toward the voices. His gaze narrowed on an open corner room.

I ran after him. Sometimes the best escape was letting them pass you. We slipped into the room. Ryker shut the door, leaving a sliver to watch through.

"If you keep sneaking into my room," a voice whispered from behind, lips nipping at my ear, "your boyfriend's going to get the wrong idea."

"Holy shit." I spun around. The dark, almond-eyed bandit stood there with a smirk on his face. Lexie and Sprig lay on the open bed. "Don't do that." I smacked his chest.

"Shut up." Ryker glared at us before looking back out the gap, his muscles rigid. We were inches from being discovered.

"Doors are open, sir. They are somewhere on this level," a man's voice I didn't recognize spoke from right outside the room. My curiosity got the better of me. I knew all the Collectors' voices. I slipped soundlessly next to Ryker, peeking through the gap.

A man a few inches taller than me stood so close on the other side I could reach out and tap his shoulder. He appeared to be of Asian descent and someone I remembered seeing in the cafeteria on the lower level a few times. But he was a scientist. Why would he be in on the search?

A muffled voice over a walkie-talkie responded. I couldn't make out the words, but I recognized Rapava's evil tone.

"I promise, sir. They will not get past us. I have men stationed at every corner and entrance. If they are here, we'll find them." He put his hand on his hip, brushing back his lab coat. On his hip he had the government-issued guns: one dart, one fae-made.

When Ryker had kidnapped me the first time, stashing me away in a grungy hotel room, the FBI had come searching for Sprig and me. I understood Rapava had access to the FBI, if needed. I never realized he had people right on the premises, undercover. How naïve had I been?

A call from down the hallway took the scientist away from the door. Ryker shut and locked it, whirling around to me. "What the hell, Zoey? Did you know Rapava had undercover agents here?"

"I had no clue." I rubbed my head. "I knew he could call on the FBI in case of emergencies, but not that they were here, posing as doctors."

"He might be a doctor, but he's also been trained to be a soldier," Ryker responded curtly.

"How do you know?"

"I just know. I've been around for a long time. They hold themselves differently."

"And I can guarantee every man he has 'stationed'"— Croygen curled his fingers in quotes—"around this level is trained as well."

I shouldn't have been surprised. Rapava's paranoia about a fae attack had long been acute. I should have expected he would have more than just the Collectors trained for battle. How many men did he have here? How many on call? I realized now I'd never known the true depth of the secrets and lies to Rapava's scheming.

"What the hell are we going to do?" Croygen broke into my thoughts. "It's not going to take them long to find us. And we can't just stroll down the hall."

"No, we won't be using *those* passages, but..." My eyes drifted up.

Croygen followed my gaze. "Oh hell no."

"We have to."

"Are you kidding me?" Croygen exclaimed, knowing what I planned. We had done it plenty of times before. "Lexie's out cold and Ryker probably won't even fit in the openings."

"What choice do we have?"

Croygen opened his mouth and then shut it with a sigh.

"We drag Lexie and Sprig on a sheet behind, like a cart."

"And let me guess, I'm the horse?" Croygen rolled his eyes at us.

"More like a nag," Ryker muttered.

I grinned. "You do like the fillies."

Croygen glowered at both of us but shrugged. There was no other way.

"It won't lead us out or to the first floor, but it will get us closer to the stairs," I continued.

"Then we jump down and go kung fu on their asses and run out." Croygen put his hands on his hips.

"Exactly."

"Excellent plan, Zoey. Stellar, really," Croygen said dryly.

"I thought so."

We all knew it would be nowhere near simple, but time was running out and our window of surprise was shrinking to a sliver.

The vents squeaked with our weight, even though we spread out as far as we could. Ryker struggled to scrunch his shoulders narrow enough to writhe through the small space. Being the leader, I checked on our location status, while poor Croygen dragged Lexie and Sprig in the middle, and Ryker brought up the rear, staying as far from me as possible.

If Rapava was aware of my use of the vents, he had yet to block them, for which I felt grateful. I couldn't believe just a few hours ago Delaney had given me the code to get Ryker out. I had crawled up into these vents and set this whole plan in motion. The "borrowed" elevator card dug into my hip. If we did get out of here, I hoped neither Kate nor Delaney would be suspected of aiding us.

I slipped down onto the pipes and peeked through a panel. *Shit.* Rapava had this place a lot more secured and ready for an attack than I thought. Five men dressed like they were about to stop a deadly bank heist blocked the door to the stairs, primed and ready for action. Armed with bulletproof vests, walkie-talkies, helmets, each appeared to be prepared to shoot the fae guns they were holding, while automatics and stun guns hung from their belts.

With a sigh I set the board down lightly and twisted to face the guys with only my head poking into the vent. It was almost pitch dark, but I could just barely make out their outlines. "Good news. We're here. Bad news. There's the cast of *S.W.A.T.* team watching the stairs."

"Dammit," Croygen whispered.

"It's clear he has his own soldiers permanently stationed here, ready to go on a moment's notice." Ryker's quiet voice held a note of annoyance.

They'd probably been here the whole time, disguised as staff or kept hidden from view.

"Croygen, Ryker and I will take care of the men. You wait here. When they're dealt with, you bring Lexie down."

"Can I leave the rodent?"

I ignored Croygen's question. "You run up those stairs to the top level. I don't care whatever locks, alarms, or blockades are put between you and freedom, go through them. We are too close now. When you exit the door, there will be a tunnel. Go to the left and just run. The outside door is a block from there. "And if anything happens to me. You get out. Rapava wants me more than anyone."

"Zoey—"

"This is not up for debate. Not this time. You get my sister out of here," I growled. He should have been gone, far from here, but he came back for me. To save me. "Ryker, you ready?" I didn't wait for a response before I bent down. The vibration of someone landing behind me shook the metal.

"I'm with you, human." His deep voice snaked up through my hair to my ear. "Till the end."

"If you have the opportunity, you better run too."

"Not a chance." He stood so close I could feel his hot breath on my neck.

"Okay, on three." I leaned over, grabbing a ceiling panel.

"One," he said and jumped down.

"Fucking fae." I grumbled and dropped down after him. My feet hit the laminated flooring, ready to fight. Five men dressed in military garb stood sentinel in front of the stairs.

Ryker pounced on the one who went for his walkie-talkie. He twisted the soldier's neck so harshly it did a one-eighty, winding his spine like a clock. *Crack.* The Wanderer pushed the limp figure away, eager for the next.

The second man came for me, drawing a gun toward my head. I spun out of the line of fire, knocking his arms, rocking him to the side. He caught himself, volleying back, bashing the weapon into the side of my face. Blood instantly coursed down my cheek. *Bastard.* I grappled for the gun, latching on to the dangerous end and twisting it out of his grip. The moment it was in my hands, his fist crashed into my face, exploding pain through my temple, his fingers greedy to take it back. *Hell. No.* I twisted around as he struck my arms; the gun slid from my fingers and away from both of us. His eyes went to the weapon. I took the moment to strike him in the stomach, ramming his groin with my knee. He hit the floor as I swiped for his dart gun. *Click.* The tranquilizer flew from the gun and embedded itself deep in his heart.

The faster it got into this blood system, the better.

He gaped in surprise, looking at his chest then up at me before he fell over. Clearly, he wasn't expecting a girl my size to kick his ass so fast.

"They're here! Stairs on the east side," one of the guards yelled into his walkie-talkie. My fist came around, plowing into the soft part of his throat. He bent over, gasping and choking. I swung my elbow up, sending it crashing down into his upper back as my knee jammed up into his face, snapping his nose against my thigh. He dropped hard.

When I turned to check on Ryker, the two other men fell to the floor like sacks of rice. Fresh cuts and bruises lined Ryker's face.

"I always forget how good you are. You didn't even need me." A slight grin hitched the side of his mouth then twisted around. "Croygen, we're about to get company," Ryker hollered up, standing below the opening. Lexie's body dropped, falling ungracefully into Ryker's arms, but she didn't even stir. The drugs kept her deeply unconscious. Sprig's sleeping form roughly landed on her, then Croygen followed. I kept quiet, thankful Croygen had pitched Sprig down at all.

Without a word, Croygen took Lexie back from Ryker, tucking her into his arms. I whirled for the door, bolting up the stairs. My body shook with fatigue, but the stone pulsed up my leg with excitement, giving me just enough to keep going. It was as though the adrenaline and fear burning through me stimulated it.

I burst through the first set of doors at the top, hitting the tunnel. There were still so many things that could go wrong, but the taste of freedom slid over my skin. Shouts and alarms rang in my ears as we bolted through the fae detectors. Men streamed behind us like ants.

A gunshot whistled by my ear as did a command I didn't stop to hear, then a hailstorm of bullets. The darkness of the tunnel kept them from finding their true targets. Their orders were shoot to kill. We weren't supposed to get this far.

We weaved, making it hard to get a clear shot on any of us. The casings bounced off the cement ground as they unloaded on us. My shoulder slammed into the final door, ready for freedom to engulf me.

It didn't budge.

Locked.

"Noooo!"

With a roaring bellow, Ryker's body seemed to triple in size along his shoulders, fury radiating off him. He ran into the doors like a linebacker, cracking the lock with a single hit. The exit flew open, all of us stumbling forward into the budding light of day.

We didn't hesitate. We burst out, bullets and shouts thundering behind us. Dawn crept over the buildings, coloring them in a golden glow. Not a good time to escape. The dark shadows we could slip into were evaporating before our eyes. Unsuspecting civilians were still snuggled in their beds, leaving us with no witnesses against DMG chasing and shooting at us.

How easy it would have been if I could still jump. But Ryker had the magic back. Didn't he? If it did go back to him, why did I feel a coil of energy lashing against my spine, giving me that tingle like it wanted to jump?

A growl came from behind me, and I shot a glance over my shoulder, Ryker's face twisted with fury.

"Can you jump?" I yelled back at him.

He shook his head, his features darkening.

"Can you guys see me?" Croygen asked, cuddling Lexie close to his chest. Sprig curled on her stomach.

"Yeah? Aren't we supposed to?"

"No," he growled. Croygen was a chameleon type of fae. He should have been able to blend so well into the background he would disappear. It made him an excellent thief and pirate. Several bullets whizzed by us. Croygen swore. "Why can't we use our powers? We're out."

Escape was the first item on our agenda. We'd worry about everything else later.

"We need to get off the streets and find a place to hide," Ryker called over his shoulder as he ran faster.

"This way. I know a place." Croygen made a sharp turn. We ran, twisting and turning through lanes, alleys, streets, and vacated buildings. I knew we had lost the soldiers, but we kept up our speed, wanting to put as much distance between us and DMG as we could.

We had done it. We'd escaped. Croygen, Sprig, and I

had gotten Lexie and Ryker out. I knew we had a long, hard journey ahead, but right then I let my heart feel the happiness, the relief. Even if Ryker still wanted to kill me, he was alive, and Lexie was here. We were all okay, though my gut sensed a catastrophe coming, like it wouldn't be long before danger came calling, smashing us into little pieces.

THREE

Croygen led us to a gutted storage warehouse under the bridge in the Fremont area, a rough-around-the-edges place. Before the big electrical storm, the region was being transformed by the twenty-something artists and computer geeks and, like in so many expanding cities, it had started to show signs of becoming hip. Now it was back in the hands of the homeless reclaiming their territory. All were fighting for space under the bridge next to the famous Fremont Troll, a stone carving, which once brought tourists to the spot by the droves.

Now people left us alone as we ran through the streets covered in blood, holding what probably appeared to be a dead girl wrapped in a blanket with a monkey sleeping on her chest. You know, pretty normal stuff. Sadly, they had probably seen worse. Everyone kept to themselves, as though too scared to get involved.

When we finally stopped, Croygen walked around to a side door, Lexie still sound asleep in his arms. Sprig curled up, snoring. "It's a safe house I used a while ago. Lots of room to hold any money or loot you want to hide until you can launder it."

"How long ago was awhile?" I asked.

"Uh... when was dropping acid the rage?"

"The sixties."

"Then somewhere around there."

My mouth gaped. "How do you know it's even a safe house anymore and not used by humans or other fae?"

"Because there's a spell on it. Humans will look past it. Other fae will feel a spell on it and move on." Handing Lexie to Ryker, Croygen went to the door and typed a code into the access buttons. "Hope this still works."

I moved closer to Croygen, watching his fingers move over the buttons. "It's been over fifty years. You really think they are going to have the same code?"

The door released from its hold, swinging open. "You were saying?" Croygen's lips turned up in a smug grin. "Remember, fifty years to a fae is like a few weeks to humans." He opened the door wider, allowing Ryker and Lexie through, then motioned for me to enter. "My lady."

I stepped inside. The two-story, rectangular-shaped building stood mostly empty except for two chairs, a table, and bare storage racks, which dotted the vast space. A filthy mattress with bunched-up blankets sat by itself like an island against one long blank wall. There were a few doors off the main room, but all opened to vacant offices, holding no more than unoccupied shelving.

No bathroom. No kitchen.

"Nice." I rubbed my arms, goosebumps rippling over my skin. "Very homey."

"Someone's a bit of a snob," Croygen mocked.

Ryker moved straight for the bed, set Lexie down, and covered her with the blanket, then placed Sprig next to her.

"Stop that... it tickles," Sprig giggled as he stirred awake.

I stepped to them, bending down to check on my sister. Ryker scurried away, putting distance between us. I tried to ignore the stabbing in my chest and focused on my sister. She

33

breathed deeply, still under heavy sedation. Croygen's suggestion that Rapava used an elephant tranquilizer on her wasn't far off. She had barely stirred the entire struggle, her eyes opening only once. She would have a shock when she woke up. I touched her forehead, feeling the warmth melting my cold hands. She felt hot but her body trembled with chills.

The place being full of metal and concrete gave off no warmth, and the crispness in the air told me fall was right on our heels. I had no idea the month or how long I had been in the DMG hole. But if I went down in the summer and came out in fall, it had to be more than two or three months.

"We should be safe here." Croygen glanced through a small opening at the side of the opaque windows, looking out at the street. "At least till we figure out our next steps. This place saved my ass a lot back in the day."

"Do I ask?" I stood from the thin mattress.

"No. Better not." Croygen winked.

Ryker moved through each room, his eyes taking in every nuance, like a trained warrior.

"Wh-where the hell am I?" Sprig popped his head up, glancing around, his eyes glazed. "Oh no. The raccoons have me again! Scary bastards. Tell them I'll pay up this time."

"Sprig, calm down." I stroked behind his ear. He took a breath, waking up more.

"Why are my nuts tingling?"

I snorted. "Welcome back, buddy."

He sat up, taking in the space. "We couldn't have chosen a diner or a grocery store?" Sprig huffed, rubbing his eyes. He crawled over Lexie to me. "Was that too much to ask?"

Our protection remained priority, but I had to admit a place with food, a bathroom, and a shower would have been nice.

I searched the area and found another filthy, scratchy

blanket. In times of need, you couldn't be picky, but I still shook out the blanket. I went over to Lexie's sleeping body and laid it over her. My fingers weaved through her naturally kinky hair. Dark and wavy and streaked with caramel, it had grown past her shoulders, but it was knotted and frizzy from lack of care.

Her eyebrows smoothed out as I stroked her face. She was such a beautiful girl. Half Puerto-Rican and half African-American, her features were striking. Even at twelve, almost thirteen, the boys had started to notice her. Though, I could only see now how scrawny and sickly she had become. Her eyes were sunken and her normally milk-chocolate skin looked ashen.

Lexie's lips parted and a small groan drifted out.

"You're safe now." I leaned over and kissed her head. "I will never let them hurt you again. I promise." I tucked the blanket tighter against her body. I heaved a sigh, stood, and turned to face the guys.

"We need to get food and water and some painkillers for her eventually." I walked to them. Ryker had settled on the windowsill, keeping sentry. Sprig sat next to him on the ledge. Croygen stood nearby. Ryker glanced over briefly, then turned back to watch the street.

"This is just for tonight," Croygen spoke, filling the painful gap between Ryker and me. "Jesus, what's up with you two? We just escaped! There should at least be a few smiles, some cheers... or undying gratitude to me." He held out his arms in wonder.

"Undying gratitude?" I lifted my eyebrows.

"Worship. Adoration. Devotion. I'm open to any one of your choosing."

"How about I don't smother you in your sleep," Ryker snipped.

35

"Or poop on your face," Sprig added. "Oh no, forget that. I will probably still do that."

"That's the spirit. See, Zoey. They're getting into the festive mood."

I smiled and let myself laugh. Croygen always improved my mood.

"I'm going to make a sweep around the building." Ryker abruptly bolted to his feet, his arm reaching over his shoulder for his axe, then stopped. A pained scowl crept up into his features. "I'll look for a vending machine while I'm out." His voice sounded gruff as he slipped by me, heading out with set determination in his shoulders.

"Wait!" Sprig scrambled after him. "I'll help. With the food thing at least."

Sprig had to work hard to catch up with Ryker but climbed up his body and settled on his shoulder. Ryker didn't respond either way to his presence. He just pushed through the doors. I opened my mouth to say something, stop him, but nothing came out as the door closed behind him.

"He'll come around." Croygen had sidled up next to me.

"Will he?" I continued to stare after him. "Should he?"

Croygen tilted his head.

"The things I did to him, Croygen... How can he ever forgive me? I can't forgive myself."

"He understands you had to do it."

"Doesn't matter."

"Look what he did to you." Croygen motioned to my neck. "He killed you. Well, sort of. And I'm still waiting for that perpetual devotion and thanks for saving your life."

I swiveled around to face Croygen. "You did save my life."

"Think I just said that."

"No." I shook my head. "I meant, if you saved my life..."

"I am no longer duty bound to you." A smirk curved Croygen's mouth. "You would be right."

"It's broken?" My eyebrows shot up.

He stayed silent for a moment before nodding, and his smile grew bigger.

"But you told Ryker if he killed me, he'd kill you."

"I'm too pretty to die." He cupped his own chin. "I mean, look at this mug. Be a waste."

"B-but I died. He wouldn't have gotten his powers back if I didn't." I rubbed my forehead. We finally had a moment so I could really concentrate on the energy I still felt inside. The more I focused on it, the more I could sense it, energy dwelling deep inside. It wasn't as strong, but it was there. His magic still resided in my core.

I tapped at my stomach, my mouth falling open. "I still have some of his powers. I can feel them. They didn't all leave me."

"Really?" His brow corked up, then bobbed his head. "Actually, that makes sense. Magic has its own will. Some of it must have grown devoted to you. Liked its new home better."

Relief settled into my heart at the thought. I had the power for a short time but had gotten attached to it. Once I hated fae, now I hated the idea of not being partly one.

"What I think is some of your human body died, but the fae magic brought you back." Croygen's smile wouldn't leave his face. "Either way, I am no longer obligated to either you or that brute. I'm free."

"Oh my god." I threw my arms around Croygen, hugging him. "That's awesome. How does it feel, after centuries?"

He closed his eyes as if he were considering what I asked him. "Amazing." He hugged me back.

"You're free to go." I leaned back, his arms still around me. "You can go back to your ship. Get away from all of this."

The smile dropped from his face. "I might not be duty bound, but until he no longer has the urge to kill you, I should probably stick around."

"Why? You can get out of here. Nothing's keeping you here."

"Yes, something is."

"What?"

He turned his gaze to mine, his dark eyes intense. "You."

"Me?"

"Whatever you do to us fae men..." He smiled. "I'm not going to just leave you, Zoey. Not until you and your sister are safe. It would feel wrong."

My eyebrows hit my hairline.

"I know. I know." He shook his head. "This is a first for me."

I pulled him into another hug. "You know what I think?"

"Not sure I want to."

"You might fight us, even Ryker, but we're your family, Croygen, your friends. And deep down that's something you want. A place to belong."

He scoffed.

"Pretend all you want. But you belong with us. With me."

The door slammed, and Croygen and I jumped apart. Ryker leaned against the doorjamb, watching us. His eyes narrowed. Sprig sat on his shoulder, his neck revolving to the three of us, his eyes wide.

Ryker's folded arms and stone face caused my mouth to blather. "It-it's not what you think."

"What do I think?" He stood straight, walking over to us. Sprig leaped off his shoulder, climbing up on the window ledge. "I'm curious. Tell me what I think." Ice started to form around the wall he set between us.

"Don't." My jaw tightened. "Don't be that guy again."

"What guy?" He fastened his arms over each other, leaning into me. It was threatening.

I would not be bullied or intimidated. "This guy." I stepped into his face, poking at his chest. "The asshole who hated me only because of his fear of feeling, of letting someone in. We've been through too much to start at the beginning again."

He bristled. "This is who I really am." Ryker lifted his top lip. "I'm a demon, little human, born to hate and destroy."

"Bullshit," I shouted.

"Whoa, you two." Croygen tried to step between us, but neither of us budged.

"What do you want from me, *human*?" Ryker's nostrils flared.

"I want Ryker back," I seethed. The tension filled the little space between us, closing the world down to the two of us.

"He's no longer here. He died back on the table where you cut him up into pieces."

I sucked in a breath, his hurtful words hitting home. "You don't think I hate myself for that? What I had to do to you to keep my sister alive?" I tapped at my chest. "Every time I cut into you, torturing you? The game I was forced to play? The revulsion I feel for myself is infinite."

"Then multiply that by seven," Ryker snarled, inching even closer to my face. "I'm the reason anyone I ever cared about died. Because of me my adoptive mother, father, my sister, the girl I loved, my unborn baby, my *real* mother are all dead."

His real mother? Right before he killed me, he had told

me his father was Vadik. But he didn't mention his mother. Did he learn who she was too?

That came only to six.

"And *you*," he continued, anger bursting off his skin. "I destroy everyone *I love*."

I felt my lungs spasm, a silent gasp choking my throat. Did he just say…?

"Do you want to hear how good it felt to sense your life draining away between my fingers? It makes me sick, but I wanted it like nothing before." His arms trembled with his fury. "The desire is still there." He stared down at his hands as his fingers knotted into tight fists. He sucked in a breath, shook out his hands, and stepped away from me.

"But you killed me. I know I was dead. And I saw you heal. You have your powers back. The promise should be broken. You fulfilled it." I watched for his reaction. Nothing.

Croygen's oath broke by saving me. Why didn't Ryker's end by killing me?

"Can I step in here?" Croygen cleared his throat, holding up his hand, stepping back into our world. "Like I said before, maybe some of your human part died, but the fae part kept you alive. It's probably why it broke and didn't break at the same time."

"What does that mean?"

"Maybe you didn't die enough. Or long enough." Croygen shrugged. "This isn't something we know. There's not a manual or anything on this. I'm most likely talking out my ass."

"Understandable. It's where your brain is," Sprig quipped. We all looked at him. He grabbed his tail and stuffed it into his mouth.

"You still aren't doing that right." Croygen sighed. "Next time try tying it around your neck."

Sprig pulled his tail from his mouth like he was going to speak but then flipped off Croygen instead.

"Guys, back here." I waved at the three.

"What Croygen said sort of makes sense. I *felt* the powers go back into me. Hurt like a bitch." Ryker shifted as if uncomfortable remembering the incident.

That had to be the pain I felt, the magic being torn from me. But what if it had just been tearing in half? They were still in me.

"I didn't get them all back." Ryker's white eyes fell on me. "Some of my powers have stayed with you, adapted to you. This might be the reason the oath doesn't feel completely out of my system."

My hand drifted up to my forehead, rubbing fiercely. Why could nothing be easy with us?

"I can feel them inside me, but when I tried to use them outside of DMG, nothing happened." Ryker's lids narrowed.

"Me too." Croygen nodded.

My fingers continued to knead my temple. "All I can think is Rapava has been playing with goblin metal so he can control fae. I thought it only sedated us, but what if he has designed it to affect the powers themselves?"

"You mean to keep us from using them *ever* again?" Croygen exclaimed.

"If he can't actually control fae, what better way than to at least put them on the same playing field as humans?" The idea struck me with force. Oh my god, no doubt this was *exactly* what he was doing. Or seeking to do. "I don't know for sure, but I got to understand Rapava's mind a bit more. This would be something he would try. While he's attempting to create humans with abilities, he would also be aiming to take away the opposition's."

"This doctor is seriously fucked up." Croygen placed a hand over his eyes.

41

"I agree, but it doesn't mean there isn't genius in it," I said.

Croygen dropped his hands. "True. Look at me. Screwed up and a genius at it."

"No, you are just genuinely fucked up," Ryker said.

"Oh, right. Keep getting those two mixed up." They exchanged brief humor-laden smiles. Then the moment was gone.

Ryker looked away. "Do you think it will last?" I could feel frustration rolling off him. What he had gone through to get the powers back might all be for naught.

"I have no idea." I shrugged. It felt horrible knowing they were there, in my grasp, but I couldn't reach them. "All we can do is keep trying and hope our abilities aren't locked away forever."

"Well, then nothing's changed for me. But we no longer have your powers to count on." Ryker motioned to Croygen and me. "And currently we have a girl who can barely walk on her own, a hoard of people, most with powers, after us, no food or water, and on top of that a really annoying monkey." A slight smirk played on Ryker's lips.

"Hey!" Sprig stood up on his hind legs. "I see the truce is over, Viking. Fine. You and the buttmuncher over there better watch out."

"Or what? You'll talk us to death?" Croygen smirked. "Stick our fingers in honey as we sleep?"

Sprig squeaked. "I would never waste my honey like that. What kind of sprite do you take me for? It is not to be wasted on your fingers. I know where those have been."

"They got lonely. Can't blame a man." Croygen shrugged.

Sprig gagged dramatically, then twisted to me. "That reminds me…"

"Let me guess. You're hungry."

Sprig's eyes widened. "It's like you're reading *my* mind."

"That's the only thing ever on your mind," Ryker quipped.

"No, sometimes I think of ways of farting on your face while you sleep. Or pooping in your boot..." Sprig drifted off, his hand rubbing his belly. "Do you think there is anything nearby? I mean, I will settle for a candy bar. Or even a cookie... oh, Izel's honey pancakes. They had good chocolate croissants too. But I always preferred the churr—"

"How about chocolate-covered espresso beans?" Ryker's mouth hitched up, his gaze darting to me, cutting off Sprig's tirade.

"Oooohhh, yes! I'll take those too." Sprig jumped up and down.

"Don't encourage him." I turned to Ryker with a glare. "Who's going to deal with him when he realizes you are only messing with him, and he can't have any of those things?"

"If I remember correctly, you were the one who got *enthusiastic* over the espresso beans." Though his face held no emotion, somehow just the fact of him looking at me sent heat rising from my center.

"Will you guys fuck each other and get it over with?" Croygen groaned, laying his head back.

"I agree with you, swashbutthole." Sprig nodded. "Though I warn you, they put fae rabbits and river fairies to shame."

Croygen turned to Sprig with surprise. "Really?"

Sprig nodded dramatically.

"Humm." Croygen seemed impressed by the notion.

Ryker's intense gaze remained on me, but he gave nothing away as to what he felt. Then he glanced away. The wall slammed back between us. What had happened to him? What had he gone through to find me? His jaw clenched as if he could hear the questions bounding around in my head. He turned, his gaze going back to the windows. I knew this was his way of saying the topic was off the table.

Suddenly I felt exhausted. We needed to talk about so many things, but my adrenaline from the escape hit bottom. Wordlessly I turned and headed for Lexie.

"I'm sorry, I don't remember adjourning the meeting."

"Good night, Croygen." I waved over my shoulder. "We can talk later. Plan for our next move." I settled down on the blanket next to my sister. Out in the world, people were rising for the day as I tucked in for a nap. My body and mind needed a little time to rest. "Wake me up when it's my time for watch."

The boys didn't respond. I heard Sprig's nails skating over the cement as he ran to me. He curled into my neck as I lay down. There were so many things wrong, so many problems ahead of us, but as I huddled closer into my sister, I had to hold on to the small victories. We were alive and we had escaped. All the rest could wait for later: the fact the man I loved was part demon, who still wanted to kill me; that we were being hunted by groups of people and had no magic; Lexie's frailty limited the distance we could put between us and DMG; I still carried the Stone of Destiny in my boot; and we stood nowhere closer to taking Rapava down.

In this moment, I got to hold the little girl I thought I had lost forever.

That was enough for now.

FOUR

It was dark outside when I finally stirred. Lexie fidgeted and groaned in her sleep, so my own rest hadn't been relaxing. With a sigh, I nudged Sprig away from my head and rolled over, my bladder demanding I get up.

Ryker still positioned himself on the sill, staring out. Hearing me move, he darted his gaze to me then back out the hole in the window.

"Do you need me to take over?" I walked over to him, rubbing my arms. Losing the heat from Lexie's and Sprig's bodies raised goosebumps up my arms. The scrubs we were all wore did nothing to keep away the chill.

"No," he replied.

"Ryker, you need to sleep too."

"Later."

He wouldn't look at me. The piece of my heart I clung to while I carved into him sank to the bottom of my soul. I hadn't expected anything different, but I hadn't let myself think about the pain of truly losing him. Maybe not in death, but I lost him just the same.

"Go back to bed, Zoey. You need to stay warm. Your body needs to rest after what it went through." He pressed his shoulders into the wall.

"No more than yours." I folded my arms over me, trying to keep in the warmth.

He twisted irritably on the ledge, feeling my eyes on him. Without his axe strapped to his back, he was like Thor without his hammer. Something felt wrong. Off. He didn't have to speak a word for me to sense his loss.

"What happened to you?" I asked.

"Nothing you need to know about."

"*Ryker.*" I clenched my palms together. "Tell me something. Please."

He finally looked over at me. "It's not going to make you feel better."

"I'm not looking to feel better." I took a step closer to him but stopped when his nose flared. "I want to know about your real mother and how you found out Vadik's your father. What happened while we were apart?"

Anger blazed from Ryker's white irises. "How do you know about Vadik?"

"You told me. Well, sort of. You told me you were part demon when…"

"When I tried to kill you," he finished my sentence. "I don't recall what I said during that time." He stared out into the dark. "It's more a feeling. The need…" He trailed off. "So yeah, I'm part demon." A strange noise came from his throat. "The son of Valefor."

"Valefor?"

"That's his real name. Duke of Thieves. I knew I was good at stealing, but it is actually in my DNA. Power, speed, dexterity, and the desire to thieve. I wasn't just good at it; I was born to do it."

"Wow." I wrapped my arms around my middle.

"I saw her, my mother. A painting of her hung in the living room when Amara and I were trying to escape."

"Amara? How is she involved with this?" Anger drilled up the base of my neck. That bitch helped him escape? But she turned us in. It didn't make sense.

Ryker didn't seem to hear me, his mind lost in the past.

"She was so beautiful," he murmured. "Seeing her face, her smile, brought back a memory. It was my third birthday. I remembered my father pouring my dinner all over my cake and shoving my face into it and forcing me to eat it till I threw up, then eat that as well."

My hand went to my mouth.

"Guess that's why I don't like mixing my food." He rubbed his head. "In the memory his face looked so clear along with his rage and need for control. He hit her."

He rolled his jaw, his gaze far off. He stayed quiet for more than a minute, but I stood there, not budging in my own stubbornness.

"After he did that, my mom snuck me into the forest where a woman waited for us. A Druid, I think. She put a spell on me to invoke my powers early and hide me from my father." He cleared his throat, shifting. "But the price was my mother's blood. Her life. She killed herself for me. To keep me safe."

I let my eyes close briefly.

"I jumped and lost my memory of her. What she did for me. Who my father was."

"I am so sorry, Ryker."

"Ryker." He snorted derisively. "Funny, I don't even know my real name."

"Ryker is your real name. The family who raised you gave you love and your name. Your mother sacrificed herself so you could grow up loved and protected. Don't take that away from her." I wanted to go to him so badly it ached, but any movement I took, he shot me a "stay back" glance.

"What's even more amusing about finding out I'm part

demon was learning my mother's part human. The two things I grew to despise, and I'm both."

"You're Ryker, the Wanderer." I put my hands on my hips. "All the other stuff doesn't matter."

"It doesn't matter I'm a demon?" Fury burst out of his mouth.

"Not to me."

He ran his hand over the top of his blond Mohawk with a grunt. "You need to stay away from me."

"Not a chance," I croaked out, toeing my boot into the ground.

His eyes dropped to my shoe, his expression growing intense. I looked down, knowing his eyes had followed.

"Why did you give it to me?" I asked.

"Because I knew it would be safe with you."

Silence grew heavy between us. "Ryker?"

"Zoey, you need to go. Now." He rubbed his hands as if he were trying to keep them from curling into fists.

I wasn't ready to walk away yet. "I am sorry about your axe. And I'm sorry about your... our... powers. That they didn't all go back to you."

His gaze darted to me. "Why are you sorry?" His forehead crinkled. He rounded his head back to the window, his voice growing so soft I could barely hear him. "I don't blame you... or them. I'd choose to stay with you too."

Tears prickled the back of my lids. "Ryker..."

"It changes nothing." He sighed. "Because of them, you lived... that is enough for me."

"And because I died for a moment, some went back to you. Saving your life. *That* is enough for me."

He rubbed his forehead, his lids blinking.

"Do you think the need to kill me will ever go away?" I asked softly.

"I don't know. Until I feel completely in control of myself, I need you far from me." His teeth gritted together.

"But you might be able to handle them? Eventually?"

He stayed silent, misery lining his forehead. Without saying it, I felt him pushing me away. Saying goodbye.

I felt and heard my heart break. It was like cracking open a clam, ripping the tendons apart in a painful wrench.

"Go back to bed, Zoey," he finally uttered. "Quickly."

Fury nibbled at my toes until I let it ride up my spine, hunching my shoulders. "Can I pee first, boss?" Anger was my default. If I couldn't use my fists, I attacked with attitude.

"Stay close," he ordered.

I stood for another beat. When he didn't turn to look at me, I whirled and stomped from the room.

Bastard. Wanderer.

"Screw him," I mumbled. *You'd like to!* my mind sang back. "Shut up," I yelled at myself.

I went outside, finding a dark corner. After I relieved myself, I stood, feeling the hair on my arms rise. All my senses tingled. I wasn't alone. I scanned the dark space, landing on outlines of dumpsters and other objects playing games on my eyes in the shadows.

A scuffling noise came from the roof, startling me, capturing a gasp in my throat. It was probably a rat or a cat, but my gaze still stayed latched on the area, trying to make out anything. At a squeak of wheels from a dumpster, I jumped in the air and rotated around. Sweat trickled down the back of my shoulders. I wouldn't be stupid and ask who was there. All the things hunting us would not be polite and respond. They would attack.

I glanced at the heavy doors down the corridor, contemplating my next move. Would Ryker hear me if I screamed? Before I could decide, a shrill squeal of nails scraped down metal, icing my bones. I took off running. As I neared the doors, a figure stepped out. The dark only gave me an outline, but a fist collided with my face and knocked me on my ass. Pain exploded along my cheekbone and nose.

"Arguing with yourself, Zoey? Not a good sign. Maybe you should have stayed locked up."

Oh. Hell. No.

"Amara," I snarled, sitting up and rubbing my nose.

Amara stepped out from the shadows, the moonlight highlighting her elegant features. A huge smile spread over her beautiful face. "I wish I could say I enjoyed seeing you again, Zoey, but we both know I'd be lying."

I scrambled to my feet. I could only see the girl who betrayed us, who turned Ryker over to Vadik and me to DMG. The torture, the pain, the heartache... A deep growl came from my throat, my body lowering itself to attack.

"Still a little mad at me, I see." She smirked

Hatred clogged my throat; I couldn't even respond. I leaped for her, my fingers itching to tear her apart. My body crashed into hers, taking us both down on the cement. My arms were already swinging, and my hand slapped her face. I couldn't feel, see, or hear anything. Fury buzzed in my brain, and the need to taste her blood drove me forward with abandon. I only got in two more hits before I flew in the air, being pulled away from her.

"No," I snarled, reaching out for her. The need to inflict pain blurred my thoughts. I struggled to get back to her, but the arm around my stomach held me tightly.

"Zoey," Ryker barked in my ear, but I ignored him as my eyes latched on to the woman on the ground. She patted at the blood coursing down her chin.

"Let me go!"

"Whoa, girl." Croygen came into sight and reached out

to calm me. My jaw snapped at his fingers, urging him back. "Holy shit!"

"Croygen, step back," Ryker ordered.

"What the hell is wrong with her?" Croygen stared at me.

"You've never seen her in crazed fighter mode, have you?"

"I've seen her fight."

"No, you actually haven't." Ryker drew me closer to his chest. His heartbeat thumped against my shoulder blade. The in and out of his breath drew my own heart into a gentle rhythm, like a sedative. "Not really."

I didn't want to be calmed. I wanted to kill her. I pushed against him, bending my head down to where he held me.

"Don't *even* think about biting me," Ryker warned, his breath hissing down the back of my neck. "Or I will bite you back."

The rage I felt quickly sizzled into something less violent, though just as primal. I sucked air through my nose harshly, my limbs shaking with built-up energy.

"I'm not going to tell you to calm down because it will only piss you off," Ryker mumbled into my ear, his voice taut. I snorted. *Damn, this man knows me.* "But I want you to breathe with me."

I could only feel his chest moving against my back. I squeezed my lids shut, and I slowed my exhalations with his.

"Are you kidd—" My eyes shot open at the sound of Amara's voice. I felt Ryker stiffen behind me. I could only imagine the look he sent her to shut her up so quickly.

She stayed quiet till my heart rate had come back down.

"Are you okay now?" Ryker stood rigid behind me, his body shaking.

I nodded, but the sight of the plum-haired turncoat in front of me plunged another dagger of fury into my system.

"Good." He loosened his grip. "Croygen, take her." Shit. He had fought his desire to kill me in order to calm me down.

"No way. She's like some wild animal."

"Croy-gen," Ryker hissed through his teeth.

"Oh shit. Right." Croygen put out his arms robotically to me.

"I'm fine!" I pulled away from both of them, but Croygen tugged me until I stood closer to him, and farther from Ryker.

"How did you find us, Amara?" Ryker's voice rumbled through the air.

"You think I didn't learn a few things from you over the *years*?" she countered. "I know you, Ryker. I knew you'd sneak out. I might have drifted off to sleep for a moment, but when you shut the door, I was up tracking you. I watched you turn yourself over to *those men*. For *her*." Her voice was thick with disgust. "I kept an eye on DMG. Finally you guys emerged, and I followed."

"Why?" Croygen asked, brows creased. "What do you want?"

Her lids narrowed. "And what is it you want, Croygen? Why are you here?" Her eyes tracked to me and back to Croygen. "Oh, I see."

Ryker's arm flexed, an irritated noise rumbling from his throat. Amara had only been here five minutes and was already causing trouble.

"You need to go." My teeth clenched. "Or I will kill you, you traitorous bitch."

Her perfectly shaped eyebrow curved up at me. I turned my head to look at the wall. Staring at her only drove more need into my muscles to end her life.

"Amara saved my life," Ryker said as he moved farther from me. "She is the only reason I am standing here now. She helped me escape Vadik."

He had told me that last night, but I didn't trust her; she bounced back and forth between sides as it suited her. "She is the only reason you were there in the first place."

"I know." Ryker kept his eyes latched on to mine.

"I-I can't believe this," I sputtered. "You're actually defending her? You've forgiven her? Think of what she's done to us."

Ryker's mouth creased into a line. "I know you can't understand, but—"

"You're right. I don't." I half turned, flipping my hand out at her. "She has deceived, lied, and separated us to be tortured and possibly killed. And you forgive her?"

"You know, I'm standing right here." Amara folded her arms.

The sound of her voice made me think of the old cliché "like nails on a chalkboard." I swung around for her. Ryker immediately stepped back to me, but Croygen grabbed me first.

"Amara, be smart for once and just shut up," Ryker snapped.

But of course she wasn't wise. "Just think, if I didn't turn you over, Zoey. You would never have known about your dear, sweet, *living* sister. You should thank me, actually."

"Oh fuck," Croygen muttered, his arms squeezed around me, but his hold wasn't tight enough to keep me back. I sprang for her like a wild animal. The power withheld from me vibrated in its case, begging for a way out. It was probably the only thing that kept her alive.

I went into a haze, my fighter instincts taking over. Amara wasn't a damsel in distress, and she fought back, landing slaps and punches to my face and body. But my love of the fight gave me drive she didn't have. I could have easily beaten her, with more time.

Once again, I was lifted off her like a hissing kitten. Ryker moved me back, shoving me once again into Croygen arms.

"Jesus, Amara. Don't be an idiot! Do you want her to kill you?" Ryker shouted, stepping away. "Keep your mouth closed for once... or leave. I'm struggling enough here."

I tracked Amara rolling to her side and spitting out blood.

"She can't kill me," Amara mumbled, wiping her chin.

"Yes, she could." Ryker put his hands on his hips. "I told you not to underestimate her. Even when she was pure human, she could have put you down. Even more so now that she's part fae."

"What?" Amara rose, grimacing in pain. "What are you talking about?"

"Some of my magic chose to stay with her. It's a part of her now." His eyes flew over to meet mine.

"Holy shit. You killed her?" Amara bent over her knees but stared up at Ryker in amazement.

"Yes."

"But she lived." Disappointment caked her words. "And some of the powers stayed?" Amara straightened. "She's becoming one of us?"

"Sort of. I can still feel her human side, but the fae is also strong. Maybe equivalent to a Druid or a human who eats fae food." He folded his arms.

"See? You didn't need Regnus after all." She smirked and cringed, her fingers tapping at her lip.

"Regnus." I forgot all about the man, the seer, whom Ryker wanted to save from Vadik. "Did you find him? Did he escape with you guys?"

Ryker stared at Amara. "Go ahead, Mar, tell her."

"Tell me what?" My head turned to look at them.

Amara's lids narrowed on Ryker, her lip curling up. "Fine. But someone better have a hold on your little pet there."

A sardonic grin inched up Ryker's lips.

Amara sighed deeply. "Regnus is dead."

I stared at her.

"And?" Ryker prompted.

"He's been dead for a couple of years. I lied and said he was alive to trap Ryker." She propped her hands onto her hips. "There, are you happy now?"

"Far from it," Ryker retorted.

I bit my lip. "Is there anything you didn't lie about?"

"Yes." She cocked her head. "I've always been perfectly honest about how I feel about you."

Croygen's fingers cinched down firmly on my arm.

"Believe me, I thought about killing Amara many nights, but she did get me out." Ryker kept his glare on Amara. "She risked her own life and took me to Elthia's to heal—"

"Elthia's?" I whirled around to face him. "As in another ex-girlfriend who is also still in love with you?" I normally wasn't a jealous person, but tonight I had hit the brink.

Croygen's sniggering cut the dense silence.

"Zoey…" Ryker spoke through his teeth. Perspiration dampened his forehead, and his hands fisted. He seemed to be fighting the urge to hurt me, I could see it, especially in the tension along his shoulders. Even being this close to me had to be difficult for him, but my temper held no sympathy.

"No. I get it." I tried to force back my attitude. Didn't work. "She's the perfect person. She could heal you. She'd do anything to keep you safe." My words didn't match the tension in my voice.

"Poor Ryker. So many women," Croygen teased. "Is

there a chance the three of you would duke it out in a ring? With mud…?"

"Shut up, Croygen," Ryker snarled.

"Or Jell-O?"

"How about both of you wres—" A deafening scream from inside the building cut me off.

My heart dropped to the ground, pulling my soul with it. "Lexie!" I raced for the doorway.

"Zoey, wait," Ryker said from behind, but I disregarded his plea. He wanted to go first to see what or who the threat was, but my mind didn't respond logically when it came to Lexie. I would fight whomever or *whatever* stood on the other side with my bare hands.

I flung the door open, crashing it into the wall, and sprinted into the room. "Lexie?" My gaze roamed to where I left her, taking in the scene before me. My feet came to a sudden halt, everyone coming in behind me. I had to blink to make certain what I saw was real

Lexie sat on the dirty mattress, her blanket wadded up in a ball a few feet away, like she had tossed it. Her gaze was locked on an object perched atop the crumpled fabric.

Sprig held a coffee stirrer in his hand, wiggling it at Lexie, as if it were a sword. "Back, you feral *Leanbh!* Back!"

My hand flew to my mouth as a choked laugh escaped. Both swung around to me.

"Zoey!"

"*Bhean!* I said hello and she threw me."

"Monkey. Talking," Lexie sputtered. Her eyes still held a blurry confusion, not able to focus on me.

I bent down. "Come here, Sprig." He stuck out his tongue at her and darted for me, crawling up my arm to my shoulder.

"Th-that thing talks," Lexie repeated, fear making her

stiff. I had forgotten she had never seen him before today. Even in Rapava's house of horrors, Sprig was an oddity.

"Thing? How dare you! I am a sprite." Sprig huffed. "My name is Spriggan-Galchobhar."

Lexie blinked.

"That is not going to help." I chuckled. I took a step toward Lexie, and she leaned back. "I promise you are safe." I held up my hands.

"What is that thing?"

"I'm a sprite." Sprig shook his head, looking at me. "Doesn't she understand English? Do I need to talk slower?"

I glared at Sprig.

"How are you feeling?" I returned to Lexie.

Her head swiveled around the room, and she didn't acknowledge me.

"Lexie?" It took a couple more calls before she finally looked at me.

"I-I know I need to tell you something…" Her brows crinkled on her forehead and she shook her head. "B-but I-I can't remember anything."

"It's okay. You just need to rest right now."

"No." Her head moved back and forth violently. "There is something…" She drifted off again, staring into the void.

"Hey." I kneeled down at the edge of the bed, cupping her cheek. "It's okay."

Her eyes flew to mine. "How did I get here? What happened?" She suddenly looked like the little girl I remembered. Emotion filled her features, bringing her to life.

"What do you last remember?" I sat back on my heels.

Her mouth opened and then she shut it. She took in a hasty breath. "Everything feels like a dream. I don't know what is real and what is not."

"It's probably the drugs DMG gave her. I'll bet it makes

her forget, so she wouldn't be able to tell anyone," Croygen spoke from behind me.

Lexie peered around me, her gaze landing on Croygen, gaping at him with a dreamy surprise. "It's you," she whispered. Croygen looked around, then pointed to himself. Lexie nodded. "You're the man from my dreams who saved me."

I groaned as I saw Croygen's face brighten. "Croygen, she's twelve. If you say anything... Actually, do not say anything at all."

"What? I wasn't... I didn't... Oh, you guys are disgusting," he grumbled. "I mean, who can blame her? I am in most girls' dreams."

"Or restraining orders," Amara muttered.

"Hey, boot-humper? What did *Bhean* say? Zip it, Lord of the Flies." Sprig pushed my hair away, to yell over at Croygen.

"How about my boot meets *your* humper."

"Okay. Enough." I held up my hands. "Jeez, it's like I'm an animal wrangler at a circus." I went back to Lexie. "I know this must be so confusing to you." My train of thought stopped when I noticed she no longer listened to me. Her attention was on Sprig.

"Lexie, this is Sprig. He was an experiment. Same as me." I nuzzled his fur. "He was once a sprite, but Rapava forced him into this monkey form."

"That's why he talks?"

"Of course I talk! Do you think I'm uneducated or something?"

"That's not what she means, Sprig. You know monkeys on Earth don't talk. It's a little strange to see at first. Remember when I first met you?"

"Oh right." He sighed in my ear.

58

"Come down and say hi."

"I only do tricks for food."

Lexie leaned in closer. "He is so little. And so cute."

"Cute? Cute?" Sprig exclaimed. "I'll have you know, *Leanbh*, I was a fierce warrior sprite."

"No, you weren't." Croygen snorted.

"Shush." He continued down my arm, his chest puffed up. "I was hunter, a great champion, feared in the forest."

"Only by the beehives," Croygen muttered.

Ignoring Croygen, Sprig bowed and then reached out his hand for Lexie's. She looked up at me, and I nodded encouragement. She giggled, taking his little hand with a finger and shook it.

"Nice to meet you, Sprig."

"You too, *Leanbh*."

"What is a *Leanbh*?" Lexie let go of his hand.

"It means child," Croygen responded.

Lexie frowned.

"Don't feel bad; he calls me girl." I leaned in closer to her. "I don't think he remembers my name."

"I know your name." Sprig put his hands on his hips, affronted. "It's... uh... it's honey—"

"If you say honey tits, I'm going to mash you up in banana pudding."

Sprig slapped his hands over his mouth, his eyes wide with horror.

I smirked and motioned over my shoulder. "Behind me are Croygen, Ryker, and Amara." She gave a little nod to them, then looked back at me. Confusion wrinkled her features.

"Where's Daniel?"

Oh god.

Her gaze loosely tracked me as I swallowed and stared

down at my feet. She wouldn't have known about his death unless Rapava told her. He clearly had not.

"He died." I exhaled, surprised at the pain I still felt recalling the moment of his murder. "The night of the big storm."

Lexie pressed her lips together. Her expression crumbled into a painful sadness.

Her response startled me a bit. She had known Daniel but not well. From what I said and the few times he helped me take her to some of her appointments, she had grown attached. I had told her my dreams of the three of us moving away together, having a life we always dreamed about. I didn't realize how much she also had counted on that fantasy. And Daniel.

"I'm sorry," I whispered. She nodded, shoulders sagging. Her lids fluttered, and her face suddenly looked drawn and tired. "I think you should get some sleep."

"Okay." Sprig responded instead. His form stiffened and he toppled over, falling headfirst onto the bed.

"Oh my god," she shrieked. "Did I kill him? Is he dead?"

I laughed and scooped him up. "No. Sprig is narcoleptic."

"He's also a tremendous pain in the ass," Ryker vocalized behind me.

"And you adore him." I craned my neck to look at him. Our eyes met, and for one brief moment I almost forgot there was anyone else in the room and we weren't really speaking. Swiftly his gaze clouded over, he whirled around, and strode out of the room. The door slammed behind him.

"And there goes the *ultimate* pain in the ass." Croygen thumbed over his shoulder at the door where Ryker exited.

I couldn't disagree.

Amara rolled her eyes and followed Ryker out.

"And there's the runner-up," Croygen grumbled. "Sometimes they tie." His crush on Amara seemed to have diminished some.

Ryker might be a pain in the ass, but at least I knew I could trust him. Amara's willingness to backstab anyone to protect herself and to get what she wanted frightened me. She wouldn't think twice about turning on me. It was in her nature. What she was.

I needed to find out why she was here, but right now Lexie stayed my priority.

"You need to rest." I eased my sister down on the mattress. "Your body is still trying to recover as the drugs leave your system."

Her gaze darted to mine, fear resonating deep in her brown eyes.

"I'll be here when you wake up. I promise."

She sighed and laid back. I pulled the scratchy blanket up to her shoulders. "Wow, luxury." She peered down, frowning at the soiled blanket. "Five stars for this place."

"Beggars can't be choosers," I replied.

"This thing is probably infested with fleas and diseases."

"So dramatic." I shook my head, smiling. She was getting back to the sassy girl I knew.

"Dramatic?" She pointed at the blanket. "Look at it, Zoey. I think it just growled at me."

She was a tough kid, but then she'd had to grow up in our neighborhood. She came to Joanne's at age three. Sometimes I forgot she never had to live on the streets or be without a bed or a meal, even after the big electrical storm. She had been tucked away underground with all her basic needs met. Unlike me.

"Lex, you are just going to have to deal." I stood, rubbing her head, making her dark wavy curls bounce around.

"Now get some sleep." I kissed her head and placed Sprig near her. She laid her head down on her arm as I strode away. Exhaustion beat out her abhorrence to our surroundings.

Croygen watched her as I walked up to him. "Has she always been that skinny? The girl could use a burger."

I sighed heavily, glancing over my shoulder. "She's always been petite boned, but this is way past that."

"Maybe feed her straight lard." He folded his arms. Both of us watched the two sleeping forms on the makeshift bed. The moon shrank deeper into the horizon, providing little light into the building, hinting at the coming dawn.

"How are you holding up?" Croygen nudged my arm.

My automatic response of "fine" sat on my tongue ready to be used. But it would be a lie, and I was sick of lying. Instead, I leaned my head against his bicep.

"Yeah." Croygen curled his arm around my shoulder and drew me in. It felt so nice. In his company, I no longer felt alone in this. We could handle whatever threat came our way.

The problem was threats came from everywhere... even from within our own group.

FIVE

When Ryker and Amara returned, I pulled them to the far end of the warehouse, away from the sleeping pair. Amara's presence remained on my list of things to deal with.

"I want you to leave." The sheer hatred I felt seeing her cramped my hands, compressing them in fists. "There is no reason for you to be here." I glowered at her. I kept my voice low as not to wake Lexie or Sprig. "None of us trust you, and I certainly don't believe your reasons for being here are unselfish. Whatever the motives are, you can take them with you as you walk out of here. Run, actually."

Amara licked her bottom lip, and a slight smile toyed at her lips, which only invoked more anger in me. Ryker stood back, but his gaze tracked us, carefully watching every nuance of our movements. Croygen looked amused as usual. He always enjoyed when Amara and I battled. Maybe a little too much.

"Do you think I'm here to turn you or your human sister back over to DMG?" She took a step toward me. "Or tell Vadik where Ryker is? Because risking my life to get him out the first time was great fun."

"I don't believe you," I countered.

"You think I had a choice in turning you over to Vadik? I agreed to the job never believing I would fall for the guy I

63

was supposed to be conning." Amara let her gaze drift briefly over to Ryker before coolly sliding back to me. "You don't just stop working for Vadik, Zoey. I did what I had to do in the circumstances given to me, but I got us out. *I* saved Ryker. So don't look at me like a righteous bitch. You have no idea what I've had to do to survive."

I didn't know what she had gone through in her life, but I still didn't think she stayed here because she suddenly had a change of heart.

"So, what do you want?" My scuffed boots nudged the tips of her stylish low-heeled booties. She was awful for the ego. My scrubs and shoes fell flat at being intimidating, especially compared to her black skinny jeans, chic shoes, tight black tank top, and leather jacket. Her long hair was pulled up in a perfect messy ponytail. She looked like the epitome of sexy badass. I, on the other hand, was just an ass. "Let me guess. The stone? Is that why you are here? You think Ryker will tell you where—"

"We all know you have it." She cut me off. "Let's not insult anyone's intelligence and pretend otherwise."

"That's it then. You came for the stone."

She sighed, and her lids closed briefly over her dark eyes. "Against everything you believe, Zoey, I'm not completely evil. Ask the two men behind me. Both seemed to be fine with me for decades... *until you.*"

I tried to respond, but she continued speaking.

"You want the real truth?" She paused, nibbling on her bottom lip. "I have nowhere to go."

My head jerked at her claim. I wasn't ready for her to show me anything but attitude.

"I lost Regnus, the man who was like a father to me. He was the only one who treated me with kindness growing up. I'm running from Vadik as you all are. *All* I have is Ryker.

I've been with him far longer than you have. He has been my family. Someone who actually cares about me."

"Seriously?" Croygen scoffed, throwing his arms out, and stared up at the ceiling in bewilderment. "I only endangered my life, my men's lives, rescued you from Vadik, all because I didn't care about you?"

"And Croygen," she added.

"Turning against the two people who, I have no idea why, actually care about you, is the way you thank them?" I demanded.

Her lids narrowed on me. "I'm not going to explain myself to you. I don't care if you like me or not, but I'm not leaving. You are just going to have to deal with it."

My neck craned over to Ryker. "You are going to let her stay? After what she's done?"

"This is not going to be Ryker's decision." Amara's face lightened with a smug smile. "*You* are going to *want* me to stay."

Laughter shot from my lips. "Are you kidding me?"

"No," she said. "You got this all wrong. It's not what I want from you, it's what you'll need from me." Amara peered down at me with superiority.

My lips hitched up in a snarl. "What could I possibly want from you?"

Her eyes glinted like she knew she had me. "I know where Vadik is keeping those girls."

"What girls?"

Ryker groaned, reaching for his head.

Amara glanced back and forth between the two of us, her expression elated. "He hasn't told you."

"Hasn't told me what?" I directed my question over to Ryker. He hadn't revealed much yet. And the fact Amara knew information I was not privy to came with a gut punch.

"That girl, Annabeth, you got all upset about... let's say Vadik is enjoying her profits at night along with the rest of the girls who are either fighting or charming the men, both human and fae."

My stomach sank, twisting into a pile of sludge. "What is she talking about?" I searched Ryker's face, hoping she was making stuff up. But his frown gave him away.

"I'm sorry. I was going to tell you." Ryker scratched his beard uneasily.

"Tell me *what* exactly?"

Ryker glanced at me warily. "Vadik may have lost you the night of the fight when you jumped back to Peru, but he came across something else instead. He realized there was profit to be made from Duc's and Marcello's old business. Fae were already there. Why not profit off them as well as the humans? He killed Duc and his men and took it over."

I struggled to take in air. A demon now ran the fight club, and the girls who couldn't fight had become escorts to the fae? "Vadik? Vadik is in charge of the underground fighting ring?"

"Yes." Ryker nodded. "He's made it an open arena for fae to pay and take advantage of humans. Feed off their sins. Drain them of their life and energy."

"Vadik moved them to a more secured place. Somewhere you would never look." Amara's smugness billowed off her.

"How do I know you aren't lying to me?"

"Go check the old place if you want. It will be vacant. If you want to waste time, be my guest." She shrugged.

"How do you know where they are?"

"I just happened to run across this information in Vadik's office while stealing the keys to his boat."

"Boat?" Croygen perked up.

"It's how Ryker and I escaped Vadik. You know, when I saved his life." Amara nodded at Ryker. "Not that he remembers much. He was out cold, bleeding all over the deck from a gunshot and a knife wound."

"What?" My mouth fell open.

"Not important right now." Ryker waved his hand. "What's imminent is it's not only those girls you need to worry about. Vadik wants you. He wanted me to find you so he could take you away from Rapava."

"What does he want me for?"

"At the time, he thought if I didn't kill you, you would make the perfect fighter and thief to add to his collection, especially with having some of my powers along with your reputation as a fighter."

I jerked my head from side to side. "But as far as he knew, if you didn't kill me, you would die."

"Actually, he preferred it that way. You were more valuable to him."

"But he's your father!"

Ryker's shoulders stiffened as he changed his footing and clenched his jaw. "That's not important to him. Or me."

I wrapped my arms around my torso. Even with this new threat to me, I could sense Ryker's pain. No matter what kind of relationship you had with your father, it had to hurt. Vadik would rather have Ryker dead so I could earn him a larger profit.

"Whatever conditions the girls lived in before, their lives will be much worse under Vadik's hold. They'll be leeched off of by fae every week and die slowly. Then he'll toss them away and get new girls." Ryker confirmed the truth I knew inside.

Annabeth's face swam in my head. The thought of her being forced to submit to these men filled me with revulsion.

Annabeth had a kind soul. She would never recover, especially if fae were feeding off her.

Duc wouldn't have done things much differently. Humans and fae could both be vile. But knowing Vadik, he would enjoy stealing her innocence and end up selling her to the top bidder. Vadik's evil had no limits. Bile gagged my throat.

"Look at you." Amara wrinkled her nose. "You're disgusted by Vadik, but you're okay with what your own doctor is doing to fae?"

My hand shot up, my fingers circling her throat. "Don't. You. Dare," I seethed. "Neither is all right. And I plan to take down both. I only hope somewhere along the way you'll get in my way." That dark, crazy, unbalanced part in me lit my skin with energy.

"Zoey." Ryker swiftly reached my side, and I shot him a deathly glare then turned back to Amara.

"Why don't you tell me where he is keeping them?" I squeezed down.

"You want to end me? Go ahead. Do it." She pushed against my hand, moving till I had to take a step back. "What are you waiting for, Zoey? Do it now."

She was baiting me. My hands shook with the need to squash her larynx.

"Come on." She heaved forward, leaning her weight on my arm. "Your threat of doing something to me before you know the location is bullshit. Plus, you won't hurt me. Not really. Ryker still cares about me, and you wouldn't do anything to hurt him. We both know it."

A growl clipped at my throat. She was right. And I hated her more for it. I dropped my hand.

"That's what I thought." She snorted, reaching up and rubbing at the indentions my fingers left.

"Don't test me, Amara."

"Some friendly advice? Your bleeding heart for those humans makes you easy to control, Zoey."

"Is that a threat?"

"No. It's a warning. I'm not the only person who will use it against you."

"I swear if you make one move I don't like I will not hesitate." I stared at her.

"Fair enough," she responded. "But know this, I won't either."

I took a moment, my gaze drilling deeper into her before I gave her a curt nod.

"Wow. This is so freakin' hot." Croygen had one hand up under his chin, the other across his stomach like he was watching a tennis match.

I glowered at him.

"Now talk, Amara."

"Oh, I'm not giving up my only leverage."

"What?" I bellowed. Ryker had retreated from me, rubbing his forehead. I was beginning to think anger from anyone, most likely me, spurred the killing oath into high gear.

Amara spun around, looking over her shoulder at me. "I will show you where it is. I'm not stupid, Zoey. Don't treat me as if I don't know the game." She glanced at Ryker. "I'm heading out now."

He nodded, an understanding passing between them.

My lungs chugged air, trying to keep my rage from taking over again. I did have to hand it to her. She was excellent at this game of deceit, betrayal, and blackmail.

I stomped off the opposite way, needing to be as far from Amara as possible. I wandered into a smaller room, off to the side. It appeared empty except some racks left behind.

Cobwebs caked the shelves and the small window at the top, shimmering in the last of the moonlight.

I can do this... just breathe, I repeated to myself. I had twisted my soul into pieces to demonstrate loyalty to Rapava. I had hidden my true feelings from a psychotic man who had me cut up Ryker to protect my sister. Rapava used Ryker as a practice dummy to inject with mind-control serums, a freaky science experiment. Amara should be easy to handle, yet something about her provoked me past reasoning.

And that something was not far behind me, following me into the dark, small space. The instant the door shut behind him, the air in the room exploded with heaviness, the oxygen so thick my teeth bit down, crunching the tension between them. The memory of the last time we were in a dark closet together convulsed my lungs and forced them to work harder for air.

He didn't make a sound, but his presence screamed through my bones. The magic we shared connected us by thousands of invisible strings. I kept my back to him, my hands strangling the frame of the racks.

I took a deep breath. "Why did you give it to me? I mean *really?*"

Like a GPS, I could feel him traveling to his destination. He stopped, his physique looming over mine. Heat seeped into the thin fabric of my scrubs. His breath knocked against my neck and traveled down my spine.

"Zoey…" My name came out like a whisper in the wind.

"What?" My lids squeezed shut.

"Why do you think I gave it to you?" his voice rumbled.

"I don't know. Because I had the nearest boot?"

"I gave it to you because you're the only one in the world I trust."

Trust. The word exploded over me like a bomb. Trust to

people like Ryker and me meant more than love. It was the ultimate compliment.

His declaration crumbled my heart like a dried leaf. But no matter what he said, I could feel the barrier between us.

"What do you want, Ryker?"

He sighed, a groan gurgling in his chest.

"I thought you wanted to stay away from me."

"I never said I wanted to." The heat from his lips brushed my ear. He didn't touch me, but his words slithered down my throat, warmth from his body pulsing against mine. My hands clasped tighter to the frame, holding me up. "It's what I have to do."

"We don't have a safe word, remember?" I whispered over my shoulder. "We take it all. Dangerous or destructive."

Ryker sucked in sharply through his nose. He reached above my head and grabbed the support beam of the shelf I was holding on to, his form rubbing roughly against mine. "Do you know how difficult this is?" The metal groaned under the pressure of his hand as he strangled the bar. "You can't imagine the things I want to do to you right now."

"Then do them." My heart thumped in my chest, my head feeling dizzy.

Ryker pressed harder into my back, forcing me to feel every inch of him. "Because some of the brutal things I want to do to you are nowhere near pleasurable. My line is still really thin. I don't have control. Until I know which way I will go, I can't be left alone with you."

"Then why did you come in here? I didn't ask you to."

"Because even against my better judgment, I can't stop myself. Where you are, human, is where I want to be."

Tears pricked under my lashes. Pain lobbied for its voice to be heard, crippling my physical body and my heart. Why was it always so tough for us to be together? The feel of him

71

against me made it even more difficult. It would be easy to tug away the two pieces of cotton between us, to let the fabric slide down my hips, feel him enter me.

Physically, the partition was thin. But emotionally? The world had built a barricade between us. Prisoners to unseen chains.

Ryker growled and stepped away from me. I stayed flattened against the shelf, letting it hold my weight.

"It's going to be day soon. We can't leave here while it's light. Amara is the only one who can glamour. I sent her to get water and something to eat for Lexie." Ryker's voice turned to ice. "But we need to plan to get proper provisions. Clothes, weapons, food."

I didn't move or answer. My throat wouldn't let me respond.

"Zoey?"

I nodded, keeping my burning eyes facing the wall. He exhaled. His boots made a squeak as they moved over the concrete. The door shut soon after.

Hearing it close felt like a bullet straight to my heart. My vision blurred, and my face crunched with agony. If I could have cut out my heart, I would have. It wailed with pain. I had never let myself love like this before. Not even Daniel. Love made you vulnerable. I had steered away from it most of my life to survive.

Daniel had been the first man I let those walls down for. I had loved him in my limited way, in the only way I thought I was capable of loving someone. But with him I always wanted to be a different person. Have a different life. Live in a fantasy where I didn't do bad things, things I secretly enjoyed. Daniel would have protected me, kept me from the big bad world, never knowing the darkness lived inside me. I would have pretended, forced myself to believe that part of me didn't exist. But nothing can stay hidden forever, and ignoring a part of myself would have eventually ended us.

Not one bit of me remained hidden from Ryker.

Without really noticing, somewhere along the way, Ryker had leaped beyond any boundary I erected. It was so subtle, like a frog slowly boiled to death. He devoured me whole. He did not shy away from the dark or light.

I loved him. Completely. Demon. Good. Bad. But fate seemed to be out for us. Keeping us apart. Even in the same room. I gritted my teeth, inhaled through my nose, and pushed off the shelving. I could sequester my feelings like the best of them. To survive, I would have to.

It took several more minutes, but I gathered my strength and walked out of the room, shoving my desires deep down. Time to focus on others—the people who needed me to be strong: Annabeth and Lexie.

I would not fail them.

SIX

"Absolutely not." Ryker threw out his arms in frustration. "What happened to focusing on food and weapons? Those are our priorities right now."

"They are, but I'm not going to sit back and let Vadik continue to harm Annabeth or any of those girls," I challenged, mirroring his movements. When I had returned to the main room, Sprig was awake, sitting on the table, bantering with Croygen. Amara left on the Wanderer's commands. And Ryker had again become the stoic, no-nonsense Viking. It should have helped me subdue my hormones when he turned into an ass, but sadly it didn't.

"Zoey, you're a good fighter. Don't let your emotions over this girl make you stupid." His jaw twitched.

"Do you guys need a timeout?" Croygen stood between Ryker and me, his hands pushing us away from each other.

"Oh man. They're at it again," Sprig climbed up to my shoulder and patted my cheek. "This happens when she doesn't get food or sex. I think it's becoming a disorder."

"Ryker," I said through clenched teeth. "I am getting Annabeth out of there. I'm not going to leave her."

"Yes, you are." He bared his, getting into my face. "At least for the time being. We need to check it out first to know what we are getting into. It's foolish. And suicidal. I have

74

fought too hard to keep you alive for you to recklessly throw it away on a girl who might *already* be dead."

A hiss of air strained through my front teeth. The thought she might be dead had skated the edges of my thoughts, but I hadn't let it settle. Ryker just pounded the idea into my gut like a cudgel.

"I don't even want you involved in this. But *if* we do, we do it *smart*." He inched his face a little closer to mine, stressing his words.

Sprig reached out and touched Ryker's cheek, muttering to Croygen. "Poor guy. It appears he is suffering from the same syndrome as *Bhean*."

Ryker glowered at Sprig and drew away from me.

"I have a brilliant idea! Food for everyone. Especially me... because, well... I. Will. Die. So, let's make it happen. I mean, before I die... kinda pointless after I die because I'd be dead and don't need to eat. Not that I still wouldn't want to. But I don't think I'd be able to chew, being dead. Hey, if you poured it down my throat I won't need to chew—"

"Sprig." I pinched the bridge of my nose.

"Oh, your boobs don't happen to be carrying the nectar of the gods? The deliverer of tasty goodness?"

Ryker stopped, his head snapping to Sprig with confusion. "What?"

"Those tiny packets of mind-blowing sweetness." Sprig stood on his hind legs, his arms up. "Please, gods, supply her bra with the magic of sugar. I bow down to the honey tits."

I groaned, which morphed into a chuckle in my chest.

"Honey tits!" Sprig sang out. "Do I get a hallelujah?"

"Hallelujah!" Croygen lifted his hands in the air with Sprig.

I looked over at him.

"What?" He shrugged. "I sing hallelujah for tits every day."

I snorted, shaking my head.

"Do I want to know why Sprig is praying to your boobs?" Ryker asked, an eyebrow angling up.

"No. You probably don't."

"Respect the honey tits, Viking." Sprig pointed down at my sports bra.

Ryker's eyes glinted as he licked his bottom lip. "Believe me. I hold them in the highest regard." Heat flushed through my body.

"Then let me hear a hallelujah."

Ryker tipped his head to the side. "Halle-fucking-lujah."

Sprig sagged down, his arms folding.

"What's wrong?" I peered at my little buddy.

"He's intercoursing with my honey!"

"Don't judge. It's been a while for him too." Croygen smirked.

I patted Sprig on the head.

"I'd feel a lot better if I had churros or a honey croissant in my belly. Or maybe some of those French fries?"

"No!" Both Ryker and I instantly refuted. Sprig's digestion did not take kindly to fast food. It took me back to the night Ryker and I sat in the dark. It had been the first time I opened up to someone and talked about my past. Even with all our prejudices and aversions to each other, he held me. Listened.

In that moment I realized Ryker was right. I was being rash. Getting Annabeth would be extremely difficult, and running off without thought or planning was stupid. It was hard to wait but necessary. But only for a day or so. My conscience wouldn't let me leave her much longer than that.

"What's your plan for getting provisions?" I leaned my hip into the table.

Ryker rapped his knuckles softly on the table. "You guys haven't been out in the city lately, but Seattle is functioning again. People are returning, rebuilding. Most electricity is back on, stores are reopened. Places aren't going to be as easy as before to sneak into or steal from."

Whatever Rapava injected us with took away the ability to glamour as well, which made stealing a lot harder. I used to do it all the time, but I didn't like the thought of stealing from people who were barely getting back on their feet.

"I miss money." Croygen put his hand to his heart. "I used to roll around naked on the piles I *inherited*. Those were the days."

"Wow, I didn't need that image in my head." I rubbed at my temple with exaggeration. It was a complete lie. The idea of Croygen naked, rolling around on anything, wasn't a bad thought at all.

But his statement triggered something in my memory. "Wait." I pushed off the table. "That's right!"

"What?" Ryker's eyebrows knitted together.

"Money. I have some." Excitement bounced me on my toes. "Daniel opened an account for me. I'm also his beneficiary if anything happened to him."

"Like how much are we talking about here?" Croygen's face lit up like a Christmas tree, but Ryker's scowl grew more dominant. It appeared so slight I was sure I imagined it, but I could swear I saw his tattoo flicker.

"I don't know, but it had to be quite a bit to cover Lexie's medical bills and for us to live on."

"Where is it?" Croygen leaned forward, his eyes dancing with dollar signs.

"The one he opened for me?" I glanced at Ryker. "Bellevue." It was in the bank we found the files and video Daniel had left for me. "The one I'm a beneficiary of is probably through a trust fund and will have to go through a lawyer or something."

"Then what are we waiting for? Bellevue, here we come."

"No." Ryker's response was immediate and ardent.

"What?" Croygen's head swung to the Wanderer. "Why the hell not?"

"Because." Ryker rolled his jaw, his expression severe.

"There better be more to it than 'because' for not getting *money*," Croygen replied.

"Because I said so."

I pinched my lips together. "Because *you* said so?"

Ryker's gaze sprang to mine like a leopard, ready to attack. "Yes."

"You are not in charge here." I slammed my palms on the table. "Nor are you the boss of me."

"Here we go again. Mommy and Daddy are fighting." Sprig jumped off my shoulder, crawling down to the table. "Retreat! Retreat!"

Ryker took no notice of Sprig. He placed his hands on the table, inclining forward, matching my pose. "Someone needs to be, especially when you are not thinking with your head."

"I think with my head." Croygen grinned.

"But neither of your heads actually holds a brain," Sprig retorted. Sprig and Croygen began to quarrel back and forth, but I ignored them and focused on Ryker as we fought for dominance in a stare-down.

"I'm going to retrieve the money, and I am going to get Annabeth," I seethed. "You can either help or get out of my way."

"Then go." Ryker folded his arms, straightening.

This was a trick.

"But this time I won't follow you back to DMG." His nose flared. "Because if you think they aren't still watching that place, waiting for you, then you're a fool."

Muscles along my back strained, and I could feel anger growing. I hated when he was right. Especially now.

"I know you want to go after Annabeth. I know you want to get your money." His voice softened and his shoulders dipped down, relaxing his stalwart stance. "But we are being hunted by a lot of smart, powerful people. DMG and Vadik will have groups scouring Seattle for us. They will not leave a stone unturned. They will expect us to go searching for resources or try to retrieve people we care about. We can't make a move without a solid plan."

I grunted. I *really* detested when he made sense. It was so unlike me to act without thinking. I had always been levelheaded and smart. Lately I felt my emotions had taken over. My heart, finally let out of its protected box, threw itself around like a whore. Damn feelings.

"Okay." I breathed out through my teeth.

"What?" Croygen spurted. "You mean we're not recovering the money?"

"No." My jaw wanted to lock down at the next part. "He's right."

"But it's *money*," Croygen whined.

"We're still getting dinner?" Sprig sat at the edge of the table. "Or breakfast... lunch... a snack... dessert. I'm really fine with any of them."

My regard ran from Sprig to Croygen. "You two really are alike."

"What?" both exclaimed in unison, flailing their arms, eyes wide.

I burst into laughter watching them look at each other, shrugging their shoulders at the same time.

Lexie groaned in her sleep, pulling my attention, watching the boney figure engulfed by the blanket.

Sighing, I turned back to the guys. "Okay. No money

79

and no powers mean we need to steal the old-fashioned way." Food and water were necessities and not something we could go without. Clothes were also important. All of us, except Amara, were still in bloodstained scrubs. Quite noticeable.

"You mean the tedious human way?" Croygen moved away from Sprig and came toward me.

"Unfortunately, yes."

"Everything humans do is tedious." Amara's voice came from behind me. My back muscles automatically clenched. I didn't bother to turn around. "What are you guys planning?" She walked up to Ryker, holding a large bottle of water and a bundle of bananas.

"What is that?" Sprig pointed to the yellow fruit. "You, purple tart, you got bananas? They taste and look like dwarf droppings. You did it on purpose, didn't you?"

We all knew she did it intentionally, but the potassium would be good for Lexie.

Amara winked at Sprig. "Oh, you don't like bananas? I totally forgot."

"She's trying to poison me." Sprig stood on his hind legs.

"Sprig, calm down," I exclaimed.

"Not with those things in the room. They will assassinate me in my sleep. Wrap their slimy peels around my neck and force me to eat them."

"What if they were coated in honey?"

"You have honey?"

"No."

"Ahhh, why, cruel world? Why?" He flopped on his back. "Is this the way I'm leaving this world? Death by banana?"

"One could only hope." Croygen grabbed one of the bananas and unpeeled it, tossing the skin onto Sprig as he stuffed the banana into his mouth. "Yum, so good."

"Ahhhhhhh!" Sprig scrambled out from under the skin.

"Croygen, really?" I shoved my hands on my hips. He only smiled at my raised eyebrow. "It's like having two five-year-olds."

"He started it!" Sprig stuck his tongue out at the pirate.

"I started it? You did, gerbil."

"Did not."

"Did too."

"Both of you stop it," Ryker shouted. "Now!"

"Uh-oh. Daddy just put his foot down." Croygen crossed his arms, sitting back on the desk.

"I'm about to put my foot up your ass," Ryker threatened, rotating his head back to Amara. "And to answer your question, we are figuring out how to get more supplies."

"I'll go with you." She placed her hand on Ryker's bicep. "You and I always made a good team."

Breathe. Breathe. Breathe, I chanted to myself. "No," I snarled. "I'm going."

"But you guys said you don't have your powers. I do." She nodded at Croygen and me with an impish smile. "Let them stay behind together. I think they want some alone time anyway."

"Hell. No," Ryker growled, his expression hard. "Zoey's the best thief even without magic."

"I'm going," I affirmed. Since Lexie was still asleep, I was all right with leaving her for an hour or two. The argument switched to who would go with me.

Ryker and I were firmly against Amara, so she was forced to stay back. Since I didn't trust her alone with Lexie for a moment, Croygen begrudgingly accepted his role as babysitter. Ryker remained terrified to be alone with me, but stated adamantly he would not let me go out into the night by myself.

"She won't be alone. She has me." Sprig ran for me.

"Sprig, stay here. We'll be back soon."

"Oh, masturbating garden gnomes. If there is food involved, I'm going."

"Masturbating garden gnomes?" My eyebrows lifted.

"Not something you want to see."

I could see both Ryker and Croygen cringe in agreement. "Now you have me curious."

Ryker motioned me to the door. "I promise you, you don't want to know. You will never look at a vegetable the same way again."

I groaned.

"Told you." Ryker smirked and held the door open for me. Even with his lightened mood, I could see the tension behind his eyes and in his shoulders. Fighting the desire to hurt me was probably worse than I could imagine. But he stayed at my side.

Sprig settled on my shoulder, gripping my hair, now back to its original brown color. I missed the purple, but with Amara here, I wouldn't dye it the same as hers again.

"Croygen." I turned back to the pirate and nodded at Lexie. "Guard her with your life."

His expression flushed solemn in a beat, his voice deep. "I will."

I knew then there was no one in the world my little sister was safer with. If you had told me in Peru not only would I see my sister again, but I would be entrusting her life without question to Croygen, I would have checked myself into an institution. But here I was. Not only did I trust my life with him, but I knew he would protect mine and Ryker's, obligation or not.

Life was seriously twisted.

I gave Lexie one last look then disappeared through the door and followed Ryker into the night, where everything hunted me.

Including him.

SEVEN

The Target store downtown was operating again, providing people with most of the essentials they lost in the storm but at gouging prices. Leave it to "the Man" to profit from the suffering, though it was nice to have so many things all in one place again. The security guards were always there, protecting the closed store from the gangs and the desperate. Ryker, Sprig, and I got in through the ventilation on the roof, moving through the ceiling ducts to the breakroom. The door was locked, but it didn't take me long to open it.

"You still have it," Ryker said, waving me in.

"Easy." I brushed my hands together with a shrug.

"No. What would be easy is if we could have jumped in here."

"Yeah, that would have been nice." I missed that power in particular, and I only had it for a brief moment. Ryker finally got most of his back and still couldn't use them.

We gathered food and water with backpacks we "borrowed." Next on our list were toiletry items, like toothbrushes, toothpaste, and soap. *Oh boy, here's to baby wipe "baths" again.* Then we moved to the clothing department.

"Should I feel bad I actually have money out there and am still sneaking in in the middle of the night robbing them blind?" I picked up a pair of soft, stretchy, skinny jeans and held them up to me.

"They will be just fine without your money. I promise." Ryker shredded off the scrub shirt and grabbed a black T-shirt. I watched him through my lashes, heat spiking up the back of my neck. No one should be that ripped. His body was the stuff of legends. Even more so because of his scars, which told a story of what he had been through in his life. *I caused some of those.* My eyes would not move away from him. I watched his tattoo ripple under his muscles as he slid his arms into the shirt.

He looked up; our eyes caught in the mirror. He stopped. Both of us went still as we stared at each other. His gaze became intense, his white eyes burning into my soul. My heart thumped, thinning my breath.

A flicker of light sparked in his eyes and down his neck, sucking the air from the room. *It's back.* I had seen it earlier, a good sign. Maybe our powers would eventually return. I also knew what the flickering meant.

Love or hate.

Kill or fuck.

It could be either, and in that moment I almost didn't care. All I could feel was my skin tingling everywhere with need. I just wanted him to touch me. To feel his hands on my body.

"*Bhean?*" Sprig exclaimed. I snapped my eyes away from Ryker back to the sprite on a shelf in the kids' section. I gulped in air, my lungs twitching. When I peered back at Ryker, the shirt was on, and he was walking away. The moment was gone.

"Yes?" I took another gulp of air and walked over to Sprig.

"Look at this bear's backpack. I have to have it!" He held up the toy, and I chuckled.

"Winnie the Pooh." A smile covered my mouth. The iconic bear had a honey jar-shaped backpack strapped to it. "Yes, you two have a lot in common. He loves his honey too."

"Winnie the poo? Like in poop?"

"Pooh."

"Poo. That's what I said." Sprig yanked at the backpack straps. "Strange name. Did he poop a lot or something? I mean, honey can do that to you sometimes." He banged the bear's head against the wood. "Take it off, Mr. Poo. It's mine. *Mine!*"

"Here, let me help you." I took the pack off the stuffed animal and hand-ed it over to Sprig. He chirped excitedly and held it to his chest. "Try it on."

He slipped his arms through and fitted the honey jar on his back.

"Perfect." I nodded.

He bounced on his legs with excitement and my grin reached my heart. Damn, this little guy made me so happy. I rubbed his head. "How did I ever live without you?"

I left him prancing and posing in the small mirror as I grabbed an outfit for myself and got dressed: dark jeans, black V-neck T-shirt, a hoodie, underwear. Simple, but much needed and appreciated after being in gray scrubs the last few months.

I laced up my old boots with the anchor inside the heel. It remained quiet right now, but most of the time I could feel it—the slight thumping of magic. Somedays it felt like it was screaming inside my head. I worried one day that anchor would pull me under.

On my way to pick up some clothes for Lexie, I spotted a shelf of knickknacks and a sale sign: *Half off zodiac animals*. I quickly ran my finger to Capricorn and almost started to cry. There under the sign lay a tiny stuffed goat. It wasn't the same as the first Pam, but it was adorable.

"This backpack is a lie." I heard Sprig screech from the other side of the room.

"Hey, furball, keep your voice down," Ryker grumbled from a dark corner.

"But-but... it's a lliiee."

I walked over to him. Sprig sat there staring down into the open bag.

"What's wrong?"

His bottom lip drooped, and he held up the pack. "Look. It's empty. No honey."

"Did you expect honey in there?"

"Hoped." He sniffed.

I leaned over, dangling the object I held up in front of him. "Well, now there can be more room for *Pam*." I said her name tentatively.

Sprig stared at the goat. Seconds ticked by and I swallowed nervously, ready to grovel and apologize, stating Pam could never be replaced. There was only one.

"Pickled gargoyles," he said evenly.

Oh no.

Sprig grabbed the goat from my fingers, holding it up, his eyes as wide as Izel's pancakes. "Pam, baby! You've had work done!" He wiggled her around. "You. Look. Fabulous!"

I clapped my hand to my mouth, trying to fight back the laughter. But Ryker's chuckle from the depths of the room was too much.

"What?" Sprig stared up at me innocently.

"Nothing." I kissed his head and turned away, giggles rocking my body. I went around the corner to see Ryker bent over his knees, laughing so hard no sound came out. Our gazes met each other, and we both burst into another fit.

Laughter felt amazing. Sometimes I forgot how good. Lately, there wasn't a lot to laugh about.

Ryker moved to the camping-and-sports section, searching for Swiss army knives and anything we could use as weapons. I rummaged through the medicine area, stocking up on antiseptic, bandages, painkillers, a sewing kit, and tampons—the necessities.

A thud from the level below broke the silence. I went still and swallowed back air, trying to listen. A door slammed shut.

I tiptoed to the end of the aisle. "Ryker?" I whispered. "Sprig?"

Only silence.

"Hey, did you hear that?" a man's voice called from the bottom of the stationary escalator. Two sets of boots pounded up the stairs.

I darted back into the clothing department, sliding up to a stand draped with the new fall clothing line, shoving my body into a mass of thick scarves, hats, and sweaters.

The two guards were dressed in uniforms: dark pants and tops, bulletproof vests and helmets, and matching automatic rifles. They bore more resemblance to SWAT team members than any security cop I'd ever seen. My gaze tracked their movements and the way they spread out and moved through the aisles, looking for burglars. These weren't the normal rent-a-cops. Things were a lot more drastic in Seattle since the storm, and they were taking protection of goods seriously. I had no doubt break-ins had been a problem since they reopened.

"Have you seen anyone come your way?" The taller man closer to me clicked his walkie-talkie, speaking into it.

"No, but we have the roof and the Pike exit covered," a crackled voice broke through the device responding.

Damn! Where were Ryker and Sprig?

"Keep your eyes open. If it's the same gang who broke in earlier this week, they're armed," he said to his partner and went around me toward the front of the store. The other man proceeded to the back.

Time to run.

I hated not knowing what happened to Sprig and Ryker, but I knew the Viking could take care of himself, and Sprig could sit on a shelf and pretend to be a stuffed animal. Still, I wanted him with me. Safe.

The men disappeared from sight, and I tore out from the fabric, bolting for the stairs. The only other outlet was on a lower level, onto Union Street.

I snuck down the steps, but every step thundered through the stillness. I reached the bottom and ran for the doors, seeing the shackles looping around the doors.

"Downstairs!" one of the men yelled.

"Shit. Shit." I pushed at the door, rattling the winding chains. Hurried footsteps headed for me. All exits were blocked, and I couldn't break through these locks without special tools, nor did I have enough time even if I had the equipment.

My heart thumped in my chest, and my gaze shifted over the room for any possible escape. "Hell!" My feet danced around like a bobblehead. *Jump, Zoey!*

"Freeze!" a man's voice boomed from the escalator, bouncing off the glass behind my head. I whirled around and spotted two dark outlines heading for me.

I was going to have to fight. Even if their guns could no longer kill me, they could certainly take me out of commission. Enough to capture and lock me up.

"I said don't move!" The sound of a gun clicked in my eardrum, sending panic throughout my body in electric tendrils. "I will shoot you."

I froze as the two security guards charged up to me.

"Hands up." The slightly shorter guard nodded his weapon at my hands, stepping close enough to see my face. He blinked. "You're a girl?"

"Well done." I put up my arms. "You must have been the top student in your class."

My gaze caught movement behind the two guards. A massive figure slunk down the steps silently, white eyes blazing in the dark. A spark of fear inched over me. I had seen him like this before. Terrifying. Now I knew it was his demon aspect taking over. His expression looked fierce; his bulk loomed over the men in front of him as he soundlessly crept up to them.

"How did a young girl like you break in here?" the taller, darker-skinned guard asked. "Where are the others?"

I tilted my head. "They are suggesting I couldn't break in here on my own. Can you believe that?"

"Stupid," Ryker growled behind them. "Never underestimate what a woman can do. Especially this one."

The men swung around, their fingers pulling at the triggers. Ryker was quicker. He tore the gun away from the shorter one, using it to club him in the head as he punched the taller guard. He hit *hard*, crumpling their bodies to the floor in an instant. Ryker's chest pumped in and out as he leaped on one of the men, grabbing his collar. The man groaned. Ryker slammed his fist into the guard's face. Over and over.

"Ryker!" I pushed from the doors, yelling. "Stop!"

His eyes shot up to mine.

Oh hell.

I stumbled back; the pure hatred consumed his

expression. He no longer saw me. Fear kicked in, taking me back to the day before when he had strangled me to death.

"Ryker…" I looked around, trying to find a way around him. Completely blocked.

Saying his name was the wrong choice. Hearing my voice sparked fire in his eyes. Even his tattoo flickered. In a blink, he sprang for me, snarling. His hand coming for my throat.

A cry tore out of my lungs.

Whoosh.

My head spun, the feel of wind crashing into my face. I didn't even have time to think before Ryker's form crashed into the glass doors, his fists knocking into the window.

I faced him. On the other side of the doors.

Holy shit, I just jumped! The powers were coming back!

The excitement was short lived. Ryker's hands beat against the glass, his face twisted with animosity. "Come back here, little human," he taunted. I took a step away from the doors.

Sprig's face peered around Ryker's feet, staring back at me. "*Bhean?*"

Oh god. Sprig.

Ryker didn't even notice him; his sight stayed on me.

Would he hurt him?

"Sprig, move away from him." I kept my gaze on Ryker as I spoke to Sprig.

"Why?" Sprig looked first at me then at Ryker.

"Just do as I say!"

"I know Vikings are assholes, but I have trained this one." Sprig ignored my words and climbed up Ryker's leg until he got to his shoulder. "Stay. Stand. Good boy." Sprig patted Ryker's cheek.

Ryker didn't even notice him; his gaze was locked on me.

"See. He just needs positive reinforcement. Honey always works. I like positive reinforcement, like in the form of honey biscuits, pancakes, candy, bread, nuts, soda, crepes, muffins, cookies, scones, fruit... well, except bananas. You know how I feel about those..."

"Sprig." Ryker dropped his head, breaking eye contact with me. "Shut up." I watched him take deep breaths, leaning against the frame of the door. When he lifted his head, his eyes were clear but quickly filled with sorrow and apologies.

I placed my palm on the glass. There wasn't much I could say.

"I'd never hurt him. I'd never hurt your sister or any of them." Ryker placed his hand on mine, even through the glass I could feel his heat. "That's not how the oath works. It's only triggered by you."

I gave a strange huffed laugh. His words actually did make me feel better.

"I think they help bring me back." Ryker lifted the shoulder where Sprig sat.

"See, *Bhean*. I have him well trained."

I snorted.

"Now can we get out of here? I am really in the need for sustenance. I want to take Pam out, show off her new figure. Though now she'll probably want a salad. Ugh. Salads. What is the point of those unless they are full of honey-coated nuts, dried fruit, and sugary dressing to soak it? The green stuff is just filler. But you could just replace the lettuce with honey mango chips or how about—"

"Sprig." I knocked on the window to get his attention, then pinched my fingers together.

Ryker straightened, tilting his head at me. "You're outside."

I nodded. "I jumped."

91

"Really?" Ryker closed his eyes, but nothing happened. His shoulders slumped as if in disappointment.

"At least they're still there. Hopefully that means they'll come back in time." Squealing tires in the distance brought me back to the urgency of our situation. "We need to get out of here before the other guards come or those wake up."

Ryker grabbed the chains lacing the doors and exhaled deeply. He could easily break the glass with his axe. If he had it. The thick safety glass was harder to put your fist through.

Sprig inched down his arm and grabbed one of the locks. In twenty seconds it fell from the door.

"Sprig!" I exclaimed. "Your powers work?"

"Yup. Because I'm awesome. Like a super sprite."

It was probably more because his little hummingbird body could work through whatever drugs Rapava had given us, but I accepted the awesome part.

He worked through a few locks before Ryker could kick the bolted door out of its frame. The moment the door opened, alarms pealed through the night air.

"Eek!" Sprig went stiff, tipping forward, falling. Ryker grabbed him quickly, cupping him in his hands.

"You. Stop right there," a woman's deep voice thundered from around the building.

"Shit." Ryker stuffed Sprig in my new bag and grabbed my arm, pulling me down the hill toward the water. Cries resounded behind us with demands for us to stop running. It felt like Peru all over again.

The messenger bag and backpack full of Sprig and the items we stole bumped against me, knocking me off kilter as I ran. A bullet whizzed past my head. Holy shit. These guys were serious about the no-stealing policy.

Ryker zipped and dodged through Pike's Place, running down the strip where empty stands lined both walls.

The guards gave up on telling us to stop, but their pursuit did not. I pumped my legs faster as another bullet zinged by me.

Ryker took a sudden turn down a passage. My boots stomped behind him, racing down the alleyway. The stone bristled with excitement under my heel, tingling my leg. It loved when my adrenaline pumped and my life's energy was at its most tangible, greedy for more. But instead of stealing it from me in those moments, it seemed to provide me with an extra boost, giving me a rush.

More. More. A part of me screamed, gluttonous for its power.

Ryker led us outside, downstairs, racing under the freeway and across the street to the tourist shops. He gripped my hand, pulling me toward a vacated booth, which probably at one point was used to sell sightseeing tickets in Seattle. Those went out of business quickly after the storm. Not much left here to see.

The booth was tiny, but I crammed myself under the desk. Ryker's massive frame stuffed in after me, his form moving on top of mine. Here we were being chased and all I could think about was his body against mine. My breath and heartbeat pounded together. The magic slipping up my leg had me shaking so bad Ryker had to press my legs down firmer with his, pinning back my arms. Slaps of feet neared us. Ryker stirred, keeping his head up and alert.

"Where did they go?" The man's voice had a thick Middle Eastern accent.

"I don't know," the woman replied. "We are so fired. Another gang break-in on our watch." There was a moment of silence. "Shit!" A bang of a shoe hit the booth by our heads.

"Well, looks like we lost them. Let's head back, check in with the others, then we can start looking in the help-wanted ads."

"Not funny, Khatri."

"Not meant to be a joke," he replied. "Come on, nothing more we can do here."

Steps faded away, but we lay there for several more minutes. The only sounds were the water lapping against the dock and random cars on the freeway.

Ryker exhaled and turned his head, peering down at me. It was as if he suddenly realized he remained on top of me. He didn't move off. He just stared, which from him was unnerving in so many ways. I didn't budge, afraid to startle the beast.

Like me, he had a hyperactive fight-or-flight response. Fighting I could handle. I enjoyed... hell, it turned me on more than I wanted to admit. This time I was more afraid of the latter. He felt so good, the weight of his body, the feel of him pushing into my thigh.

Our lips were only an inch apart, one tiny movement forward and my mouth would claim his. With what just happened in Target, I understood he had to be the one to make the first move. My heart thumped in my chest; my breath grew shallow. He exhaled, his breath sliding down my neck like tickling fingers. Without my mind's consent, my hips opened up wider, allowing more of him to fit between my legs. His hand gripped my thigh, sliding up to my waist.

Desire hit me so hard I had to squeeze my lids shut. Ryker produced a soft moan. His lips brushed the corner of mine, lifting my eyes. His hand continued to trail up my side, pushing underneath my T-shirt. Even the butterfly touch affected me. He didn't kiss me, but the brush of his lips, his fingers, the sensation of his breath skating to the sensitive part behind my ear and trailing between my breasts made me groan. We filled the small space with short, forceful breaths.

Ryker only had to look at me and I came undone. We both loved the high of the chase, got off on close calls, and were turned on by fierceness. It was nice to know I didn't have to hide that part of myself or push it away and pretend it didn't exist. With Ryker I could roll in it, getting as dirty as I wanted, and he would respond in kind.

My back arched as his palm skimmed my stomach then wandered back, dipping below my jeans. He tugged at the button, letting his fingers trail underneath the band of my underwear. Then he moved lower.

"Oh gods," he whispered, his hand cupping the heat between my thighs. His hand moved deeper between my legs. I gasped. His touch was too much. I could no longer wait.

"Ryker," I choked out, lust coating my throat. "Please."

My voice caused him to lift his head. His eyes flickered with light. His hands went to my hips as he stood, tossing me up on the counter, my butt landing hard on the wood. His hands skated roughly up my neck, pulling my hair up as he went. He yanked my head back. The moment our eyes connected I knew he was no longer there.

"Ryker?"

He leaned over into my ear. "How about I fuck you while I'm killing you." He bit my ear.

I shoved him back, giving me enough room to pull up my leg. The sole of my boot slammed into his chest. He stumbled back, hitting the wall.

"I like it rough." A smile turned up his mouth as he came back for me. That was the problem. We both did.

I jumped off the table. There was nowhere to go in the tiny room. He easily reached out, wrapped his arms around me, and brought me back into his body. One hand coming up for my neck.

I didn't say a word. There seemed no point pleading. He stayed a slave to the oath.

I thought of only one thing to break his trance. My teeth sank into the soft spot between his finger and thumb, sawing together.

Ryker shouted in pain, his arm dropping away from my neck. I crunched down tighter, the taste of blood exploding over my tongue.

"Zo-ey. Stop." He hissed in pain.

My name. He said my name.

When I let go, blood oozed from the puncture holes. I moved away, spinning to face him.

Pain etched deep into his face as he held his bleeding hand to his chest. "Fuck, woman. You are worse than a Chihuahua."

I wiped the blood from my chin. My body vibrating with life. "At least let me be a pit bull or something cool."

Ryker lifted an eyebrow. We both stood there, breathless, our eyes locked. The small space couldn't seem to contain us, spitting back the sounds of us gasping for air, echoing the thumps of adrenaline pumping in our veins.

Want.

Desire.

Lust.

Carnage.

It was always there with us. The passion mixed with fierceness, tearing at the seams, breaking me in pieces till I didn't know which one I wanted more. My hot skin screamed to be touched again, to feel his rubbing against mine.

His tattoo flickered, his nose flared, and he jerked his head to the side.

"You have blood on your nose."

"You have a tendon sticking out of your hand." My voice wobbled, still rough with craving.

"You have a wicked bite." Ryker inspected his hand, the blood already slowing.

"Why you love me," I replied coyly, not realizing what I had said.

Oh, holy shit. Did I just say that?

"I didn't mean it like *love*. I meant like love. You know…" Crap! I was babbling. I think I giggled too. *Shut up, Zoey.*

"I know what you meant." His tone sounded unemotional. He dropped his eyes to his hand. It had already stopped bleeding. "We need to get back. Get far away from here."

I nodded and picked up the messenger bag where Sprig curled at the bottom.

Ryker collected his things, unlocked the latch, and stepped out into the early dawn.

I heaved the strap over my head, chiding myself quietly. A head poked out from the bag. "Hey, bud. You're awake." I rubbed his ears.

"Where the hell are we? Do we live in a tollbooth now?" He glanced around. "Small. Might be a little awkward with all of us, but hey, still a lot less awkward than the painful moment I just witnessed." He patted my arm.

"You heard, huh?"

Sprig waggled his head and peered at me with concern. "Tragic."

"Yeah. Story of my life."

"The giggle was a nice touch."

"Shut up."

I buttoned my pants and proceeded out into the night, still reeling from the whiplash of our encounter.

We only walked for two blocks when I felt a sensation slither up my spine, like boney fingers up the back of my neck. We were being watched. I stopped, my gaze roamed over the black alleyway and dimly lit street.

"What?" Ryker glanced over at me, his expression unreadable.

The itchy, uncomfortable feeling of eyes on me prickled my skin. My gaze wandered around, reaching in the dark corners. Nothing was there, but the unease would not dissolve.

"Zoey?" Irritation twisted through my name.

"It feels like we are being watched." I gripped the strap of my new bag, feeling the comforting weight of Sprig inside. He talked softly to Pam 2.0, catching her up on all she had missed since Peru.

Ryker tensed, turning slowly in a circle, taking in the space around us. "I don't see or sense anything."

If it were DMG, they would come right for us, no playing around. This energy had the presence of a cat playing with its food. Garrett would enjoy messing with us, but his power was strong. I couldn't even tell if this was human or fae. I rubbed my head, a slight headache thumping at my temple, the energy I had earlier depleted, leaving me feeling drained and a little depressed.

"Let's get off the street," Ryker barked. He moved in front of me, walking deeper into the shadows, his shoulders curling up toward his ears, worsening my mood.

That damn oath still controlled him. *Us.* I hated it. Why couldn't it just break? What if it started getting worse again, to the point where he lost himself in the bloodlust? How long would it be before he really tried to kill me? Would I survive? Would it break, or would I keep rising back to life, never fulfilling the oath? Was this twisted cycle the best we could hope for?

I pushed back the thought, picking up my pace to catch up with him. As I rounded a corner to follow him, I glanced over my shoulder. In the depths of the alley, a pair of black eyes stared back into mine, a faint glow of aura hinted at his skin, but I couldn't tell if it was human or fae.

Air caught in my throat.

"Hurry up," Ryker shouted, shattering my attention on the figure.

"I'm coming," I snapped at him and quickly looked back behind me. The eyes were gone, the alley empty. I blinked a few times.

I wanted to believe my sight was playing tricks on me, my pounding head making me see things, but my intuition told me different. It was probably a homeless person or someone looking to score drugs, sex, or goods. With everything we had been through today, I pushed it away and followed Ryker back to the safe house, forgetting about it the moment we walked into the warehouse.

EIGHT

My attention went straight to the pair sitting on the floor. Lexie leaned against the wall, bundled up under the dirty blankets while Croygen sat on the ground facing her.

Croygen didn't even look up, but I knew he sensed our presence.

"Full house." He chuckled, placing some cards between them. "Beat that!"

A sly smile curled up Lexie's face, a look I knew well, as she spread her cards down. "Four of a kind."

"Seriously?" Croygen groaned. "No one can be this lucky."

"That's seven in a row, pirate." She snickered, then took a deep breath, her face pale and clammy. "You owe me fifty bucks."

Croygen turned to me. "I think I'm going to take this girl to a casino. She's kicking my ass."

"She's twelve." I folded my arms, stepping farther into the room.

"I'll be thirteen in a week," Lexie retorted.

Jeez, was it already late September? I'd lost more time underground than I thought.

"Still illegal."

"Well, kid, no matter your age, you are a freaking card shark." Croygen shook his head admiringly.

"She was gambling for kids' lunch money at the age of seven." I let my eyes roam proudly over her. She looked so frail and sickly, sweat beading her hairline, her usual creamy caramel skin a pallid color.

"Six," she corrected me.

One guy I'd been "seeing" had taught Lexie cards and dice. She learned quickly. She gambled for objects she coveted, whereas I stole them. We were quite a pair in our neighborhood. Two sweet-looking girls, one disabled, who would rob you blind without you even realizing it. It was also another reason I picked up fighting.

I had to fight us out of sticky situations when the loser wasn't too keen about forfeiting the pot to a little girl. Many times it didn't go in our favor, and I'd end up back in the hospital or the police station. People, especially men, did not like being beaten by a young girl over the table, while another one robbed him. Our ruse didn't last long when they figured us out, but Lexie never stopped gaming with kids to win their Christmas gifts.

"Where did you get the cards?" I asked.

"Left in a drawer." Croygen tipped his head toward the desk. "Probably from the last person who hid out here."

"Speaking of hiding," Ryker huffed from behind me. "Glad you are keeping guard."

"Amara's shift." Croygen pointed over to the corner. Her lithe figure stood in the shadows, blending in so well I hadn't seen her.

"I knew you guys were coming." Amara leaned against the wall, keeping her gaze out the window.

"Fifty bucks, Hook." Lexie held out her hand, her jaw set firmly as she looked at him.

"Oh, were we playing for real money?" Croygen took a step back.

"Pay up."

"Wouldn't you rather have a doll or something?"

"I decapitate dolls."

Croygen's eyebrows shot up.

"She does." I moved in closer, realizing a smile was plastered on my face. It felt so good to have her back. She was alive! That in itself had been enough, but seeing the saucy tween I knew so well lightened my heart.

"Oh, look. I think it's my shift." Croygen pointed over to the window.

"No, it's not." Amara folded her arms.

"Yes, it is," Croygen replied.

"Running scared from a twelve-year-old girl." Amara rolled her eyes. "Pathetic, Croygen."

"She's a hell of a lot more intimidating than most grown women I've met," Croygen mumbled.

"That's because I'm already smarter than you." Lexie's smile was soft, and she struggled to keep it on her face. She sank down, exhausted and weak. "Still owe me my winnings."

"I'll get back to you on that."

Hiding my amusement, I kneeled down in the empty spot he left. "Never trust a pirate."

"Tradesman!"

"Dickhead. Assmuncher. All the same." Sprig tugged himself out of the bag around my hip.

Lexie went still, her eyes centering on Sprig.

"I-I thought I dreamed him."

Sprig climbed out onto my knees. "I missed the card game? What was the bet? Honey? Or honey-filled doughnuts? Those are so good. Have you ever tried churros dipped in honey? Holy gnome ass!"

Lexie eyes widened the faster he talked.

I covered his mouth. "He can get a little excitable."

"Sprig," Ryker called, walking over to the beat-up desk against the wall. His back stayed rigid, the fence between us locked firmly in place. "Come here, furball."

Sprig slipped off my lap, heading for Ryker. "How about addressing me as Captain? Or Master Sprig. Super Sprite works as well."

"The only thing you are a master at is licking your own balls." Croygen sat back on the windowsill.

"Only if they are coated with honey." Sprig flipped his middle finger at him and climbed up Ryker's leg, plopping on the desk.

Ryker snorted. "Admit it, you're kind of jealous, Croygen."

"Hell yeah. Would you leave the house if you could lick your own balls?"

"Honey-dipped ones," Sprig chirped.

"Guys," I growled, rubbing at my aching head again. My hands quaked against my forehead, the tremble growing steadier. Dropping them, I rolled my shoulders back, shoving aside my restless, yucky mood.

Lexie watched the banter with an incredulous smile on her face. Sadly, this wasn't even close to the worse conversation she'd ever heard or participated in. She had quite a mouth on her thanks to life in our neighborhood.

My hand reached up and cupped her face. Her flesh burned my skin. I didn't need a thermometer to know she had a fever. My life had been so in tune to Lexie's health I knew the signs.

"I have missed you so much."

"I missed you too." Lexie's gaze darted to me.

All the unsaid words weaved between us like cobwebs.

"Here." I took the bags off my shoulder, opening the one with water and food. "You need to get something in your system. I got the strongest painkillers I could."

"Thanks."

"Get out of there, furball," Ryker's voice ordered from the other side of the room. With the help of Sprig, Ryker tried to display the items we stole on the table.

"Here." Ryker picked up a plastic bear filled with honey, wiggling it between his fingers.

"Honey! The deities love me," Sprig cried out, bouncing on the table, his arms flailing in the air. "Oh sweet tasty bear, let me suck out your guts." Sprig grabbed the bear from Ryker's fingers, ripped off the safety top, and began chugging it.

"Only half, Sprig." I shot over my shoulder, knowing my request would be completely ignored. He made only a chirped moan as he guzzled the nectar.

"I'm going to walk around and check to see if everything is okay." Ryker's voice sounded gruff like both heaven and hell at once. The distance between us made me feel like I had been banished. I understood why he needed to. Twice tonight he had tried to kill me, but that didn't ease my pain. His eyes went to me then he spun around and marched out the door. Amara quickly followed, slipping into the night.

My molars ground together. Of course she'd go after him.

"I see you two made up." Croygen chuckled and headed for the table, picked through the clothes and food, and changed into the black cargo pants we got him.

Ignoring him, I turned back to Lexie.

"How are you feeling?" I put the back of my hand to Lexie's forehead. *Shit.*

"Still really out of it."

"Dizzy?"

She nodded.

"Cold and hot flashes?"

"Yeah. Right now I'm freezing."

I drew the blankets tighter around her shoulders.

"You need to eat something." I put a power bar in her hand. It was one for bodybuilders, extremely high in calories and protein. "I got you other stuff, but I think you should start with this. We need to get as many calories into you as we can."

She scrunched her nose, sniffing it before taking a bite. "Eww." She shook her head, gagging.

"I know it doesn't taste good, but you need to eat."

"But I'm not hungry." She flinched, swallowing. "I want to throw up."

"I still need you to try." I gently brushed her wild, knotted hair flatter to her head. "What did they feed you at DMG?"

Her mouth opened to talk, but nothing came out. Her brows furrowed. "I-I don't know."

"You don't know what you ate?"

She rubbed her temples and shivered hard.

"I don't remember."

My stomach plunged to my toes.

Lexie bit down on her lip, her brow creasing. "It all feels like a faraway dream, as if it happened to someone else."

"Tell me anything you remember. When did they operate on your legs?"

"A week, a month? I don't... I don't know."

"Can you remember anything?"

"I remember Rapava and tons of people coming into my room all the time, but when I try to center on anything specific..." Her fingers began to rub violently over her brow.

"Why can't I remember? How can I not have even one memory of getting these legs? Or what I ate last..." Her eyes widened, filling with tears. "Oh god. Why don't I remember anything?" Her voice grew high and agitated.

"Shhh. It's okay." I pulled her against me, my hand running over her back, trying to soothe her. "Calm down."

"No." Her head brushed back and forth against my shoulder. "It's not all right."

"You're right. None of what he did to you is okay." I sucked on my bottom lip. It was what I feared. The mind control and all the drugs had messed with her memory. I hoped it was temporary, but I wouldn't put it past Rapava to make sure it lasted. Just in case she did escape, she wouldn't be able to clearly tell anyone anything. "Rapava drugged you to control your mind. This must be another effect of it so you wouldn't be able to remember anything of your time in the lab."

She pulled away from me and licked her lips. "I let him drug me."

"What? You let him?" The words burst out of my mouth like a bomb.

"He said the injections would help me. I didn't know he would take away my memories." Her lips quivered. "He told me I would be benefitting human lives, that my help was crucial. My aid could benefit every kid like me. He said I would walk again."

"What an asshole!" Croygen spoke, stepping back over to us. "Manipulating a little girl's mind so he can run tests on her."

"Croygen." I shook my head, telling him to shut up.

Lexie slid her hands over her face, then dropped them to her lap. "Everything before the night of the storm is crystal clear." A tear pushed from the corner of her eyes, trailing down her cheek. "I was so mad at you for lying to me. For knowing there could be a cure and not telling me. Letting me die…"

Ice stabbed into my heart. Was that what she thought? I would let her die?

"Lexie." I gripped her hands in mine. "You have to know there isn't anything I wouldn't do for you. They were still only testing. There was *no* cure."

"That's not what Dr. Rapava told me. He said they had successful transplant cases and felt positive he could make me walk. That he could save my life, and I wouldn't be sick anymore."

Hatred and disgust coated my throat, choking me.

"He said he didn't understand why you kept me from getting better." Tears glided down her face. "There was no reason for me to live the rest of my life in a chair."

"Are you fucking kidding me?" Croygen exclaimed, his voice booming behind me, his new shirt halfway over his head. "That evil, lying, deceitful fucker!"

"He wanted to help me and convinced me not to tell you. He said you would be glad once I got better." Lines ground into her forehead. "I am so sorry, Zoey. All I thought about was the fact I could possibly walk again and be healthy."

"I don't blame you, Lex. Of course you'd want that." I was livid that a grown man turned my sister's mind against me, but hadn't I also fallen under the spell of Rapava's manipulating power? I could not fault a desperate, scared twelve-year-old for wanting to believe his words. "What happened the night they came for you?"

"After the storm hit, they came to the house." She wiped away the tears on her face, taking a deep breath. "Joanne tried to fight them with a bat, but they knocked her out. I think they must have injected me with something because everything after is jumbled. I don't know what they did to Jo. But I do have this blurry memory of our house on fire as we drove off."

The fire they set was to kill Jo and to make it look like Lexie had died in the flames as well. Perfect cover.

Her delicate hand rubbed her face roughly. She sighed, exhaustion drooping her shoulders. "I don't even remember when I first saw you. It's all bits and flashes, but nothing seems real."

"Don't worry about it right now."

"I'm sorry, Zoey," she whispered. "I'm so sorry for everything."

"Hey." I put my hand up to her face. "You are safe and with me. That's all that is important."

She nodded. A bead of sweat trickled down her face.

"Take these and get some sleep." I handed her some painkillers and bottled water. She downed both and lay back on the blanket.

"I'm scared, Zoey," she whispered.

I squeezed my jaw together. I would not cry in front of her. "Go to sleep." I leaned over and brushed my lips against her forehead. She exhaled and buried herself deeper into the covers.

The moment I felt her slip into a slumber, I jumped up and marched over to the far side of the room. My palm pushed firmly on my chest so it wouldn't crack open and spill all over the floor. I leaned my head into the wall, trying to breathe.

Croygen's hand touched my shoulder.

"I can't do this." My voice broke. "I can't go through losing her again." Or losing any of them. Annabeth was never far from my mind either, her peril just as grave. The world seemed to be crashing onto my shoulders, determined to bury me under it.

"We'll figure it out." Croygen rubbed my back.

"Will we?" I could feel anger slowly absorbing my sadness.

"Yes."

"How?" I whipped around, my hands on my hips. "DMG and Vadik are hunting us. We probably have a price on our heads. We aren't even strong within ourselves. I don't trust Amara. Ryker can't be around me without trying to kill me. Lexie needs better care and medication…" I burst into tears. I couldn't take care of her this time. Everything else I could deal with, but failing Lexie again was not among them. She was getting sicker, and I could do nothing to stop it. I only wanted to get her away from DMG, but what if that had been the precise thing keeping her alive?

Croygen pulled me in, wrapping his arms around me.

"What if I made a mistake?" I sobbed into his chest. "Was she better there?"

"No one is better there."

"Croygen…"

"You are not alone. I'm here, Zoey. I'm not leaving. Even your dick of a boyfriend is here. Neither of us are going anywhere." He kissed the top of my head. "I have known him a long, long time. Believe me when I say that man is not leaving your side. No matter how painful it is. And like me, he will do anything in his power to help your sister."

His words only caused more tears to flow down my face. I pushed deeper into his chest, my heart wanting to dissolve into him. I knew so little of love or trust. Even to depend on people. To have friends. A family.

Somehow these two menacing fae had let me in. Brought me within their walls, protecting and loving me.

"How did I get so lucky?" I muttered into Croygen's damp shirt.

109

"You and I have different versions of lucky." He loosened his hold on me. "But if you want to try the whole face in my crotch again…"

I snorted and pulled away from him. I wiped away my tears, letting a smile push at my lips.

"Dangling bee nuts. You mole rats are frisky tonight," Sprig muttered from the table. I leaned around Croygen. Sprig sprawled on his side, his new backpack facing me with Pam's head sticking out. He cuddled the empty bottle against him.

"Stop. That tickles." He giggled, his feet kicking out.

"And here I thought *my* mind was a scary place to be." Croygen shuddered.

I walked over to Sprig, took Pam out of his bag, and switched the bear bottle for her. I held up the hollow container. "We're so going to pay for this."

"You still have a receipt, right? We can return him?"

"Think the warranty is up. We're stuck with the little bugger."

"But it came broken. There's got to be a policy for that." Croygen waved at Sprig.

I turned around, wagging my head.

"The zoo might take him."

Yeah, a talking, narcoleptic, ADD, honey-addicted sprite-monkey would go over well.

"Adopted by a troop of monkeys in Brazil?"

I continued to head for the corner.

"Hell! He could be their leader. He'd love it. He'd be a king of the baboons there."

"Night, Croygen."

Dawn licked at the night sky, blushing the darkness with light as I curled up on the dirty mattress. Lexie's body felt fragile next to mine. The night of the fae storm, I'd watched

110

the only place I stayed at long enough to call home burn down, with the reason I called it home inside. Now I watched her chest move raggedly up and down. The sense of her being taken away from me for a second time washed over me.

I gripped her to me, hoping if I held on tight enough, she wouldn't slip through my fingers again.

NINE

Screams tore me out of sleep, jolting my eyes open to the muted light. My heart crawled up my throat as another terror-filled cry came from the figure next to me. I sat up and turned to face her. Her eyes were closed. Tears and sweat coated her face. A strangled, pained wail arose from her, her arms lashing out at an invisible attacker.

"Lexie." Terror filled my chest. I reached down, touching her shoulder. "Wake up."

She batted at my hand, screaming in terror.

"Lexie! Wake up."

Ryker was suddenly beside me, grabbing her hands and holding them down. Croygen came to Lexie's head. He pressed his fingers in the space between her brows and then rubbed his hand soothingly over her temples in an arch motion.

"Shhh," he whispered softly. Lexie's cries died in her throat, her body stilling as her breathing slowed. A peaceful expression lightened her face.

My mouth cracked open, staring first at the sleeping girl then at the pirate. "How did you do that?"

Croygen looked at me through his lashes. "You learn a lot in the Orient." He winked, as his hands continued to trace from the bridge of her nose to her temples. "The pressure point they call the third eye helps calm a person."

Ryker's awed expression matched mine. We both stared at Croygen. Every day these men surprised me.

"Well, thank you."

"Welcome." Croygen's brow furrowed. "The kid has been through a lot. I can't imagine the horrors she's endured. She might not remember right now, but her subconscious does."

"Yeah." Guilt climbed on my back. I tried so hard to provide a better life. Make the best of the crappy hand she was dealt. She appeared strong, but I knew too well that fine line between tough and brittle.

I reached out, feathering my fingers over Lexie's face. Heat rolled off her skin like a scorching desert. Her fever had gone up.

"When the sun sets, we need to move. We can't stay at any location for more than a night or two." Ryker stood, moving away from me. "I know of a place owned by dark fae. We should be safe there."

"Where?" Croygen rose.

"Across town. An old car garage."

"Joey's place?" Croygen's eyebrow hitched up. "Sure we'd be safe?"

Ryker folded his arms.

"Why?" I glanced between them.

"Joey, from what I heard, is not too happy with our boy here."

"Shocker." I got to my feet, careful not to disturb Lexie. "Ryker doesn't have a lot of male fans, fae or human."

Croygen snorted.

"Just be ready to go in two hours." Ryker turned around and left the room. I hated he couldn't be near me for more than a few minutes. Every time he walked away a piece of my soul followed.

Croygen stared at me with a knowing grin.

"What?"

He chuckled under his breath, walking away. "Joey's a woman."

Ah. Croygen didn't need to say any more. Here was another one of Ryker's forsaken lovers, probably another passionately pissed-off woman. Speaking of those, I noticed Amara was nowhere to be found. Hopefully she'd run away.

"Maybe we should go somewhere else."

Croygen only laughed harder, purposely nudging the desk where Sprig passed out.

"Bears! They're coming for me," Sprig squeaked in his sleep, his legs and arms twitching. "No. No, don't eat me!"

"All those honey bears he's eaten are finally retaliating." Croygen hit the desk again. "Get him, bears. Suck out the mush he calls brains."

"Croygen. Stop." I moved over to the table. "We have enough people in here who need therapy."

"Too late for this one."

"Sprig?" I touched the soft fur by his ear.

"Ahhhhh! Zombie honey bears. Eating. My. Brains!" He jerked and jumped up, fists forward. "Get back, Teddy!" He blinked at Croygen and me. When he realized where he was, Sprig dropped his arms, the grimace smoothed away. "Hey. Is it breakfast time? Oh look, a granola bar." He pointed down the desk at the loot we took. "Is Izel's close? I really want some of her pancakes. Damn, that woman can cook. Pam? Oh gods, did she leave me again?"

"She's right here." I picked her up and placed the goat into his outstretched arms.

"Pammy." He hugged her tight. "What?" He put his ear to her mouth. "She wants to go to Izel's too."

"We are nowhere near Izel's." My mind flashed back to the previous night when I had jumped. Again it was purely out of self-protection and not by choice, but I hoped that meant someday Ryker and I would be able to control them again. Izel's for breakfast would be a possibility.

The sun dipped below the horizon. Our situation had turned us into night crawlers.

Amara sauntered in the room; her hands wrapped around a coffee cup. My mouth watered as the strong, rich aroma wafted into my nose, and I had to bite my lip to keep from snatching the cup out of her hands.

"Did you get us any?" Croygen sat on the edge of the desk.

"I got it for the people who needed it, who were actually on guard all night." She smiled, taking a gulp of coffee.

"Bitch," Croygen snarled.

"Wow. It's like you can read my mind." I tapped his arm.

We shared a smile. Amara's gaze darted back and forth between us, smugness glinting in her eyes. I knew what she was hoping, what she wanted to happen—that the bond between Croygen and me would push Ryker and me apart.

"You two are really adorable." She smiled.

"Back off," Sprig huffed, coming to my side on the desk, glaring at Amara. "Your desperation is making me want to fling poo at you."

"You are disgusting."

"And you are a carton full of bat-shitting bananas."

"Hmmm. I like that one." Croygen gave Sprig an approving nod.

Amara glared at both, her mouth open as though to speak, but at Ryker's entrance, she shut it.

A coffee cup in hand, he strolled in. In an instant she

pulled a flirty smile on her lips and flicked her ponytail over her shoulder. He walked by her, not even giving her a look. He took a sip then placed the coffee in my hand as he passed, going to the bags and wordlessly packing the stuff on the table.

I couldn't fight back my smile for the fact that he knew me so well and my love for coffee... or more accurately, for caffeine.

Even with the oath in place, we were still a team. I was so freaking in love with this man. Seeing Amara's bitter expression didn't hurt either.

I took a swallow, letting the strong acrid flavor coat my tongue. It wasn't great coffee, but I missed it too much to care. Black, cheap, lukewarm, I'd take it. A small sigh came from my throat.

"Do we need to leave you alone, *Bhean*?" Sprig patted my arm. "I totally get it. Honey—"

A liquid-filled cough cut off Sprig's words. I spun instantly. Setting down the coffee, I ran for Lexie. She leaned over and began retching on the floor. Everything she had eaten or drunk in the last day came out in violent waves, until there was nothing but bile.

I held her hair with one hand, rubbed her back with the other. It reminded me of the many times I'd done just this after a treatment or when she dealt with the side effects of a new medication. It didn't even faze me anymore, especially when I looked into her face and saw the pain and exhaustion streaking her features.

Her arms shook as she held herself up. Vomit covered the floor and left splatter on her top. "I'm sorry." A tiny, childlike whimper came from her.

"Don't be sorry. Never be sorry." I softly massaged her shoulders. She always got extremely emotional after she was sick. "Remember what I used to tell you."

She nodded. "Just my body filtering out the bad to make room for good." Lexie took in a shaky breath and glanced at her audience. A fever flushed her cheeks, but I could also see embarrassment in her eyes.

Luckily no one seemed horrified. Croygen ventured over first.

"Oh god. Don't look at me like this." Lexie squeezed her lids closed, turning her head away from him.

"Are you kidding, little card shark?" He squatted down next to her. "You know how many times I've hurled? I didn't look half as graceful as you. You have style."

She snorted and wiped her mouth.

Ryker handed me a towel, wipes, and a shirt I had picked out for Lexie. I took the items.

"I didn't think we could get that blanket filthier. Good job." Croygen patted her back. His humor had relaxed her shoulders, helped her embarrassment fall away.

"All right. Let's get you cleaned up." Afterward I hoped I could get more liquids, painkillers, antibiotics, and eventually food down her.

Without a word, Croygen scooped her up, lifting her away from the mess on the floor. Ryker hooked the blanket with his foot and covered the puddle. It was simple, but for Lexie, it would make a difference not having to see it. I gave his wrist a squeeze as I passed, his body going rigid at my touch. I ignored it and headed for my sister. Croygen set her down on the table.

"Impressive projection." Sprig held up his hand.

"Thanks." Lexie high-fived him.

"All you boys, out." I pointed to the door. I wanted to give Lexie some privacy as I cleaned her up.

Sprig grabbed Pam and walked back to Lexie. "This is Pam. We got back together last night. She's had some work done, but we don't talk about it."

117

Lexie looked at me. I gave her a smile. She turned back to Sprig and the goat. "Nice to meet you, Pam."

"She told me she'd like to hang out with you. Girl bonding stuff, you know." He held Pam up to Lexie. My heart fluttered. I knew what he was doing. Pam was his security when he felt scared. He wanted Lexie to have the same.

"Cool. I'd love to hang out with Pam." Lexie took her.

"Don't let her have a drink, no matter how much she begs. She gets soggy. Then I hear all day how fat and bloated she feels. Ugh. Women."

"Tell me about it." Ryker grabbed Sprig by the scruff, plopping him on his shoulder, and headed out of the room.

"And don't touch my honey. Wait, shouldn't I have some to go? Takeaway honey tits?" His voice faded away as everyone left the room.

Lexie stared after the vanished group.

"You'll get used to this crazy group." I carefully took off her soiled scrub top.

"This is all…"

"Overwhelming? Scary? Screwed up?"

"All of the above." She giggled softly, but with little energy. "What's strange is I don't find it weird that you have a talking monkey and are hanging out with fae."

"After what you've seen, I'm sure this is nothing." I handed her a wipe for her face as I started on her arms.

"I wished I remembered more. I don't recall being told about fae, but I know about them. It's in there." She tapped at her head and then wiped off her face.

"Are you all right with them? Do they scare you?"

"Bad-boy version of Thor is terrifying, but no… I'm not scared. I feel protected." She wiped at her hands, then leaned over. "I don't like her though, the one with the purple hair. She looks like one of those bitches I wanted to hit in school."

118

I tugged Lexie's head forward and kissed the top with a laugh.

"You always had good instincts, kiddo."

She grinned faintly, her gaze rolling over me. "Are you okay?"

"Yeah, of course," I responded quickly. She narrowed her stare on me. "Why do you ask?"

"Because. You've lost weight and I've noticed your hands shake a lot. You look really tired."

"Wow, thanks." My shoulders stiffened. My eyes dropping to my fingers. They vibrated with a slight tremor. Lexie could see through me. She knew something was wrong. I couldn't tell her about the stone, what it was doing to me, but I couldn't lie to her either. "It's nothing I can't handle. Don't worry about me. We need to concentrate on you getting better."

She nodded, letting the topic drop. I continued to wash her, several minutes passing in silence.

"Is Jo dead?" Lexie blurted.

I bit my lip and nodded. "Yes. She is."

"I should feel sad or something, shouldn't I?" She held up her arms as I slipped her new shirt over her scrawny body. "I mean, I do. But not really for her. More for our home, the room you and I shared."

"You feel how you feel." I understood her fear of losing empathy. When you were so used to loss, you put up walls to protect yourself. One day those walls became so thick, you stopped feeling completely.

"I am really sorry about Daniel. I know how much you cared about him."

"I did." I nodded.

"You're in love with the Viking dude, aren't you? I can see it."

119

"Lexie, you've been with us for less than twenty-four hours and most of it you were asleep."

"It's that freakin' obvious." She smoothed her T-shirt. "I thought you were in love with Daniel, but this is different. The way you look at him. Hell! The way he looks at you when you don't know it."

"Ryker and I are... complicated."

"What's difficult about it? You go down on him. Man is yours."

"Lexie." I groaned into my hands.

"What? Tell me what's so complicated about it? Don't say it's because of her. Is he sleeping with her?"

"No." Not anymore.

"Well…"

"Well, for one, he wants nothing more than to kill me. And I mean that in the literal sense." I explained to Lexie about how oaths worked in the fae world and how and why I forced Ryker into binding himself to one.

"You've been busy, girl." She shook her head, and then had to grip the table to steady herself. Every word she spoke seemed to zap energy from her.

"You could say that."

"So this oath works on you even though you're human?"

"Well, it works on human or fae, but there's something else. I'm not completely... uhhh…" I trailed off. "I'm not exactly human anymore."

There was a long pause. Lexie's eyes went wide. "Are you freaking kidding me? You are fae?"

"Yes. Part fae."

"Holy shit! My sister's a fairy."

"Fae. Not fairy. Difference." I sponged at the heavy perspiration along her hairline with her old scrub shirt.

"Whatever. Do you have powers?"

"I do, except they're not exactly working right now. Rapava did something to screw them up. Neither Ryker nor I can jump right now."

"Jump?"

"Ryker is a Wanderer. It gives him the ability to jump to anyplace in the world with a merely thought. I took on his traits when some of his powers stayed with me."

"Oh my god. This is the coolest thing ever," she whispered hoarsely.

"What's the coolest thing ever?" Croygen walked into the room.

"My sister's a fairy."

"Fae," we said in unison.

"Don't lump her with those righteous fuckers," Croygen snarled. "She's dark fae."

"We can give Lexie a history lesson on fae later. What do you need?" I asked.

"Oh, Wanderer has his panties in a twist. Something about spotting Garrett nearby."

"What?" I screeched. "Don't you think you should have started with that?"

Croygen shrugged, heading for Lexie. "You ready, little shark?" Her face reddened when she realized what he was doing. He shoved his arms under her legs, picking her up like she weighed no more than a doll. "Time to move."

I snatched the packed bags, giving a couple to Lexie to hold, then stuffed a hunting knife in the back of my pants. We bolted into the evening, where the big bad monsters lurked, waiting for a meal.

TEN

Croygen steered us to Ryker and Amara, who were hiding in an alley. Tendons along Ryker's neck and arms were taut with strain. Sprig huddled on his shoulder.

Ryker seethed in a whisper, "Garrett, Maxen, and Cadoc are a block up, both on the ground and rooflines. There is another group of them two blocks over." Ryker pointed to the left and right of us. "They're doing a sweep."

"What's your plan?" I pulled out my blade.

"Try to slip out under their noses," he replied flatly. "Keep low and to the shadows."

"Sprig." I pointed to my messenger bag. He wordlessly jumped from Ryker to me, crawling in my bag, where his backpack and Pam awaited.

I looked at Croygen to be sure Lexie stayed tucked safely in his arms. Her eyes were already half-mast, struggling to fight back the sleep the fever demanded of her.

I felt like we were some unusual family, like the von Trapps, trying to escape in the middle of the night from a horrendous dictator's regime.

Oh right, we kind of were.

We crept along together, stealthy and silent. The night buzzed with energy but was spookily quiet.

Ryker was leading, and at every corner he would stop

and check to see if the coast was clear. Amara constantly scanned the tops of the buildings, while I brought up the rear, watching our backs. With every step my chest tightened in anticipation of fae coming closer.

We passed an alley. When I glanced across the entrance, the glow of a slight-built fae stepped into it from the other side of the block.

"Hey," he yelled.

Shit.

"Boss! I spotted them," he bellowed, his feet pounding for us.

"Fuck!" Ryker turned back for Croygen. "You remember where Joey's place is?" Ryker didn't even let him answer. "Run. Get her out of here. We'll distract them."

Croygen did not hesitate, and with Lexie in his arms, he sprinted forward. Ryker waited for the fae to come from the alley before turning the opposite way Croygen went. I had to trust he would keep her safe.

"Boss, they are heading toward you," the guy shouted into the night. Footsteps and yelling voices filled the air.

"You think Vadik will ever give up searching for you?" a thick Irish accent hollered into the night. "There is nowhere you can go he won't find you. *Or her*," Garrett called out, his voice echoing off the buildings.

Ryker's jaw clenched as he turned Amara and me down another alley. We weaved in and out of lanes, the blond, skinny fae right on our tail, yelling out our location. He had to go. I stopped and spun around. My sudden switch in direction startled the boy. I didn't recognize him from Garrett's normal gang. He looked no older than seventeen but was probably hundreds of years old.

"Zoey!" Ryker's voice boomed.

"Come on, pretty boy." I shoved up my sleeves,

disregarding Ryker's call. I yanked the messenger bag off me, curling my fingers around the knife. Sprig squeaked when I set him down but stayed put.

The fae grinned and came straight for me. I stood my ground. The moment he was on me, his sword swiping for my chest, I fell to the ground, kicking out. My boots slammed into his ankles, and he stumbled back. The boy had to be fairly new, not even seasoned enough to know simple fighting tricks. I jumped up and smashed the hilt of my knife into his forehead. He hit the ground. I pounced on him, striking him with everything I had. The blood in my veins sparked to life. Adrenaline propelled force down my arm, expanding my chest with exhilaration.

The high of the fight bloomed under my skin. The world disappeared.

His head bounced off the cement like a ball. His body went limp, his head rolling to the side.

"Zoey, enough." Ryker's voice startled me out of my tunnel vision. "He's unconscious. Let's go." He pulled me to my feet. The body on the ground lay bloody and beaten. He was fae. He would be fine, but it still chilled me how easily I could hurt someone. And feel nothing about it.

Shaking out my hands I turned around.

Amara stood with her mouth open. "Damn."

"Told you not to mess with her, Mar." Ryker waved me forward.

"She wasn't that good when I fought her last."

"Yes, I was." I grabbed the bag, hearing snores inside, and knocked into her shoulder. "I went easy on you."

A huff came from her as she followed Ryker and me. The tingling of my skin told me more fae were descending on us. Anxiety danced in my bones. The three of us rounded a corner and came to a sudden stop.

Garrett, Cadoc, and Maxen stood in front of us.

The Irishman's eyes wandered over each of us, a smug smile on his face. "How nice. The three I was looking for. Thank you for meeting me here. Much easier to capture you when you come to me."

Ryker gripped the large hunter's knife in his hand.

"Seriously?" Garrett chuckled at the weapon. "You think that is supposed to scare me? A human breadknife? Where is your axe, almighty Wanderer? Did it leave you too, because you weren't fae enough to handle it?"

Ryker inhaled, staying silent.

My back prickled sensing fae moving around us. Shit. We were surrounded.

"Always so loquacious." Garrett took a step forward. "Sorry. Was that too big a word to use?"

Garrett wasn't especially tall or built, so he played the clever card as if he had to make up for not being brawny.

My gaze went wildly around us. More and more men moved from the shadows, boxing us in.

"Why should I bother when all you want is to hear yourself talk?" Ryker's eyes darted to the side, picking up on the force coming in on us. At least twenty fae moved in closer, all with swords or spears. Wolves rounding us up like sheep.

Shit. Shit. Shit.

Ryker stepped closer to Amara and me, brushing up against my back. It was the best position. The three of us, our backs to each other, were going to have to fight.

"True." Garrett grinned. "You won't understand anyway. So let me put this in a language you do." He jerked his head for his men to act. They reacted instantly, springing for us. We were outnumbered and certainly out-gunned.

From every direction swords, spears, daggers, and sticks

with multiple spikes came for us. I whipped my head around, trying to gauge the leading threat. Our knives only shrank under the menacing weapons, doing little but quivering in our hands against the odds.

I swung my arm wildly, striking my blade at anything reaching my space. I quickly acknowledged the odds. But even when I had no hope, I still never quit. I always fought till my body shut down, which was why the bosses in charge of the fights always enjoyed me in the ring. No matter my odds, I fought to the end.

And I would do it here as well.

With my back to Ryker's, three men were on me. A sword drove for my gut. I jumped, lurching a low side kick into the tall, blue-haired man with the spear, my boot hitting the tendon behind his knee with force. He stumbled back with a cry. I rebounded, centering myself for the next attack. I ducked as a curved blade whooshed toward my neck, the tip slicing across my temple. Blood oozed down my face.

I didn't feel anything through my adrenaline and fear. I didn't even see faces anymore as reflex impelled me deeper into survival mode, my muscles moving like a machine. I felt the hits, the knife marks the fae engraved to say they had been there, but I also sensed my comrades fighting next to me. Mostly I focused on the men coming at me in multitudes.

"Zoey!" My name rang through the air with a terrorized crispness. My head automatically jerked out of my fighting haze. And that's when I saw it. The blue-haired fae's arm pointed in my direction, his javelin hurtling through the air, the arrow heading straight for my chest. I didn't even have time to blink before the tip was a breath away from kissing my skin, embedding itself into my heart. A hand yanked me so roughly, I flew back. Ryker's arms grasped me as our collective force toppled us like dominos, his body crashing into Amara's back, taking her down.

With a whoosh my world spun as if someone had thrown me into a spinning dryer. My lids shut as the earth whirled.

My ass hit hard concrete with a painful bite. Warm arms shielded the rest of me from the impact, holding me so firmly I lost my breath.

I heard Amara cry out. The sound of skin and fabric slapping cement.

The spiraling stopped.

Quiet and darkness.

I cracked open my lids. The buildings in front of me swayed before they righted themselves, revealing a quiet alley. Overflowing dumpsters and the smell of molding food, piss, and foraging rats were our only threats.

The sensation of Sprig's warmth on my lap drew me out of my haze. I placed my hand on my bag, feeling him breathing inside. I exhaled with relief that he was okay.

A noise came from behind me, and I craned my neck to see Ryker, with Amara lying face-first on the ground, halfway underneath him. Garrett's men were gone, no attackers descending on us. The grungy setting of Fremont no longer surrounded us.

"Holy shit." I gaped. "You jumped us."

"Yeah." He frowned, searching the alley. "But not on purpose."

"Fear," I responded, remembering the many times I had accidentally jumped because of fear. For the longest time it seemed the only time my powers kicked in. "It triggered the jump."

His gaze landed on mine, a pointed look deep in his eyes. *Fear for me.*

"Are you hurt?" He let his arms drop from me, his fingers grazing the cut at my head.

"No." I touched the tender slice into my hairline. "It'll heal."

"Yeah, yeah. Your concern is so sweet I want to puke. Now could you both get your heavy asses off of me?" Amara growled, struggling to move under our combined weight. "Now."

I climbed to my feet, taking inventory of the rest of my body. The wound was closing at my temple, blood congealing there. Other than a few cuts and bruises, I was fine. And most of all I didn't have an arrow sticking out of my chest. If it had touched me, it would have come with us, and I'd have been dead, jump or no.

Ryker saved me. Saved all of us.

He got his feet, helping Amara up.

"You guys all right?" I asked.

"Yeah." They both nodded. They also had surface nicks, but nothing serious. I took a relieved breath.

"Where are we?" Amara asked, brushing herself off, twirling her head around, and looking down the lane.

"Pioneer Square," Ryker responded, heading toward the alley opening. "The guy I was fighting reminded me of this son of a bitch I did a job for years ago. He owns the Mediterranean restaurant right there." Ryker pointed to the back entrance of a hole-in-the-wall joint. "Obviously why we ended up here."

"Huh. That's kind of funny."

"Why?" Ryker glanced over his shoulder at me.

"Well, I was about to be speared like a shish kabob. Kind of fitting, don't you think?"

Ryker's lips thinned and he turned away, checking the street, and then motioned us forward. "The garage is actually not far from here."

Amara brushed by me. "I think it's hilarious."

Yeah. Even more so if I actually had been impaled.

On our ten-minute walk, Sprig's snores provided traveling music. When we finally made it to Joey's, my feet hastened the moment I saw the sign. Two people remained on my mind.

"Croygen?" I ran into the garage. Tools, cars, and parts stuffed the place. The smell of oil, metal, and gasoline saturated my senses, stinging my nose.

"We're here," his voice rang back.

Relief zipped through me when I saw him. He sat on a bench seat that had been pulled out of a car. Lexie curled up on her side next to him, her head on his lap.

I rushed to them and dropped to the ground, needing to touch her and make certain she was really there. Sweat beaded on her face, and she struggled to breathe.

"She's burning up." He frowned. "She's gotten a little worse just since we've been here."

I brushed back her hair, her labored breaths slashed at my heart. What did I do? Was getting her out of DMG actually her death sentence? I pulled Sprig from my bag and placed him next to Lexie. He nuzzled into her stomach, falling into a deeper slumber.

"We'll let her sleep for a bit more, but she needs to drink something soon to stay hydrated. If we can get food down her, even better."

He nodded in agreement. Amara's and Ryker's footsteps sounded behind me.

"Garrett found you guys, clearly." Croygen tipped his chin at our wounds.

"Yeah, but Ryker jumped us." I stood up.

"Really? That's good. Your powers are coming back then." Hopefulness clipped Croygen's words.

"Yeah, but we both are still poor at controlling them." Ryker scoured his thumb over his forehead.

129

"Still, it's something." Croygen shrugged.

I twirled around taking in our new location. "Are you sure Joey is all right with us being here? She doesn't need to work or anything?"

"Not lately. Not many needing an oil change." Ryker wandered around, investigating the dark corners and hiding places. He thumbed back toward a door. "There's a shower in the employee bathroom. The hot is actually cold, just warning you."

Amara immediately darted in the direction he pointed.

"Not going to ask how you know that," I replied.

"Good thing. I'd rather not sleep with one eye open all night." Ryker poked his head into a room, flicking at a light switch. "Great. No electricity."

"Shower doesn't work either." Amara stomped back into the room. "And with no electricity, the refrigerator and microwave in the breakroom are useless."

"Those taunting little sluts." Croygen stretched his arms above his head, yawning.

Amara rolled her eyes, mumbling under her breath. She made her way to where Ryker was, helping him search the other rooms attached to the garage.

I grabbed the bags and took them to the windowless breakroom. While in Target, I added flashlights and candles to our plunder, considering we might have to stay in places like this. I struck a match and lit one of the candles. The walls glowed with dim yellow light. The room contained a table with four chairs, and cabinets lined one wall. A sink and a microwave were next to a refrigerator. The bathroom entrance was to the right. Posters about customer service and a board with the employees' schedules covered the walls.

Turning back to the sacks, I set out the food, water, and

medication, finding the wipes and cleaning the blood off my face, losing myself in thoughts.

"I'll sleep in here during the day." A deep voice came from behind. I twisted around to see Ryker stepping into the room, the candlelight flickering off his features. "And do the guard shifts at night."

"I can do them too."

He shook his head. "Amara will help."

My jaw cracked.

"You can't be guarding and taking care of your sister. She needs you more."

The bristling anger evaporated as fast as it came. "She *is* getting worse." My voice splintered.

"We'll figure it out." Ryker took a step then stopped, balling his hands into fists. He looked down at his shoes. "Garrett is on our trail, and Vadik won't stop till he has us." He shoved his hands in his pockets, his voice cool. "I know you want to take down DMG, but right now I'm thinking we need to get out of Seattle for a while. Get some distance."

My head bolted up, my mouth opening.

"Before you speak." His eyebrows went up. "I'm not suggesting we leave Annabeth to her fate. We go after her. Soon. Maybe tomorrow night we check Vadik's place out. Figure how best to get her and then get us the hell out of here. We are just sitting targets in this town."

Maybe if we had a chance to breathe, Lexie would have time to get better, to heal. I could get her stronger drugs. We could have a moment to plan how to destroy DMG.

"Yeah." I met his eyes. "Sounds like a plan." Our gazes remained on each other. Desire was always there, boiling like a volcano, but this time I also felt its pain, the raw agony of being so close, yet so far apart. His white eyes pierced into mine, holding me prisoner. Neither of us moved nor spoke.

Love and hate. Pain and pleasure. The air crackled, simmering over my skin, caressing my nerve endings.

"When I saw that spear heading for you…" He trailed off, his voice a rough whisper. He ran a hand over his head. "I want to touch you."

I sucked in through my teeth. "I want to be touched."

Ryker's pupils dilated, his tattoo flickering down his neck. A growl hummed in the air. He stood in front of me before I could even blink, shoving me with his bulk until my back slammed into the counter.

"Where?" He licked his lips.

"What?" My head spun at his nearness, wanting to feel his heat seeping into my body.

"Where do you want to be touched?"

Air. Thoughts. Logic. They all vanished. I knew if I had them, I would know we were playing with fire, and one of us would end up barbequed.

"Show me." He placed his palms on either side of the counter, boxing me in.

A warning bell deep in the back of my brain went off.

"Ryker…"

"Show me," he demanded, his eyes blazing hotter. There was a fine line between the brutal Wanderer and his oath, between the man who liked it rough and kinky to the murderous robot who just wanted to strangle the life from me. But the danger, the thin line between the two, only urged me on.

I trailed my hands down my body to my jeans, slowly unzipping my pants. Ryker leaned in farther, rumbling as my fingers trailed along my underwear line. "Where do you want my fingers, human? My tongue?"

I dipped below the fabric, a breath exhaling from me, imagining it was him. The man didn't even have to touch me and I was beyond ready.

"Deeper." His voice strained with gruffness. His words became unclear. More alarms were going off, but I could only respond to his demand. "Harder."

I groaned as my fingers moved quicker. On either side of me, the lip of the counter snapped, crumbled into bits, falling onto the linoleum.

"Imagine that's my tongue." He leaned into my ear. "Licking you." My head fell back, his hot breath on my neck was too much. He whispered and breathed in my ear until I climaxed.

"Ryker. Please," I whimpered. "I want it to be you touching me... inside me."

A strangled sound came from his chest. "I can't." The words were so soft I barely heard them.

"Yes. You can." My body felt like a live wire, and it didn't care about the repercussions. It just wanted him.

He went still for a moment, then grabbed my hand, pulling it from my underwear. He brought it up to his mouth, curling his tongue around my fingers and nipped them.

I was done. Thankfully the counter behind held me up.

His grip on my hand constricted, his eyes shutting. "You taste so damn good," he muttered, his lids squeezing together. When he opened his eyes, the man was gone. The robot had taken his place.

"Shit," I said under my breath. I didn't even get the whole word out before his body crushed into mine.

"I should have made you get me off first." He snarled, his eyes cold, but his touch heated as his hands skimmed up my chest to my neck, his thumbs pressing down lightly on my vocal cords, as if he got off flirting with my demise.

"Go ahead." I stared straight at him, pushing against my instincts to kick and fight back. My voice struggled to talk. "Kill me. End this." Maybe if I died again my fae side would save me, looping this whole cycle into action again, or maybe I would truly die this time. I was willing to find out. I was tired of fighting him.

My eyes closed, compelling my arms to stay limp at my sides. He squeezed tighter, then his hands froze. A roar bellowed from him, forcing my lashes open. Ryker's fingers dropped away, stepping back from me. His face twisted with pain. I inhaled air into my lungs but didn't move, my gaze burning into him. The fae part quickly healed the pain in my throat.

He leaned over his knees, groaning and pounding his fist into his leg. Then he stilled.

"Fuck!" Ryker raked his hands over his face, standing back up. He kept his face covered, his breaths becoming measured. He dropped his arms, but his eyes would not meet mine. We stood in heavy silence for a long time. Then he finally spoke.

"When this is all over." He cleared his throat, his arms locked down at his sides. "I'm going away."

It felt like someone dumped a bucket of ice water on me. "What?"

"I can't do this to you. I'm not just hurting you; I'm killing you." He swallowed; his gaze still not able to meet mine. "I can't do this to myself either. Do you know how hard it is to be around you? How torturous this is?" He set his jaw.

"Where would you go anyway? The oath will always draw you to me."

"It eases a bit the farther away I go. I'll have to live with it. But I can't be this close to you and not be able to touch you."

I saw the verdict was settled. He pushed out his chest. "You've already decided this. Nothing I can say will change your mind?"

"No." He shook his head and rolled his shoulders back, his expression cool and firm. "I will stay till we get Annabeth and can find you guys a safe place to lay low for a while."

"You aren't going to help with DMG?" I snapped. My defenses bucking up. "They still have your axe."

He shifted on his feet.

"You're just going to abandon us when I... we need you." I was being completely unfair, I understood that, but my pain lashed out.

"Zoey, don't make this harder. I've talked to Croygen. He will stay with you and help with Lexie. I'll come back and assist when you are ready to fight DMG. Croygen knows how to contact me."

He was actually leaving! All my past insecurities flamed up in my chest, clogging my air waves. "No."

"I don't want to." He glanced at his boots. "I have to."

"What about the stone?"

"I'll be taking it. You don't need that burden as well."

"No!" My reaction blurted out with fire. Possessive energy chewed up my throat. "You're not going to take it from me!"

"Take it from you?" His lips thinned. "Jesus, Zoey. Do you even hear yourself?" He lifted his arms toward me. "Do you even notice what it's doing to you?"

"What are you talking about? It's not doing anything."

He snorted crudely. "You don't even see it. You've lost weight, you get the shakes like a druggie. Headaches, moody. Possessive. It's slowly destroying you." He took a step toward me. "I should have never given it to you. It was selfish of me to make you carry the burden. I can't watch it continue to hurt you. Give it to me." He held out his hand.

A crazed overprotective feeling fumed up, engulfing me till I couldn't breathe. I took several steps back.

"No."

"Hand it over or I will take it." He regained the space I put between us.

My hand went to the small blade in my boot, tugging it out, my brain not even taking in what I was doing or saying. Only reacting.

"If you dare try." I held up the knife to his chest, the tip poking into his breastbone. "Don't fucking touch me *or* the stone. I will kill you, Ryker. Don't test me. I will. I swear." I strained through my teeth, fury lurching down my arm.

"And don't fucking *challenge* me, human." His tattoo and eyes both sparked, his nostrils flaring. "It will end far worse for you."

"I'm warning you, Viking. The stone stays with me."

"Oh really?" He licked his lips. "Stop me."

My body came alive, understanding the moment before someone is about to strike. This was something I knew. I understood. And I wanted it. I wanted his blood.

His hand shot out for my wrist, going for the weapon. My arm blocked it, my leg kicking out for his stomach. He dodged out of the way, giving me more room to spring back and to stab my knife out for him. He dipped to the side, my blade nicking his shirt. I sprang forward, twisting back around, and swiped the back of his leg. The knife cut a line through his jeans; the edge of my blade came back red. Ryker snarled, ramming his elbow into my ribs, his power flinging me to the side.

He was huge and I was tiny. But I knew how to fight men far bigger than me and still win.

Bring. It. Adrenaline and fury pumped in my veins. The stone rang with energy, salivating at every punch that met its mark.

That's right, Zoey. Don't let him take us away from each other, the stone taunted in my head.

I danced in closer, my fist cutting up into his Adam's apple. Ryker cracked his head forward, knocking into my face. Blood instantly gushed from my nose. I howled, punching directly into his kidney. He gasped, stepping back.

Keeping low, I jabbed the knife into the side of his knee. He snapped his jaw and grabbed the weapon, ripping it from his leg and tossing it on the floor. His eyes blazed with light, his shoulders rolled back, and a snarl curled his lips. He raced for me, grabbing my arms. He yanked me into him, aligning our bodies. Heat, rage, and violence throbbed between us. We both froze, breaths heavy. His grasp on my wrists constricted. He licked his lips, his gaze wild.

Fuck. I was so angry and turned on.

"Give it to me." His voice thick and rough.

Wrong thing to say.

My knee went up, colliding brutally with his groin. Dropping him to his knees with a groan. I shoved him back and pounced on top of him, leaning in, I grabbed the knife off the floor and held it to his throat. "*It's mine... mmiiinnee,*" I growled. Rage I couldn't contain vibrated my muscles.

The door swung open.

"Holy shit!" I heard Croygen exclaim and bolted into the room. "Stop. Now." Croygen grabbed me, tearing me off Ryker, dragging me back against the far wall. Ryker sprang up, his pupils dilated, a twisted smile on his face. "Ryker... stay back." Croygen kept hold of me, but put himself between me and the Wanderer. "Don't let it control you. Take a moment and realize what you are doing. You too." He gripped the front of my arm firmer. "What the hell has gotten into you?"

My throat let out a rumble as I wiped the blood from my nose.

"*Bhean?*" Sprig scrambled into the room, followed by Amara. "What in the honey-fried frog nuggets is going on?"

"Uh-oh, relationship trouble already?" Amara clicked her tongue. I ignored her. Seeing Sprig felt like getting electrocuted. I came hurling out of the cloud I was in, seeing everything in color.

"Oh my god." I put a hand over my mouth. I was about to stab the man I loved over a rock. Embarrassment and guilt coated my cheeks, turning my head to the ground in shame.

A string of swear words spouted from Ryker. I watched his boots start to pace the room.

"Seriously, you two need a timeout," Croygen huffed. "Isn't it enough everyone else is trying to kill us?"

"It's. The. Syndrome," Sprig fake whispered to Croygen. "They need food."

"They need a kick in the ass," Croygen grumbled. "Ryker, take a walk and cool off."

"Let us have a moment." Ryker's words jerked up my head. His expression a mix of frustration and sorrow.

"Not a good idea." Croygen shook his head.

"I will stay on my side. I swear." He planted his feet. "Please. I need a moment alone with Zoey."

"Shit. If I have to come in and pull you guys off each other..." Croygen folded his arms.

"I'll be referee!" Sprig raised his hand. "We can play honey-wrestling wars!"

"No," Ryker responded.

"Actually..." Croygen tilted his head in thought.

"Go. All of you," Ryker demanded, nodding to the door.

Croygen begrudgingly agreed, tugging Amara and Sprig out with him. Amara's smug expression slipped into one of exasperation and irritation.

Croygen shut the door, leaving only the two of us. The room was crowded with an uncomfortable strain.

Ryker ran his hand over the top of his head, letting out

air. "You know I'm right about the stone." He stared at the floor. "I won't take it now... but I will. When I go... I won't let it consume you any more than it already has. I should have never let you have it. It is my burden; I won't let it be yours."

When he goes.

"Well, aren't you the self-sacrificing hero," I whispered, acid dripping in my tone.

"Don't." He ground his teeth. "Right now all I want to be is the villain. Take what I want. Fuck. Fight. Kill. Steal. Do everything I'm good at."

Heartbreak threatened to crawl from my eyes. I shoved it back, covering my grief with bitterness. "Fine. Go. It's what you're good at. Probably wouldn't have been long before you left me anyway."

"Fuck, Zoey! What do you want from me?" He held his head between his palms, like he had a pounding headache. "You think this is easy? That I'm fine with leaving you?" Anguish rolled through his eyes. The torment I saw there shut me up, the ire ebbing away. "I am fighting for control every second. We have so many battles outside us, and I can barely keep it together. All of me wants to stay. To be with you. Only one tiny piece of my brain is trying to be logical. To be safe. And I am holding on to that by my fingers. Please don't push me."

My shoulders drooped with overwhelming sadness, and I inhaled a trembling breath.

"I will make sure you are settled before I go." He rubbed a hand over his mouth. "Tomorrow when we go to Vadik's warehouse, it will be more of a surveillance night to get the lay of the land. We need to understand what we are getting into first. The night after we can go after her."

I lifted my chin, acknowledging his plan.

He observed me for a few moments before he headed to

the door. "At the end of this week, I will be gone." He left, shutting the door.

I stood for a while, drenched in grief and shame. The stone was turning me into this. Changing me into a monster. *How could I let myself attack him?* What was worse and disgusting me further, I knew I would do it again. I would fight him when he came to claim the stone again.

Itching to move, I walked to the counter, my finger running over the gouges he had created. The flame of the candle flickered, and I was tempted to touch it so I could match the pain inside. I blew out the ember, enveloping myself in darkness like a shield, giving me freedom to feel. My knees crumpled to the floor. I clutched desperately onto the broken tabletop, my head leaning against the lower cabinets.

I sobbed silently, keeping my pain contained inside my fragmented chest.

ELEVEN

The night was rough. Ryker and Amara kept sentry as Croygen and I took turns with Lexie. When she did sleep it was fitful. Each time we got water in her or a tiny piece of bread, it came back up. We kept a bucket by her head after the second time she rejected the nourishment.

Every time she threw up, I felt a piece of hope go into the bucket with it. I had pushed away Ryker's future departure the moment I walked out of the room. But I felt cracked. Bleeding. Watching my little sister, someone I loved more than anything, diminish in front of my eyes ripped open my already feeble heart, tearing at the strong façade I tried to keep up. It only made me push firmer against the truth. Deny it even harder.

Finally, a Tylenol PM calmed her down and reduced her fever just enough for her to sleep a couple of hours. Croygen forced me to sleep in the breakroom, assuring me he'd stay near her. As I moved, I heard Sprig's snores come from one of the gutted cars. He had passed out in the auto's glove box wrapped around Pam.

With pads and blankets found around the shop, I assembled a bed in the corner of the breakroom and curled into it like a kitten. It seemed as if my lids closed just for a moment when the door opened, and daylight streamed in. I didn't have to look. I could feel him like a breeze over my skin. I parted my lashes, glancing over at the entrance. The Wanderer filled the doorway, his body rigid like an iceberg. A blank slate of blue-white eyes watched me.

"I need to get a few hours of sleep if you still want to go tonight. Amara has agreed to show us the location."

"Of course I do." I pushed myself up. "What time is it?"

He stepped into the room, setting his weapons on the table. "I think it's around two."

"In the afternoon?" I blurted. It wasn't really a question, just shock at how long I slept. I rose to my feet, rubbing the sleep from my eyes.

"You don't have to leave." He kept his back to me, leaning over the table as he kicked off his boots. "I'll sleep over here." He nodded to the opposite corner.

"No." *Yes. I'll stay.* "I should check on Lexie, and I'm sure Amara also needs some sleep." I made for the door, pausing close to him. *Leave, Zoey. Walk out now.*

"She's passed out in the bed of a truck in the other room. I let her go to sleep hours ago." He reached over his head and tugged his shirt off.

Oh. Holy. Hell. The sight of his back muscles came with an enormous amount of sadness. I stared at the lines of his tattoo curling down his shoulder blade, and my intimate knowledge of how far down it went on his thigh, what they felt like against my fingertips. My hands had a mind of their own and reached up to lightly trace the black ink. He sucked in a sharp breath, his muscles constricting. I barely made contact, but the electricity sizzled under my palm.

"Zoey." He breathed out my name, telling me both to stop and to keep going. I went with the latter, causing his chest to move in and out rapidly. "Zoey. Stop."

142

The sorrow and hunger I held quickly metamorphosed into fury. My hand jerked away from him, and I stepped back.

He glanced over his shoulder.

"I'll wake you up when it gets dark." I looked away from his intrusive gaze. "We need to go over our plan before we head out."

He nodded as he turned back to the table.

I swallowed the paralyzing scream and walked out the door and shut it behind me. This was why I never let people in. The pain of their loss seemed too much to endure. Was this how normal people felt, or had I been made different? You'd think being created in a lab I'd be less emotional in order to function. Perhaps they stuffed me with extra feelings. The need to fight and love with the same ferocity.

Croygen sat on a cushy bench with his head back, mouth open, sound asleep. Lexie's head used his leg as a pillow. I bent down in front of her to feel her forehead. Her skin seared under my touch. Her fever was back and worse than before.

"How is she doing?" Croygen's voice whispered. I glanced up at him as he rubbed his face.

"Not good." I patted the sweat off Lexie's head. "She feels hotter."

Croygen watched Lexie, worry flickering over his face.

"Tonight Amara's going to show me where Annabeth is. We need to check it out and get the layout."

"And you want me to stay?" he responded. "With Lexie."

My gaze went up to his. "I know it's a lot to ask. And it's probably the last thing you want to do. But there's no one else and…" I motioned to the sleeping form on his lap. "She clearly feels safe with you. I don't trust anyone else to watch her."

His head jolted back, eyes widening in surprise. "You trust me with your sister's life?"

"Yes." I didn't hesitate. "And mine."

"Wow." Croygen rubbed his neck, glancing away. "Don't think I've ever heard anyone say that to me."

"Well, I do. Unequivocally."

Sprig jumped on the back of the bench seat. "That means absolutely, in case you were wondering."

"Thanks, ass-licker. I got it." Croygen batted at him, but Sprig leaped out of his grasp.

"Sprig, I want you to stay here too."

"What?" His mouth fell open. "No way, *Bhean*. You need me."

"This is just a scouting mission." I rubbed Lexie's leg. "You would be great comfort for her. Please, Sprig."

His eyes narrowed on me.

Croygen laid his arms on the back of the bench. "Yep, she just played the sick sister card on your ass."

"I will leave you three packets of honey," I offered, sweetening the pot.

"Wait, I didn't know there were bribes being offered." Croygen jerked to look at me.

"I know what kind of enticements you would want."

"Same as him." Croygen winked. "Some sweet *honey*. Heard your tits offer it freely."

"Honey chalices of love," Sprig chirped. "Oh, speaking of that…"

"Thanks." I glowered at Croygen. "You had to bring up the H-word."

"I'm starving! No one has fed me all day." Sprig rubbed his tummy.

"You were sleeping for all of it," Croygen challenged.

"Not the point!" Sprig waved him off. "Listen. My tummy is angry. It's so empty. You know what sounds good?"

"Honey?" Croygen and I said together.

"Yes, but why am I suddenly craving kabobs?" He scratched his head, then his eyes widened. "Oh, honey-coated doughnut kabobs wrapped in honey bacon and sugar! And for dessert I want cookies... no, cakes... maybe scones... sweet bread? Corn brea—"

"How about a packet of honey and a granola bar?"

"Okay, but I was thinking more of honey-stuffed croissants... warm. Also, I want one of those cola thingies. Oh, what about a bag of chocolate-covered caramels, wrapped in hon—"

Croygen swiped him from the bench and shoved him inside his jacket pocket. I could hear Sprig muttering words, none nice.

"He'll poop in your coat for that." I nodded to his pocket.

"Not the worst thing I've ever done in or on a coat." He shrugged. "Time to break it in."

"Ugh." I pinched my nose.

After rescuing a pissed-off sprite, I forced Croygen to go sleep in the breakroom, grabbing enough food to keep Sprig's stomach quiet for at least a few hours.

Lexie woke up needing the bathroom, which was not easy. It wasn't the first time I'd carried her. She had lost weight, but the limpness of her muscles made the task difficult. When I settled her back down, I tried to get her to eat and drink again. Ten minutes later she was vomiting. Her body shook, tears streaming down her face. I felt helpless, which kicked in my urge to fight. It was always my initial reaction. I did not handle powerlessness well.

When everyone got up, they found me wound up like a fish on a line, bobbing around the garage at a constant pace. I acted as if I had eaten a dozen espresso beans again. By checking on Lexie so often I probably contributed to her already restless sleep. My anxiety saturated the air.

We had an unheated dinner of canned spaghetti, peas, and pineapple chunks. Not mixed together of course. Ryker even kept his tin cans from touching. Knowing what happened to him, what Vadik did, changed how I viewed his particular problem with food touching. The torment that little boy went through when all he wanted was to enjoy his birthday and eat cake like most kids do. I could also see how he related that night to losing his mother. It wasn't just the food but the loss of the family, the life he knew.

"Amara and I are going to do a last look around the garage. Check to see that everything is fine." He tossed his empty cans in the trash and proceeded out the door. Amara rolled her hair up in a messy bun and followed him. The more he called on her, said her name, the smugger her smile became. I wasn't the only one who noticed.

"He says her name, and she acts like her kitty is about to get the cream."

"Croygen," I snarled, tossing my trash away. "Don't need thoughts like that in my mind, especially when I'm stuck with the pair of them tonight."

"He'd never go back to her."

"Do you know that for sure?" I pulled on my jacket, zipping it up. "I know he told you he's leaving."

Croygen nodded stiffly.

"She'll follow him." I stuffed a knife into my boot. "We can't be together. He'll eventually move on. She'll ensure it's back to her."

"You know he doesn't love her, right?"

146

"Not sure if that makes it worse or better." I rolled my shoulders trying to loosen the knots, my hands trembling. Damn, I was ready to fight. The stone buzzed in my heel, feeling angry energy pulsing off me in violent waves. I could almost hear its excitement.

"Zoey?" My name floated lightly to me. I spun to Lexie and moved to her side in an instant.

"Hey, trouble." I brushed her cheek. "You're awake."

"Where are you going?"

Guilt twisted my heart. "I'm just going to be gone for a few hours. My friend Annabeth is being held by really bad men. She needs our help," I whispered to her. "Croygen is going to stay with you. Is that okay?"

She nodded, squeezing my hand. "Be careful."

"I will. Tonight we are only checking things out."

She licked her dry lips. "I love you, Zoey."

"I love you too," I responded, but fear crackled through me. It sounded too much like a goodbye. "Hey, kiddo, what's wrong? You're freaking me out."

"Zoey... You know... I'm dying." She put her hand on mine. "I can feel it."

"No, you aren't." My shoulders bristled. "I didn't get you back to lose you again."

"Some things even *you* can't fight."

"I'll get you more painkillers. Maybe break into a hospital and get real medication."

"It won't help. They don't have what I need." Lexie's eyes filled with sorrow, but it seemed like it was for me, as if she felt sad I couldn't see the truth.

And she was right. I wouldn't... couldn't... accept it.

"Then what do you need? I will get you anything!" I could hear the shrillness in my voice. The desperation. Ryker was leaving. I would not let Lexie leave me too.

147

"Zoey." Croygen touched my shoulder. "You know I hate to say this, but she needs whatever medication Rapava gave her and the daily blood transfusions."

"Then I'll get them." I stood, swinging to Croygen.

"You can't get blood for her."

"I'll get her the medicines. We'll start with that."

"How?"

"I will break into DMG and get them."

"Break in? Are you serious? If they catch you, you're dead."

"Then I won't let them catch me."

"Do you hear yourself?" Croygen placed both palms on my shoulders, slightly shaking me. "Don't be stupid. The place is lined with alarms and goblin metal. We barely got out the first time."

"Then what? I'm not going to let her die." I jerked away from him. "I am getting her this medication, Croygen. You can't stop me."

"No." Lexie cried, barely able to get words out. "They... they will capture you. He won't let you leave. He will kill you, Zoey."

"I am a lot harder to kill than you think."

"Shit. You are not invincible!" Croygen threw up his arms in frustration. "You will crumple to your knees the moment he cuffs you with goblin metal. You'll become his pet again. And I promise you, death would be the easy way. He will make certain you can never escape again and be forever his test monkey." Anger flared through Croygen's expression. "Then we are left with no medication. And no you. Ryker will go after you, you know that."

"I have no choice." I shoved my hands onto his chest. "You may be willing to let her die, pirate, but I'm not."

Rage burned in his eyes, his whole frame filling the

space as he went motionless. "I am trying to keep *both* of you alive." He said it so slowly and determined a chill ran down my spine.

The door swung open as Amara and Ryker came into the room, armed and ready to go. I looked at Croygen. "I appreciate everything you've done. I seriously couldn't have gotten through this without you. But she is my sister. This is my choice." I walked over and gave Lexie a kiss on the head. "I'll be back later."

She watched me, her body quaking with fever.

"Sprig?" I patted the sprite's head as he sat on Lexie's shoulder. "Stay close. Take care of her for me."

"Eye-matty." He saluted me while petting Lexie's curly hair. "On *Leanbh* duty."

I gave him a smile then turned back to Croygen. "Thank you." I squeezed his arm, walked around him, and joined my teammates for the night.

I was ready to fight. To battle for the lives of both my girls. Lie, cheat, steal, torture, kill.

Whatever it took.

TWELVE

The hike felt like it went on forever, and my feet ached. I wanted to ask Amara if she was taking us someplace or if she was making us walk till I was too tired to strangle her. She weaved down streets and roads until we hit the industrial district. The streetlights thinned to only one every so often. It was not the nice part of the city and the dark only increased the creepy, seedy factor.

Finally she turned and went around to the side of a building and climbed up the fire escape. Ryker silently followed her, bristling at my nearness as I grabbed a ring and pulled myself up behind him. I sensed the anger increasing again, building under his skin, like lumber doused in gasoline ready for a spark to become flames.

He got to the roof and quickly moved to Amara. I came up on the other side, letting her buffer the tension vibrating off Ryker.

"There." Amara pointed at a large building. "He's keeping them in there."

My eyes scanned the structure. No lights shone outside. Only a dim glow from inside hinted at life behind the walls. It was surrounded by identical structures, making it even more invisible. Not that it mattered. It was tucked against a hill and so far off the main street that no one would come back here. The structure built right next to it looked to be a victim of the storm or maybe just time and decay. All the windows were busted, and the building sagged with neglect.

Only Vadik could keep his shady business protected from sight right in the middle of Seattle. With the downtown and outer areas rebuilding and property owners returning to their vacated places, people were everywhere. He was smart to leave the other warehouse near the stadium.

My gaze caught on a dark figure moving along the building. A guard. Fae. My sight picked up a semiautomatic rifle over his shoulder and a knife in his belt. More fae moved around the building. These weren't the old security Marcello or Duc had. No little boys playing dress up, but fae who were trained to kill.

Shit. This did not look good for us.

"He owns this whole space," Amara whispered, waving her hand in a wide arc. "And every bit of it is under surveillance." As much as I hated to admit it, her knowledge of Vadik's business was helpful. At least I didn't feel we were going in completely blind.

"Remember, this is only a surveillance mission, Zoey," Ryker stated. "We need to see what we're up against: number of men, changing of guards, weaknesses."

I pressed my lips together, not answering either way. I didn't know if I resented him treating me like a child or that he had the right to. My need to slam the fae guard against the wall and run in and rescue Annabeth twitched from my toes up to my fists.

Fighting had been easy for me. I stayed cool, calm, rational, and quick to pick up on others' weaknesses and emotions. I hurt people all the time, but they stepped into the ring knowing what they were getting into. They chose to be there. These girls had not chosen this. When it came to people

I cared about, I became a loose cannon, reacting before thinking. I shoved my shoulders back, clinging to the vacant coldness I knew well.

"Well, I'm out of here. Have fun guys." Amara stepped back.

"What? Where are you going?" Fear painted Ryker's words like an Easter egg. His gaze darted to me then back to her.

"I'm not going to hang out on the roof all night. Boring." She walked backward. "This is not my thing. I couldn't care less about these girls. I showed you where they are, now I'm leaving. Maybe I'll stop at a bar on the way back. Get laid."

"Amara," Ryker growled. "You can't."

"You're not screwing me. So, *yes*, I can."

His jaw sawed together. "Not what I meant. You can't be seen either. You are being hunted just as much as we are."

"Well, I need a drink and sex. Unless you're willing to change your sudden stance on abstinence, I'm going." For a moment I could see the hope in her face.

Ryker clenched his fists but did not respond.

"That's what I thought." She tipped her head with attitude and whirled around. "I'm not stupid. I know how to keep under the radar. Have fun up here." She slipped over the railing and down the ladder.

"Fuck," Ryker swore under his breath and went back to the edge of the roof, staring at the building.

I didn't know what to say. His anger appeared palpable. But he stayed here. For me. This wasn't his quest either, but he stood here because he knew how much Annabeth meant to me. My hurt was temporarily quelled. I faced the building, both of us staying quiet.

Time ticked by. We watched every detail, every new guard, and only talked when we had to. It was boring and extremely uncomfortable.

I was about to throw myself off the roof when a guard walked out of the front doors, standing at taut attention, like a soldier. Only a few seconds later the sound of a car rumbled up the lane. Ryker and I dropped behind the wall, gradually inching back up, peering over.

Voices spoke from below while the car idled.

"Take her upstairs. Another one at the club strung up on heroin and getting out of control. I have to stay under the radar."

Ryker stiffened next to me, his gaze drilling into the man below.

Vadik slipped out of the town car and dragged a girl behind him.

"Shit," Ryker mumbled. The anxiety in his voice snapped my eyes to his. "Being this close, he might sense me."

Great. I worked my jaw and glanced back over the top. The chances of Vadik sensing him were good; Ryker was part demon, extremely powerful, and Vadik's son after all. Right now I hoped our abilities were still mostly sequestered by Rapava's magic-dampening medications.

"I'm endangering you," Ryker muttered. My hand came down on his, and he flinched.

"Too late now." I withdrew my hand and stared down at Vadik.

Vadik walked toward the front of the building, his hand clutched around a girl's thin arm. Her overly dyed, black hair was ironed straight and left scraggly at the ends. She stumbled in her six-inch heels. The tiny, skintight black dress she wore made her resemble a skeleton. Her eyes appeared sunken, her skin a greenish-blue color.

"Give her just enough to keep her going. Soon she will find that fae feeding off her is far more powerful than any drug humans can produce."

153

Fury filled my mouth with the taste of bile. I knew humans were capable of this and worse, but Vadik's cruelty inspired a deeper hate and disgust.

"Yes, sir." The guard who came out to meet him nodded. Vadik pushed her toward the man, her boney figure flying into the man's chest. Vadik turned back to the opened car door. He took a step then stopped. Cold navy eyes zipped up to where we were hiding, sealing off my lungs.

Ryker and I ducked, hiding behind the wall. My muscles seemed to turn to ice, my spine a rigid pole. Ryker's lids squeezed together, and his lips pinched.

"Sir, is everything all right?" the guard asked.

It was just a moment, a glitch in time. But it felt like the entire world stopped, waiting for him to respond. My heartbeat throbbed in my ears.

"Yes," he said slowly. "Fine."

The closing of the car door echoed through the air before the expensive town car rolled away.

I leaned my forehead against the cement partition. "That was close."

"Too close." Ryker still didn't look relieved, a frown lining his forehead.

"You think he knows we're here?"

Ryker lifted his head, staring over the wall, and I followed suit. The guard and the girl were gone, already deep inside the structure.

"I don't know, but it's time to get out of here."

"I just want to look in, see what's going on. See how many girls he has in there, how many guards."

"Zoey, we almost got caught."

"But we didn't," I retorted. "We're here. I'm not going till I know what we are dealing with."

"You mean see Annabeth. You understand even if we see her, you probably won't be able to get her."

A snarl clipped at my lips. "How do you know?"

His mouth flattened, and he tipped his head. "Because I know Vadik. He's going to be sure it's pretty much impossible to get in or out."

"But not *totally* impossible."

Ryker rubbed the creases between his eyes. "I want you to be prepared that she might not be here anymore."

My head snapped away from his. "Yes. I'm prepared." It was a lie. My heart was riding a wave of hope, gripping it with all my might. Before he could say anything else, I scampered for the ladder. The only place I could get a look through the top windows appeared to be from the crumbling building next to the warehouse.

Ryker silently followed me, but I could feel his resistance like a band pulling me backward. Slipping around the building, I watched a guard stroll around the front, his gun in his hands, ready to discharge. During the hour, I watched the handful of security pacing around the property and realized they had a pattern. One would turn a corner and in five seconds another one would walk around the front of the building. They moved in sync, one or two always had eyes on an area. That left me with only a few seconds to dart from my location to cross the lane before a guard would come.

Ryker pressed against the wall beside me. His breathing grew heavier. I glanced over my shoulder at him. He gripped his knife so tightly his knuckles were white, his eyes closed.

"If it's too hard for you to be near me, you can go." I clung to my own knife. It would be a lie to say I didn't miss having a gun.

His lids barely opened and his eyes slid to me, flashing bright with anger. "I am not leaving you."

"You'd rather stay to make sure I'm all right so you can kill me later. Love the plan." I waggled my head. "Stubborn ass."

"I'm stubborn?" he scoffed.

A guard strolled down the street, nearing us. I slammed my head back against the wall, wanting to blend in with the shadows. He passed us and curved around the opposite building.

"Now." I sprinted across the way and headed straight for the fire escape. This building stood at least seven stories, a floor taller than the one next door. From the top, we could look into the windows of the other.

We had a lot of rungs to climb before we were safely out of view. My heart thumped, adrenaline sweat dampening the back of my neck. Any second a guard could come around and spot us. My back prickled, waiting for a bullet to find its way into my spine.

I hauled myself over the top and, without looking, leaped over the wall, rolling to my knees on the roof floor. A shrill chirp of fear tried to exit my throat, but unease locked down all my muscles.

Ryker dropped beside me. "Holy shit."

Both of us gawked in alarm at the colossal gap only a few feet away from us. It looked as if someone dropped a bomb on the building. A massive hole was ripped through the metal and concrete, leaving the roof buckling.

Slowly I edged back, pushing my back up against the roof wall.

Ryker moved to me; his gaze on the ground far below.

"Looks like they use it as a fight ring."

That would make sense. The girls he used as fighters had to train and keep in shape enough to attract a crowd.

"The rim along the roof looks sturdy enough." Ryker kept low and followed the edge to the other side. I copied his movements.

When we finally reached the far side near the main

building, I exhaled. Heights didn't scare me, but falling from them did.

We gazed at the building across from us. The top had windows, which gave us a view into the structure. The space reminded me of a high-security prison. The entire middle was open all the way to the bottom, metal tables and chairs filled the lowest level with what looked like an eating area. Circling this main area were levels and levels of jail cells.

I stepped forward, making out human forms pushing through the bars. My heart squeezed. Bone-thin arms stretched out from some of the cells, reaching for something I couldn't see. Then the guard from outside came into view dragging the new girl to a chamber. It was a split second when he opened the cell door that I saw her lying on the lower bunk bed, curled in a ball. Her blonde hair spread over the thin mattress under her. Her face void of emotion. She looked dead.

Annabeth.

A sound came from my throat.

"Zoey!" Ryker tried to grab for my arm, but I was already gone. Dashing for the corner of the roof, I figured out that the best way to get there was where the structures almost touched.

I shoved the knife into the back of my pants and bolted for the ledge. I pushed myself off and flung my body toward the opposite roofline. Grunts and moans hurled from my throat as I landed, rolling several times. Damn. Still hurt. I did this once before when Ryker and I were trying to escape the Collectors. It hurt when I had been human, and it hurt being half fae. But this time I bounced up much faster, scurrying for the roof door without even a limp.

I had never acted so foolishly, but I couldn't seem to stop myself.

I heard my name along with some words not even I would repeat, but I ignored the pissed-off Viking and advanced down the stairs to the cells below. My shoes padded down the pinging echo of the steps. The stone felt my adrenaline and hummed along the base of my foot and up my leg. It pushed more power and drive into each step.

Do you feel it, Zoey? The high you sense right now? It could always be like this.

I did feel the high. It thrummed into my head. The rush of blood. The sensation of being truly alive, like when I fought. But this was on a whole new level. I needed more. I needed a bigger high.

I can give that to you.

I bit down on my lip. I knew it could.

Say it. Say "Yes, I am yours." I already have you, Zoey. You know it. Just make it official.

I could taste blood. *Stop!* I yelled in my head, but my voice sounded soft, even to me. Pain slashed through my head like a zap of electricity, so quickly bile coated my throat. My legs gave out and I hit a stair. My back slid down the wall, and I groaned.

No. You won't have me, I growled in my head. Pressure built against my brain, filling along my skull, until I thought it would explode. Sweat beaded my hairline, my teeth gritted, and a cry escaped. *Stop. Now... please,* I whimpered.

Soon, Zoey. I will not wait much longer it whispered and then went silent.

The buzzing in my mind vanished, and the pain dissolved into only a slight pulse in my head, sending relief throughout my body. I took in a breath, my muscles still tense after the sudden shock of pain.

It took me a full minute before I felt confident my legs could hold me. They still shook, along with my hands, like I was some kind of junkie coming down from a high. The magic it contained was like a drug, and when the stone took it totally away from me, I sensed myself crashing. Emotional and trembling, I rolled my shoulders and stood, trying to push the need for another hit.

All I need is a little, just a small dose to get me through the night.

Jesus. I did sound like a junkie. And like everyone who suffered an addiction, I wondered how much longer I could resist its call.

The lack of time and the extreme danger tossed me back on my path. *Annabeth. Remember Annabeth.* The image of her face stilled my hands. I snuck to the door leading to the cells and twisted the knob. Slowly I peered around it, assessing my surroundings. A large man was stationed on the opposite side at the far end. *Crap.* I grabbed my weapon.

At least Annabeth was on the end of the building closest to me, with no guards. I went low, plastering my back to the wall, letting the dark prison engulf me. I slunk down the row, my breath tight in my chest.

The first cell I passed was empty. The next one held a single girl who stared at the wall, vacant of life. I recognized her as one of Duc's girls. She wore leggings and a gray sweatshirt, dirty, ripped, and worn, with her frizzy hair knotted in a bun on her head. We had sparred once in the practice ring. She had been decent enough to be an opening fight but not to headline a match. I couldn't think of her name, and even though it stung to leave her, she was not why I came here. I wanted to help them all eventually, but Annabeth remained my first priority.

I slipped by one more cell, which held two girls, both curled on their sides asleep. No blankets or pillows, only a thin dirty mattress for comfort, a true prison. I never thought

159

I would say it, but they had been better off with Duc. At least Maria had made sure they were comfortable, clean, and healthy.

The cell where I spotted Annabeth was close. My heart slammed against my ribs, sweat dampening my back, as I slithered slowly up, grabbed the bars, and looked in. This cell appeared larger with two sets of bunk beds perpendicular to each other, a toilet and sink on the opposite wall.

Annabeth still lay on her side, indifferent to the new girl sitting in the corner crying. Another girl curled on the top of the other bunk, her back to me.

"Annabeth?" I whispered her name almost inaudible. Her complexion had been naturally pale, but now she was the waxy white of parchment. Bruises puffed her right cheek, but her features were sharp with malnutrition. Her leggings and hoodie did little to hide the bones under her skin.

She didn't flinch.

I moved closer, desperation flooding my lungs. "Annabeth." The girl in the corner stopped crying, her eyes unfocused as she glanced up.

"I shouldn't be here," she sobbed. "I want to go home."

"Shhh." I put my finger to my lips.

Annabeth slowly lifted her head, then sluggishly turned to the bars. It was several beats before her eyes widened, and she sat up.

"Zoey?"

Relief sucker-punched my heart. "Yes."

The girl on the top bunk jerked at my name and twisted over. My initial reaction was to lurch back, but I held the bars, forcing myself not to move.

Maria.

Her figure was a rail compared to her former curves. Her highlights had grown out giving her curly hair dark roots to her temples and golden brown to her shoulders, her skin pasty and eyes dull and lifeless.

"Help me!" The crying girl started to crawl over to me but only made it a few feet before stopping.

"Quiet," I hissed. She would draw the attention of the guard.

Maria's eyes were wide with shock then tapered, her lips curling up. "Why am I not surprised it would be you of all people? The Avenging Angel has come down from the heavens for us. Praise the day."

Her bitterness was not lost on me.

"What are you doing here, Zoey?" Annabeth didn't rise from her bed, but she leaned over, staring out toward where the guard was stationed, her eyes flitting frantically. The new girl continued to wail.

"I'm getting you out of here."

Maria snorted. "Always the hero, aren't you?"

I glared at Maria, then looked back at Annabeth. "I can break these locks, but she needs to shut up." I motioned at the wailing girl.

Again, Maria laughed harshly. "They don't hear our cries."

"She's still bringing attention over here."

"No. No. You can't be here!" Annabeth's eyes pleaded with mine. "Zoey, you need to get out of here now."

I shook my head. "I'm not leaving without you. I can get you out."

Sorrow flittered over Annabeth's features. "You can't."

Then Annabeth moved her leg, and I saw she was chained to the bed by her ankle. My gaze drifted to Maria then down to the new girl. They were all chained to the bunk beds, giving them only a few feet of freedom to move.

"Help me. Please. I didn't do anything wrong. I

shouldn't be here. I never took money. It was just sex." If not for the bars I probably would have punched the new girl unconscious just to shut her up. She appeared high as a kite and blathering loudly, unaware of the true danger.

"Hey, bitch. Shut up," Maria growled at the sobbing mess on the floor.

My hope was deflating like a balloon.

"Zoey. Go," Annabeth demanded. "You don't understand... they've been—"

The black-haired girl started to screech, pounding the floor and tearing at her hair. Shit, she was coming off the drugs and coming down hard. Guards would be heading here soon. But how could I leave Annabeth knowing where she was and what was happening?

"Annabeth..."

"Zoey. Run. They've been waiting for you. They knew you'd eventually come here for me."

That's when I heard the pounding of feet coming my way.

Holy hell.

Annabeth set her jaw. "I'm a trap for you. I'm so sorry."

A cry broke from my lips with realization.

"You can't help me if you get caught." Annabeth's voice rose. "Girls are disappearing from here daily, never to be seen again. We all need your help, but you won't be able to if you're behind these bars with us. Now run!"

"Freeze!" a man down the walk yelled, as he pointed the gun in my direction. A group clumped behind him, some with fae swords, but most had guns. I wasn't about to test if the bullets were goblin made or not.

I gave Annabeth one last look. "I *will* be back."

She nodded. "I know you will."

I whirled around and ran.

For my life and every girl locked in this hellhole.

THIRTEEN

Fuck. Fuck. Fuck.

A bullet whistled by my ear as I darted back for the roof door, flinging it open. The sound of footsteps gaining on me bounced off the walls in loud, shrill noises. I hated going back to the roof, limiting my exits, but I had no choice.

I shut the door behind me, fastening the flimsy lock. It would only hold them for a brief moment, but any time I could gain, I would take.

I took the steps two at a time, and my short legs strained to push harder. I reached the top, grasping for the knob. I barely touched it before it swung open, and I stumbled out into the night.

My hope that it was Ryker immediately vanished when a gun was pressed to my forehead. "Step out," the man barked. The familiarity of his voice rolled over me. "Drop your weapon."

"Carlos?" The man who followed Maria around like a lovesick puppy, the one who had actually been decent enough to me under Duc's rule, stood in front of me, pushing a gun to my head.

He stirred at hearing his name, but his expression stayed hard and ruthless. "I said drop your weapon."

"Okay." I lifted my arms, easing down to lower my blade. "Carlos, it's me."

"I know who you are: the girl Boss wants." His words were rote and emotionless, as if he didn't really know me more than what he had been told.

Shit. Carlos had been glamoured.

The door banged below. They would break through in a moment. Some were probably already making their way to the roof from outside. I didn't have much time.

"Carlos, look at me. You know me. You helped me." I kept my hands up. "I was one of the fighters. The Avenging Angel."

"Avenging Angel?" he repeated, tilting his head.

"Yes. I'm not your enemy. I only want to help." I licked my lips. "I want to help the girls... I want to help *Maria*."

"Maria?" He took a step back, longing imbued in her name. He might not totally remember me, but there was a reason he stayed here as one of Vadik's guards. And that was the curly-haired girl in the cell block below our feet. He probably talked Vadik into keeping him on. He would want to be where Maria was. Little did he know they would glamour him to try and forget her.

Love was more powerful than any glamour in the world. He just needed a little reminding. Quickly.

"Carlos, you love Maria. You would want me to help her."

His arms began to shake, his mind and heart opposing each other.

"Please, just let me go and I swear I will come back and get them out. Safely."

He grunted, his gun lowering slightly. A loud clang tore up the stairwell followed by pounding footsteps. They were coming. Crap. This was taking too long. "Sorry, Carlos. I can't wait for you to come to your senses."

I took advantage of his sinking arm. I grabbed the barrel of the gun and punched him hard in the face. I swung my leg, taking his feet out from under him. But he held on to his weapon as if it were his lifeline. I grabbed my knife off the ground and ran.

"Stop!" I heard him scream as my toes hit the roof wall. I glanced over my shoulder. He lay on his stomach, the gun pointed at my back. Our eyes met. It was a second, but something in his expression shifted, and his finger slid off the trigger.

I swung around and jumped. As I rolled onto the opposite roof, I heard men filing out the stairway onto the roof, shouting. I scrambled to my feet and started to run, my eyes on the group of men shooting at me.

"Zoey! Stop!" I heard my name bellowed from the across the roof. My head snapped forward to see Ryker and the reason terror was etched over his features. I skidded to a stop.

I hit the rim, my arms waggling, trying to keep from falling through the giant hole.

"Zo-ey!" Ryker screamed. Fear curled around my name from far away. Then suddenly he was there. His figure slammed into my back. The ground disappeared under my feet. My stomach plunged as my body flayed in the air, plummeting down the hole of the building. Like a drop of water, gravity tugged me down with speed. The ground came up fast; my head and shoulders slammed into the cement floor with a crunch. The impact was so violent, my nerves went numb, flattening my form to the floor.

Everything went black.

Nothing.

It could have been seconds or years when I sensed a tickling in my soul.

Then agony. A shitload of it. Scorching up my veins, shredding me from my body.

Death really, really didn't like me.

Something tugged me from the peacefulness of nothing, where I had no thoughts or pain. There was no me.

"Zoey." My name rang in my ears, buzzing my head, tugging me further from the tranquility. "Open your eyes."

I tried, but only a groan stung my throat. I heard my name again. Felt a strong awareness my body was being cradled. Warmth.

My nose filled with strong smells of trees, asphalt, Italian food, Chinese takeout, rotting garbage, and piss. It seemed as if each smell developed a picture in my head of exactly what it was and how far away from me. *Okay, weird.*

"Don't you dare leave me," a deep voice whispered in my ear.

Ryker. My heart cried out.

The pull of him carried me through the last bit of murkiness. My lids fluttered, and I looked up to blazing white eyes. The night sky moved behind his head, becoming so clear and crisp I felt like I had never seen the stars before. My lashes fluttered a few times, the sharpness almost uncomfortable at first, but my sight quickly adjusted and landed fully on the breathtaking man bending over me.

"Hey," I croaked.

His lids squeezed together and then he opened them again, his brows furrowing. "Thank the gods." It took me a moment to remember why he was thanking his deities, and why he carried me in his arms.

"We got out?" I let my head drop to the side to see around me.

"Yes."

"Yay, us." It was difficult to concentrate on a landmark, but I finally recognized the area. We were near Pioneer Square. "I've been out for a while."

"You've been dead awhile."

I twisted my head to look back up at him. His jaw looked like it was crushing his teeth, grinding them into dust.

"Hey, it's okay. We made it out. I'm alive."

He shook his head. "I jumped... I had no control. I jumped right into you."

This had to be strange and frustrating for him, having no command over his powers, as if he were a child again. I spent more time with sporadic powers than I did controlling them.

"It's okay."

He growled, a strange expression deepening the anger flaming under the surface. He moved quickly through the city, heading back to our hideout.

I experienced some dizziness, but I actually didn't feel too bad. Every minute my body continued to heal and regain energy. Actually a lot of energy. My muscles buzzed with a strange abundance of force, wanting to move and run.

"You can set me down. I can walk on my own."

He gritted his teeth and ignored me.

He carried me the entire way, holding me close, which I found extremely nice, but also curious. Was he fighting our proximity right now?

Damn this bullheaded Viking. I reached up, brushing the lines from his forehead away. He tipped his head in my hand, tension releasing from his jaw and eyes. He actually looked at peace.

When we got back to the warehouse, I heard Amara call

for us. She was either really quick at getting laid or she never went. Sadly, it was probably the latter. It had likely been more a test for Ryker to see if he would stop her.

"Not right now," he shouted back.

"But—"

"Not the fuck now!" Ryker roared, then took me into the breakroom, slamming the door. I cringed from the shrill sound, my eardrums pulsing. He set me down on the blankets and stepped across the pitch-black room, lighting a candle. The space illuminated in a hazy glow.

He turned to the door and placed his palms on it, leaning forward. The energy shifted in the room. Anger. Fury.

I sat up with a groan, rubbing my hands over my face. My senses were in overdrive, causing me to feel restless and strange. My body and head ached from the fall, but I felt no worse than the aftermath of a fight. I had fallen at least seven stories. My head should have splattered like a watermelon. My body should be broken in tiny pieces.

I should be dead.

Like dead, dead.

But here I sat feeling no more than slightly bruised all over.

Ryker's breaths became heavy, causing me to pull my hands away from my face and glance up. He pushed off the wall and turned to lean back against the spot, folding his arms over his chest. He was pissed.

"What?" My words came out with annoyance. It had already been a rough day and by the look on his face it wasn't going to get better. Ryker wore his lecture expression. Anger flared in his eyes, and he looked away. "Don't tell me. You're mad at me." I stood, biting back the moan wanting to follow. Okay, I hurt a little more than I first thought, but I was standing. That was a plus.

His silence picked at my irritation button like a scab.

"Oh, for fuck's sake, Ryker. Just get it out. Tell me I was stupid. What I did was foolish and rash. Go ahead. You know you want to," I taunted, but my voice sounded hot with anger. "Look me in the eyes and tell me you wouldn't have done the same to try and save someone you care about. Did you see them? Any of them? Vadik is sucking the life out of them, literally. Annabeth is chained to a bed—" My voice broke with emotion recalling the memory. "She's being used as a prostitute. She's fourteen! What if it had been your sister? Tell me you wouldn't have tried to save her, no matter the costs."

It wasn't till that moment I realized that was exactly how I thought of Annabeth. I barely knew her, but in the little time we had spent together, she lodged deep inside me. Her strength reminded me so much of Lexie, and she created her own spot in my heart. She and Lexie were the little sisters, the family, I never had. I would fight for her just as hard.

"Screw you." His silence caused my emotions to mushroom. "I do not regret trying to get her out of there. I would do it again."

His feet moved toward me, swallowing the space between us in three strides. Instinct slammed into me, wanting to retreat. I forced myself to stay as his feet flushed up to mine, and I kept my head high. His chest heaved as his eyes wandered over me, really taking me in. His strong fingers cupped my face, turning my head more up to his. Feeling his touch with his warm body so close to mine flooded me with familiar contrasting sensations. Hunger and bliss.

Home. My heart sang.

He didn't speak while his fingers explored my face, his thumb dragging slowly across my bottom lip. My skin burned as his penetrating gaze rolled over every inch of me, making me feel naked and vulnerable.

"I am furious," he spoke low and husky. "But not for trying to save someone you care about."

"Then why?" I struggled to talk, his touch clogging all thoughts.

"Because there was a moment I thought I lost you. No. I did lose you." He swallowed, his Adam's apple bobbing. "Again."

My forehead crunched up in slight confusion.

"No one was there to save you, human. I felt the oath break. For good."

My mouth opened, but nothing came out. I had died before. Well, sort of. Croygen and the fae magic brought me back to life.

"Your human body completely died tonight." He licked his lip, a shot of fear pinching the corner of his eyes. "I felt it. The link. Our oath broke. It must have been connected to the human you. Not the fae you. When your human part died, so did the promise."

"Wait. What?" My mouth gaped open. "Are you saying I'm completely fae now?" That's why my senses were on steroids. Why energy poured through me like Gatorade. It was magic.

Holy shit. I was entirely fae?

"Even more than me." His mouth twitched with a smile. "Your life is no longer counted in human years."

Whoa. I hadn't thought about that. The moment the powers decided to stay, choosing to permanently live with me, they had altered me. My life. My DNA. I would not age like a human anymore. Ryker and I were on even terrain.

I was a Wanderer.

Holy hell. I was one hundred percent fae? The same

thing I spent most of my life against, trained to hate and kill. My brain couldn't fully wrap around the fact I remained no longer human.

I waited for a wave of sadness, a feeling of loss, possibly a sense of horror. I didn't. At all. That actually upset me the most. All those years of hating and killing fae, I should have had some adverse reaction to the fact I was totally one of them now. Maybe having Ryker's powers for the past several months had me accustomed to being "semi" fae, I don't know. But against everything I had been taught, I felt oddly relieved. Even happy, like this is what I was supposed to be all along.

"The curse broke because *I* killed you. I was the reason you fell. Your death was by my hand." Ryker pressed his mouth together, his jaw twitching. If the curse broke, it meant he no longer had the desire to kill me. "If some of my powers hadn't decided to stay with you…" His lids squeezed shut, his head shaking slightly.

I suddenly got it—his bristling anger. That's where the true anger lay—with himself and with his fear. It was exactly how I reacted to things. "That's why you're mad." I couldn't get my voice above a whisper. His hands gripped my face forcefully.

He inclined his head, tapping his forehead against mine. His warm breath fluttered down my neck. My lids squeezed together as his hand slid around to my neck and gripped me tightly. The world disappeared around us… one of those moments it was only us.

"Now that it's broken, are you…?"

"I'm not going anywhere."

He always seemed to know exactly what I was thinking. Relief came out in a shaky breath.

"Not sure I would have been able to anyway." He

brushed his nose against mine. "I don't know how you did it or when…" he muttered. Our mouths were so close, but neither of us moved to fuse the distance. I reached up, sliding my hand down his cheek, his scruff tickling my hand.

"What?"

His throat bobbed again, but his words came out strong and hard. "You made me fall in love with you."

My chest clenched, air expanding in my throat. *Did I hear him right?* "What did you say?"

"I'm in love with you, *human*." He growled, his mouth so close I could feel the vibration.

The declaration took a moment to cascade down and soak in. Ryker, the Wanderer, the feared Viking, the man who was a demon fae with a touch of human, just told me he loved me.

He was also the man who held me when I was scared and turned himself over to DMG because he'd rather be near me than safe. The man who put a candle in a loaf of bread for my birthday, patched me up, took me up to Machu Picchu because he knew I wanted to see it, and who fought and loved me with a ferocity nothing in this world could match.

And I was completely in love with him as well. My lips parted to tell him, but he spoke first.

"I swear to the gods, Zoey. If anything happens to you…" His grip turned brutal. "I hate this. I hate knowing you completely have me by the ball sac."

I smiled. "I promise to be somewhat gentle."

"No safe words. Ever."

"That I can *promise*."

He lifted his head; his lids narrowed. "That's the last time you will use that word ever again. You are fae now. The word holds a lot of power. You can't say it anymore. You got it?"

"I promi—"

His lips came down on mine, stomping out my sentence. The feel of his mouth on mine turned my body to butter. Heat pulsed from my breasts to my thighs.

It felt as if someone detonated a bomb inside me. The need for him became so overwhelming and instantaneous my head spun. His tongue and lips tugged at my top lip, and a needy, desperate noise escaped my throat as if of its own volition. His fingers dug into my scalp as he pulled me closer.

It was not enough. My fingers shoved his coat off his shoulders. He let it drop to the floor as my hands dove under his shirt, running over the ridges of his abs and around to his rear end. Oh man, how I missed his perky tush.

A hand dropped from my head and trailed down my torso. Everywhere his fingers brushed, fire burned, tightening the need in my abdomen. Holy hell did I want this. I nipped at his bottom lip. My hands pushed past jeans and boxer briefs, roaming over his bare ass, my nails skimming over to his V-line.

Ryker swore under his breath, his grip on me burned into my skin. His legs pushed mine toward the blankets. My fingers tugged at the buttons of his jeans as we stumbled backward.

"Ahem." Someone cleared their throat behind Ryker, and we both froze. "Sorry to interrupt, but I think you'll find what I have to say more important than a quick fuck." Amara's tone could not hide her hurt, which surprised me.

Ryker jerked away from me, his arms dropping as he turned to look over his shoulder. My body's reaction to his sudden absence shocked me. Handling him with violence and indifference had been torture after being so close to him for so long. Now given the opportunity to let my guard down, I never wanted to stop touching him. I clenched my hands and peered around Ryker.

"What?" I snapped, my irritation only rising when I saw Ryker buttoning his pants before fully facing her. Did she interrupt us on purpose? Her reason had better be epic or she would see what happened when my lust turned to violence.

Amara stood in the doorway watching us. There was a slight lift to her shoulders. I thought maybe I saw tears brimming under her aloof gaze, her lips pressed in a firm thin line. She quickly held her chin up, her face and tone unemotional.

"I thought you guys might want to know... but if you are too busy getting it on to care about your sister or Croygen." She shrugged.

"What is it, Amara?" Ryker gritted his jaw.

"They're not here."

"What?" I moved alongside Ryker. "What do you mean?"

"Just what I said. They. Are. Gone."

"They can't be." I crossed my arms, confusion pushing away the meaning of her words.

A smugness lifted one of Amara's eyebrows. "Well, they are. They left a note."

My feet were moving before my brain caught up with them. "Lexie? Croygen?" I screamed as I ran into the main room. Silence greeted me back. A few bubbles of alarm floated up.

"Sprig?" Again, nothing responded.

"He's still here." Amara motioned over to the table.

My gaze went to the tiny, furry figure on the counter. Lying on his back, a dozen empty packets of honey fanned out around him, Sprig snored softly.

They were all the packets I had been storing up for Sprig to be eaten over time. Everyone knew he couldn't eat more than three without going into a sugar overdose and narcoleptic sleep. Sometimes he only needed one.

"Sprig!" I ran to him, my hand rubbing his soft belly. There was no point. Sprig seemed to be down for the count.

"You said there was a note?" Ryker came up, addressing Amara.

Amara picked a piece of folded paper off the table and handed it to him. I snatched it from him, my fingers trembling as I tried to unfold it.

Scratchy handwriting scrawled on the paper. I knew Lexie's loopy, girly handwriting instantly. My eyes scanned over the words, my brain struggling to understand.

Zoey,

I will not let you risk your life for me again. You can keep denying it, but you know the truth. I am sick. I need medication and help, which only Dr. Rapava can give me. It was a fantasy, a wish, to think you could simply go in and get it. But I know you. You won't stop till I'm okay. I can't let you do that. Not when I can do it for myself. Don't worry about me. I will be okay. They won't hurt me. They need me for research too much. And I'm not going alone. Croygen would not let me go unless he went with me. He made me promise. Told me someone needed to protect me. So I've got my very own sexy pirate escorting me! Take that, stupid bitches at school!

Don't forget, I love you, Zoey. More than you could ever know. That's why I have to go. And I'm sorry for all the pain I caused you.

Lexie

P.S. I still think you should paint your

toenails. Fire red. Might get Ryker's head out of his ass. You'll thank me!

P.P.S. Sorry about Sprig. Only way we could get out. Wow... does he go off the rails after four honey packets!

"Are you kidding me?" I spoke, my hands shaking. "Are you fucking kidding me?" I screamed. I felt gutted and drained. Panic for my sister stirred my feet. How could Croygen betray me like that? "I have to stop them."

"How?" Amara lifted her arms. "You have no idea where they went. Besides, they are probably long gone by now. They weren't here when I got back."

"When did you return?" I demanded.

"About ten minutes before you. I stopped for a drink on the..." She kept talking, but my mind and body were already gone. Desperation to find them had me bolt for the door.

"Zoey!" Ryker bellowed after me.

I kept running. I had to at least try. I sprinted out of the building and down the street on instinct. My mind would not let logic in yet, so I relied completely on my intuition. In my soul I knew it was more than instinct that led me forward. My new deeper fae ability heightened an urge I felt in my gut.

I heard feet pounding pavement behind me; Ryker. I wound us through the alley, coming out on a main road.

Croygen was smart. He would not let DMG know where we were staying, but he would have to carry Lexie. They would still have to be relatively close. Night or not, DMG would not meet on an open street. They would use a parking structure or a side street.

The streets were silent, everyone tucked away for the night as I sprinted down Second Avenue, nearing Pike's

Place. A few streetlights illuminated our path. My gaze flashed over the outlines of cranes and bulldozers. New and old buildings with large empty gaps hulked down the dark boulevards. I turned up a side street.

"Zoey, what are you doing?" Ryker grabbed my hips, yanking me to a stop. He twirled me to face him, both of us gasping for breath.

"Let go!" I pulled against him. "You're letting them get away."

"How do you know? They might have left hours ago." His voice was steady as he tried to get me to see reason. When it came to my sister, I had no logic. I had none with him either.

"What if it were me?"

He panted, but I quickly realized it was with strong emotion, not breathlessness. "It had been once."

I forgot he had gone through something like this when I jumped from Peru to Seattle, except he had no idea where I went and if I would ever come back. There were many hints that he'd gone a little nuts trying to find me.

Still, Ryker let me go.

As I led us down another alley, I heard a van door open, cutting through the quiet night. My head popped up.

Across the street, through the darkness and deep in a covered parking lot, I saw the strong but slender figure of Croygen lit with a bright fae aura. My new senses saw and heard way past any normal human senses. Hugo, Marv, Matt, and Peter stood around him, their human auras almost nonexistent next to Croygen's fae one. The Collectors held their weapons on him as he lifted his leg to crawl into the van.

"Stop!" I screamed. "Croygen!"

All heads shot toward me.

Arms wrapped around me, a hand over my mouth, Ryker darted us back into a doorway. "Fuck, Zoey," he whispered hoarsely. "They will shoot you before you can even get close. I lost you once tonight. I will not lose you again."

Yelling came from the garage, feet sounding off concrete.

Ryker swore under his breath, peeking out. Matt and Marv shoved Croygen in. The other two trained military men headed directly for us. A bullet struck the corner of the building.

"Run, you assholes!" Croygen yelled at us, his head poking back out of the van.

Ryker didn't hesitate. He grabbed my arm, tugging me out of the doorway and around the corner. More bullets whizzed by us, one nicking my ear. I yelped as warm blood oozed down my neck. Another clipped Ryker's calf.

Shit. I really hoped they weren't fae bullets.

I trucked after Ryker, the men behind us nearing. Ryker steered me into a construction site, outlines of structures rising up to the sky. My heart thumped, the stone sparking underfoot. The hit it gave me pushed my short legs par with Ryker.

"Zoey. Stop!" Peter's voice rang out, vibrating off the steel. Ryker tugged me behind a pile of structure beams, keeping us low as he darted farther into the building.

"Fighting us is only going to hurt your sister," Hugo yelled. "You really want her to take the punishment for your wrongs?"

Ryker gripped my hand tighter, yanking me closer to him. He slipped us around equipment and material. We darted in the next room.

"Shit." I bounced on my feet. The room was walled off. No exits.

Fuck. Fuck. Fuck.

Hugo's and Peter's footsteps grew near. My heart slammed against my chest in panic. What the hell were we going to do? We had no weapons. They did.

Frantically, I searched the room. Against the far wall piles of tubes for air ducts lay deep in the shadows. My feet were moving before I could think. Ryker trailed behind me as I ran for them.

"They'll look here," he exclaimed.

"We don't have a choice." I waved around at the blocked room. "They are not seers. They won't see our auras."

He pressed his mouth together then nodded and went for the ducts. Grabbing me, he picked me up, my legs wrapping around him as he slid us both into the pipe, settling us far into the darkness.

It was only a moment before I heard Hugo and Peter enter the room. "Did they come this way?"

"Shit. We can't lose them." Footsteps neared us. "Look in those. They couldn't have gone far."

I could feel Ryker's heart pounding against mine, his breath heavy in my ear. I shut my eyes. *You don't see anything. You don't see anything,* I chanted in my head. *Please, glamour, work tonight.*

"I can't see anything." Peter let out a string of swear words.

"We know they are close. We'll do a sweep of this area tomorrow," Hugo said. "We better get back to the van. I don't trust that fucking fae. The girl I can see; she needs Rapava. She's good as dead, but why would he turn himself in?"

"Good question."

"Let's go." Hugo's boots shuffled over the floor.

"Hold on a moment."

I heard the sound of a gun clicking.

Oh. Fuck.

Shrill wails of shots rang out, reverberating over the huge space, shredding through the huge plastic pipes we were in. Holes tore through the tubing like connect the dots. Ryker wrapped me tighter against him, but he couldn't cover me completely.

Piercing pain shot through my hip, my body jerked, my mouth opened to scream. Ryker's hand slammed over my lips, covering the wail of agony my body wanted to express. The bangs of the gun covered up my muffled cry. The gun clicked again.

"Feel better?" Hugo chuckled.

"Yeah. You know. Just in case."

"Rapava wants her alive."

"She's his weakness. She's better off dead. I should have killed her a long time ago."

"Yeah. Well, next time we won't make that mistake," Hugo replied. "Let's go."

Boots resounded over the floor, then disappeared. Ryker held me close, my breathing labored, his hand still over my mouth, the other brushing the back of my head softly. Liquid leaked from my eyes as I bit down against the pain. Another five minutes passed before Ryker pulled me out of the duct, a trail of blood following me. He sat me on the tube, tugging down my pants to check my wound. His finger was frantic as he tried to find the bullet.

"I don't feel sick. I think it's a human bullet." I flinched against his touch. My ear was already healing, and I didn't feel any goblin metal effects from that either.

"I think so too. It was also a clean shot. Went all the way through." He let out an exhale, his shoulders drooping. "You've already stopped bleeding. It will be sore, but you'll be fine."

Fine? I was far from fine.

The realization Lexie and Croygen were truly gone slammed into me. I leaned forward, my head knocking into Ryker's chest. Ryker brought me into him, holding me till my sobs went quiet.

I welcomed Ryker's silence. He didn't give me platitudes or try to take away my pain. He shared it with me and held me tighter as I clung to his chest.

Even if it didn't help or change anything, I still needed it. I needed him.

FOURTEEN

The mood stayed bitter and defeated when we reached the garage. Amara jumped up the moment we walked in. Ryker held up his hand, telling her not to speak. It was for her own safety. My temper was on the cusp, and she would push me over. I staggered over to Sprig, who still snored on top of the table, gathered him in my hands and moved to the bench seat. I lay down with him on my good hip. He eased some of the pain storming inside, like a security blanket. When I felt his heart flutter against my chest, I let my eyes close.

Laying there, the night's drama flooded me. Losing Lexie and Croygen, my earlier death, and the demise of my human self finally soaked in. A hole drilled into my chest, forcing tears to my eyes. The urge to call for the stone traveled over me. Desperation for its power to get my sister or just to feel the numbness of its magic was hard to ignore. Now that I was fae, would my strength against it be stronger or weaker? I was scared to find out.

An acute headache filled my forehead as my muscles twitched. Rolling into a tight ball, trying to combat the fervent craving, I shut down.

Sleep came quickly, but it didn't keep me. I skimmed the line between slumber and wakefulness. My mind tormented me with the memory of the fire when I thought I lost Lexie the first time. I saw her and Croygen being tortured. Rapava asking over and over where I was hiding. Lexie screaming. Needing me. *Zoey, help me!* Lexie's voice called, then her face morphed into Annabeth's. I whimpered, then gasped, my eyes shooting open.

A hand came down and pressed on my thigh, immediately calming me. I twisted over looking at Ryker, who sat on the windowsill above me. Somehow while I slept, he dragged the bench closer to the window so he could watch over me and the street. His hand drifted down to where I had been shot, the wound closed up but still a little tender. His thumb rubbed soothingly over the injury, like he was trying to make it disappear under his soft touch. I covered his hand with mine. Telling him without words I was fine. Being all fae, my healing time had doubled. I couldn't say it wasn't awesome.

Sprig curled into me, and I shifted him higher on the hoodie I used for a pillow, careful not to wake him. Ryker looped an arm around my waist, helping me stand.

"You really should try and sleep as much as you can," he muttered quietly. "Your body needs to heal. It's been through a lot tonight."

"I can't."

Rhythmic breathing from Sprig drifted up. I glanced over my shoulder to see Amara curled into a blanket in the back of the truck. She appeared to be asleep, but there existed a good chance she was awake, listening.

I recalled the tears brimming in her eyes earlier when she walked in on Ryker and me. Surprising as it was, I didn't really enjoy hurting her, but I would not hold back with Ryker either. There remained no pretense anymore. No more staying away from each other because of a stupid oath or for Amara's sake.

"My mind will not let me sleep." I scoured my eyebrow. "My sister, Annabeth, Croygen… you."

"None of this was your fault."

"You know that never stops the guilt." I licked my lips nervously, staring into his eyes, then down his torso. "Guilt consumes you even if you know there was no choice."

Ryker's head shook. "Don't…"

"I have to." I shifted my feet, his arms still holding me steady. "We've never talked about it. What I did to you. What I had been capable of doing. How can you ever forgive me?"

"You did what you had to." He brushed a strand of lose hair behind my ear. "Like you said, we are survivors. We do what we need to live and protect our loved ones."

"I didn't protect you."

His gaze snapped to mine, taking in my meaning. He twisted, letting his legs drop over the sill and tugging me between them. "I could handle it. Lexie was your first priority. She should always be." His rough hands skimmed up my thighs, lighting every nerve ending. The friction through my jeans sent a thousand tiny electric shocks through me. "If it makes you feel better, I would have done the same."

My eyebrow curved up in a taunting *really*?

"Because you could have handled it. You are strong. Amazingly so... inside and out."

I didn't feel strong.

"They're gone." The thought stabbed at my heart just as cruelly. I still did not want to believe it. I twisted and slid down the wall to the floor next to the bench. Sprig snored louder. "Why would Croygen let her go? Why would he go with her?"

Ryker slipped off the sill and sat down next to me, his arm brushing my shoulder.

"I would have gotten the medication for her. She didn't have to give herself up."

"She's really sick, Zoey. She had to go back. You understand that deep down." Ryker leaned his bent leg against mine. "She's as stubborn as you. There would have been no way to stop her. Croygen understood as well as me that with you sisters, if you can't stop them, you join them."

I wanted to punch Croygen, but I also wanted to hug him. "I can't believe he did that. Croygen knowingly went back to DMG to be tortured and experimented on because he wouldn't allow Lexie to go back by herself."

"I'm as stunned as you. I have known him for centuries and have never seen him do anything so self-sacrificing for anyone. With Amara he always did it in hopes she would love him, or for the fame. This is completely against his personality." Ryker rubbed his thumb over my knee. "Well, that was until you. He didn't have to follow you either. But he did." Ryker's voice tightened at the end.

"Do I detect a note of jealousy?" A small smile inched my mouth.

"Should I be?"

I threaded my fingers through his. "No."

We stayed silent for a moment.

"He's lost his freedom and risks death just to protect her. How does someone ever repay that?" I leaned into Ryker's shoulder.

"You don't. It was his choice." Ryker leaned his head back against the wall. "But dammit. He's making me respect the fucker. I don't like that feeling."

I laughed bitterly, dropped his fingers, and pressed the heels of my hands into my eyes. "I'm supposed to be the one who protects her."

Ryker pulled me into him.

"It's my job to keep her safe." I burrowed into his chest. "I have failed both Annabeth and Lexie."

185

"We will get them." He kissed the top of my head. His arms felt like the warmest blanket. The love I felt for this man frightened me, but there was no way I wouldn't leap straight in. It was too late for me to be saved. I wanted to drown in him. Whatever pain would come, I would be willing to take on. He was worth everything to me.

"Her birthday is the day after tomorrow," I said absently. "I had planned on stealing a birthday cake from the bakery a couple blocks away."

Ryker squeezed me tighter, perhaps knowing there was no need for a response. He held me until I fell asleep in his warm arms—the only place in the world I felt truly safe.

When I woke up, it was still dark outside, and he was gone. The old reaction of feeling abandoned struck me but no longer controlled me. Ryker wouldn't leave me. Not unless he had to. The sureness of my trust in him gave me solid ground to walk on.

I wandered through the shadowy automotive repair shop. Looking through the window, the dimness of the sky told me dawn was coming. We would have to move locations today. We really shouldn't be here now, the risk too great of being found. DMG would start searching a ten-block radius in all directions where they picked up Croygen and Lexie. It was protocol.

Amara stayed asleep in the truck and Sprig on the bench. The overdose of sugar would keep him asleep till late morning.

I continued to walk through the building and found the Viking holding sentry at a window overlooking the street at the far end of the building. He peered sideways at me when I entered the room but turned back to keep guard.

I weaved around frames and car engines, positioning myself directly behind him. My hand reached out, roaming over his firm derriere. His back went straight at my touch, but he didn't move away.

"I forgot to say something earlier." My fingers trailed up, crawling under his shirt, sliding up his back. His shoulder blades flexed. Without thinking I leaned in, my lips touching his spine softly. He sucked in sharply as my mouth moved up his skin, and my tongue traced the lines of his tattoo.

A deep sigh pulled from his lungs, his head falling forward. "What was that?"

I stepped around in front of him, my hands finding their way to his abs. My heart thumped in my throat, forcing me to swallow. "That I'm in love with you too."

His white eyes stared down at me with radiating light. The tattoo on his neck flickered. I loved it was back.

"So, damn you, Viking, for making me fall in love with you. Not that I had any chance. I was pretty much doomed the moment you tied me to a bathtub faucet." I grinned mischievously.

"I knew you liked it that way," he muttered, a smirk inching up the side of his mouth.

I reached up, running my fingers softly over his features. The scars, the lines in his eyebrows, over his lips. "Whatever is ahead of us, I want to be with you. As long as you want me."

He watched me as I traced the light emanating from his tattoo. His breath sounded clipped, the heat between our bodies sparking in the cool air.

"Is forever good?" he whispered.

"I guess that will do." I shrugged, licking my bottom lip.

His eyes locked on my mouth. I stood on my toes to come closer to his face. "No safe words," I muttered.

"No safe words." He grabbed my face, pulling me to him. His lips met mine and the fire in my belly swelled. His tongue parted my lips, opening my mouth to fully take him. My entire body flooded with desire and need. The need to feel him overwhelmed me. His hands skated up to my ass, pushing me firmer into him. A low moan filled my throat when I felt him hard against me.

The day's situation only increased my urge for him. You never knew what tomorrow would bring. I might be harder to kill, but both of us could still die. I wouldn't waste the time we had.

Tonight we were *alive*.

He lifted me up, my legs wrapping around him. His warm mouth devoured mine. Taking our time would have to wait. The raw passion consumed us, turning our thoughts primal and desperate. My ass slammed onto the hood of a Chevrolet Chevelle as he pushed me up. My fingers frantically gripped the bottom of his shirt. He sucked in air as I ripped it over his head.

My fingers slid over a slash running over his heart. *I did that.*

"Stop, Zoey," he growled. "I'm fine."

"But…"

"No. No more guilt or blame." He shook his head, ripping my shirt over my head, taking my bra with it. He tossed them to the side and lay me back on the hood, the icy metal against my hot skin. He loosened the buttons, lowered the zipper of my jeans, and then drew them down my legs. The fabric and his fingers sending trails of desire over my skin. He tossed my boots across the room, ripping the jeans off me.

I shoved guilt, regret, and anger to the background as his lips kissed my inner thigh, his beard tickling me. I sat up, grabbing him. "Foreplay can wait." I wrapped myself around him, my hands pushing down his pants, my mouth not wanting to break from his.

His pants and briefs fell to his ankles, leaving him naked. I couldn't help but lean back and take him in. A blissful sigh escaped my lips. He was unbelievable. Seeing him so ready for me was the only thing that stopped me looking and pushed me to act. I reached for him. His hands grabbed the sides of my underwear, wiggling me out of them. Our mouths crashed back together. Biting. Sucking. Nipping. Our hands exploring, gripping, and tearing at each other to get closer.

Nothing stood between us now when I wrapped my legs back around him. The couple of times we had sex before, I knew how dedicated he was to pleasing me first, but now was not that time. And I was glad. I moaned when I felt the tip of him. Hearing me only made his grip on me tighten. Then he drove in deep, filling me completely. I sucked in sharply. The unbelievable pleasure of him sliding inside sent me over.

"Holy fuck," he whispered hoarsely in my ear as he pushed in deeper. Then he started moving, his motions raw, rough, and desperate.

I groaned and arched my back as he laid me back on the car, the hood creaking in protest at our frantic motion and weight.

I pulled his ass to me. As he went deeper, ecstatic sounds vaulted out of me I never knew I could make. He grabbed my hips, picked me up, sliding deeper into me. He walked us over to a truck, ramming me against the grill. I laced my fingers through the grill, holding me in place as he pushed in. We both became wild and frantic. My climax rumbled in as my body tightened around him. A roar exited Ryker's throat, and his fingers dug into my skin as he released, not relenting till mine followed right behind. Shattering me.

We did not stop. Flipping between slow and exploring to rough and desperate. We were making up for lost time. Energy from him, pain and pleasure, continued my need for him. And he ruthlessly took it and gave it back.

We used every car, bench, back seat, hood, and table in the room, and we were not quiet or shy. I had been afraid someone living nearby would call the cops. I had no doubt Amara could hear us in the other room, but I couldn't feel bad enough to stop.

The sun was above the horizon before we slowed down, and finally exhaustion closed my lids for a moment, my head laying on his chest.

He lay across the back seat of the four-door Chevelle, and I sprawled over him, breathing deeply.

"Damn." He kissed the top of my head. "That... that was..."

"Insane, hot, incredible." I slipped my chin up his chest to look at him.

"Which time?" His eyes glinted, and he grinned. He cupped my face, pulling me to him, his lips soft, but the kiss was deep and strong. "I want you naked all the time." He moved to my ear. "Straddling, bent over, under, on top, from behind."

"We would get nothing done."

"You call this nothing? I feel extremely accomplished." He nipped my earlobe and my breath caught again, fire shooting through me.

"We have to get out of here. It's dangerous. We've already stayed way too long." I sat up, tugging his bottom lip in my teeth, then straddled him. Hugo had said they would do a sweep of the area. We should have left hours ago.

"Yeah." His mouth found my breast. "We should go now."

I closed my eyes, taking a breath. "I'm not kidding."

"I'm not either." His lips moved to the other one.

"Ryker, you need to stop," I said weakly, my breath spiking straight to the center of me. "We need to relocate. Make a plan to get Annabeth, Lexie, and Croygen and to shut down both Vadik and Rapava."

"Wow. That sounds like a lot of work." He lifted me by the ass and, flipped me flat on my back. He leaned over me, kissing my stomach. "I think I need to eat something, have a solid breakfast, before I can do any of those things." His hands pushed at my thighs, opening my legs, his mouth trailing down, kissing, and nipping.

I sucked in sharply, clutching for the door handle behind my head.

Oh my god... I was pretty sure I screamed that several times out loud, but I wasn't paying attention to any of the words or noises that erupted from me. I wasn't even sure I stayed in this universe.

But reality loomed, waiting for us, knocking on the car door for us to let it in. Literally. A few minutes after Ryker made me cry out, I heard a knock against the Chevelle.

"*Bhean?*"

"What do you want, furball?" Ryker sighed, sitting up.

"I said *Bhean*, not seal clubber."

"What do you want, Sprig?" I curled up, leaning my bare chest into Ryker's shoulder. Our clothes were far away, scattered across the room.

Being fae, neither Ryker nor Sprig thought twice about nudity, but I still held a human bashfulness, which seemed silly since many strangers had seen me naked at DMG when they ran tests on me for two weeks. But now my shyness wasn't just about being undressed; it was why we were naked, and the fact they probably heard us quite clearly.

"Well, I wanted to let you know Purple Dumpling is gone."

Ryker leaned his head back, his hand rubbing my knee. "Not really surprised."

I felt a tiny rush of guilt for Amara. "Do you know when she left?"

"No. I woke up and she wasn't here," he replied. "And what happened to the assprick and *Leanbh*? I woke up and no one was here. I would have thought you left me, but then I heard the sound of rutting pigs and—"

"Okay, thanks, Sprig. We'll be out in a moment." I cut him off, laying my temple on the back of the seat, looking at Ryker. He turned his head, staring back.

"We aren't especially nice."

"Don't think for one moment she wouldn't have done the same or worse."

I felt briefly nauseated at the thought of Amara naked in the car with Ryker instead of me.

"Don't." He tilted forward and kissed me, then lifted his head, reaching for the door handle. "Come on. Time to deal with shit." He opened the door and climbed out, stretching his arms up to the sky, unabashed. Nor should he be ashamed with that physique.

I climbed out of the car behind Ryker, Sprig already gone.

Ryker swung around, wrapping his arms around me, pulling me to him. "Whatever is ahead, we'll deal with it. We will rescue your sister and Annabeth."

"And Croygen?" I lifted an eyebrow.

"If we have to."

I smiled, rising on my toes and kissing him. "Wherever we go, can we be sure it has a shower? I feel extremely dirty."

"Just the way I like you." He grinned. I had never seen him smile so much. It made my heart patter. "Though you literally have grease and oil marks all over you. What did you do to get that one there? Or the tire marks across your stomach?" His eyebrows shot up in mock wonder.

I smacked his ass and stepped out of his hold, going for my clothes. He went to grab his discarded jeans in the corner.

"Where are my boots? Do you see them over there?" I searched the space for my shoes, finding my bra on a carburetor.

"Got them," he responded from the corner, pulling up his jeans.

We had our night—and morning—in a bubble, and now it was late morning. But I couldn't push away the face of my sister or the tears in Annabeth's eyes.

The night was long gone, and we needed to focus on what was really important.

What loomed ahead was frightening and overwhelming, but there wasn't a choice.

Lives depended on me.

FIFTEEN

"Where did all the honey go?" Sprig dug through the box on the table when I ventured out of the room, mostly dressed.

"You ate it all." I ran my fingers through my hair, knotting it up in a bun. I seriously needed a shower. I knew I smelled of sweat, sex, and motor oil.

"No, I didn't."

"Yes, you did."

"There were ten packets left. You never allow me more than three."

"You don't remember." He sometimes lost bits of time before he went into one of his honey frenzies. "Croygen and Lexie fed them all to you, so you'd pass out."

"Why?"

I conveyed to him everything that happened while he had been out, that they wanted him to go to sleep so they could sneak out on him.

His mouth hung open. "They tricked me?"

"Yes, I'm sorry."

"But all my honey is gone, and I don't even remember eating it."

"We'll get you more." Ryker came beside me, handing me my boots.

Sprig's face lit up as he licked his lips. "It's way past

194

breakfast. I need to catch up. Can we get breakfast and lunch?"

"You mean brunch?" I said, slipping my feet into my shoes, tying them up.

"Nooooo." He looked aghast at my question. "Brunch is still only one meal."

"We'll see." I touched my head; a sudden thumping began in my skull.

"I ate my breakfast like a good boy." Ryker smirked, looking at me intently. "It tasted delicious."

Heat flamed my cheeks, burning my face.

"Wha-what?" Sprig stood up on his hind legs. "You ate without me?"

"Sorry, buddy. It was too tasty to stop."

"Oh my god." I put my face in my palms.

"Is he intercoursing with me, *Bhean*?" Sprig looked between us.

I groaned louder, which caused Ryker to chuckle.

"You better not be intercoursing with me, Viking, or I will fart on your face in the middle of the night."

"Now, that's territory I haven't gone to before."

"Okay. Stop." I held up my hands, then pointed at Sprig. "You, stop talking. And you." I narrowed my lids on Ryker. "You just *stop*."

His mischievous smile forced me to inhale and glance up at the ceiling, gathering strength.

"Right now we are going to get our shit together, get something to eat, and move to a different location where we will plan what to do next. On the way, we will try to find Amara," I stated firmly. "All right?"

"Can I have more to ea—?"

"Zip it!" I cut off Ryker, holding my fingers together. "I didn't say you could open your mouth."

He arched a brow.

"Not. A. Word." I knew where his mind went because mine was already there.

He ran his hand over his mouth and chuckled.

"Now, do you have any idea where Amara would go, and should we be concerned she's gone?"

"Amara," a woman's voice spoke behind me, "didn't need to hear her former lover and his new girlfriend fucking each other's brains out all night."

I whirled around to see Amara leaning against the doorjamb, holding a white paper bag in her hand. Her expression was anything but teasing. "So I went for a walk. Then I thought on my way back to grab something to eat for everyone."

My jaw went slack, and Sprig sat back on his hindquarters, eyes wide.

She ignored our expressions and walked to the table, tossing a bag of doughnuts on it. Sometimes people could surprise you.

I had to admit I wouldn't have done something like that. I probably wouldn't have come back. In that moment I realized how alone Amara really was. How painful it had to be for her to stay with us. She no longer had Ryker as a boyfriend, but she still clung to him. He was the only thing she had left. I didn't really like her or trust her, but I couldn't deny my heart softened toward her right then.

It could have easily been me in Amara's shoes, the one who had to watch and listen. "I'm sorry," I whispered so softly only she could hear me.

Her eyes darted to mine, then away. She pushed back her shoulders and continued laying out the containers.

It wasn't a truce or even close. But I took it.

Today was one of those gorgeous fall days, but typical of this area a hint of change was in the air as clouds gathered in the distance, indicating an impending storm. Autumn in the Pacific Northwest jumbled sunny and cloudy days like a blender.

Even in the crisp afternoon my black hoodie became a sauna. Beads of sweat trickled down my back. I wanted to rip it off, peel it away from my hot, sticky skin, but it was the only protection I had to keep from being noticed. Crowds of people swarmed around me creating a thicker cocoon of heat, sharpening my headache. My body trembled, showing the signs of withdrawal, which I recognized more and more after the stone gave me a boost. I hadn't realized I took so much of a hit from it the night before.

The city had blocked off several streets and opened it to a huge farmers' market for people to buy, sell, or trade goods. Citizens of Seattle and the surrounding areas were getting back on their feet, lifting us back into the land of the living. Stands and tents dotted the area along with the food trucks, offering anything from herbal medicines to clothes. People also offered their services, like carpentry or physical labor, for room and board. I heard many of the hospitals reopened and that much of the electricity had been restored. The city still bore scars, and the already bulging homeless problem had tripled.

Tempting odors from the food trucks pervaded the streets and caused my empty stomach to growl. Lines curled and weaved around the entire area, hindering the people trying to walk through.

The smell of Mexican food drifted over to me,

reminding me of my hollow stomach. I had barely eaten what Amara had brought back to us, my stomach queasy. Dying had also rattled my system a bit. Go figure. I really needed to stop dying. It messed up my day and only contributed to the monster-size headache, jittery, restless, and irritable feeling. The only thing bringing a smile to my face and a flush to my cheeks was Ryker, along with the memories of what we did and how he felt.

Damn. Another round of desire ran through me like a drunken squirrel, my stare drilling into the massive hooded figure a dozen yards away. And as if he could sense my gaze, his neck twisted back, his white irises narrowing straight on me. Our eyes connected briefly, but I sensed the intensity, the unspoken words. The promise for more to come. He turned back, snaking through the cluster of bodies, his shoulders tense and alert.

I could sense that Ryker wanted to get away. He didn't feel safe this close to so many humans. Even though my sight picked up a lot of fae around, it was better to hide in the masses than stand out on our own. Also lifting goods from the vendors came easy to me. Each stolen item smacked on Sprig's head as it plopped in my bag.

"*Bhean*, if you're going to have it rain food, make it something softer," he hissed at me through my messenger bag. He sat at the bottom, holding his honey jar backpack with Pam inside.

"Like honey?" I mumbled back.

"I swear you can read my mind."

I tossed in another pinched item.

"Ugh, fairy farts, is that a banana?"

"Shush."

I glanced over the crowd, keeping the large Viking in my view. The three of us spread out because we were too noticeable moving together. Ryker led us, while Amara brought up the rear. Having her watch my back was not terribly comfortable for me, but Ryker demanded I be in the middle. I hoped it was because of the stone I carried and not because he was being an overbearing caveman.

Right.

Nudging through the gaps, I already felt edgy, but I kept fighting the feeling of being watched. A strange chill skated over my spine and stabbed at the base of my neck. My head jerked around, and I searched for the source, following the line of trees shading the area behind the food trucks. The pull of someone's intense gaze dragged my focus to a space between a large shrub and truck.

I stopped dead in my tracks.

Dark, beady eyes cut through the people, ramming into me. A gasp pelted from my lungs. A lanky man stood there, with scraggy, long, dark hair and beard, looking like he could be one of the homeless. But the puckered scar zigzagging down his face knotted my airways.

I blinked. A scream built in my chest.

A body slammed into my shoulder, tripping me. Hands shot out and grabbed me, keeping me upright. He was taller than me and built, but the baseball hat dipped low over the man's brow and kept his face obstructed from view.

"Sorry," he mumbled, a hint of an accent sprang off the one word before he slipped by me. My gaze trailed after him, but the crowd quickly absorbed his large frame. I spun back to where I spotted the other man.

The location looked empty.

I scanned the space, looking for a hint of who I thought I saw.

"Hey, what's the holdup?" Amara reached me, her voice low. "Who are you looking for?"

"N-no one." I pushed myself forward, the familiar scarred face flashing in my mind.

There's no way. It was just stress and tension creating paranoia that we were being hunted by everyone. Old and new.

But Arlo's face and the memory of the last time we saw him in Peru stuck in my mind...

Arlo held a lot of resentment toward Ryker, and I'd brought him a great deal of humiliation when I beat him up in front of his men. Would it drive him to the far edges of the earth to seek revenge?

Ryker found a rundown motel away from the main thoroughfare in an area called Atlantic. It reminded me of where he took me the first night he caught me when he tied me to the bathtub. Now if he did, I would want him to.

Amara glamoured the front clerk to give us a room in back then forget he ever saw us. She was the only one who could control her powers right now. Ryker and I were too sporadic to rely on.

"Shower!" Amara was the first to dart for the bathroom. I placed my bag on the table, taking Sprig out. He had broken into the stolen candied walnuts and ate half the bag before passing out. Sugared chunks stuck to his hands, tail, and face. I brushed off what I could before setting him on a pillow.

"How are you feeling?" Ryker sidled up behind me, putting his hands on my hips.

"Crappy." I leaned back into him.

"Not surprised. I really should have forced you to sleep last night. Your system needs to recover after injury."

I twisted to face him. "You mean after dying."

He frowned.

"But, hey, look at the positive side. You don't want to kill me anymore."

He half smiled.

"True." He unzipped my jacket, pulling the hood off my head. "But now I want to do other things to you."

He kissed my neck.

We both knew it wasn't only my "death" which had me restless and fevered. But after our last fight, neither of us wanted to bring up the stone.

"I thought I saw Arlo at the market."

His body went rigid. "What?"

"I swear I saw him behind one of the food trucks." I rubbed my aching head. "Maybe it's lack of food and sleep affecting my brain."

"Arlo?" Ryker's grip on my waist constricted. "Are you sure?"

"Yes." My arms dropped. "No. It happened so fast. He was there, then he was gone. I'm probably just imagining things."

Ryker sucked in a deep breath. "Maybe, but it's still good to be on guard."

"As if we don't already have enough people gunning for us." I heard the water in the bathroom turn on. I so wanted, *needed*, a shower. "Do you think he would track us down?"

"Yes," Ryker responded quickly. "We embarrassed him. Fae kill each other for a lot less. Between his hatred and wanting the stone, I have no doubt he'd come for us. *I* should have killed him when I had the chance. Teaches me to be nice."

"You?" I lifted my eyebrows.

"Fine. I could have let you finish him off." He smirked,

leaning over, grazing my ear. "But Arlo is the least of our problems. I'll be on the lookout, but he's the last thing I'm worried about right now. Not on my radar."

"Oh?" I grabbed his sweatshirt, his breath tickling my neck. I knew one thing which would help me feel better. "And what's on your radar?"

"Right this moment?" Ryker moved slowly to my breastbone. "You."

I smiled, whispering low. "We have at least eight to ten minutes before Amara gets out."

"Not enough for what I really want to do, but I can work with it." He hooked his hands in the shoulders of my hoodie, pushing it slowly over my arms. He tugged at fabric, drawing my arms out of it, and tossed it on the bed next to us.

A flicker of off-white fell out of the pocket and fluttered to the floor. I looked down at it.

"What?" Ryker noticed he no longer had my attention.

I bent over and picked up the item. It was a thick, parchment type of paper folded neatly several times.

"What is that?"

"I don't know. It wasn't in my pocket earlier." I peered up at him. "You leaving me love notes now?"

Ryker laughed. "Do I look like the love-note type?" He took a small step back. "I'd much rather show you than write about it."

"Me too." I grinned at him before turning back to the note, unfolding it slowly. Cursive scrolled over the page. It looked to me like male handwriting. Both the parchment and handwriting looked old fashioned, like he learned penmanship back in Shakespeare's day.

Tomorrow night. Sunset. I have imperative information. Near Chittenden Locks. Your companion will know the place. Be sure you are not followed.

My eyes went up to Ryker's, his gaze still roaming over the page.

"Imperative information?" Ryker took it from my fingers, rereading it. "Who put this in your pocket? Who could have known where to find you?"

"I don't know." I pushed past Ryker, needing to move my feet. "I get this note and think I see Arlo. Is that just a coincidence?"

"This is not Arlo's style." Ryker rubbed the back of his neck with one hand. "Not sure he even knows the word imperative. And he's not one to plan. He just slinks in on someone else's raid and steals it."

"Then who else?" I tossed up my arms with irritation. "It's not like we have a lot of people on our side."

"Do we have any?"

"Exactly!"

"Think back. I know there were a lot of people, but do you remember anyone getting exceptionally close?"

"I don't know, Ryker." A sudden burst of irritation lashed up my body, streaming out of my mouth. "We were in a market *full* of people. I got close to a lot!"

His lids narrowed; his jaw clenched. He sucked in through his nose, keeping his expression guarded.

"Sorry," I huffed, pinching my eyebrows together. "I'm just tired." It was true, but we both knew it wasn't what had me lashing out.

Tension took hold of the room, lasting what felt like forever, my gaze on the floor, before Ryker spoke evenly. "I meant anyone bumping or knocking into you."

My head lifted, my eyes widening with a sudden memory.

"Yes." I nodded. "At the same time I saw Arlo. This man knocked into me hard enough that he had to grab on to me so

203

I wouldn't fall over. He must have put it in then." Another realization hit me. "Man, I had been so focused on Arlo, it didn't even register then. I'm so used to seeing it with you guys."

"What?"

"He was fae. It was sunny out, but he had a glow."

"What did he look like?"

"He had on a hat and kept his chin dipped so I didn't see his face. He was tall, built, but I don't remember much else. Nothing useful." I paced the room. "When he said sorry, I heard a slight accent."

"What kind?" Ryker sat on the corner of the bed, the note still between his fingers.

I squeezed my lids closed, replaying the moment, trying to hear his voice in my head. "English. Scottish... maybe Irish."

"Yeah, that narrows it down. Pretty much covers most fae."

"It doesn't matter. I'm pretty certain I didn't know him. His aura was new to me."

Auras were as different as human fingerprints, everyone giving off their own. The more magic you possessed, the brighter it was. When I first met Ryker, his almost blinded me. Now, because of the magic that had chosen me, I could look at it more clearly.

"You want to check it out, don't you?"

"There's something telling me to go." I nibbled my fingernail. "I can't explain it, but yes, I want to check it out."

"Even if it might be a trap?"

I padded over to him, not responding. He knew me better than that.

He rolled forward till the top of his head pressed into my stomach. "You can't stay out of trouble for a moment, can you?"

"I'll let you have tonight off." I laced my fingers through his silky hair.

"Gee. Thanks." He turned his gaze up to me.

I placed my hands on the sides of his face, running my fingers over his brows and temples. "Thank you."

He huffed, wrapping his arms around my hips, pulling me into a hug.

"Flamingo tulips, don't insult me, beaver. My wood is perfectly good," Sprig muttered in his sleep, rolling over. "The woodpeckers are quite fond of it."

I chuckled, letting my forehead fall to the top of Ryker's head. "Oh, please say he is gambling in his sleep again."

Ryker grabbed my thighs, pitching me onto the bed. My back bounced against the mattress as he crawled up, leaning over me. "The number of dirty puns I could make off that. Too easy." He kissed me.

"Easy? My monkey is trading his pecker wood to a bunch of beavers," I said evenly. "I don't see where you'd get any dirty puns from that. Sounds perfectly normal to me."

"That is normal for us."

"Sadly, so true." I inched up, meeting my mouth with his. "We still have at least three minutes left."

"What I want to do will take way more than that."

"I'm still feeling a little dizzy and shaky. I might need a shower monitor, to supervise."

"I take my duty very seriously." He nipped my lip. "Oversee, inspect, and examine."

We were teasing and laughing, but my thoughts never ran far from Lexie, Annabeth, and Croygen. So much had happened in the last day, I needed to find the humor, to relish this time with Ryker. Because if I didn't, I would fall apart.

The hurt and darkness I carried was as molten as lava and as liable to explode, burning my heart and soul beyond repair.

SIXTEEN

"Are you sure we're in the right place?" I looked around the deserted section near the water. Boats bobbed and weaved against the wind that brought in the storm. Yesterday's sun was now eclipsed by dark clouds and torrential downpours.

Amara didn't appear to be overly thrilled when Ryker and I took off, giving her few details about where we were going. She whined about being left behind, but Sprig moaned even louder when he found out he was being left with her. I assured Sprig I would bring him back a treat if I could.

Rain flowed heavily off the roof. Not one person stirred around the area, and there was no indication of a pub here at all.

"Yes," Ryker replied. Only a hint of his face peeked out from his hood. "Heard a lot of stories about this place."

"What place?"

"Headless Queen." He nodded toward stairs leading below. "A pub."

"Headless Queen?"

"Not too subtle coming from dark fae, huh?" he replied. "Haven't been there."

"Really?"

"It's full of thieves, murderers, and scoundrels." He turned to me with a hint of a smile on his face.

"Sounds like your type of place."

"No, sounds like yours." He bumped me playfully before returning his focus to the dilapidated building. "I'm better skilled than any of those in there. Wouldn't benefit me. Actually, I would be a target."

"You? A target?" My eyebrows lifted. "Sorry, I can't picture it."

"Lace my drink with a little goblin metal. Kidnap me and force me to work for them." A nerve in his neck twitched.

"I'm thinking this is not hypothetical."

"There is no honor among thieves. Believe me." He took a step forward, glancing back at me. His gaze was serious, his eyes roaming over my body.

In an instant lust bloomed through me. Ryker could tap into my emotions, altering them with just a look. He was another thing I was addicted to.

Sex had been a no-go the night before. My headache and tremors had grown so bad, all I could do to ease the pain was sleep. Also spending the night in the room with the woman who used to sleep with your man made for awkward bedfellows. Being kind to Amara, we took our showers separately and as soon as my throbbing head hit the pillow, I was out for the rest of the night.

However, waking up with his muscular build touching me… To say I struggled was not a strong enough word.

Today I felt a little better, but still off. Fidgety and irritated. Looking to release my edgy mood, my hormones were working overtime. Ryker seemed to be the only thing able to reduce my agitation.

He turned to stand in front of me, grabbing the edges of my jacket.

"This is completely a dark fae pub. Keep the hood on and try to blend in with the scenery. You being a beautiful, young girl are just asking for trouble." He grabbed my hood, pulling it forward. "This is not a place where you fool around. I don't want to spend the whole time defending your honor."

I nodded. I had been raised on the streets so I understood better than he thought. There were times you just needed to be smart, stay quiet, and not attract attention. My small frame and heart-shaped face had always caused people to challenge me, thinking I was a sweet, fragile girl, an easy victim. I was all for being a strong woman, but sometimes it was better to let the huge Viking fae take the lead.

"I would prefer you not even be here, but I know there is no way you wouldn't come or that this person would talk to me without you." His fingers drifted to the zipper of my jacket, tugging it up. "Plus, I know you can take care of yourself." His voice went softer, and I stared into his eyes.

Ryker's fingers slid under my jaw, tipping my head back. He closed the gap between our bodies, pressing against me. He leaned his forehead against mine, his lips grazing my own.

My lungs decided to stop working as his breath traced over my lips and down my neck like fingers. I thought he was going to kiss me, but instead he spoke. "Stay close to me. If I feel anything is off or wrong, we are out. No questions asked. Okay?"

I tilted my head, inching us even closer. "Yes, but the same goes for you. My seer senses are good detectors too. I don't want to have to defend *your* honor the entire time either."

I felt his mouth twitch with a smile. "I don't know. I find it hot when you protect me."

"Well, then maybe I'll pick a fight." I brushed my lips against his.

His throat tightened, and he struggled to swallow.

"Dammit, human," he mumbled before stepping back and taking a deep breath. "I am really wishing we didn't have to meet up with this contact, and I could just take you to the alley right now."

"Oh, now an alley is all right?" I said, recalling the night we first were together.

He gave me a look. "Then I didn't know... now I do. No place is safe anymore."

"Let's get this over with, then we can talk about the alley," I said as I passed him, keeping my voice nonchalant. I heard a slight moan behind me before his footsteps joined mine on the pavement.

"Stay behind me." He quickly lapped up my lead, surpassing me. "Let's try to get in and out without any life-and-death incidents."

"You're talking to me."

"Exactly." He sighed, beating down the steps to the tavern.

The smell of dank wood, stale beer, and smoke from a chimney climbed into my nose. The stairs creaked underneath us. The entrance was unmarked and just slightly off kilter, adding to the feeling this building was extremely old.

Ryker opened the door, ducking to step in, his shoulders barely fitting through the lopsided doorway. Like a shadow, I followed close behind him, dwarfed by his huge frame.

As my eyes adjusted to the dark room, I saw it wasn't a large space. A fire blazed in an old stone fireplace on the wall opposite the door. The bar stood on our left, filling most of the wall. To my right were at least twenty small, round tables with chairs, and against the far right built-in seats with a line of rectangle wood tables butted against each other. Either Scottish or Celtic music filled the room loud enough to drown conversations to a general murmur. It looked exactly what I pictured as an old pirate-type tavern.

In the early rainy evening, the bar was busy enough so our arrival didn't attract too much focus. Only a few heads turned our way, assessing us. Wary eyes watched Ryker. He wore jeans, a hoodie, black leather jacket, and biker boots. Nothing which stood out here, but his size alone made people nervous. His magic was still being blocked, but you could not deny the power in his stance, which was intimidating as hell. I would know.

"Do you see him?" Ryker muttered to me.

"No." I checked for any familiar auras. The glow of fae encompassed the room. Shifters, trolls, and dark Otherworlders occupied the seats. This place was obscure and secretive, far too dangerous for even a partial human to come. Good thing I wasn't one anymore.

"Can I help you?" The bartender's unfriendly tone spun my head back to the counter.

I tried to hold in a gasp. The fae did not need to hide his true form here. He stood shorter than Ryker, but muscular enough to be menacing. I guessed him to be in his thirties, although with fae you never knew their true age. He wore a tight black T-shirt and jeans. From a distance it looked like his shoulder-length hair was gelled into a bunch of spikes around his head, but where I stood, I knew they were black twisted bones protruding out of his scalp. His squashed nose had a bull ring through it, and he was covered in tattoos.

I shivered at the sight of him up close.

"Just a drink," Ryker replied, keeping his tone hard.

The bartender crossed his arms, looking us both up and down, like he was considering if we were trouble. Finally he flicked his head toward the room. "Take a seat. What'd you want?"

"Two scotch whiskies." Ryker headed for the back of the room, snaking between the tables. Sconces hanging on the wall gave off a dull light, but most of it came from the huge crackling fire. Ryker sat us in the farthest, darkest corner, where we blended into the shadows. I slid into the booth against the wall, and he sat down next to me. I hated being pinned in the corner, but it was better to be able to see the room and know what threat was coming.

Every head turned to me. "I feel like I'm wearing Christmas lights," I said quietly.

"Just keep your head lowered." Both of us kept our hoods up. After a few moments the stares moved off me.

An Amazon-sized woman came up to the table, a tray of drinks in her hand. She stood over seven feet tall and had the shoulders of a linebacker. Her long blonde hair coiled into a beautiful braid and hung past her ass. She had a pretty face, but her blue eyes held a "don't mess with me" expression. She banged the glasses on the table, splashing out a tiny bit of liquid. She huffed, looking Ryker up and down, then turned around and stomped away.

"Something tells me she doesn't have problems with men taking advantage of her." I wiped rainwater off my face.

Ryker snorted. "It's the other way around with her kind."

"She's an Amazon, huh?"

"A descendant. A true Amazon was a lot taller and tougher. They originated in Greece. But let me tell you, the present Amazons take after their ancestors. They decide who they want and take him. He doesn't get a choice."

My head jerked to him. "Don't tell me some Amazon woman did that to you?" My teeth locked together.

He chuckled, twisting his neck to look down at me. "Why? Jealous?"

211

My instinct was to fight this Amazon bitch, but at the smug look on Ryker's face, I picked up my drink and smiled. "No, I hoped I could volunteer you again. Get you off my hands."

A ghost of a smile played on his mouth. He picked up his glass, knocking it against mine. "Well, here's to getting me off... your hands."

I smirked before slamming back a sip of whiskey. The liquid burned down my throat, warming my chest.

A figure nearing our table caught my attention. He was dressed in dark pants and a long, dark, woolen cloak, his face hidden under a hood. Though he could have stepped out of the past, he also fit strangely in with the present. He grabbed the back of the chair across from us and slipped into the seat.

Ryker went rigid. He set his glass calmly back on the table, acting like we knew the stranger. His body vibrated next to mine with tension.

"Were you followed?" The man's voice was gravely.

"No," Ryker replied. "We made sure."

The man's head lifted and by the light of the fire I could make out his features. He was a lot younger than his voice portrayed, appearing to be in the mid-thirties. He had a strong rectangular jaw and face. Dark brown eyes stared at me from under his hood. I couldn't see his hair, but if I were to guess by his scruff, it was a reddish-blond color.

"Who are you?" I stared back, not lowering my gaze from the intensity of his.

"Dunn." He leaned his elbows on the table, keeping his voice low. "But I don't think that is what you meant, did you, Zoey?"

It was my turn to stiffen. "How do you know me? Why did you want to meet?"

"I know all about you."

Ryker shifted next to me, but he kept his mouth shut.

Dunn gave a quick glance around then came back to me. "Kate asked me to."

My mouth parted. My seer sense had seldom been wrong, and it now told me he was dark fae. How would he know Kate? DMG and fae, light or dark, were not on friendly terms by any means. Even if she was sensitive to fae, I still couldn't see her befriending one.

"Kate?" I repeated. "How do you know Kate?"

His gaze drifted to the side. "Our relationship goes back over thirty-five years."

"What?" Shock at his claim caused my words to fumble out of my mouth. "Thirty-five years? How long had Kate secretly fought for fae? How did she come to work at DMG? Why did she start to work for DMG if she was for fae in the beginning?" I didn't realize all these questions came storming out in a jumble until Ryker placed his hand on my leg, quieting me.

Dunn grimaced. "She told me you were inquisitive and wouldn't relent unless I told you everything."

Ryker chuckled, and I shot him a glare.

"I don't know you. I do not feel comfortable telling you anything." Dunn adjusted his shoulders. "But Kate insisted you were someone to trust and that I tell you her story." He took in a steady breath. "Kate and I met when she was twenty. She had just finished school and was going for her PhD in science and genetics. I can't tell you what drew me to her. She was human. I tried to stay away from them. But her energy stood out bright like a beacon. I found myself following her wherever she was. Like a thorn in my side, I couldn't seem to stop thinking about her."

"Humans can be irritating like that." Ryker squeezed my leg. Dunn and Ryker exchanged a look of understanding.

"Our relationship was intense, and I loved that woman something fierce." Dunn sat back in his chair. "But I knew it couldn't last; I was fae, she was human. But every day that I convinced myself today would be the day I'd break it off, I would find a reason not to. By this time, she had earned her PhD and started searching for a job. When she told me she was moving to Chicago, I decided it was the perfect time to end things." Dunn swallowed, his Adam's apple bobbing. "Then she turned my world upside down..."

I leaned closer, adsorbed in his story. This all sounded so unbelievable to me.

"She told me she was pregnant." He huffed out a long breath.

My jaw went slack again, my eyes widening. I knew Kate had a daughter, Elsbeth, who now had a daughter, Kiera.

"Are you telling me...?"

"Elsbeth is my daughter?" He sat up. "Yes."

"But that would make her..."

"Half fae." He finished for me. "It does. Elsbeth was my mother's name."

Ryker's hand left my thigh and went to rub his face. I sat motionless, stunned into silence.

"With a baby coming, I could no longer keep my world from Kate, especially because it was rare for humans to live through a pregnancy not alone the birth of a fae child. I wanted her to understand why I didn't want her to keep it."

He grabbed Ryker's drink and took a sip, when he pushed it back, Ryker shook his head, saying, "Have it."

Dunn nodded a thank you and took another sip.

"After a long time of convincing her about the truth of fae, she still remained firm on keeping the baby. Even knowing it might kill her, she was certain, and all I could do was sit back and wait, wracked with terror that I would lose them both.

"We moved to Chicago and had the baby. Against all odds, she and the baby survived. When Elsbeth turned three she was diagnosed with leukemia, but her fae power healed her over time, to the shock of all her doctors. They couldn't figure it out. This is when Kate became obsessed with fae genetics and how she could save other children.

"As years went by, she threw herself into work, which caused our happiness to be short lived. She spent extra time at work, and I grew more restless at home. Not because I didn't enjoy being a father, but because I did. I could see them aging every day while I wasn't. Kate and I began to fight all the time about it. Even though she said it didn't bother her, when people would ask if I was her nephew or younger brother, it would upset her. A lot. I knew things had started to shift when she introduced me as a 'friend.' It wasn't till she learned about Dr. Rapava and his work that I really lost her. They began to email and contact each other all the time. She was too easily swayed by this man who claimed he wanted to help cure humans of diseases and defects. It had been the end of us. When Rapava offered her a job in Seattle, Kate took it without hesitation." Dunn's gaze drifted away, like the memory still pained him. "She told me that night she didn't want me to follow."

Ouch.

"Kate wanted to keep Elsbeth ignorant of the fae world because Elsbeth has more human traits than fae. She will age and die similar to a human. Kate thought it would only make her life difficult knowing the truth. It was the one thing we both agreed on. We also realized my *not* aging would become a problem.

"So, I let her walk out the door. I secretly checked on Elsbeth every once in a while over the years, watching her grow up and have a baby of her own. Kate, on the other hand, completely fell into Rapava's world, and I lost all touch with her. Over time I heard what she was doing, the sick testing on fae, and we became enemies. I rallied against DMG. I knew she heard about me but never tried to contact me. That was until two years ago when she reached out saying she needed my help. Elsbeth was in danger. Kate told me what had been happening, how deep she was in, and her fear that Rapava would find out about our child. Even our granddaughter is one quarter fae. She's in danger too. I became Kate's informant. She notified me when the hunters were coming to get anyone I knew, and I would also help her catch some really nasty ones, so she could keep her cover. After this long, after all she had done, there wasn't anything I wouldn't do for her."

Kate had been living her life acting like a flaky mad scientist while she had been carrying the biggest secret of all. Her daughter and granddaughter were part fae. No wonder she was so scared.

"What's messed up is I still love that woman completely, but she treats me like a grandson." He shook his head. "She forgets I'm technically hundreds of years older than her."

"I can't believe this." What horror to watch the woman and child he loved grow older, and he couldn't do anything but watch them die. I understood Ryker's resistance to me at the beginning more clearly. Now that I had fae powers my life cycle would slow down to be equal with his.

"She couldn't tell you any of this while inside DMG." He downed the rest of the whiskey. "But I'm not here just to tell you her past. Kathryn contacted me to come deliver a message to you."

I waited for him to continue; my hand gripped my drink.

"Rapava has hunters searching for you everywhere."

"That's nothing we don't know." Ryker swiped the glass from my hand and took a mouthful then plopped it between my fingers again.

"There are also officials keeping an eye out for you."

"What do you mean?" I inched forward.

"Government officials. The conspiracy goes further up than you think. Rapava's connections and people who believe in his work are in the highest echelons of government. If you go to them, you might find yourself hushed and taken care of. It's another reason Kate couldn't get out. She figured it best to stay close and continue to work with him."

"Why didn't she just leave when she realized how far he had fallen?" I asked.

"Kate knew too much. She realized what happened to the scientist who tried to escape before. Rapava had his whole family killed." My heart lurched painfully in my chest, knowing which family he was referring to. "Kate was not willing to take the chance, especially when Rapava had hinted at the safety of her family." Dunn glanced over his shoulder. "She believes in you, Zoey. She feels you are the one smart enough and strong enough to find a way to take him down for good."

I gulped back the rest of the brown liquor, scorching my throat.

"But you need to hurry." Dunn dark eyes leveled into mine. "Your sister's life depends on it."

I sucked in. "Lexie?" She had only been gone two days. All day I thought about it being Lexie's birthday. Today she turned thirteen. And I wasn't there with her. "Is she all right?"

"Kate told me they ran tests as soon as she came in. You know she is dying. Her body is rejecting the legs and the fae-blood injections."

I opened my mouth to speak, but Ryker beat me to it.

"How long?"

Dunn pressed his mouth together. "No more than a few weeks. Kate thinks it might be less. You don't have long. I'm sorry." He scooted back his chair. "That's all I can tell you. I better go."

"We appreciate you meeting with us," Ryker said for me, my shattered heart keeping me mute.

Dunn bobbed his head, standing up. "You two watch your backs. You're being tracked."

"By more than you know." Ryker clasped his hand. "Thank you."

"Take care." Dunn reached over and took my hand. He was a daunting man, but his touch felt gentle and kind. I could see what Kate had loved in him.

He dropped my hand and turned to go.

"Wait. How do we contact Kate or you again?" I asked.

He turned enough for me to see his profile. "You don't." With that he slunk across the room and vanished into the stormy evening.

Ryker and I stepped into the night. The rain thumped down on my hood, and my boots sloshed through newly formed puddles. But I didn't notice the cold or the wet. My soul felt sick.

Lexie was truly dying. Hearing it made it final. There was no pretending anymore. I was going to lose my sister again.

Ryker hadn't said much. Nothing would make this better. Telling me we'd figure something out was just a crock of shit. This wasn't something we could work out. The only thing I wanted was to undo the operation, take away Lexie's new legs and remove the fae blood poisoning her.

"What if we removed them?" I grabbed Ryker's arm as we reached the top of the stairs. "Got rid of the thing killing her?"

He contemplated my idea. "Might work, but we need to get to her before it's too late."

That was the problem. Could we get to her in time? And if we did, who would do it? We couldn't just take her to a regular hospital. They would have no idea what to do with a human who had been given another human's legs along with foreign magical blood.

Ryker watched my shoulders slump.

"It's something. We *will* get her out of there." He left out dead or alive, but I got his meaning. No matter what, we would not leave Lexie there. He took a few steps into the parking lot and twisted around to look at me, cupping my face in his hands. His eyes told me the words that didn't cross his lips. *I'm sorry.*

I swallowed back the lump in my throat as he drew me into his arms, engulfing me in the warmth of his body, holding me tight. It was the only place I felt safe and momentarily comforted. All other issues disappeared, and I felt his love wrap around me in a protective bubble.

Then, Ryker stiffened, the muscles in his back coiling. I jolted.

"What?"

He kept his arms around me, but his head jerked around the parking lot, nostrils flared, his eyes bright.

"Ryker?" Fear strangled my vocal cords.

"I don't know," he muttered. "But something is off."

I sent out my senses, feeling only fae, which was not a surprise here. But then the hair on the back of my neck prickled. Magic crept over my skin. A lot of fae energy surrounded us, but this felt powerful. Danger discharged down my spine like a warning bell.

Ryker stepped away from me, sliding out a knife from his coat. A lamp from the street outlined his movement. His white eyes glowed under his hood.

I tugged out the blade strapped to my back. My heart thudded in my chest. Did Vadik find us? Did Dunn lead them right to us? It didn't make sense, but my mind still ran over the possibility. Could it be Arlo, or did DMG finally locate us?

The fact we still couldn't jump on command made me crazy. *Jump dammit!*

Ryker touched my back, moving us to the top of the lot in hurried steps, my legs barely able to keep up. With a clanking noise behind me I swung my head to look over my shoulder. In the depths of the parking lot, a hideous figure slunk toward us, small eyes boiling with hatred. I whipped back, my mouth opening to tell Ryker when a black van squealed to a stop in front of us, blocking our way. Men in dark clothing ascended out.

Panic resounded through my brain, never reaching my throat. A dark windowless van had me recalling my time at DMG, but the amount of magic pounding off each individual didn't back up the theory. These were pure fae.

Ryker and I didn't need to communicate to understand each other's next move. We twisted around and ran for the alley between the bar and another building. He grabbed my arm, pulling me in front of him as the lane narrowed only enough for one. I pushed my legs to move double time so I wouldn't hold him back and darted down another path. The men gained on us, sounding like a troop of soldiers as they pounded behind us.

"Faster!" Ryker hissed.

I bit down on my lip and impelled my legs to go quicker. As I curved around another bend, I took a second to look behind us. They were shadowed, but I was sure I didn't know them. These were not Garrett's men. I knew most of their faces. And Arlo was nothing more than a second-rate pirate. He could not command this kind of military precision.

Who were they?

"Zoey!" Ryker yelled. My eyes flicked to him, then to what he stared at. I spun my head forward to see a dumpster and wall ahead, hindering our escape.

Of course.

I picked up my speed, pumping my arms. I felt as if I were back on a hunt, chasing fae, when I worked for DMG. I leaped for the dumpster, stretching out my arms to grasp the top, my feet kicking at the side, pushing me up.

Ryker scaled to the top faster, grabbing the back of my coat, pulling me to my feet. I was waiting to hear gunshots as we scaled the wall, but they never came. Most fae tended to like old-school hand-to-hand combat. There was even an honor code among enemies. Guns didn't take much skill. Vadik no longer seemed to hold this policy. His men at the warehouse had their weapons loaded, ready to shoot and kill. Another reason, my instinct told me, these were not his men.

Ryker dropped to the ground as I landed next to him. Both of us rose to sprint for the buildings before us and lose ourselves in the maze of streets, alleyways, and hiding spots.

We took three steps before a massive figure moved in front of us. He was so enormous, with muscles bigger than my head. A scream choked my throat, and I stumbled back.

"Fuck," I heard Ryker mumble as he leaned back to take in the huge form. The man had to be more than eight feet tall and five hundred pounds of solid muscle. Large gashes covered his face and bald head. His chest was bare, and his legs were covered in a mishmash of fabric sewn together to construct pants to fit him.

Panic lodged in my arms and legs and froze me in place as the massive figure wrapped his oversized hands around a club the size of, well, me. He huffed, dipping his head toward us, his dark skin almost blending with the night. "Stay."

Even if I wanted to disobey him, my body wouldn't oblige. It stood stock still, air caught in my throat. I didn't even blink till men came from all sides, corralling Ryker and me back to the wall.

"What do you want?" Ryker puffed up his chest, keeping his blade ready.

A sandy-blond man stepped up. War wounds lined his face as well. He appeared to be a tiny bit smaller than Ryker, but his coiled muscles told me he had been trained to take down his enemy in mere seconds.

"That's not for us to explain." He edged closer.

"Then whose is it?" Ryker demanded.

"You will have to wait and see." As soon as the words came out of the man's mouth, the dozen men advancing toward us rushed forward. Ryker tried to fight, but the men were quick and precise. Three grabbed me before I could even try to fight back.

A bag was shoved over my head, and I sucked in a suffocating gasp as darkness engulfed me. Ryker roared with anger beside me.

My body wanted to jump. Yet, as I took in a deep breath my mind started to swirl with fog. With each breath I took the mist grew into thick clouds, my legs bending underneath me.

My tongue felt coated, swelling as a hint of something skated down my throat. *The bags are lined with some kind of drug.*

The last thing I heard was my name being screamed out into the night before a muffled yelp gave way to silence.

Fate had us in its hands, and all I could do was let it lead me.

SEVENTEEN

Whatever they treated the bag with wasn't strong enough to completely take me under. I stayed conscious but woozy the entire trip with no willpower to fight. Fear stayed knotted in my stomach, but I knew it was pointless to fight this group. The men never handcuffed us, but they took all our weapons. They were highly trained and powerful.

We rode in the van for about ten minutes before we stopped. They picked me up, my legs lightly touching the ground. The scuffling and grumbling told me they were dragging Ryker behind me. The gravel gave way to smooth concrete, my boots finding more solid footing with every step. The slamming of doors behind me and the faraway echoes of our shoes suggested we were in a large warehouse of some sort.

An arm brushed my shoulder and my heart leaped at Ryker's touch. His closeness gave me strength. The bag was ripped from my head, and I blinked at the solitary light hanging in the room. I glanced over to see Ryker's hood being torn away, causing his eyes to blink against the sudden light.

When he caught my eyes, his shoulders relaxed slightly. I scanned the space and found I had been right. It was an empty warehouse, probably left that way after the storm. Like much of this area, it looked like it had once been used to fix or store boats.

The room was quiet, and the men stood straight as if the Queen of England was about to enter the room. Movement stirred to the side, and another group of men entered. This time the hair all over my body went straight, driven upward by fear. The air in the room seemed to thicken with magic so dense I started to gag. My shoulders felt weighed down, and I stirred, trying to escape the energy pounding on me.

Ryker shifted, and I could tell he sensed the same thing. My apprehension shot up when I felt a strange anxiety bound off him and slam into me. I turned my head to look at him. He kept his head forward, his hands clenching and unclenching, his feet bobbing nervously. I'd never seen Ryker anxious. Not like this.

Shoes snapped over the floor, nearing us. The handful of men dressed in black entered and spread out, with one man walking down the middle demanding our attention. A harsh gasp ran roughly up my esophagus, and I stepped back. I heard Ryker swear next to me.

The gentleman coming for us appeared to be the source of the energy. He possessed power unlike anything I had ever come across in the fae world. It pumped off him, crashing into every object around him. He was tall, nicely built, and held his head with dominion, as though the world was his for the taking.

The effect of his magic on me felt like I'd consumed several pots of coffee. He also was one of the most attractive men I had ever seen. I assessed him to be in his late thirties, with black, wavy hair and a light olive complexion. He wore a suit of such fine blue fabric I guessed it cost more than a car. He embodied sophistication, wealth, elegance, class, and intimidation.

When he looked over at us, I heard Ryker suck in a breath. Then, his piercing, yellowish-green eyes fixed on me. He was a demon. Remembering my studies and what Ryker once told me, he was no ordinary demon. He stood at the top of the food chain.

"Holy shit," Ryker whispered and sank down to his knees, bowing his head. Seeing Ryker react like this sent more terror into my bones than the actual man did.

The man walked up in front of Ryker and me. "You may stand," his deep, sultry voice ordered Ryker. As Ryker stood back up, the man's eyes went to me, and I couldn't help but shift nervously. "I will forgive you this one time for not addressing me properly, since you are... or *were* human." He tilted his head, analyzing me. "But in the presence of a King, you kneel."

King? My gaze darted in confusion to Ryker then back to the man.

"Zoey, this is our Unseelie King."

My mouth dipped open, closed, then fell open again. "Un-un-seelie King?" I stuttered. I had heard all about him. Lars, King of the dark fae. All the rumors passed around were so frightening you hoped they were tales to scare children. But standing in front of him I knew—hell, I *felt*—they had not been made up. My hands trembled at my side, and I forced my bladder not to react to him. In my life I had dealt with a lot of unstable or scary people and situations, but no one inspired such a primal animal terror as he did.

Unfortunately when I got scared, I got defensive and combative. My anger took over my nerves, my hands stopped shaking and my lids narrowed. "What do you want with us?"

One of the King's perfectly sculpted eyebrows curved up.

"Zoey." Ryker shook his head next to me.

"What?" I turned back to Ryker. "It's a perfectly reasonable question to ask a man who just kidnapped us."

Ryker tilted his head, then looked back at the King, like "fair enough."

The King stayed quiet for a moment, adding tension to the air. "Be careful, Zoey." He said my name with warning. The fact he knew my name didn't shock me for more than a second. There was a reason he became King. He would know everything about everyone, especially if they drew his attention. And to get a personal call from the Unseelie King, we had to be high on his interest list. "My patience is thin. I've had my fill of lippy, tenacious young ladies lately. Do not disrespect me."

"O-kay. What do you want with us, *Your Highness*?" I asked evenly.

Slowly a smirk hinted at his lips and eyes, and he shook his head, almost as if he was amused. I still understood it was a perilous line to walk, and I wasn't stupid enough to push it.

He rubbed his hands together, his eyes never breaking from mine. "I want the stone."

"Get in line," I spouted off before I could stop myself. I sucked back my bottom lip with a hiss. "Sir."

Ryker let out a soft groan next to me.

"Yes. You two have created a long list of enemies." A shadow of amusement filtered over the King's beautiful features, then it was gone. "Do not make me one." I didn't dare respond, and Lars did not seem to be looking for one. He shoved a hand in his pocket and started to stroll around us. "The difference is, in the end, you will hand it over to me."

I gulped as he walked close. He turned and faced me. I wondered if he could sense the stone in my shoe. It had been quiet for the last day, but a man as powerful as he must be able to sense the magic pulsing off it. Of all people, wouldn't the stone want to be taken by one of the most powerful men in the Otherworld? If he could feel it, why didn't he get one of his men to tug off my shoe and take it? He could easily do it, and Ryker and I couldn't fight.

"I never go into a situation without knowing my outcome. I always win, Ms. Daniels." He didn't move, but I suddenly felt like I was being suffocated. I tried to draw in more air without success. Ryker dropped to his knees next to me, reaching for his throat.

Ryker! My cry stuck in my throat as I tried to move to him. My muscles ignored my commands, keeping me locked in a frozen prison.

Ryker clawed at his throat, trying to breathe, driving terror deep into my body.

Lars was doing this with his mind. I had heard of the Unseelie King's tremendous powers. Now I was getting a firsthand account of them. He wanted us to get a taste of what he could do.

A subtle threat.

Lars stared at me, examining me, his chartreuse eyes boring into my soul, digging around. Then the grip he had on my neck loosened, giving permission for my words to leave my tongue.

"Stop!" I choked out. Liquid leaked out the corners of my eyes as I struggled. Ryker slumped over his hands, gasping like a fish for air. "Please, stop."

It lasted only a few more seconds, but to me it seemed like an eternity watching Ryker suffer.

Then in an instant, the pressure vanished. Air zoomed into my lungs; movement came back into my muscles. I heard Ryker suck in, coughing. He quickly looked over at me, his eyes blazing. My fingers massaged the invisible handprints on my throat, and my eyes narrowed on Lars.

"I get what I want. Always." Lars took a step toward me. "However, I also can be fair. Most simple leaders command by fear. I like to invoke respect, as well. But never doubt what I am capable of, Ms. Daniels."

Ryker climbed to his feet, holding himself even taller than before. He remained pissed but was far too smart to do anything but stand there obediently. It wasn't something a Wanderer did well, but even he understood the Unseelie King was top dog.

"I'm willing to offer you my help, in exchange for the Lia Fáil."

"Your help?" Ryker's voice came out low and gravelly.

"Yes." Lars's eyes darted to the Viking. "I am well aware that my attention on my city has slipped. More pressing matters have taken precedence in the past few months, but I can no longer overlook what is going on. A few have taken my lack of attentiveness as an invitation to take possession of my city in hopes to dethrone me."

"Vadik." Ryker pressed his lips together.

An eerie smile turned up Lars's mouth.

"Yes, my dear old friend *Valefor.*" He crunched down on the name like a beetle between his teeth. Lars took deliberate steps toward Ryker. "And here stands Valefor's long-lost son. The formidable Wanderer."

Ryker flinched at the word *son.*

"I see the demon in you. But you are your mother's son too."

"You knew my mother?" Ryker tried to keep his voice even, but I could hear a crack of emotion in it.

"Yes." Lars nodded. "She was an amazing woman. Strong, smart, beautiful. Everything your father didn't earn. He tricked her into marrying him. She didn't know he was the demon Valefor until it was too late. She was carrying his child. She deserved much better than him."

Ryker's face held no reaction, but I knew how much this meant to him to hear about her from someone who knew her. Liked her.

"Vadik needs to be reined in." Lars placed both of his hands in his pockets and began walking around us again. "To be reminded of *his* place."

"Or we could just kill him." Ryker folded his arms over his chest.

"No love lost between you two, I gather." One eyebrow curved up. "There was a time I should have killed him, but chose not to. I have come to regret my choice. However, there are things *far* worse than death."

"Yes, there are. I have seen too much of it in the last few months," Ryker replied.

"Is this an acceptable deal then?" Lars's glance bounced between Ryker and me. I knew it really wasn't up for us to decide, but once again, I had to open my mouth.

"No." Every head swung my way, all probably thinking: *How dare you say no to the Unseelie King?* Fair enough. It was pretty stupid.

"No?" Lars replied coolly.

I nodded. "The stone is one of the most powerful weapons in the Otherworld. Vadik is a third-rate demon. He's not worth the stone."

Out of the corner of my eye I saw Ryker's mouth dip open, but he quickly slammed it shut, a twitch of a grin on his lips.

Lars's gaze burned into me. His face looked chiseled and cold as ice. If he felt any emotions, they were hidden. I shifted on my feet, my tongue curling up, ready to apologize for my insolence.

Then the most bone-chilling thing happened.

Lars laughed. A deep, husky chuckle detonated out of

his chest and bounced off the bare walls. He moved to me, less than a foot away from my face.

"In spite of myself, I am intrigued, Ms. Daniels. What would you feel is a fair deal?"

He appeared to be the kind of man who would smile as he cut off your head. A part of me understood it because in much humbler terms, it was the game I played with my opponents. It kept them out of step, off kilter. You smile and laugh and people instantly feel safer, like someone joking couldn't possibly hurt you. Right. They were the ones to watch out for.

"You help us with Vadik *and* DMG." I inhaled, pushing out my chest to appear bigger than I was. "Help take them down, and the stone is yours." I waited for Ryker to refute my offer to the King, but he held up his head higher and stared at Lars expectantly.

"You have completely surprised me, Ms. Daniels." Lars's piercing eyes analyzed me. "I did not expect you to be smart and suave in our dealings."

"I'm used to being underestimated."

"I will certainly keep that in mind." Lars smiled. "I should know better than to misjudge a young girl with intelligence and gumption."

I kept my mouth shut. He hadn't killed me yet, and I wanted to keep it that way.

"I would hold on to this one," Lars said to Ryker. "She is cleverer than you."

"I plan on it." Ryker said every syllable without the slightest hesitation. "And women usually are, sir. Over all of us men."

Another short chuckle came from Lars. "Don't I know it."

He drifted away from us, his fingers steepled beneath his

chin. "Very wise, Ms. Daniels. I cannot deny bringing down DMG would benefit me as well. They need to be dealt with. Terminated. I haven't had the advantage of someone who's been one of them and knows how to get in. It's time I take my city back." He let his arms drop, turning to me. "What do you have in mind, Ms. Daniels?"

Damn. I hadn't really thought that far. I figured I'd be a corpse on the ground by now. "Uh," I stuttered.

"We need weapons, men, a distraction to get into DMG. Her sister and our friend are being held there. We'd like to get them out safely." Ryker picked up my scattered thoughts.

"That can be arranged. When were you planning this attack?"

"Soon," I responded. "My sister is dying. I need to get her out immediately."

"I do these two things for you and the stone is mine."

I inhaled hard.

"Yes." Ryker nodded.

"I need to hear it from you as well." Lars faced me.

"Yes."

A pressure so heavy pushed down my throat, bending my knees. I curled over and placed my hands on my legs. It wasn't exactly painful but unbelievably uncomfortable. It felt similar to when you were close to crying and got a huge knot in your throat, making it difficult to swallow. This was similar, but ten times worse, like someone cinched my throat with a zip tie, trapping particular words.

"You bound us," Ryker hissed through gritted teeth.

The Unseelie King made a low sound, almost like a purr. "Like I said earlier, I'm always sure there is no question I get what I want."

232

The van door slid shut and the wheels tore over the wet pavement away from us, leaving Ryker and me in the exact spot where they'd grabbed us. The rain pattered on my hood, breaking the silence. We both stood there in utter shock until Ryker swore under his breath.

"Did that just happen?" A bubbled laugh caught in my throat. Did we really just spend an hour planning a raid with the Unseelie King? It was beyond my brain's capacity. "Did the freaking Unseelie King, the most powerful man in the Otherworld, just make a deal with us? Is he really helping?"

"I swear, if I hadn't been standing right next to you, I would say no." Ryker still stared into the night, the brake lights long gone from view. "But we did just promise to give him the stone. We are bound to give the most powerful man one of the most powerful weapons."

"Not that we had much choice, but we just did the stupidest thing ever, huh?"

"Oh yeah. Without a doubt." He turned me. "But like you said, we didn't really have much of an option on the matter."

"Damn. He's sexy and *so* freaking scary."

I thought Ryker would laugh, but his muscles twitched around his neck.

"Come on. Let's get out of here." I turned toward where we needed to head.

He grabbed my arm, swinging me back around to face him. "If you *ever* do something so stupid again… What were you thinking talking back to the King like that? How could you be so foolish?" His shoulders coiled high around his ears. "Don't ever scare me like that again. He could have killed you with a snap of his fingers, without a thought, simply for you getting sassy."

"I know." I cringed. "It's just a reflex. Fear makes me angry. I'm sorry."

Ryker's expression flashed with pain, and I saw his true fear. "I'm not losing you," he barked. He took a long breath. "I can't... got it?"

My hand stroked his face, feeling his thick stubble under my hand. I drew him to me. "Got it."

His forehead knocked into mine, and he blew out air, his neck relaxing a bit. "I swear, human, fae don't have heart attacks, but I am convinced you could give me one."

I rose on tiptoes, closing my mouth over his, trying to reassure him. He quickly grabbed the back of my head, pressing his lips hungrily against mine. In his kiss I felt words he did not say out loud. Tremors ran down my spine, into every nerve, stimulating my body. It ended far too quickly for me.

"We can't tell Amara anything that happened tonight," he said quietly, pulling away to see me. "I mean, literally we can't. I know you've never had a bind on you before. I have. You try to tell someone and the words get painfully stuck in your throat."

"So that wasn't just a warning to keep his visit secret?"

"No." He shook his head. "You and I can talk about it with each other, but if anyone else walked up right now, our mouths would shut. Nothing would come out."

"Wow, that's creepy." The whole scene felt surreal, except that the pressure of the King's fingers still throbbed around my throat.

"We need to get out of here." He kissed me again softly and stepped away.

I nodded and followed him into the dark, damp night.

EIGHTEEN

"*Bhean!*" Sprig ran for me as we entered the room. I bent over and took him in my arms. "Don't ever leave me alone with *her* again."

"I could say the same, chimp." Amara lay on the bed watching TV, a bottle of scotch next to her on the nightstand.

"I'm not a chimp!"

Amara smirked, taking a swig straight from the bottle. "So how was your *meeting*?"

"Uh." How do you even answer that?

"We're going after Vadik tomorrow night." Ryker entered the room behind me.

"What?" Amara pushed up against the headboard. Her lids narrowed, and her gaze shifted between Ryker and me. "Who did you meet with? Why is this suddenly a plan?"

I would never have confessed anything to Amara, but the moment I even thought to say something, I could feel the words turn into water, falling off my tongue and back down my throat. The more I tried to force the words, the more painful it became. My throat constricted and closed, choking around the invisible gag muzzling me. I began to retch, and coughs tore my throat. Fae bonds, oaths, and promises all could suck my ass.

"You can stay or come; it's up to you," said Ryker, patting my back as my gagging eased.

She huffed as irritation blanketed her features. "I'll go."

"*Bhean? Bhean?*" Sprig tugged at my arm. "Besides Medusa not feeding me, she ate all my nuts, the honey-sugar ones."

"Oh, were those yours?" Amara's lips lifted in a smirk.

"It's malicious... almost teetering on abuse. No, forget that. It was cruelty. But I stayed strong—"

"Sprig," I cut him off.

"Your tit-carriers don't happen to be full of honey, do they?"

"Sprig."

"I'm just saying it would be nice right now. Do you hear it?" He pointed at his stomach. "It's getting angry."

"So am I," I growled.

"Stuff it, furball." Ryker rubbed his head, collapsed on the bed, and lay back.

Sprig leaped from my arms to Ryker's chest. "These crimes should be punishable by death!" He grabbed Ryker's jacket lapels. "Do you hear me, Viking? She *starved* me. On purpose! You know what happens when I get hungry? I jabber... I *talk*." He shoved his face into Ryker's.

Ryker rolled his eyes back, then sat up. "Fine." He rose to his feet with Sprig on his shoulder and moved to the door.

"Where are you going?" I lifted my arms.

"Out," Ryker grumbled. "Before this little guy pops like a tick."

Sprig pointed at Amara then flipped her off with the other hand before the door closed.

"That was weird." I stared at the door and shook my head.

"You find that weird? Of all the things *it* does? He is

dating a *stuffed goat*." Amara took a huge gulp of alcohol. "Which, sadly, is still more action than I'm getting."

"I know this has to be hard for you—"

"Just stop right there." Amara dropped the bottle on the table, whipping her feet to the floor. "I don't want to hear any false sympathies or have some heartfelt moment with you."

Well, that made two of us.

"Enjoy your time with him. The sex is seriously unbelievable. I know." Amara stood. She only wore a long T-shirt, which barely made it to her upper thighs. "But he will come back to me. It's inevitable. We belong together." She stumbled for the door, clearly drunk. "Now, I'm going to go skinny-dipping in that tragic thing they call a pool, in case Ryker is wondering where I am. I'm sure it will cause him to think of Prague." She winked then slammed the door behind her.

My temper had handled enough bullshit tonight. I reached for the door handle. "You are such a narcissistic bitch." I flung the door open and froze.

A gun barrel was pointed at my head.

"Yes, you are." The man pressed the revolver into my forehead, pushing me back into the room.

"Arlo," I whispered.

"You remember. I feel so honored." His lopsided mouth grinned, a horrific picture.

I could never forget that cruel face. A scar, which Ryker had given him, cut through his face like a ragged mountain range and ran into his scalp. Arlo's black hair had grown long and hung in greasy clumps. A beard sprouted in splotchy patches around his uneven jaw. His back curved slightly, more animal than human. His dirty, worn clothes hung off his boney frame. He looked awful and smelled even worse.

He shoved me back hard, slammed the door, and locked

it. "I don't want anyone to disturb our reunion. So much to catch up on."

Terror burrowed down my throat to my stomach like a mole, settling into my gut. So it had been him in the parking lot at the pub when we first came out. He must have followed us back here.

"What do you want?" I had to stall to gather my thoughts.

"Oh, pet. It's more what I don't want." He staggered forward. "Like you breathing anymore. I've been following you for weeks, waiting for one moment to be alone with you." His foul breath sputtered into my face. "But let's cut the chitchat, and I'll get straight to killing you." He kept the gun on my head, but with his other hand he tugged out a knife.

A long, sharp knife.

"If you kill me, you won't get the stone. Isn't that what you want?"

"I want to painfully rip the flesh from your skin. To watch you suffer as I have." His mouth bared in a chilling grin, displaying yellow teeth. "How beautiful would it be for the Wanderer to return and find his beloved in tiny little pieces?"

"Not sure beautiful is the phrase I'd use." I licked my lips, my heart thumping wildly in my chest. *Please jump. Please for once just work.* Apparently my magic was giving me a big "screw you," being a stubborn child, not wanting to do what it was told.

"If you yell, scream, cry, or move an inch, I will carve into your face like you were going to do to mine," he snarled. "Then I will shoot you in the stomach, causing a slow and painful death. And if you were wondering, fae bullets are in here, pet."

I kept my hands up, trying to casually look around the room. Was there anything I could use to defend myself?

"After your boyfriend finds you in chunks, it will be his turn." Arlo licked his lips, smacking them excitedly. "I've been waiting for this day for a long time."

"Did we hurt your feelings that much?"

"Shut up, bitch." He slammed the gun into my head, throwing me back on the bed. He quickly climbed over me, pushing me down. "I will enjoy this so much."

"Good, I'd hate for you to come all this way for nothing." I struggled to keep my voice from wobbling, fear clawing at my facade. The weight of his body on mine, the feeling of being helpless, stabbed at the deep-seated nightmares I kept locked away.

"You should have killed me," he screeched, tiny bits of saliva sprayed out. "You and the Wanderer took everything from me."

Ryker was right. A fae would rather be dead than embarrassed or affronted.

"I've lost respect, my men, my business." His eyes darted crazily as if he'd been lost in the wild far too long. "You took it from me. A stupid human girl. They laugh when I walk in a room."

My stomach flipped. I was as good as dead.

His legs cinched around my hips as he kept the gun to my head and slowly traced the blade of the knife down my throat. Then he pressed in, slicing little cuts into my skin.

Pain built behind my eyelids, but I pressed my lips together, trying to barricade a cry from breaking out. He cut in deeper. A tear leaked out the side of my eye.

He sat back, grabbing my shirt, his knife sliced through the fabric, exposing my chest. The scared little girl I confined to the depths of my being began to shriek, fear wrenching her loose. My body reacted, wiggling against his hold.

"I don't think so." He rammed the pistol into my

forehead, indenting my skin. "I am going to do what you did to me. You fucked me in the ass... it's only fair, bitch."

My lungs halted, icy hot waves of terror flushed logic, my system going into sheer panic. Screaming, I crawled and bit at him.

"Stop it, bitch!" He slammed the butt of the gun into my temple. "The more you fight, the deeper I cut!"

His blade traced between my breasts. Arlo smirked, licking his lips, before he dragged the blade across my chest, leaving a deep trench through my breastbone. My lips drove apart, cries tore from my throat, my eyes leaking with pain, fear, and anger. Blood oozed from the cuts, trickling down my sides to the comforter. The violence and the control he had over me excited him. I could feel his arousal as he ground into me. He lifted off me just enough to flip me over on my stomach, one hand tugging at my jeans. With the other hand he shoved the gun into the back of my neck, pushing my face into the blankets. The horrors of his declaration came to life.

No... not again.

"Oh yeah. I'm going to enjoy this."

My past roared in like a bull, snorting and knocking everything, colliding straight into my anger. I would not let this disgusting piece of garbage make me that girl again. Old nightmares filled my chest, images of my eleven-year-old self at the mercy of... A growl deep and raw emerged from my gut. I bucked back when I felt him slide my pants over my ass.

Nooooooo!

Air hissed in my ear, and suddenly I was across the room, standing up facing the sink. The mirror in front of me showed a girl with a shirt ripped open, blood trailing down her exposed torso, anger entrenched on her features, and her eyes bright with hate and revenge.

It also displayed the man right behind her. Arlo's startled expression reflected in the glass over my shoulder. His moment of hesitation was all I needed. I slammed my elbows into his gut, causing him to stumble back. I twisted around and ploughed into him, taking us both to the ground with a thud. The gun slid out of his grip and skidded toward the door. We both scrambled for it.

He swung the knife at me, slashing a cut from my ribs to my hip. Blood poured from the wound onto the carpet and saturated my clothes. I felt nothing. My heartbeat thumped in my ears.

I punched out and struck him in the nose, which I had broken before. He grunted, red liquid gushing from it. I could not feel or think. My brain went primal, protecting the young girl who couldn't defend herself back then, fighting against everyone who hurt or took advantage of her.

Ryker's words came flooding back to me: *He was a grown man, a repulsive human who took advantage of a young, innocent girl. He is the sick fuck. You are not to blame.* It had been the night I told him of my darkest secret, of the abuse. For years I carried guilt that I had deserved it. Now I channeled that fury into my fists. I had been so angry at myself for so long. I felt weak, mad. I hadn't stopped it. Let it happen to me.

I am not to blame.

I no longer saw Arlo, but the man who abused me.

Arlo's abhorrence for me and mine for him painted the walls and floor red. Hate, blame, pain, isolation could turn you into the precise animal they claimed you were.

Knuckles cut across my face, a blade sliced my shoulder, but I continued to fight. Punching, clawing, and kicking, I completely lost myself in the violence, no longer a girl, but a wounded animal seeking release from all the pain.

The sound of a gun blasted through the room, wrenching us apart. Consciousness slammed back in, and I sucked in the air I had forgotten to breathe. I blinked and opened my eyes to see Amara standing in the doorway, the lock broken, Arlo's gun in her hand, the ground smoking.

"Get the fuck away from her." Amara aimed the gun straight at Arlo. "Now!"

Arlo slowly got to his feet, holding up his hands, covered in blood. He limped toward Amara instead of away.

"Amara. Come on. You of all people wanted to get rid of this human. With her out of the way, you can have everything you ever wanted." He struggled to talk, his face looking like minced meat. "Like Ryker. Take him back, Amara, steal him away from this human bitch."

I wanted to run after him, but even the slightest movement sent pain slamming into the wound in my torso.

A smile edged at her mouth. "Steal Ryker?"

"Yes. Kill her and you will never have to deal with this wretched human again."

"Hmmm." Amara tilted her head as if she was considering it.

My lungs clenched, sadness prickled my eyes, but I held my head up. This was what she always wanted. "Go ahead."

Amara rolled her eyes. "You are so fucking righteous. It's really annoying."

Boom! The gun discharged, vibrating the room. I closed my eyes, and I waited to feel the bullet explode in my brain. Did you feel something like that, or did it just go dark? Instead, I felt a spray of liquid cover my face.

Thump.

My lids bolted open to see Arlo's body fall to the floor, his head a mess of pulp. Okay. Wow.

"We're definitely going to have to change rooms now.

Blood is really hard to clean. And brain matter is impossible to get out of carpet."

My mouth gaped. "You shot him."

"Clearly." She looked over at me like I was crazy.

"But... but..."

"I may not like you, Zoey, but killing you will just make Ryker mope. He's a bear when he's sulking." She turned to me, then snarled at the dead body on the floor. "And this asshole suggests I *steal* Ryker back? I only steal goods. I'm not pathetic. Ryker will come back to me. There's a difference."

"You saved my life."

"Yeah, that was an unforeseeable event." Amara moved to the table, setting the gun down.

"Zoey!" Ryker's voice rang over the parking lot to the room, his boots hitting the pavement. He reached the doorway and stopped. Sprig looked frozen in shock, holding a doughnut halfway to his mouth. Ryker's eyes scoured the room.

"Holy shit." Ryker came to my side before I took another breath.

"*Bhean?*" Sprig jumped from Ryker's shoulder onto the bed, looking overwhelmed and terrified by all the blood.

"I'm fine, buddy."

"Your guts are coming out," he said, then pointed down to Arlo. "And his brains are all over... oh my turtle puffs... his brain is all over my honey packets. That's really not cool." Sprig bent over, breathing deeply. "Oh, raven turds." I counted three more seconds before he fell face-first into the comforter. Out cold.

"Poor guy."

"Poor guy?" Ryker's hands tore at my clothes trying to find the source of all the blood. "Fuck." He peeled away my torn shirt. "You've been stabbed."

I pushed myself against the dresser, taking slow breaths.

"Amara, can you get all the towels from the bathroom? And the bottle of scotch."

"My scotch?" she whined, but stepped over me, padding through the blood with her bare feet. "Maybe I should have shot her."

"Not funny," Ryker snarled.

Amara swiped the bottle off the table and handed it over to Ryker.

"Drink this." He placed it in my hands. I clutched the bottle, my fingers smearing bloody fingerprints over the glass, and downed a gulp of the liquor. It burned down my gullet.

Amara disappeared into the bathroom.

"Seriously, human, I leave you for five minutes..." Ryker tried to joke, but his expression looked tense. His jaw worked back and forth.

"Hey." My stained fingers slid over his face and pulled up his chin to look at me. "I'm okay. I'll live. I'm probably already healing."

"Still need to stitch it up. It's really deep."

"Aww..." I giggled. "We'll have matching scars." I pointed to where I had stitched him up months before.

"I think you are in shock." He pushed the bottle back to my lips, and I drank more. "Do you have any thread and needle?"

"In my bag." I blinked, my lids suddenly heavy. I took another huge swallow. Ryker grabbed my bag off the table, tossing out my last pair of clean underwear, and finding the sewing kit in the side pocket.

My head started to spin. Along with the room. "I'm not feeling so great."

Ryker made a noise, coming back to me.

"This is all I could find." Amara came out holding a hand towel.

"It took you that long to get *one*?"

"The rest were dirty! You were the one who put the 'no room service' sign up."

"Go to the front desk and get more."

"I have blood all over my feet, and I'm only wearing a T-shirt."

"Glamour him, Amara." Ryker's voice strained. "Now!" Ryker didn't even try to hide his impatience.

"Fine." She stomped past us to the door, then threw the cloth at Ryker. "Remember, I saved her life, so don't get so testy with me. She's fae now; she'll survive." Amara slammed the door behind her.

He growled, took the scotch from me, and soaked the towel in it. "This is going to sting."

"Wow. This really is *déjà vu*." I clenched my teeth as the alcohol hit my open wound, like fire that burned hot and cold at once. He cleaned around the gash. "But this feels a lot less sexy."

"What happened?" He continued to clean, his eyes not meeting mine.

"You were right. Arlo wanted revenge." I pushed out the words. Sleep yanked on my arm to follow it. "I was it."

"Did he do anything? Did he *hurt* you?"

Ryker meant did he touch me, rape me. I let my lids drift close and a thin smile turned up my lips. "No. No one will ever hurt me like that again."

"No. They won't." Ryker's words soaked over me. "I'm sorry I wasn't here."

Sleep began to curl around me protectively.

"I've finally forgiven myself." I felt my mouth move, a peacefulness slipping over me. "I was just a kid… It wasn't my fault… I need to let go. To move on." As I drifted off, all the pain I had possessed for so long finally released me.

NINETEEN

Gray light appeared through the curtains as I opened my eyes. I stared at the soft glow, my brain slow and groggy.

I stretched out my legs, pain tugging at my stomach and hip. In a flash everything from the previous night came back in jagged images, and I sat up with a jolt.

Scanning the room, I was aware I was alone. The faucet dripped a steady rhythmic ticking, like a clock. I looked down to see I wore Ryker's extra shirt and my underwear but nothing else.

For the first time, anxiety filled me not because I was alone, but the room where I lay was completely different from where I passed out. The comforter and color scheme were dark and heavy, and there was no blood, no body, no signs of struggle at all.

My gaze landed on my bag sitting on the nightstand across from me. I swung my legs over the edge of the bed, my feet resting on an ugly patterned brown-and-maroon carpet. The room was laid out like every cheap motel, but this one still had the eighties-style design used to disguise the stains and age of the room. Dark colors swathed the flowery comforters and curtains. Heavy wood furniture lined the rectangular room, giving the space a cavelike feel.

I padded over to my bag. Every step strained the skin

over my torso. The mirror above the desk reflected a sallow version of me. Like I had been drained of blood. Oh right, I had.

I lifted my shirt, my fingers following the ridges of the basic stitches across my side. Crusted blood still caked on my skin in places, but the wound looked spotless. Ryker did a decent job of sewing me back together. The white lines running from my neck to my breastbone were healing, but I wouldn't be surprised if some of the marks, especially on my stomach, would leave permanent scars. Scars didn't bother me. They were like a storyboard of my experiences.

The door to the room swung open, flooding it with light. My neck snapped to the door, adrenaline powering through me in a sickening lurch. Then eased the moment I saw him. Ryker paused, his huge figure filling the doorframe. His white eyes pinned me in place. His dark shirt and jeans hid the stains, but it didn't conceal the stiffness of the dried blood left behind. He had a bag slung over his shoulder.

"Hey." My voice sounded quiet even to me.

He didn't respond but stepped into the room, shutting the door.

"Where were you?" I suddenly felt shy. Energy slipped off the Viking, but I couldn't make out what emotion lay behind it.

"Getting more clothes and supplies," he said low, matching my volume. He placed the bag down on the bed and pulled out items of clothing. "We burned everything you had on."

"Burned?"

"Along with Arlo." He kept his eyes off me. "Making sure he could never come back."

"What? When did you do this?" I gaped.

"After I sewed you up, Amara and I tossed Arlo into the

dumpster next to the room, set it on fire then the room. We wanted it to look like a dumpster fire that got out of control."

My mouth opened then closed. I was void of emotion, even with the grotesque images of burning bodies rolling through my mind. The only thing I possibly felt was relief, and that scared me. Had I grown numb to such violence? It wasn't that Arlo didn't deserve to die, he did. But I felt I shouldn't be so nonchalant about tossing a dead body in a dumpster.

"Where are we?"

"We're near the stadium in the SoDo area. I knew if Arlo found us, others could."

"Sprig and Amara?"

"Amara stayed outside watching the room until I got back. Then she took off. Needed to get out of here for a moment. And the furball…" Ryker tugged out a new hoodie from the bag. A tiny form curled up around his backpack, sound asleep. My feet instantly carried me over to him, needing to feel his soft fur between my fingers.

"I let him have four packets of honey, a doughnut, and two granola bars."

I groaned mockingly. "You always give him whatever he wants, and *I'm* the one who has to deal with the aftermath."

"Yep. I'm the nice parent. Deal with it." He finally looked at me, our gazes connecting.

He watched me for a long time, lines forming around his eyes like he was in pain.

"What?" I asked breathlessly.

"I wasn't there."

Guilt. That was the sensation radiating off him like cologne. "It's not your fault."

His chest rose in indignation.

"Some things happen." I realized the words were for me

as well as him. "You can't control everything. You deal and move on."

He breathed in and out of his mouth, strong emotions building under the surface.

"I'm all right." I took a tentative step toward him as if approaching a cornered animal. "And if you haven't noticed, I can take care of myself."

"I know you can." He curled his hands into fists.

I reached out, taking a hand in mine, straightening his fingers.

"But you're still mad?"

"I'm not mad at you."

"No, you're mad at yourself. Because once again you felt you weren't there for someone you care about and they got hurt."

In one night, the ghosts of both our pasts came back to haunt us. I could only imagine him standing there, watching the room go up in flames with me limp and bleeding in his arms.

Ryker stiffened under my touch, his eyes sliding to the side.

"Do you think my rape was my fault?"

He jerked violently back to look at me with softness in his eyes. "What? No!"

"Then why do you think what happened to you is your fault?"

"Those are two completely different things," he rumbled.

"The acts are, but we were both victims of circumstance. We only have control over ourselves, not others. You couldn't have prevented it any more than I could. We can spend the rest of our lives with what-ifs and being afraid of it happening again, or we can let ourselves off the hook.

"Last night I forgave myself," I continued. "I always felt if I were stronger, if I fought back, if I weren't such a bad girl it wouldn't have happened. But you showed me that punishing myself only gave him more strength. I was playing the victim. Now it's your turn to forgive yourself."

His body was rigid, but his shoulders slowly sank, letting the anger leak out. His hand trembled slightly in mine.

"Let the ghosts go." I took another step to him, pressing the back of his hand to my lips. "Let me in."

A groan erupted from him, his fingers ran under my jaw, tilting my head back before his lips crashed down on mine. The kiss was first filled with pain and anger, but soon it slowed down, deep and exploring.

It detonated something inside me. Love. Complete and unconditional. I knew I had fallen in love with him, but now it embedded itself so deep in my soul, I couldn't breathe. This was something new to me. It should have felt foreign or scary, but it didn't. Not with Ryker.

He grabbed the hem of my shirt, pulling it gently over my head, leaving me only in my underwear.

"I need to get this blood off me first," I mumbled against his mouth, my hands running through the braids on either side of his head, releasing them from their binds. His hair fell down, brushing his shoulders.

"How about during?" His mouth never left mine as we made our way to the bathroom. He shut the door and locked it.

He leaned past me and turned on the shower. I undressed him, peeling away his jacket, sticky shirt, and jeans, which fell to the floor after he kicked off his boots. He broke the kiss to trail his lips down my chest, paying extra care and attention to all my healing wounds. His fingers crept between my skin and my underwear and slipped them slowly down my legs.

Every nerve ending exploded at his touch. I stepped out of them, moving back into the shower, where warm water made a blissful cascade down my bruised frame.

He climbed into the tub, sliding the curtain closed. My heart thumped, watching trails of water descend down his body. His hands slid up my thighs, curving over my sides. He turned me around, pressing his chest into my back as he grabbed the motel shampoo and poured it into his hands. His fingers skated through my hair, massaging my scalp. Dark red water pooled at our feet until it ran clear of blood as he worked through my knots. His hands soothed me as he washed and conditioned my tresses.

Once my hair was clean, his knuckles glided down my spine, his breath hot on my neck. His teeth skated and nipped up the curve of my neck.

My breath became rapid. He pulled me closer, his hands slithering over my stomach, moving lower, parting my legs. My palm struck the tile wall, keeping me from falling over.

"I want you," I whispered, my free hand running over his hip, pulling his amazing ass closer to me. He was so hard he felt like marble against my lower back.

"You sure about that? I've heard I'm a lot to handle." He nipped my ear, positioning himself. His tip hinting at entering.

I grinned and inhaled. "I think I can manage it."

"I have no doubt of that, but do you want to? Your life is a lot longer now." His husky voice rippled through me.

I looked over my shoulder at him. The love I felt for him seemed almost crippling. "Always, Viking."

Magic flickered up his tattoo, and he inhaled sharply. He whipped me around to face him. He cupped my face, kissing me so deeply and powerfully I could no longer feel the boundary that separated him from me. He breathed me in, consuming me.

He lifted me, and I wrapped my legs around his waist then lowered me gradually down on him; every cell in me burned. He moved deliberately at first, driving me insane, in a very good way. Neither of us could get close enough, kiss enough, touch enough.

He shattered me, my body trembling, brought me back, and did it over again. And then again.

We'd had sex several times now, but this was different. I never used or liked the phrase "make love." It sounded so cheesy and overly sweet and romantic. I wasn't those things. I was the girl who rolled in the dark. Lived off aggression. Enjoyed it actually. And I liked it in sex too. So did he. With Ryker and me, violence would always be there, nipping at our heels, under the surface of our skin, part of who we were. But this time the passion was healing. Instead of wanting to break or combust, we let the fire take us, consume us, and burn hotter.

A fire that would never burn out.

TWENTY

Tap. Tap. Tap.

I opened my eyes, a noise stirring me from my nap. The darkening sky shaded the room in heavy shadows. I sat up, my feet tangling in the sheets. I glanced at the clock on the nightstand and 5:20 flashed back at me. "Hell."

"What?" Ryker's sleepy voice asked. He rolled onto his side, propping his head up with his hand.

"We should start getting ready for tonight. Get something to eat."

Ryker flopped back on his stomach, mumbling something into the pillow.

Tap. Tap. Tap.

I looked around the room. Where was that sound comin—?

"Shit!" I didn't even finish the thought before I stood. I grabbed Ryker's new shirt, which had been tossed on the floor along with the comforter, and shoved it on, jogging to the bathroom door.

I swung the door open, and beneath guilt-laden eyebrows, I gazed at six inches of pissed-off monkey. He sat there with his arms folded.

"I am *so* sorry, Sprig."

"You locked me in the bathroom. Again," he huffed at

me. Technically he wasn't "locked in." The bolt hung on the inside, and he could have easily unlatched it, but that wasn't what he meant.

I put my face in my hand. "I feel awful."

When we moved from the shower to the bedroom, Ryker quickly rolled Sprig up in a towel, placing him and Pam in the bathroom.

"We left you a granola bar." I shrugged, shamefaced.

"You think that makes it okay to confine me in a bathroom with no windows? I couldn't even escape outside."

"No." I dropped my head.

"I'm just kidding. Being locked up with a granola bar is like my ideal night." He chirped and ran past me to the bedroom. "Hey, seal clubber, it's time to put the weapon away or PETA will start protesting." Sprig jumped on the opposite bed, then leaped to the table by the window. Three new packets of honey sat on the surface.

"Oh no." I ran for him, but he tore into them before I reached him, sucking on all of them at once. Ryker had already let him have four beforehand. "Sprig, let me have them." I held out my hand.

He shook his head.

"*Sprig.*" Shit. It turned out I did have a "mom" voice. I reached for them, and he sprinted off the table, slipping out of my fingers.

"Dammit. You know what happens when you eat too much in one day." I wasn't really upset; it was more of a game. Sprig twittered as he jumped, leaped, and fluttered all over the room like a trapped bird.

Then the sugar really kicked in. "Ahhhh!" he screamed, chasing his tail, and knocked the clock off the nightstand. "More. More. More!"

Ryker smirked when I crossed my arms and cocked my

hip to one side. He leaned over the bed, snatched the sprite, and held him in the air.

Sprig's legs and arms continued to shimmy as if he was running. "Look in the sky. It's a pixie. It's a hummingbird. No, it's Supersprite! Dah-dah-dah! The deity's warrior of sweet nectar."

"It's more like your kryptonite," I teased.

"I need a cape! Ahhhh. Honey, I will save you!"

Ryker's white eyes glinted, and he sat up, placing Sprig next to him. He leaned over and grabbed the brand-new package of underwear he had stolen for me. "You want a cape?"

"Yes. Yes. Yes!" Sprig spun in a circle. "Honey Hero needs a cape!"

"What are you doing?" My hand went to my laughing lips.

Ryker tore open the package and grabbed one of the black cotton bikini-style undies. Looping the leg holes together, he slipped it over Sprig's head. "There. A cape."

Sprig went still, his eyes widening, then his body began to tremble. "Oh. My. Gods. This. Is... Awesome!" He zoomed around the bed like a windup toy.

Laughter heaved out of my tender stomach, and Ryker struggled to keep a straight face.

"Suuupperrspprriittee," Sprig sang. "I'm so badass. Like a honey-crunch, double-dipped-doughnut, rolled-in-sugar, fried-in-honey badass. Bees will be my pollen posse."

A pair of underwear flew behind him as he zipped around the bed. He was about to leap on Ryker, when his head fell forward, face-planting onto Ryker's arm. Deep snores vibrated from his little chest, his tongue hanging out the side of his mouth.

"His superpower is being a pain." Ryker placed him on the pillow.

I went to the bathroom and snatched Pam. "Supersprite and his sidekick, Pam the Goat." I placed her next to him. "Has a catchy ring to it."

"Pretty much defines our screwed-up world."

I tapped my forehead, chuckling. "Just wait till he adds his honey backpack to the ensemble."

"Weirdo." Ryker winked. "Definitely takes after your side."

I sat on the bed, crossing my legs in front of me. Ryker lay on his back, one arm behind his head, the other on my knee, rubbing my leg.

"What would I do without him?" I watched Sprig sleep. I felt like the Grinch whose heart grew three sizes in one day. My family was so important to me. They were my air, my world. But my family was in pieces, separated. Tonight I hoped that would change.

"We'll get her." Ryker's fingers moved over my bare skin. He knew without a word what I was thinking. I nodded, pushing back my shoulders.

"Yes. We will." There was no room for doubt.

"Please stay close to me tonight." Ryker sat up, leaning his head against mine. His damp hair fell loose and tickled my cheek. "I know she is important to you, so she's important to me." He inhaled. "But if it's your life or hers, please don't hate me later for picking yours. You will always be first, above everyone else."

I let my head fall onto his shoulder. How could I hate someone for that? I nodded against him, and I felt him kiss my temple.

"Okay, let's find Amara and go over our plans."

I sat back as he climbed out of bed, strolling over to the pile of clothes he nicked earlier. I watched the fluidity of his naked figure in awe. This man picked me. Loved me.

Sometimes life came out of nowhere and clobbered you, tearing down your preconceived ideas and prejudices, till all you could see was the truth behind the labels.

I had started out despising fae, treating them like beasts whose lives weren't equal to humans. Now as I thought of anything happening to the fae standing before me or the one sleeping on the pillow next to me, I could barely stand it.

"What?" Ryker had stopped, watching me.

I walked over to him, wrapped my arms around him, and burrowed my head into his chest. He submerged me in his embrace, leaning his chin on my head. We stood there for a long time just holding each other.

"I'm gonna need that shirt back," he finally muttered into my ear, his fingers running along the hem, brushing the back of my thighs.

"Come and get it," I whispered against his neck.

He took claim of his shirt and me. Fiercely. Like the end of the world was coming. He made sure everyone in the vicinity heard our passion. While vehement cries tore from my throat, I silently thanked fate for putting this man in my path. For showing me it was okay to love someone so much you almost couldn't breathe. And more, to let myself be loved in kind.

Amara returned thirty minutes later with a greasy pizza. Sprig still snored from the bed as we went over every detail of our raid ... at least what Ryker and I could talk about. There was no mention of Lars as the bind blocked our mouths from even hinting. It surprised me a little that Amara didn't even question our plan. I had no doubt her willingness stemmed mostly from wanting to please Ryker, but I sensed it was also about Vadik. From Ryker's brief accounts of their capture and what Vadik did to her, I had no doubt he remained the driving force for the both of them.

"You know our odds are not good with only three of us." Amara frowned, leaning over the makeshift map of the inside I had drawn from my memory. Ryker did a hasty sketch of the outside, giving Amara the rundown of the guards' routine. "That person you met? They're not helping out with this attack, are they?" Her eyebrow curved up questioningly.

Amara wasn't stupid. She connected the dots when we came back from some secret meeting, saying we were going to raid Vadik's warehouse. She knew there was more to the story.

"The person we went to meet?" Ryker kept his eyes level on hers. "No. We will not be receiving aid from him in this."

I wanted to snort. *Well played.* It technically was true. We went to meet Dunn. He would not be helping us with Vadik. *The Unseelie King is,* I wanted to scream. At the same time I couldn't fight a twinge of doubt from forcing its way up. Would he actually follow through? He might have made a deal with us, but he was a demon, a ruthless, extremely powerful one. Demons were not known for being trustworthy or fair. He could be setting us up. For all I knew, he and Vadik were allies.

It didn't make sense. Why didn't he just take the stone from me the night he kidnapped us? Maybe he didn't feel it? That seemed unlikely, but I really didn't know. I knew I had to go forward. Enough sitting and talking; it was time to act.

"It's not three. It's four." Sprig popped up from the pillow as if he had been awake the whole time, the underwear trailing behind him.

"You're not coming with us. You'll just get in the way." Amara leaned back in the chair, sipping her soda.

"Excuse me, huckleberry witch. Who are you to tell me I can't go? I'm an important part of this team."

"What the hell are you wearing? Is that underwear?"

"Cape."

"It's gross."

"They're new." I shrugged.

She glared at me, shaking her head.

Sprig sat on the edge of the bed, holding up his hands. "You all need me. I've got magical fingers. Pam tells me so. One of my superpowers."

"Wow." I slapped my hand on my face. "So many dark, bad images."

"Thought you said that was *my* magical power?" Ryker mumbled into my ear, his eyes sparking with mischief.

"Ugh. Please." Amara's nose crinkled. "Stop before I vomit all over. I can barely sit in this room. It's saturated with sex."

I wasn't one bit sorry about that. My mind drifted briefly to what we did in this room after the shower. I smirked. If she only knew how we used that chair, she would not be sitting in it. Nor would she touch the dresser, the table, or either bed.

"I'm more needed than you are." Sprig leaped on the table near me. "We should leave you behind. How about in the dumpster with the other dead body? It is put-out-the-trash day, right, *Bhean*?"

"Shut up, freak," Amara spat back. "Why don't you go get some of the honey packets they got you and see if any of them are poisoned?"

Sprig made a huge gasp. "You wouldn't."

"Hmm... would I do something like that?" She tapped her lips and tilted her head, a cruel smile on her mouth.

Sprig's fingers clasped over his mouth in shock, then he tore across the table for her.

"Whoa!" Ryker snatched him off the counter the moment he scampered past.

"Let me down!" Sprig twisted and clawed, still reaching for Amara. "That witch needs to be taught a lesson."

Amara burst out laughing. "You're going to teach me a lesson? You're wearing underwear around your neck and carry around a stuffed animal."

A high-pitched cry came from Sprig. "Let me down!"

"No." Ryker cupped his hands around him, cocooning him. Sprig immediately quieted down, but his chest heaved with panting.

"But how can she even tease about that?" he whimpered. "You don't mess with honey. It's just wrong."

"I know," Ryker spoke quietly, his voice rumbling and soothing.

"You hear that, purple she-devil? Respect the honey."

"Sprig?" Ryker said. "Calm down. She didn't touch the honey."

"It's okay?" His voice sounded full of hope.

"Yes."

"Oh good." Sprig barely got that last word out before his head fell back, his mouth opened, and snores stormed out. The mere thought of ruined honey caused too much stress. And with the overdose of sugar today, he was sleeping more than he was awake. I lifted an eyebrow at Ryker as if to say, *See, what did I tell you? You never listen.*

He only winked back.

Damn Viking.

"That seriously is freaky," Amara grumbled, nodding at Sprig.

"Enough, Amara." Ryker's attention went back to the

map, but I watched him draw Sprig into his chest with one hand. A wave of tenderness hit me at the idea of Ryker as a father. Not that I wanted a baby right now, if we even could. But it was still sweet to see. Like, *look, my man can hold his baby and set up a heist at the same time*. I found that seriously hot.

"Are we all set? Everyone feel they know what they are doing?" Ryker stabbed his finger into the paper. We all nodded, an edgy tension in the air. "All right. Let's get ready. We leave in twenty."

Sprig's head bolted up from Ryker's arm. "Damn you, pixies! Stop grabbing my berries... they're attached!" Sprig blinked, glancing around at all of us. "Huh? What?" Then his forehead crashed back down. He was sound asleep, mouth open like a drunkard.

Yes, ladies and gentlemen. That's my best friend.

TWENTY-ONE

"Look." Amara pointed to the building with the hole in the roof. We took point on the building across from it to assess what was happening at Vadik's torture camp before we put our plan into action. "They're all there."

More than two dozen girls mulled around the space, either sparring, stretching, or working the bags draped around the room. Even if not all the girls were there, this was a bit of good news; we didn't have to break into each individual cell to get them out.

"There are seven guards. All with automatic weapons." Ryker narrowed his lids, inspecting the space.

"Seven down there, a dozen guarding the building, and who knows how many inside." I touched the gun on my hip. Arlo's. He didn't need it anymore.

"We need to get in there... *undetected*, knock out seven guards... *undetected*... and get out with a bunch of girls... *undetected*." Amara snorted, bumping Ryker's shoulder. "Kind of reminds me of Sarajevo."

"*Slightly* different." Ryker chuckled.

They had a past. A long one, but I clenched my jaw a little too hard. His hand slid against mine, entwining our fingers, as if he sensed my mood. I couldn't seem to hide anything from him anymore.

"I miss my axe, especially on nights like this," he muttered under his breath.

"You miss your axe every night." I squeezed his hand.

"And day."

"We'll get it back."

He nodded, keeping his gaze on the girls below. He stood in full warrior mode—his braids tight against his scalp, the top pulled back, wrapped up in a bun. He wore all black clothing and boots, with a new holster, which held several knives, but none of them bigger than a butcher knife. You'd be surprised how fast the weapons were taken after the storm, so I was pleased he found those in Target's kitchen section.

Amara had three knives, while I had the gun and one knife. Ryker hated fighting with guns, so he gave Arlo's to me. I was still more comfortable with a gun in my hands than a sword or tiny knife. Too many years of training and hunting didn't go away overnight. Vadik didn't seem to play by fae rules. All his men had guns. Most likely filled with fae bullets.

"Do you see her down there?" Amara zipped up her jacket to her chin.

"No." I moved my head from side to side. "But she isn't a fighter. They might still have her in the cell."

"We start with them. Get them running before we go for the cell," Ryker stated. "It will cause a distraction, pulling any guards from the warehouse so we can slip in."

We had been waiting for Lars and his men to show up, but the clock was ticking. The opportunity of these girls being out of their cells was limited. We needed to act now. The knot of fear doubled in my throat. "You ready, buddy?" I opened my jacket where Sprig lay tucked safely inside.

"Yeah, I'm ready. I guess." He pouted. "Though a lot less super." We forced him to take off his cape and put it in his backpack with Pam. He would be too easy to grab and possibly strangle with the cloth around his throat. He was not happy.

"That's the spirit." He crawled onto my shoulder.

The four of us stared down, taking in these last quiet, non-life-threatening moments.

"Okay, let's do this." I unlaced my fingers from Ryker's and turned for the ladder down to the ground level. There was no turning back now.

We moved silently to the building. The girls' grunts and jeers arose from the practice ring. We skated along the wall, playing hide-and-seek with the guards patrolling the grounds. Five of the guards in the workout room were near the exit. The other two milled around the edges of the ring.

"Try not to use the gun. That will bring attention to us far too quickly," Ryker said into my ear. "Amara will take the two on the right, I'll take the three on the left. The other two guys will come for me. I'm physically the bigger threat. Zoey, you get the girls out."

"What do you want me to do?" Sprig grabbed my ponytail.

"Not die," Ryker grumbled.

"Sprig, we're going to need you in the cells. I want you to sit this one out."

"What?"

"You are too important to the mission. You need to stay safe."

"Wow, that was a bunch of banana mush," Sprig quipped. "But fine. I will stay back, but if anything happens, I'm coming to save you."

"My hero."

"Ugh." He rolled his eyes and hopped down from my arm, his backpack strapped tight to his body, and vanished into the shadows.

Ryker twisted the door handle and, like a ghost, slipped into the room, Amara and me trailing behind.

The guards were all facing the girls. Most of the men leered at them in their tiny shorts and sports bras wrestling on the ground.

As big as Ryker was, you'd think people could sense him coming, but he was so swift and precise in his movements, he twisted the neck of the biggest guard before anyone noticed. But the moment the guard dropped, everything changed.

Shouts, groans, and the sound of bones crunching echoed around the area as Amara and Ryker descended on the guards. Like Ryker predicted, the two roaming men ran directly for him.

I sprinted past them and straight for the girls. "Come on!" I bellowed. They all turned around and stared at me. "What are you waiting for? Run!"

"What the shit? Is that the Avenging Angel?" A blonde girl on the mat tilted her head.

"Seriously?" My mouth fell open. That was what concerned them at this moment? I was trying to save them, and they all stood there like sheep. "Do you want to get out of here or not?"

"Yes." A girl pushed her way through the crowd. Her round face looked sunken and pinched, her stringy hair tied up in a loose bun.

"Maria."

"You always come back, don't you, Angel? Can't get away from it, can you?"

"No," I said, staring straight into her eyes. "It's who I am."

"Finally you realize it." Maria nodded, a smirk twitching her lips. She glanced at the girls, who stared at her like she was the Messiah. "Come on, girls."

A gunshot snapped through the air behind me, and I whirled around to see a guard drop to the floor, his gun bouncing off the cement, Ryker standing over him. Every guard lay crumpled below Amara and Ryker.

"Time to go." Ryker wiped the blood off his face. The sound of that gunshot would have every guard heading our way in seconds.

Alarm burst up my spine. "Go. Now!" Twenty-plus girls turned into a screaming, babbling mess as fear set in. Voices boomed from outside, heading for us. *Shit*. This could go bad fast.

"Amara and I will take the guards, you get the girls out of here," Ryker barked and whirled around, running out the door. Amara swiped up another gun and hurried after Ryker.

"Maria, get them away from here. I need to go inside and get Annabeth."

"She's not there." Maria grabbed my wrist.

"What? Where is she?" Acid bubbled into my lungs.

"I don't know. She disappeared a couple of days ago." As Maria talked, her eyes wandered around the room, watching her girls. She was still their leader, even when locked up with them.

"You have no idea where?"

"No. She was too sick to work our last fight. When I got back, she had gone."

No. No-no-no-no-no. It's can't be true. Was I too late?

"Sorry to say she's probably dead." Her voice turned cold. "They killed my brother without a thought. If you aren't good for anything, then you are discarded."

Marcello was dead. I felt neutral about his demise. He had become a drooling shell of the man he once was because of Ryker and me, but that could never overshadow what he had done to me, his cruelty.

"What does it say about me that I am relieved?" Her lips hooked up in disgust at herself.

"Maria!" a man shouted from the door.

Her grimace broke open into a huge smile. "Carlos!"

It was like watching a romantic movie as the pair ran for each other. She jumped into his arms. The relief on his face at seeing her filled my heart and then broke it. I knew they had been through a lot together. He willingly became a controlled soldier to stay near her. But once I had helped him break through the glamour, he was back to himself. He was still here and alive, which probably meant he was smart enough to fake being under fae control.

I wanted their love to have a chance. Reaching their side, I ripped a knife from my bootleg. They let each other go, and I handed her one of my knives. "Take this. Help the girls and run as fast and far as you can."

She stared down at the weapon then back at me in wonder. "You're helping me?"

"Yes."

"Why?" Her expression appeared confounded. "I locked you up. I *tortured* you."

"Because you are a survivor like me. And no one should die here. Not like this. Now run. Go!" I waved my hands forward. Maria gave me one last look but nodded. Fate wove our lives together with threads of death, hate, and violence. But somehow we had saved each other. She could have killed me many times, and I could let her die now, but there existed a similarity in each other we recognized. Possibly an exceptionally thin line of respect.

"Come on," she bellowed to the cluster of frightened girls, taking the lead. Maria and Carlos led her troops into the dead of the night. I heard more shouts and shots fired into the night.

267

I bit my lip, hoping with all my heart she could get them away from here. If anyone could, it would be Maria.

I whirled back around, moving toward the other building. I wouldn't believe Annabeth was dead. Maybe they put her in another cell. I couldn't leave without checking. Hope was a powerful force.

I eased out of the building, my gun aimed and ready. "Sprig?" I stepped out, my gaze roaming over the space. "Sprig?"

I could hear only yells and gunfire in the distance. Ryker had done a great job getting the men away from here.

Where was Lars? Would he come? Did he betray us? I didn't have time to dwell on it.

"Sprig, where are you?" No response. Shit. I didn't have time to look for him. My opportunity to find Annabeth narrowed with every tick of the clock. I started to dart for the main building.

"Zoey!" Amara's voice from the alley broke my course.

"Amara?"

"This way!" She waved me toward the back of the building. "I remember in the plans a backdoor to the stairs here."

I changed my direction toward her. "Where's Ryker?" I hated not being the one who had his back.

"We got separated." Worry creased her forehead. "I was coming back to look for him when I saw you. There's an easier way into the building. It takes you to the stairs, leading to the cells." She turned, heading for the door.

"Have you seen Sprig?"

"No." She shook her head. "I'm sure he's fine. Probably passed out in the bushes."

Sadly that was a real possibility. I hoped it was true. He'd at least be safe.

I trailed after Amara, following her through the door, into a hallway.

"Wait." Alarm beeped in the back of my mind. "The door wasn't locked?"

When the door shut behind us, it took my eyes a moment to adjust to the pitch darkness enveloping me. Amara's dark eyes glinted in the dark, and gradually my advanced sight identified her outline in the blackness.

"Yeah…" She tapered off. "They probably just forgot to lock it."

His men wouldn't forget anything, least of all a door where people could sneak in and out. My desire to find Annabeth pushed me forward, deeper into the building, but logic kept jumping in my face, screaming at me. My skin itched, my gut twisting. Something felt wrong.

"Amara…" I had just called her name when I felt more prickles at the back of my neck. The sound of feet moving for us.

Shit. Fae.

"Amara!" I yelped. Right then the light blasted overhead, the bulbs crackling awake. Men came from all directions, so fast my eyes couldn't track them. One grabbed me from behind. I could sense my body wanting to jump, but nothing happened.

"Not so fast," a thick, familiar Irish brogue whispered in my ear. Garrett. His arms swiftly grasped me and slipped goblin metal around my wrists. Then he tugged the gun out of my hands, and put it in the waistband of his jeans. "Don't want you taking me to some exotic resort in Tahiti… well, not quite yet. We'll have time for that later, sweetheart."

I grunted as I fell against him, my magic subdued by the

metal. Cadoc, Maxen, and all the rest of his nameless cronies surrounded us. One I didn't know patted me down. Cadoc held Amara by the throat, her eyes slanted in anger.

"Always good to see you, Mar." Garrett settled his chin on my shoulder, keeping me pressed against him.

"Can't say the same."

"Come on, luv. We've had some good times together. Even you can't deny that."

"It's called faking it, Garrett. You probably wouldn't be able to tell though, since all the girls do it with you."

"Deny all you want, luv. But it was you crawling into my bed each night. Begging me." She scrunched her face and looked away, and Garrett laughed wickedly.

"Come on, li'l sis. Daddy is going to lock you in your room for disobeying him." Garrett yanked my cuffed arm and pulled me forward. When Ryker and I were first on the run, Garrett showed a picture of me to locate us, pretending I was his missing sister.

As we passed Amara, he slapped her ass. "I'll be punishing you later, but Vadik wants to see you first."

She glowered at Garrett with ferocity, but he didn't appear to care. He and one of his nameless goons shoved me up the stairs. I knew they were taking me to a cell. My mind ran through any possibility, any hope, to get out of this. I had goblin metal stealing my powers, which were sporadic anyway. I had no weapons, and a gun was pressed against the back of my head. Sometimes you were just screwed.

Garrett took me to the second floor, to a room far in the corner. This room held no beds or chairs, only chains pressed against the walls on either side. I gulped as he pulled me in. My body was slammed against the wall, and the click of metal cuffs around my legs and wrists sounded before I could even take a breath.

270

Garrett's speed was his advantage. His blurry form stopped in front of me. A smile spread over his striking face. A perfectly trimmed red beard lined his jaw. "So much trouble crammed into such a tiny, cute package."

I pulled my arms, rattling the chains holding me to the wall. My fury emanated in a snarl.

"Easy, sweetheart." Garrett patted my head. "Why don't you hang out here and think about what you've done?" He turned for the door and stepped out with the other fae. He slid the cell door close, the lock snapping in place.

"Oh, and don't you worry your pretty head about your *boyfriend*." Garrett smirked, wrapping his hands around the bars. "He's getting some father-son bonding time."

As if on cue, a pained roar tore through the building.

Ryker!

My soul sank to my toes and my body instinctively struggled to move toward him. To get to him. The shackles clanked as I tried to fight them. I knew what bonding time meant. Torture.

"Go ahead, wear yourself out." Garrett winked and turned for the stairs. "I'll be back for you soon after I gather up the humans you set free. You thought you saved them?" He clicked his tongue. "You just got them killed." Garrett blew me a kiss and disappeared along with his minion.

Another bellow came from below, tearing out my heart. Hearing Ryker being tortured was more painful than if it was me. My arms and legs failed against their restraints, bucking and slamming against the wall until I gasped for air, a strangled cry twisting my vocal cords. All I was doing was hemorrhaging energy. The chains weren't meant to hold fae, but that didn't mean I could get out of them. Being fae didn't suddenly turn me into the Hulk or Superman.

I wish.

The sounds, grunts, and voices rose to me in waves from the room where they were holding Ryker, punishing my mind with images. Every cry from Ryker created a despairing whimper from me. I hated that all I could do was wait to be released from the chains. It was my only possibility to get away. Finding Annabeth and getting Ryker and Sprig were at the top of my plan, but I had no idea how to accomplish any of it.

A shadow obstructed the light briefly, and I jerked my head toward the shape moving to my cell door. Purple hair high in a ponytail swished across her black leather jacket.

"Amara!" I exhaled with relief. "Never thought I'd be so happy to see you. How did you get away?"

She tugged a key out of her pocket, unlocking the cell door, sliding it open.

"You have a key?" I hissed excitedly. "Where did you get it? Never mind, just help me get out of these. Then we can go get Ryker and find Sprig."

"Why would I do that?" She tilted her head. "You're exactly where I want you."

Trepidation fluttered in my chest. "I know you don't like me, but we need to go after Ryker."

"You are both where I need you to be for the moment."

"What are you talking about?" My throat struggled to get words out.

"Ryker is finally away from you. And all their attention is on him. Not you."

"This is all because of you?" I rattled against my chains. "*You* set us up. You led me down that hallway on purpose, didn't you? Why?"

"Because you have two things I want." She crossed the room. A knife hung off her belt loop, a guard's gun tucked in her back belt. Weapons, I realized, that Garrett's gang never took away from her. This had been all an act, and she went to great lengths to keep Ryker and me believing she remained on our side, even killing one of the nameless guards in the training room.

"And what is that?" It really wasn't a question. Her desires were transparent.

"Ryker and the stone, of course," she answered. "And both were always with you."

"You thought it best to work with the man who tortured Ryker, almost killed you, just so you could get me away from Ryker?"

"I am not really working with Vadik." Her upper lip hooked up in disgust. "He might think I am, and I allowed him to believe so. I needed to be sure you and Ryker were separated." Her dark eyes glinted with rage. "Because he never left your side. Ever. It was disgusting."

"And you're an idiot," I stated. "You think Vadik is just going to let you have the stone? Or Ryker?"

"Vadik doesn't know about the stone's true whereabouts. I led him to the conclusion it wasn't with you, and Ryker is the only one who knows where it is. Why do you think Ryker is downstairs and you are here with little security?" She held her arms out in the tiny space. "All in all, this worked better than I imagined. Now you and I can have some quality girl time."

"You want to braid my hair?" I lifted an eyebrow. "Sure, go for it, but don't be surprised when it becomes your noose."

Amara put her hands on her hips, strands of her plum hair hanging down. Even covered in dirt and blood, she looked as if she were posing for a magazine. "Oh, Zoey. Aren't you just the cutest thing?"

"That's what I hear." I shrugged, the manacles jangling. "But let's get past the bullshit. Get to what you want, Amara."

"I already told you."

"Neither one is for me to give, nor are they for the taking."

"Big words coming from a girl restrained to a wall. Defenseless."

She did have me there.

"The entire time you were with us, you were scheming to bring us back here?"

"No." The word burst out of her mouth as she moved closer to me. She stopped, taking a breath. "I hate Vadik, what he's done to me, but I work with what I am given. Your little human friend locked up here gave me great opportunity."

"Where is she?"

"That I don't know. Like you, I thought she was still here. I have no idea what happened to her, nor do I care."

I jammed my lids together, breathing out. *One thing at a time, Zoey.* I needed to get out of these chains and this cell before I could help anyone.

"All of this," I opened my eyes, looking around the space, "is just to get Ryker back? He *doesn't* love you, Amara. Let him go."

Her nostrils flared.

"Was saving me the other night only to gain my trust and his appreciation? Make us less inclined to suspect you?"

"Yes and no. Like I said before, I've always been honest with how I feel about you. I don't like you, but killing you would not benefit me. I understood that when Ryker followed you down into DMG. Helping you is another thing..." She let the sentence drift off. "Arlo was a viral dog who needed to be put down. He presented a great opportunity. I wasn't going to let him really hurt you. I just needed you to be threatened enough to need me."

My jaw went slack. *How did I not see this coming?* "You were working with Arlo?"

"You think he would have found us otherwise?" she exclaimed. "He couldn't find his ass if he tried."

I felt so stupid. Amara was a trickster, a deceiver. It was in her DNA; she couldn't help herself. And we walked right into it. She used Basic Magic 101: create a distraction so they won't see the trick you pulled right in front of their eyes. Arlo had been the distraction, an unaware pawn. She had set him up as well.

"You are psychotic."

"No, I'm a survivor." Amara sauntered up to me, a smugness drawn over her features. "You are so easy to play with, Zoey. You practically walk into traps without my help. Your weakness for people makes you incredibly vulnerable."

"At least they don't turn me into a cold-hearted bitch no one cares about. Even the man whom I never thought would stop loving you, no matter what awful things you did, doesn't care about you anymore." I leaned forward, the chains only allowing an insignificant amount of leeway. "Even *he* chose *me*."

Low blow.

She snarled. "Croygen is a fool. He always has been." Her nose twitched. "He never got me. He made it too easy with his love and his willingness to be at my beck and call."

I tilted my head back, taking her in, understanding twitching my lips. "I get it. Ryker was the unattainable. A game to you. If he ever had turned around and told you he loved you, you probably would have left him too."

"Shut up," she snarled, glaring at me.

"But you knew deep down he would *never* love you. That became the draw. The desire to make him truly and fully want you. But he never did... or would."

"I said shut up," she yelled and stepped closer to me.

"It must have killed you to watch him with me." I

grinned, knowing perfectly well I was poking her. "To see him love someone. To know a *human* got the exact thing you wanted for so long. His heart."

Her hand clashed against my cheek, which first went numb, then ached. I twisted my head back to her, our faces only inches apart, and I smiled.

"Is that why I'm here, Amara? Because you're a sore loser?" I tipped my head in closer, keeping my voice low. Seductive.

I had come to terms with the dark, twisted part of me who loved a good fight, the taste of blood, learning how best to get under the skin of your opponent. It made me feel alive, and like a dog in mud, I rolled in it with glee.

Amara was a good opponent. Most people I fought were easy to read. Either I stayed silent, letting them waste their energy with meaningless words, or I found their Achilles heel and clamped down on it until they lost. Amara's only weakness was Ryker. And sadly it wasn't even about him.

Fury flamed in her eyes, but then her mouth twisted in a superior grin. "Do you know how many nights he yelled out my name? How many beds we broke? You can pretend all you want, little girl, that he cares about you, but he will grow so *unbelievably* bored of you. You don't think I haven't seen it before? The list of women he has been with is endless, but he *always* came back to me. And he will again."

Pretending her words didn't bother me was difficult, but I kept my face complacent. "You are pathetic, Amara." I chuckled. "You don't even see it. The way you treat Croygen? It's how Ryker treats you. He's used you because you were there and more than willing. A doormat."

"Shut up!" She shoved me back against the wall. My laugh echoed off the wall, like a demented witch. "I said shut up!"

I turned off my cackle like a light switch and leered at

her. "Come on, Amara. You think having us captured by Vadik is the best way to get Ryker? You just handed him over to be tortured and killed."

"Vadik won't kill him. He assured me. No matter what he says, Ryker *is* his son. But he will kill you. That was part of our deal." She lifted her hand, brushing my hair back off my face. Icicles rushed down my spine. "Too bad I won't be around to see it. But to answer your question, my plan does end with Ryker coming for me. He's forgiven me for a lot worse. And I promise you, he *will* follow me again."

Her confidence unsettled me. Either she was truly nuts or she knew something I didn't. It wasn't long till I got her meaning.

Amara dropped to her knees in front of me, reaching for my right boot. Fear struck like a belt to my back, air catching in my throat. *Oh shit.*

She winked up at me as she undid my laces. I tried to pull back, but there was nowhere I could go. "Amara, don't."

Her fingers gripped my heel, pulling on the shoe.

"You don't know what you are doing." I thrashed against the chains.

"I know exactly what I am doing." She slipped the boot off my foot. She was taking the stone from me. Panic struck at my magic, but it was under the weight of the goblin metal still poisoning my system. I sensed it wanting to explode from its hold, but it still couldn't fully break through.

"No, you don't." She had no idea the power the stone retained and unlike others, she didn't have the strength to fight its call. She would be the stone's perfect victim, too self-absorbed to see or care about the consequences. "It's not just its power. There are—" My throat choked over my words, shutting down. Lars's bond keeping me silent. "*Others.* Extremely powerful people are after it."

She tugged a cloth from her back pocket. "That's why I will be holding it. I'm not going to use it. But the girl with the biggest toy will be in control." Amara lifted the sole of my boot, my stomach sinking as the smooth gray stone slid into view, as though waiting patiently.

"Please," I begged. "You have no idea what you are getting yourself into."

"All this fuss for such a little thing." She stood, staring down at it with awe. "Why can't I feel it? Shouldn't it be emanating magic?"

"Only if it wants to." I had experienced its temperamental mood. It could go silent, gauging the carrier, or it could grow loud and demanding. The last few days it had been unbelievably silent. "It's alive, Amara. It will mess with you. Play on your weaknesses."

"Don't tell me about a fae relic. You've only been one of us for a week. I've studied and pursued it most of my life." She folded it in the cloth and put it in her jacket pocket. She glanced up, catching my eyes and cocked her head, stepping back toward me. She lifted her hand to my face, and I fought back my recoil. Her fingers tucked a piece of my hair behind my ear. "Ryker, Croygen, every man you come across is completely taken with you. I don't get it. What is so special about you?" Her anger dissipated as she studied my face. "Tell me, Zoey. What is it about you that made Ryker love you? Even when you were a weak human, you captivated him."

"That's your problem, Amara, you keep thinking there's something you can do to make people love you. Love doesn't work like that." A part of me pitied her. She had probably never known real love. It might have started out with her bad childhood, but now she who would never let herself love. Her trust had been broken a long time ago, the walls built. She didn't understand relationships without deception, cruelty, and lies.

She stepped back, dropping her arms away from me, then patted her pocket. "Now I will get everything I want." She walked to the door and turned around. "Because you know Ryker *will* come for me now. He will spend so much time thinking and obsessing about me. How to find me. When do you think his thoughts of me will destroy whatever you think you have with him? Love and hate walk a fine line. Let's see what side he falls on in the end." She winked, slipping out of the cell door. She slid it closed behind her, the clank of the lock turning over. She held up the keys, stuffing them in her pocket.

"Thanks, Zoey." She winked before disappearing.

"Amara!" I bellowed, thrashing against my chains. My gut wrenched at the thought of the stone leaving me. Angry. Hurt. It had fought to stay with me so many times before, even caused me to attack Ryker. This time it was silent, not calling for me. It was probably happy to go with her. She would give in to its desires. It could control her. My relationship with the stone wasn't healthy, I was fully aware of that. But I couldn't stop the longing to feel the pulse under my heel, its power seeping into me.

The hours I hung there didn't diminish the sense of loss, but the sporadic bellows from below intensified my cries for Ryker. Every time I heard him bellow out in pain, my own followed. I was not one to give up, but I couldn't stop the reality of our situation from seeping in. All our plans to get Lexie and Croygen, take down DMG, save Annabeth with the help of the Unseelie King were gone.

Lars had not shown up. The stone was gone, along with Amara. Annabeth had vanished and was probably dead. The only good thing we'd done was to get the other girls out. I

279

wanted to believe they would make it to freedom, away from Vadik's reach.

My shoulders slumped forward, and my lids shut heavily with fatigue and stress. My mind started to drift, trying to find a moment of peace, when I heard a rattling at the door. My head shot up. Was Vadik here to show me a preview of my fate?

My heart thumped so loudly in my ears, I could have sworn I heard Sprig call for me.

"*Bhean?*" The voice came louder this time.

I froze. *Did I actually hear him?*

Through the shadows an outline of a creature scampered to the cell, sliding easily through the bars.

"Sprig!" I cried out, then slammed my lips together.

"No." He scuttled to me. "It's Supersprite. I know you probably didn't recognize me without my cape."

"Yes, my underwear would have given away your identity."

"I'm undercover."

"I won't tell." I listened keenly for any footsteps or voices heading my way.

"Guards?" I asked.

"Most are still out after the girls. A few are downstairs."

"Where did you go?"

"Medusa caught me and gave me to that redheaded fart face. He locked me in a box."

"What? How did you get free?"

"People always underestimate sprites." He reached my feet and started to climb up my leg. "Like I can't get out of that poor excuse of a lock. Huh! Showed those banana-nutters. Stupid fruit and stupid men." He reached my shoulder.

"It is so good to see you." I blinked back a swell of love

for this little bugger. I rubbed my chin against his fur before he darted up my arms, working on those locks that held my arms in the air. Sprig quickly freed me of the cuffs. They were made for human girls, not for fae. The blood rushed into my arm with tiny pricks of pain. I rubbed them. "Thank you."

"Easy as pie... oh pie. That sounds good right now, doesn't it? Honey-custard pie, honey-apple pie, honey-blueberry pie, honey—"

"Sprig? Focus." I waved my fingers in his face.

"Right." He shook his head. "Pie later. Even though it would be so nice right now... yummmm."

I proceeded to the cell door. "Do you think you can work your magic on this?"

"Cake." Sprig swished his hand, crawling down my arm to the lock on the other side of the door. "Oh, cake sounds delicious too."

"Sprig," I groaned.

"Sorry."

In less than thirty seconds, the lock popped on the door. Damn, he was good. I inched it open, a low whine vibrating off the hinges. I gritted my teeth, keeping my arm steady.

A thump downstairs jolted me, my anxiety skyrocketing. Sounds of boots clipping the cement echoed up.

"We'll give him a moment to consider his options. Have you found any of the girls yet?" Vadik's voice was low but throbbed off the walls.

"We have located a few," a familiar Irish accent replied. Garrett. "Maxen and Cadoc are heading back here with them. We will keep searching for the rest, sir."

"Thank you, Garrett. And when you round them all up, kill them. They were becoming useless anyway. We can easily start over with healthier ones."

"Consider it done."

Footsteps. A door slamming. Silence.

My heart lodged in my throat. All those girls I thought I saved were headed to a faster grave.

Think, Zoey. Don't fall apart now. My mind zoned in on survival.

Number one—get Ryker.

Number two—find weapons.

Number three—

Okay, let's start with one and two first.

"Okay, Supersprite, let's go save our Viking."

"As usual, *we* have to save the day." Sprig jumped back onto my shoulder. "This better not be his way of wiggling out of our deal."

"What deal?" I darted Sprig a look.

His mouth opened, then he shook his head. "Nothing, *Bhean*."

Normally I would have pressed it, but right now it was not important. Ryker was. I slunk down, leading us toward the stairs to the pit. I moved blindly, unaware of the dangers that lay ahead. But nothing would keep me from Ryker.

Nothing.

TWENTY-TWO

I felt like a snake as I slithered down each set of stairs. With the girls gone, the hallways all but oozed a heavy silence that chilled me. The place felt as if ghosts of old prisoners continued to walk around.

Sprig scampered ahead of me, my first line of defense, warning me of any unknown guard or trap. I breathed out in relief when my feet finally hit the ground level. My goals were basic: Get out of cell. Check. Get downstairs without being found. Check. Sprint across the large space to get to the room where Ryker was held.

Sprig darted in front of me, beelining for the office. In the dim light you'd mistake him for a rat. I could not pass for the same.

Setting my jaw, I bolted through the area, dashed for the office wall, and crouched beneath the window. Like the ones at DMG, this one was tinted, so those on the inside could look out, but no one could see in. I had no idea if Ryker was alone.

"Damn you, Viking," I grumbled, slipping over the wall. My heart pounded. At any moment someone could walk in and I'd be done. I reached for the doorknob, twisting it so slowly I hoped no one on the inside would notice. I guess they figured it would be pointless to lock a thin door on the

Wanderer. It was like paper to him, but they wouldn't leave him free to roam around.

Okay, Zoey, this is probably the dumbest thing you've ever done. No weapon or idea what's behind this door. Bring on the stupid. If we are going to die, I'd rather it be together.

The door released and drifted a few inches away from its frame. Sprig darted inside, and I quickly followed. The room was dark, but the light from the gaping door spotlighted the crumpled shape on the ground before I shut it behind me.

"Ryker!" I whispered, running for him. He was on his knees, his head bent forward, both his arms above his head, pulled tight by the chains cuffing him to the ceiling. Slashes and burn marks covered his bare chest. I crashed to my knees in front of him, my hands cupping his jaw. He grunted as I lifted his face.

"Oh my god."

His face was mangled. Blood leaked from the side of his mouth. One eye was completely swollen shut. I struggled to make out his features. Gashes, cuts, and bruises covered him, and the open wounds over his torso crisscrossed with his old ones.

"Fuck." I felt vomit rise in the back of my throat.

"Voey," Ryker slurred out my name, his body tensing. "Gooo."

"Not on your life, Wanderer."

"Damn, Viking, you looked like minced pie." Sprig climbed up Ryker's shoulder. "Oh man, I shouldn't have said the word pie again. Now I'm hungry."

"You're always hungry," I replied. "Sprig?" I nodded to the shackles straining Ryker's arms.

"Eye-Eye Matty!" He saluted me and climbed up the chains.

"We're going to get you out of here." I kept my gaze

locked on the Wanderer. My heart hurt at the sight of his ruined state.

"Rvun." Ryker's one eye bored into me, tension twitched at his temples. "U've gwat tu go."

"I'm not leaving you," I retorted. "When will you get it through your thick skull that we are a team? We save each other. And right now I am saving your ass. So shut up and play the damsel in distress like a good boy."

He watched me for a moment before his mouth parted, his top lip curving in a smirk. The action caused him to grimace in pain and reopen his split lip. He leaned over and spit. Blood and saliva pooled on the ground. A click sounded above, his left arm falling to his side. He groaned at the sharp movement. I glanced up at Sprig swinging from the chain before he leaped across for Ryker's other wrist.

A door banged from the front of the building. I jerked to my feet, panic thumping my heart. *Shit*. They were back. I frantically scanned the room for a weapon. Anything that could stab, knock out, or hurt someone. I rushed to the desk, pulling at the top drawer. My eyes zeroed in on an item. Scissors. I grabbed them, shoving them in my back pocket, and pulled at another drawer. Only files.

The door banged again, voices volleying outside the door.

Shit. Shit. Shit.

Terror often crippled people. But I had pushed that reflex back years before. One moment of uncertainty could be your last.

There was a pop. "Aha. Supersprite to the rescue!" Ryker's right arm fell, tipping him forward. I dashed for him, catching him before his face hit the cement. He righted himself, and I eased him back.

A lump of fur landed on Ryker's other side. Voices grew

closer, and I could distinguish Vadik's deep voice. We were really screwed, but I wouldn't go down without a fight. If Ryker was up to par and had his axe, we'd have a lot better odds. Neither of those things were going to happen.

"Stay here," I whispered in his ear and zipped to the door, placing myself behind it. I tugged at my back pocket, palming the item. I only had the element of surprise to my advantage. Leaving Ryker in place would at first lower suspicion. In the moment between seeing him and then noticing his arms were no longer confined I would strike.

"Let's see if my son is ready to negotiate. Go retrieve his little half-breed pet. Slitting her throat will help motivate him."

I saw Ryker's shoulders constrict as his fists rolled into balls.

The handle of the door moved, my heart scaling my throat.

Creak. The door opened.

A figure stepped into the room.

Three.

Two.

One.

No battle cry or noise escaped my throat as I slipped behind the demon. He stiffened and turned back toward me. Too late. I drove the scissors into the side of his neck with a gruesome squelching sound. Blood sprayed over my face. Vadik stumbled to the side, and I followed as I pushed the metal in deeper. I snarled, wanting to inflict triple the pain he'd ever caused Ryker and me.

The second his men got past the shock of my attack, chaos ensued. Men yelled behind me. Some crashed into me. My body went flying, slamming on the ground. Ryker bulldozed past me and hurtled for the man who hit me. The large, dark-haired muscleman sprang for Ryker, their large forms colliding midair in a crunch. Cadoc.

Vadik lay on the floor, blood gushing out of his neck as he tried to wiggle out the scissors. Garrett leaped around the two men and advanced toward me. I rolled forward, using my momentum to hit Garret at his knees and push him backward, the tendons behind his knee snapping. He howled, his elbows slamming into my back. I grunted but didn't let go until we rammed against the wall.

Another figure entered the room, reaching for me. Maxen. A brown ball of fur came flying at his face, clawing and biting like a cat. Sprig got some deep slashes across the fae's face before Maxen ripped him away, his fingers wrapping around his neck. *Oh. God. No.* Maxen smirked at me, then twisted. *Crack.* The sound of Sprig's neck breaking echoed in my head and detonated my heart.

NOOOOOOO!

Maxen threw my best friend across the room like a baseball. Sprig's body hit the cupboard with a crunch and fell to the ground.

Lifeless.

A sound drove up from my soul out of my mouth. It rang in my ears and shredded my throat. I shook with wrath and whirled around, pouncing on Maxen. We both hit the ground. This man had killed Daniel. And now… Another crazed scream soared free of me, and I tore into him like a frenzied Tasmanian devil. There was no skill or thought, simply blind rage and wrath thumping in my fingers.

Maxen fought back, but I didn't feel any of his strikes, only the desire for his death. Revenge burned through me for Daniel, the man I had once loved, my friend, my partner, my fantasy of what could have been. And for Sprig.

All I could feel was bottomless violence and rage. He

killed Sprig. Took my best friend from me. Death would be the least of his problems.

Vadik hunkered down near me, his hand trying to slow the blood gushing from his neck like a river. Seeing him there, my hands moved on instinct. Vadik wailed as I twisted and ripped the scissors from his body, creating a flow of blood that surged in waves out of his neck.

I flew back, my head smacking the ground as Maxen bore down on me, his punches knocking me onto the floor. He leaned over me. His face was torn, and he was missing a tooth.

"You fucking little bitch. I will enjoy taking your life like I did your partner's." He cupped my neck, his thumbs squashing my vocal cords. He banged my head back onto the ground over and over as he strangled the last bit of air from my throat. My legs kicked wildly underneath him, my nails tearing at his hands.

I had died before like this, but I knew he wouldn't just leave it at that. Before I woke, he'd probably cut off my head or burn me.

It's what I would have done.

My vision started to blur, my ears ringing.

"Die," he seethed. "Go join your freak pet. Say hi for me."

"You first." I lifted my hands and drove the scissors right into his heart.

He froze, losing his grip as he looked down at his chest. His jaw slackened, and his eyes darted back up to mine in shock.

I twisted the handles, rotated the shears, and dug in deeper. The deep shade of scarlet began to soak in and color his shirt. I shoved him off me. Maxen tumbled to the ground, his eyes wide with panic.

"I will enjoy watching *you* die," I said hoarsely, straddling him. I tugged the shears out of his chest. "This is for Daniel." With all the force I could muster, I propelled the scissors down into his throat till the handle halted. His lips parted for air. His body jerked and flapped. I yanked them out of his neck. "And this is for Sprig!" My arms swung back down, the metal sliding through his gaping mouth, embedding into the back of his throat with a gurgling tear as it ripped through to the floor. I kept pressure on the scissors till he went still, his eyes void of life.

My hands shook as I let go of the shears and scrambled backward off his frame. I stared at the horror before me, only the tips of the handles sticking out of his mouth. My darkness could still frighten me. My gaze was unfocused as I scanned the room. Ryker was fighting. His shoulders rolled as he battled against four fae. Blood covered his torso, dripping down his back like sweat. He would not last.

At the sight of Sprig's crumpled form on the floor, fury flooded bone deep. *Get up, Zoey. Keep fighting.* I got to my feet, ready to join Ryker, when a tall form suddenly blocked mine.

"I am a demon, little girl. You think a pair of scissors is going to bring *me* down?" Vadik's navy eyes turned black, his skin paper thin, displaying the bones and veins under it.

A desk leg scraped across the cement floor, drawing white lines as it moved across the floor. Lars's power could actually move people, control them. Vadik's level of demon could only move inanimate objects. Still, he was incredibly powerful. And fast.

My mind barely grasped what I saw before the desk collided into me, pushing me back into the wall, pinning me in place. I yelped as the edges dug into my skin.

"I can see why my son picked you. You remind me so

much of his mother. Strong, defiant, smart, self-sacrificing. You impress me, Zoey, but you will lose. In the end you will forfeit your life for his just like she did."

A sucking slurp sounded as the scissors wiggled free of Maxen's throat. Goo and blood matter dripped from the blades. Vadik was controlling them with his mind. They flew for me, stopping at the base of my throat, their sharp tips tapping at my skin.

I heard a roar from across the room that sounded like my name. My gaze found Ryker through the chaos. His white eyes blistered like a neon sign, ignoring all the men punching and stabbing him. He drove forward, dragging some with him.

"I wouldn't do that, *son*." Vadik's words broke my attention from Ryker. "You move another inch, so does the blade."

He stopped.

"Here we are again." Vadik gazed at me then back to his son. "But unlike Peru, you two will have a dreadfully tragic ending." The scissors twirled like a screwdriver, digging in.

I screamed.

"Stop," Ryker snarled, barely able to stand fully straight. His fae magic was probably trying to heal him, but it could only stay even as a flood of new wounds descended upon him.

"Not this time." Vadik shook his head, his blond hair sticking up in bloody points. "Look at what my generosity got me last time."

Another cry broke from me as the sharp edge of the scissors pierced past the skin of my neck, hitting muscle. Pain eclipsed my vision, blurring the room. Ryker bellowed.

Then noise and commotion at the door broke Vadik's attention from me. The scissors dropped to the ground, tearing a larger hole in my flesh as they fell. Vadik whirled toward the entrance.

The door to the office burst open. Figures rushed into the room.

I blinked a few times, regaining my vision. My eyes locked on a tall, scarred blond man. I knew him. Goran. Lars's men were here. I almost burst into tears with relief.

Vadik stood in place, which surprised me. He watched his men go down one by one but did nothing. His eyes moved wildly around the room, but not a finger twitched.

The fae, Rimmon, who was the size of Goliath, crashed into the room, tearing down half the wall with him. Rimmon swung his arm and knocked into Garrett, smashing him against the wall. Garrett's body collapsed to the ground in a heap.

Cadoc leaped over and slashed his sword at Rimmon's waist. Rimmon's eyes flashed with anger, his fist slamming down on Cadoc's head. Cadoc stumbled trying to keep upright but teetered to the side and fell. His head knocked into the desk.

More and more men pushed their way into the room like silent ninjas. They didn't say a word. They didn't have to. There were so many of them, trained and efficient, and quickly took control.

Vadik and the rest of his men halted, finally seeming to realize they were outmanned and overpowered. Goran and another man moved to each of Vadik's men, disarmed them, and lined them up against the wall.

Vadik didn't flinch a muscle, as if he were actually frozen in place.

"Everything is secured, sir." Goran spoke into a walkie-talkie.

"Took you long enough," Ryker snarled and limped

over to me. His one eye stayed swollen shut, and fresh bruises and cuts bloomed across his face and body. He clutched the desk and shoved it away, kicking the shears.

"We've been here for several hours now," Goran replied.

"You knew the whole time we were here? Caught?" Ryker snapped over his shoulder, then returned to me, reaching up to cup my face. His thumb brushed over the hole in my neck, and I gasped at the stinging pain. "You okay?"

I nodded. I couldn't quite make myself speak yet.

Sprig. My feet went to where his body was. "Sprig! Oh god. No." I went down on my knees, sobbing, scooping him up in my arms. "I am so sorry. I didn't protect you." I buried my face in his fur, tears racking my chest.

My buddy. My best friend was dead.

I sensed Ryker squat down next to me, leaning his head into mine. He reached over and ran his fingers over Sprig's fur. His hand stopped.

"Holy shit."

"What?" My head shot up, tears streaming down my face.

"I can feel him breathing. He's alive, Zoey."

A joyous whimper bent me over farther, cradling him closer to my heart. It was soft, but I could feel his heart patter against mine. Relief so tangible wound my broken heart back together. I kissed his head softly. "You're okay, buddy. I'm here," I whispered.

"He'll be okay. He's still fae. He'll heal," Ryker whispered and kissed my temple. I let my forehead fall onto Ryker's shoulder. *My boys were all right.* He rubbed my arms, peering over at Goran.

"Did you know we were being held prisoner? Tortured?"

"Yes." Goran nodded.

"They were waiting on my orders, Wanderer. I don't rush into situations without knowing my outcome." A deep voice spoke from behind Goran. Goran stepped to the side, letting his King pass.

Ryker and I scrambled to our feet. Magic so thick I could taste it on my tongue crowded my lungs. My seer qualities went into overload as the King's magic pressed down on my shoulders. My gaze locked on to the man strolling in. The whole room focused on him. He commanded attention. His power and confidence gave you no choice.

"I told you before I'm always sure things are in my favor." Lars stepped into the room, stealing my breath for a whole other reason. He was seriously one of the most striking men I had ever seen. Today he wore a dark gray suit with a buttery yellow tie, which blended with his green-yellow eyes. With his wavy hair styled perfectly, he looked like he stepped out of a *GQ* magazine.

His attention snapped to the other demon. "Valefor, my old friend," his voice mocked. "You are giving me yet another reason to regret my decision to let you live. I showed you kindness, and this is how you repay me? Trying to take over *my* city?"

Vadik's eyes flashed black, but he didn't respond.

"I already know I am going to regret this." Lars tugged at his cuffs. Vadik's body drooped, and he leaned over his knees, sucking in air.

Ah, Vadik hadn't moved or spoken because he couldn't. I knew the feel of the King's control.

"Kindness?" Vadik's nose flared, and he glared up at the ruler. "Is that what you call it?"

"Yes," Lars snapped. "A while back, I allowed you to live. I warned you what I would do. I should have taken care of you then. For Rez. A mistake I will not make again."

"And one I would never have made." Vadik stood up, pushing his shoulders back, looking like a puffer fish. "*Your city*, as you call it, has fallen apart. And you have done nothing. I did what needed to be done. You are a sad excuse for a king. You let the humans have control, have free will, and look what happened? Chaos. I put order back in this city. What were you doing, Lars?"

Vadik's body flew back against the wall near me, his feet hanging off the ground. His fingers clawed at the invisible fingers around his throat, croaking out choked noises. Ryker tugged me away, inching us both out of Vadik's reach.

"You address me as King." As Lars walked up to him, the King's fury made my knees bend. "You are a disgrace, Valefor. You have always been a vile weasel. A man trying to wear his father's pants. And you know you never will." Lars smirked as Vadik gasped for breath. "You keep pretending you're in the big boys' club, but you can't play at our level. The inferiority complex you struggle with will always be your downfall. I am grateful to see your son has taken after his mother. She had strength, true fire, and fierceness I respected.

"I may have become distracted, but I have known every move you have made: trading fae and humans to that human doctor, the little fight club, your secret dealings with the Seelie Queen."

Vadik gasped for air, his face a shade of purple from the lack of air. "I am a demon. Dark!" Vadik struggled to talk. "I do not deal with the Seelie."

"No?" One eyebrow curved up elegantly on Lars's face. "Really?"

"No! I've never even seen her before. I would never do that." Vadik uselessly continued to struggle against Lars's hold.

"At every turn, Valefor, you make the wrong choice."

Lars pressed his lips together. "I know you have never met with her in person, because if she found out those letters *I intercepted* were from a demon, she would not have been as welcoming to your turncoat ways."

"I swear. It was not m—" A strangled cry came out of Vadik, and I could see his throat begin to crush inward.

"Enough. I am tired of you, Valefor." Lars clenched his hand tighter. Vadik's legs kicked wildly where he hung, his back ramming against the wall.

I hated Vadik. I wanted him to die. But it was hard to watch his eyes bug out, vessels popping, saliva trickling down his chin, his tongue darting out. I gripped Ryker's hand and turned my head slightly to the side.

Ryker's body rocked next to me. "Wait!" he called, letting go of my hand and stepping closer to Lars.

The Unseelie King's eyebrows shot up.

"He is my father, my responsibility."

Lars stared at Ryker for a couple of beats, then Vadik fell to the floor. Vadik grabbed for his neck, hacking and grappling for air.

"I will honor your request, Wanderer." Lars bobbed his head. "You may deal with him in whatever way you see fit by the dark laws, but I can't leave without him being punished. He has gone too far. And I do not go soft on those who disrespect or challenge me."

Ryker nodded in agreement.

Lars turned back to the man on the floor. Gone was the imposing man, the feared, cruel, ruthless demon. In his place stood a bully, pathetic and stripped of his dominance.

Vadik's eyes were wide with fear as realization of his situation set in. He held up his hands in plea, as if he were waving the white flag. "No, my King. I promise. I will not do anything against you. I will be your faithful servant."

Lars shook his head with disgust. "I would have had more respect if you defied me to the end. No one likes a coward."

Glancing around the room at Vadik's men, most wore frowns of disdain at their pitiless leader, who was nothing more than a sniveling child when roles were reversed.

"You open your mouth one more time, and I will forgo your son's request." Lars leaned over him. "And I swear to you, you will much rather him kill you than me."

Vadik stupidly opened his mouth to speak, but before he could say anything, Lars crumpled his hand into a fist. Vadik put his hands up to his neck, his legs jerking out. It unnerved me to watch someone fighting against nothing. I had experienced it, so I knew something was there or at least in the mind of the victim. But Vadik only clawed at air.

"As a trader of the dark, you are hereby banned from Earth and the Dark side of the Otherworld, if your son does not sympathetically end your life for you." Lars spoke low, but the words still boomed through the room. "You have challenged the Unseelie King and lost. Your title has been stripped and everything you own is now mine. Enjoy your fate with the Seelie, *old friend*. See how accommodating the Queen can be to demons."

In my studies of the fae, I remembered reading something about how the Light and Dark couldn't live on each other's sides without massive consequences. They would grow weak and eventually die an especially painful death.

Lars straightened. Vadik's struggle relented, and he slumped over, his head slid to the floor, and he passed out from the weight of Lars's creed.

"To the rest of you," Lars circled around, speaking to Vadik's minions, ignoring the monster on the floor. Garrett and Cadoc were both back on their feet, dried blood coating their heads and necks. "As law states, your fate would be the same as the one you pledged your obedience to."

I watched as Garrett swallowed, his forehead wrinkling as if he tried to fight back the fear. Almost all the men bore wide-eyed expressions of terror. Except Cadoc. He was the picture of indifference. He held his chin high, accepting his fate.

"However, situations are currently changing, and I am in need of men willing to go into battle."

Garrett's head lifted, his green eyes sparking with hope.

"I warn you. You will commit to me completely. An oath bond. Your loyalty will be the only thing that keeps you alive. If you break it, death will be more painful than you ever imagined. For saving you, I own you and you are mine to rule. Death is likely but not immediate, but if you choose not to go with this option, you die here." Lars stared at each man, each of whom wiggled beneath his penetrating gaze. "I am being quite generous. What do you choose?"

"My life is yours, sir." Garrett licked his lips, leaning forward.

Ryker snorted behind me. We both knew Garrett would jump at this. His life was far more important than any belief he had, if he actually had any. He went where the money and power might trickle down to him.

One by one each of Garrett's men pledged themselves to the Unseelie King, except Cadoc.

Lars walked up to the burly man. Even though he looked puny next to Rimmon, he was still big. "Will you follow me?"

Cadoc's eyes drifted to Vadik, then back to Lars. "No. I swore my loyalty previously, sir."

Lars lips turned down. "That is too bad. Your size and skills would have been an asset. And your honor to duty is exactly what I want."

"Cadoc, don't be an idiot. You don't owe Vadik anything. You follow me," Garrett hissed at him. Cadoc's chin lifted in defiance, ignoring Garrett.

"I could force you, you know?" Lars took one more step closer to Cadoc.

"I know, sir," Cadoc replied.

"The one man here I actually want tells me no." Lars contemplated him. "Normally, I would honor your wish, but I no longer have the luxury. I need every trained fighter I can get."

Cadoc's head jerked to really take in Lars. "You are going to force me, sir?"

"War is coming. I need soldiers."

Cadoc shifted on his feet, turning his head forward, his eyes full of hate, but he gave Lars a curt nod.

"Rimmon." Lars only said his name, and the large man gathered the new recruits and herded them toward the door, emptying the tiny office of Vadik's old followers.

Rimmon had just left the room when another man entered, his sword against another man's throat. "Sir, I found this one creeping around the side. He's *human*." The dark-haired fae stated, but his lip inched up at the last word. "What do you want me to do with him?"

The prisoner held up his chin, but his hands shook at his sides.

"Carlos!" His name flew out of my mouth. His eyes went to mine, relief softening them.

"Kill him." Lars waved turning back to me.

"No." I took a step to the Unseelie King, keeping Sprig close to my chest. "Please, he only came here to protect someone. He's been under Vadik's glamour." Lars stared at me, making me feel like a piece of paper in a stove.

Lars clasped his hands together and whirled around,

stepping up to Carlos till he leered over him. "Do you feel I should allow you to live?"

The only true human in the room lifted his chin, staring back in the demon's eyes. "You can do what you want with my life. I only ask you save Maria's."

Even Lars appeared taken back. "You will die for this woman?"

"Yes." Carlos didn't even flinch.

Lars nodded, pressing his mouth, he wandered away. "Where is this Maria?"

"She was recaptured and locked in the cell below, in the hole."

"The hole?" I repeated. "Are there more cells in this building? Is Annabeth down there?"

Carlos shook his head. "No. Men came here and took her away."

I was in his face before I realized I moved. "What men?"

"I didn't know them, but I had seen the black van here before."

My throat wouldn't let me swallow. "Black van?"

"One with no windows and a government license plate," Carlos replied. "That's all I know."

Bile burned up my esophagus, and I stumbled back. I set Sprig down on the desk so I could grip it and keep my balance. My eyes drifted over to Vadik. His chin hung slack against his chest.

"Was it DMG?" I stomped up to him, but he didn't move.

"Wake up! Answer me! Did you give her to DMG?" I kicked Vadik's leg, which only bobbled his head. My foot dove into his shin over and over, but he never woke.

"Zoey." Ryker grabbed me, pulling me back. "Even unconscious he still can feed off your anger. It only gives him strength."

My nose flared. Ryker forced me to turn around. Those in the room gaped at me. Lars was the only one who looked amused.

Lars curved around to the human man. "You understand what we are?" Lars asked, his voice icy.

"Yes." Carlos nodded.

"You also understand why humans must not be aware of us?"

"Yes." Carlos's hands continued to shake, but his chin never wavered.

Lars watched Carlos intensely before a hint of a smile lifted his lips. "You humans really do surprise me sometimes." He shifted his gaze to the fae holding him. "Take him down to this Maria. If she is anything like him, they might be helpful."

The fae soldier nodded and led Carlos from the room.

"What are you going to do with him?"

The King slowly turned to me, his lids narrowing. "That is my business. Do not mistake our dealings as an invitation to know about any of my other affairs."

I really needed to learn to shut up.

"But to ease your curiosity, I will not kill him."

It shouldn't have made me feel better because he could do a lot worse to him, but it did.

"Now, for the last bit of our deal." Lars eyed both Ryker and me. "It looks as if you might need some time to recuperate."

"No." I shook my head with desperation, thinking about Annabeth. "Lives are in danger. And now I'm afraid they have someone else I care about. We need to go as soon as possible."

Lars steepled his fingers at the bridge of his nose, lowering his head in thought. He exhaled and drew up, staring at us. "You may have my men as we talked about, but by the end of the day, I will come for what is mine. No matter what."

I gulped. That didn't give us a lot of time to break into a well-guarded lab protected from fae magic, save Lexie, Croygen, and Annabeth, destroy the lab, take down Rapava, and get the stone back from Amara.

"We are grateful for your help," Ryker replied, still struggling to talk without flinching. "But we might need a few things…"

TWENTY-THREE

After our plans with Lars were confirmed, he left with his newfound followers. Garrett's men might come to regret their choice, but they would at least live a little longer.

Only a few of the King's guards went with their ruler. The rest waited outside for Ryker and me to join them. We wanted to attack DMG with the least amount of people in the building, the least defense, which was now. The night was waning, and we needed to get there before dawn.

Our biggest battle still lay ahead of us. Ryker and I already looked and felt like utter shit. Our bodies demanded sleep to heal fully, but we couldn't, which spread our energy thinner. *Great start.*

"Are you really ready for this?" Hands came down on my arms, twisting me to face the man I loved. He stood in front of me, one eye half-mast.

I laughed. "*You're* asking *me?*"

His fingers roamed over my face, taking in all the wounds with his fingers like he needed to be sure they weren't killing me.

"Are you?" I stared up into his swollen face.

"I'll be fine. I can see a little out of this eye now." He brushed the hair off my face. "I'm really asking."

"Basic answer is yes. You and Sprig are alive." I nibbled

on my lip. With all the activity I had not told him the other bad news.

"What? Just tell me."

"Amara. She set us up again."

Ryker lifted one eyebrow.

"That's not the bad thing." I inhaled. "She knew. The stone. She took it."

Ryker stared at me, his mouth opening to respond when another voice spoke instead.

"Can't ever trust a con artist." Vadik chuckled from where he sat against the wall. Ryker swiftly stepped in front of me. "Got to admire a girl like that. She even fooled me."

Ryker didn't respond, just pushed me farther back behind him.

"She has the stone now, huh? That is interesting." A spark danced in Vadik's eyes. Then he let his head fall toward us, his lids tapered. "At least *she* stays true to who she is."

"Gee, I don't have my father's respect? I am so crushed," Ryker sneered.

"Aligning with the Unseelie King." Vadik spat like he swallowed something vile. "Why am I surprised? Too weak to fight your own battles, *son*?"

The muscles along Ryker's back twisted. He stomped forward till his boots hit Vadik's shoes. Anger pumped his shoulders like a hot-air balloon. Ryker leaned over, clutching Vadik's neck. "I am *not* your son."

"You can deny it, but my blood is in your veins. *Demon* blood."

"Shut up." Ryker hit Vadik's head against the wall. "My father is the man who raised me. You were just a sperm donor. Probably by force."

"I made a deal with her father. She belonged to me. So did you, until she hid you from me. I can do what I wish with *my* property."

303

"Oh. Noooo..." I seethed. I wanted to kick the shit out of him, but Ryker blocked my path.

The "monster" as Ryker called it, now knowing it was his demon side inside, flourished, pressing under his skin, his eyes glowing with hate.

"There he is. My son. The demon." Vadik grinned sardonically. "Come on, son, kill me. Go ahead."

The tension in the room pulled like a strained violin string. I was ready for it to break, for Ryker's fist to pummel into Vadik till he became puree on the ground. Ryker leaned farther over, his face inches from him. "It would be a favor to the world of I killed you. Death would be easy compared to what you will experience living in the Light."

Vadik blinked; the smugness fell from his face.

"I won't be that kind to you, *Father*." Ryker patted his cheek, then stood up, learning over the man. "I. Will. *Not*. Kill. You." The moment Ryker said, it Vadik howled gut-wrenching shrieks. The hair on my arms stood up. Vadik struggled to get to his feet, his arms clawing at his body, as though trying to get rid of an invisible force.

Ryker retreated, showing Vadik he would not be there to help him.

The cry tearing from Vadik's mouth filled me with anxiety. "What is happening to him?"

"Because I declared I'd let him live, the King's curse is now taking over. He's banned from Earth, so until he finds a door and gets to the Light side of the Otherworld, he will feel like his insides are being shredded. Which is like the demon equivalent of tearing out pumpkin guts."

I glanced at Ryker. He shrugged. "Or so I've heard."

"You will..." Vadik huffed, spit flying out of his mouth. "Regret this."

"Probably. I wanted to be the one to kill you. But

knowing you are still alive, slowly and painfully being tortured to death will help me sleep better at night." Ryker's expression and voice were stone cold and hard. "For what you did to my mother, to me... you deserve worse. I do not have time or energy for your pathetic self. You are nothing to me."

Vadik frantically scratched at his neck and face, his eyes growing black. He looked like he was debating. He rocked back and forth on his feet as if he might come bowling for Ryker.

Ryker stared back. "Do it. I dare you." His voice was low and harsh.

Vadik's neck veins bulged. A piercing growl tore from him and then he bolted from the room. The door to the building slammed behind him, bringing silence.

Air I held in my lungs skated out in a quiet exhale. Ryker and I stood in a sort of daze. So much had happened in the last hour my brain struggled to keep up.

I ran my hand down Ryker's bicep. "You okay?"

"Yeah. I am." He pivoted to me, grabbing my hips. "I want to forget him."

I nodded.

"Now about the stone..."

"Shit." I blurted out. "Lars. What do we do about him? He will come for it later, and I don't have it." I would possibly die before he even could claim it, which was better than what he would do to me when he found me empty handed. "Damn it! Why can't we get a break?"

"Hey." Ryker grabbed my flaying arms. "Calm down. Amara doesn't have anything significant."

"The stone is not significant?" My eyes darted to his. "One of the most powerful weapons in the world is in the hands of a lying, selfish bitch. That's not important?"

Ryker had the audacity to grin at me.

"Why do you find this funny? She has the stone. Lars will kill us," I screeched.

"Breathe, Zoey." His unruffled demeanor only evoked another tirade from me. "Stop," he said more firmly. "Haven't you notice you've been even more cranky, not feeling well, and irritable the last couple of days."

"*If* you say anything about me 'being on the rag,' I. Will. Kill. You."

He smirked, shaking his head.

"The morning after our all-nighter in the garage, when you weren't looking, I switched out the stone with a fake."

"Wh-what?" My jaw dropped, anger igniting my brain. "Switched? Where is the real stone? What does Amara have?"

"Amara has a fake." He rubbed my arms. "It's been close so you wouldn't feel the withdrawal too badly."

Now I understood the reasons why I didn't feel any magic from it when she stole it. Why it had been so quiet for the last couple of days. Why I had felt off and edgy.

"Wait. Is that the reason Lars didn't sense it on me? Because I didn't have it?"

Ryker nodded.

"Where is it? If you have it, how did he not sense it on you then?"

"I don't have it either."

"Where is it, Ryker?" A surge of possessive rage fueled me. "It's mine." *I need it. I need it.* My hands opened and closed desperate to have it back. "Tell me."

Ryker frowned, folding his arms, his jaw rolling. I could sense his apprehension, his displeasure at my words, but knowing the stone was close fostered a frantic feeling in me. Where could he have hidden it if not on himself?

A snore broke the silence, and I turned to the sprite on

the table—a monkey wearing a backpack. Neither had been in the warehouse with the King.

"Oh. My. God." I turned and walked over to Sprig.

"Leave it, Zoey. It's in safest place it can be." Ryker took a step up to Sprig, blocking my hand. "It doesn't seem to affect him like it does you."

Zoey, I'm here. Please take me back. Claim me. I swore I heard the stone calling me, driving my hand to reach again.

Ryker grabbed my hands, turning me to him. "Amara figured out the stone's location before I even went to DMG. It was only a matter of time before she would try to take it from you." He let my arms drop. "When I realized he could hold it without it influencing him, I knew he was the ideal carrier. He's always near you, which I hoped would help keep you from figuring things out."

"The deal he spoke of..." Comprehension settled over me. So many confusing details suddenly made sense.

Ryker rolled his one working eye back, turning to face Sprig. "That furball is set for life. He drives a hard bargain."

"Yeah, because you're so tough when it comes to him."

Ryker shrugged, staring at the curled-up monkey. "I knew Amara would betray us again. Did I see Arlo coming? No. I regret she caused that. But I used her for what she could give us as well. She will find out fast she has a phony and realize with a gut-wrenching sickness she played her last hand and came up short. We won. And no one will be chasing her. *Ever.*"

I should have felt relived. Happy. But a lash of anger and betrayal strangled me. "It belonged to me. You had no right to take it."

"I have *every* right." A nerve along his jaw twitched. "You would never have given it to me freely. That became clear the night at the garage." He eyed me sternly. "I thought it was best. With your attachment to it, knowing you would never let it go, I had to steal it. I wasn't going to let it hurt you anymore. It was slowly killing you. So be mad at me. Fine. I'd rather you pissed than dead."

He was right. I wouldn't have. Even now my hands were shaking to take it back, to know it remained in my care. I tucked my arms around each other, fighting the feeling it physically pulled me toward. I understood his reasoning, but it was still hard not to feel the duplicity. Though I would have done the same.

"Why do you think the King didn't feel it this time?"

"I don't know. There was so much magic in the room already, and I also think Sprig neutralizes it. That's probably how it stayed hidden for so many centuries. Maybe lower fae diffuse the power coming off it."

His theory made sense. Even I didn't know it was gone, but I did now. I wanted it back. I wanted to see it. To touch it.

Take it, Zoey. You need it and it needs you.

Ryker swung to me. "We ought to get going."

"Yeah." I pulled air in through my nose, rolling my shoulders back. "I'm ready."

Ryker tucked a stand of loose hair behind my ear.

A snort came from the desk. "No, Mother, I want to wear the *pink* bloomers with lace," Sprig whined, then his head bolted off the table, and his bright eyes stared at Ryker and me. "What? Huh? What were you saying?" He rubbed the lump on his head. "It was something about dinner, right? Or dessert? Both sound awesome to me." He climbed to his feet.

"Sprig!" I gathered him up, nuzzling my face to his. Utter joy coursed through my body at hearing his voice, seeing his sweet animated face. "I am so happy you're okay. I love you, buddy."

"Are you okay, *Bhean*? Your eyes are leaking all over

me." He shifted under my smothering grip. "My head and neck hurt. Did I drink too much mead again? I have a sensitive system."

"No." I softly rubbed the mending wound. "I wish it was the reason."

He picked up his chin and looked over the room. "Wh-what in the... dingle berry, nut-crusted, toad-stooled biscuits happened?" Sprig exclaimed, his mouth hanging open.

"It's over. That's all you need to know."

"Did we win this time?"

"We actually did."

"Yay. Victory dinner then? I'm hungry. Aren't you guys? It's been days, right?"

Ryker snorted, rubbing Sprig on his back. "Food is going to have to wait. Right now we have two girls and a pirate to save."

"How about everything you said minus the pirate and add dinner along the way, then I say we have a plan." Sprig crawled up onto my shoulder.

Ryker tilted his head, looking like he was pondering the thought.

"Don't even think about it." I elbowed Ryker in the stomach.

"What?" Ryker's eyes widened. "The sprite has some good ideas there. Be a shame to disregard them so quickly." A grin tugged at my mouth. Ryker was all talk. There would be no way he'd leave Croygen there.

I turned around to face the Wanderer, my smile fading. "This is going to be extremely dangerous. Especially since none of our powers will even remotely work once we are down in that hellhole."

"Then we rely on our brains and brawn." Ryker grinned.

"We're so screwed." Sprig tossed up his arms in defeat.

"Wow, for being such a heroic *warrior*, you're a pansy," Ryker taunted.

"Did I say warrior?" Sprig pointed at himself. "I meant guardian."

"Guardian of what?"

"Did I say guardian? I meant caretaker."

"Caretaker?"

"Part-time…" He twisted his hands together, his gaze rolling to the ceiling. "Okay, I was fired!"

"Fired because?" I asked.

"Because I kept getting caught eating the town's supply of honey for the winter months."

"You were a monitor of the honey supply?" Ryker hands drifted down to my waist, pulling me closer to him. "Which idiot decided that?"

"Uh… I did."

"Yep, we're screwed." I stared up into Ryker's eyes with a smile.

"So screwed," he muttered as he brushed his lips over mine.

In an hour we all might be dead. I wanted to enjoy these tiny moments. They might be all I had left.

TWENTY-FOUR

Ryker sent me out first. He stayed behind to be certain Maxen stayed dead. I figured Ryker would set fire to the place, clearing the building of any trace of the fae who ran it or what had been happening there. In an old building like this, an electrical fire would not seem strange. Sure enough, when he came out, smoke billowed after him.

"Is everyone out?" I asked. The girls, Maria, and Carlos were gone when we exited the building.

"I made sure," Ryker confirmed, strolling up to my side.

Goran gave him a nod of thanks. "I was about to send my men in to do that." He handed us weapons from a pile on the ground, a gun and several knives we could tuck away. All the things we requested from Lars.

"Wanted to be sure one person never got the chance to escape," Ryker replied.

I lifted an eyebrow.

"I needed kindling to start a blaze," he replied to my unvoiced question. "Maxen worked well."

I flicked my chin and turned to face the men milling around the lane. Sprig held on tightly against my neck. "All right." I cleared my throat, pushing authority into my voice. "I know you are here on the request of your King, but I still appreciate each one of you for fighting next to me.

311

"What we are doing is going to be difficult. Yes, these people we'll face are human, but *do not* underestimate them. DMG is well secured, and the people who protect it are highly trained. Many are top elite in the military, and they know the terrain. Each one will have guns that can kill fae. And they will not hesitate." All of Lars's men were pinned on my every word. Not one condescending expression, like *why is this little girl speaking to us like she is the authority?*

They all faced me like soldiers. My soldiers. "If it was only them, it would make our job easier, but a lot of innocent civilians are in the building."

"Innocent?" a man scoffed from deep in the group.

"As much as you think all the humans working there are evil, some don't realize how far Rapava has gone. They think they are helping their country. They were given orders, and they are doing their duty." I knew many of the innocent probably would not get out. The line between those who knew the evil truth and those who didn't would be undistinguishable, especially to these bloodthirsty fae.

A few lives to save the masses. I heard Rapava's voice taunt me in my head. I pushed away the sick feeling. No. This wasn't the same.

"Focus on the ones who want to fight back. Once we get in, most of the scientists will try to flee. Let them. The ones trained for combat, the hunters, even the seers will not run. They have been waiting for this fight for a long time. *They* are your focus." I rubbed my hands together. The weight in my voice echoed off the buildings around us. Fire crackled behind me. "This place is far more guarded than I was ever led to believe. There are not a lot of options to enter. The tunnel we have to use to enter will only give them more time to prepare for us. They are always watching. We have to attack immediately and fast. Once we have broken through the door, some of you will stay above ground and some will follow me down. Remember, the Collectors have caught *many* of your kind, so don't let your guard down for a second.

"Okay. Let's do this." I clapped my palms and turned down the lane. "Follow me."

They snapped to at my voice, turned with me, and quietly shadowed me without question. *Hell.* I had not expected them to take an order from me so easily.

"We're going through a drive-thru on the way, right?" Sprig said into my ear. "Like a last meal kind of thing?"

I just patted his head.

Lars's men stayed close, following me every step of the way down into the pits of hell, from where none of us might crawl out again.

"That's the door?" Goran whispered next to me, nodding at the pair of taupe doors blending in with the structure. The nondescript doors on the side of a building down an alley were so unnoticeable your eye would naturally move on.

"The hidden camera is there." Ryker pointed behind an advertisement, where it blended in with the wall. "They're going to know we're here the moment we enter the alley."

"That's why we need to strike fast." I gripped the round object in my hand.

"You want me to do it?" He tapped the device in my hand.

"No. I need to do it." My fingers clutched the detonator. The back side was already gummed up, ready to stick to a surface. Lars had provided us with grenades, smoke bombs, and a few low- and medium-grade detonators.

Ryker and Goran crouched next to me in the bushes, the rest of Goran's men close behind.

Sprig had refused to stay back and remained perched on my shoulder. "This is my battle too, *Bhean*, after the things he's done to me and my kind, I am not sitting out of this fight. Plus, you might need these magic fingers, remember?" As much as I wanted to refuse him, keep him in bubble wrap far away from here, he had every right to be involved, and I would not take that away from him.

The door was bolted and made of thick steel. After we got through it, we still had a short tunnel then layers of doors and levels to move through to get to the center of DMG. The only staircase I knew to get down was from the first two levels. For safety there had to be more stairways hidden, but I never asked and no one showed me. I hadn't ventured farther than those few levels when I worked as a Collector.

"Once we are in, I will start dispersing my men so each level will be covered," Goran stated.

"But Rapava's mine," I said to both men.

"I will try to honor your wish, but I will not guarantee it. I have been told to shoot him on sight." Goran tipped back on his heels.

"I understand." I nodded.

"And I can't say if I see him I won't cut off his head," Ryker huffed.

"All right. Are you ready?" Goran asked.

I took in a deep breath. "Yes." I stood and slid my finger softly over the button. One little slip or push and I would be blown into fragments.

"Sprig, stay with Ryker," I ordered.

With one look at my face, he didn't make a peep. He leaped over to the Viking and wrapped his tail around himself. I moved out from the brush, leaving our hiding place. Ryker grabbed my free hand as I moved around him. I met his gaze, his white eyes igniting the dark, staring intently into mine.

"We're going to get through this." He squeezed my fingers. "Together."

I tried to smile, but it felt more like a grimace. I released his grip and turned back to the doors. I couldn't think of anything but my target. It was finally here. The day. The moment. The fight I had talked about for so long.

My heart thumped in my chest as I moved against the brick wall, slinking down the alley. The moonless night left no shadow behind me. I shut off my brain. I didn't want to think about what lay ahead. How many of us might die? Would I find Lexie and Croygen alive? Would I be able to do what I set out to?

The only thing I knew was in a few hours, when the sun kissed the earth, this would probably be over.

The doors were in sight. I only had about five seconds to get away once I stabbed the button and only thirty to return and get through the doors before Rapava's men responded. I sucked cool night air deep into my lungs, my hands shaking, sensing the hidden camera raking over me. Did they already know we were here?

I slammed the bomb between the two doors, pressing the red key. Then I swiveled and ran, pumping my arms hard, though I felt like I was moving through quicksand.

Five.

Four. *Move faster!*

Three.

Two. *Shit! I'm not even to the alley entrance yet.*

One.

BOOM!

My body flew into the air. Fire and heat curled behind me, licking my back. My arms windmilled through empty space and then I hit the ground, rolling over the rough concrete with painful thuds. When I stopped rolling, I looked back at the doors, which had exploded, were open and smoke wafted out.

"Now!" I heard Goran yell, and in a blink, a horde of men headed for the doors.

"Zoey?" Ryker raced up to me, helping me to my feet. "You all right?"

"Yes." I regained my footing though my head swam.

"Damn, *Bhean*. You might need to borrow my cape. You went flying!" Sprig leaped back onto my shoulder, gripping strands of my hair.

"You do need to work on the landing." Ryker winked then grabbed the back of my head. His mouth crashed into me, his lips taking mine. Then he broke away, leaving me breathless. "Let's do this."

I nodded, feeling dizzy. I grabbed the gun out of the back of my pants and both of us ran for the entry.

Goran led his men, moving them through the fae detectors. We didn't care about the blazing alarms ringing through the passage; we didn't really care to keep our arrival a secret once we were in.

I led them to the stairs that brought us to the first level. Boots thumped behind me, mimicking my heart, as we went down. A handful stayed in the passage watching it and the elevators, ready for those who would flood out of the rat trap.

I swung the door open, my gun pointed. We entered an empty hallway. At this time of night, I hoped some of the nurses and lab technicians were home in bed. But I knew Rapava was here. He was always here.

We moved out slowly, inching down the corridor. Corner after corner we were met with nothing. The silence felt unnerving. My skin crawled with intuition.

Even when I had been here at three or four in the morning, this place was still more active than this. Twenty-four hours a day DMG was filled with employees. Rapava had a revolving staff that worked days, nights, and graveyard shifts.

There were fewer workers at night, but this seemed epically silent. That's when it hit me. I had no idea how he knew, but he did. Rapava knew we were coming.

This was a trap.

I had just opened my mouth to tell Goran, when a tin object rolled down the hallway toward us, sizzling with smoke. Then it detonated. My back hit the floor, Sprig tumbling off my shoulder with a cry. Haze consumed the air, obscuring our vision.

"Sprig?" I bolted back up to my feet. Blurry figures and loud voices were coming straight for us. A lot of them. A bullet whizzed past my head. I dove back to the ground, keeping my gun pointed toward the hazy outlines approaching.

"Zoey." Ryker's voice came from behind me. "I have Sprig."

Relief washed over me, my lungs hacking up the smoke, my eyes watering.

"Come on." He grabbed my ankle and tugged it toward him. He and I had to keep going lower. Rapava would hide like a coward in the belly of his creation. Take out the kingpin and his followers would follow.

I wiggled back, the vapor slowly clearing, giving us less cover in which to hide.

"Go! Go!" Goran waved us off and moved to the place I vacated. We shifted back until it was safe to stand.

Ryker held Sprig, who was out cold, as we ran for the elevator on the other side of the hallway. Before we dealt with

Rapava, we had to find my sister and Croygen. We stepped in, and I shoved in the key card Kate had given me. *Please still work.* The elevator dinged and the doors closed.

"We split up. The floor is huge. They could be anywhere." I bobbed up and down nervously as the elevator lowered us into the earth.

"We need to release all the other fae he has down there." Ryker placed Sprig's sleeping body in my hoodie pocket.

"I know. Not easy. Each room is locked, and the Plexiglas in each one will not break."

He rubbed his face with aggravation.

"We take down Rapava, then we can go back and let them all free."

He nodded, pulling out his gun as the elevator came to a stop. Usually fae didn't fight with guns, preferring swords or something that takes skill. But we weren't playing with fae. Humans would shoot to kill us. We needed to shoot first.

The doors slid open, and we both stepped out cautiously.

The smells, the buzz of the lights overhead, the sound of my boots squeaking over the floor, it all inflicted me with memories, with trauma. My skin prickled; my lungs clenched.

"You take that hallway. I'll take this one." I pointed my gun down each path.

"I really don't want to separate," Ryker growled.

"We have to. And we have to move fast."

Ryker gave me a curt nod then proceeded down his designated passage. I swung down the opposite one. The hall I chose was mostly vacant. I didn't know if I should be relieved or sickened. Had it been full at one time? If it had been, I understood all too well those people, or fae, weren't alive anymore.

"Sweet honey and butternut biscuits, stop touching my

ass." After a few beats Sprig's head peeked out of my pocket. I put my finger to my lips. He nodded, then slipped out, crawling up to my shoulder, his backpack hitting my cheek as he settled.

"What are we doing?" He leaned into my ear.

"Looking for Lexie and Croygen."

"*Except* the pirate, right?"

I ignored him and continued to move past each window. There were a few fae, most sleeping. When I reached the end room, it appeared to be slightly bigger and set up more like a testing room. The eggshell-colored room was embellished with lab equipment. A robot machine was positioned above the lone hospital bed, decked with needles, blades, and a Taser.

A shirtless man was pulled into an eagle pose with all his limbs chained to the bed. I moved to the glass, feeling my stomach spin like a washer. Dark hair, slender but muscular frame, a tattoo on his shoulder and chest.

My hand slapped over my mouth. "Croygen." I reached for the door, shaking the bolted lock furiously. "No!"

Sprig sighed and moved down my arm. "Don't say I never did anything for the pirate." Sprig stuck his tongue out as he worked on the lock.

"Can you do it? Is it coated?"

"This one doesn't have goblin metal. Just an ordinary lock."

Finally one thing went in our favor.

"Hold on." His tongue stuck out farther. "Like honey." The lock inside snapped, the door sliding open.

"I love you, monkey-man."

"I know." Sprig leaped back on my neck as I slunk inside the room, shutting it behind me.

"Croygen?" My feet moved quickly toward the form on

319

the bed. Blood leaked out of open wounds, bruises covered his face and body. Like Ryker they left him shirtless, using his torso as a battering ram. "Oh my god." My hand reached for his face.

"Is he alive?" Sprig scuttled down to Croygen's chest. "Hey, butt-bandit." Sprig jammed his finger into Croygen's ribs. "You dead?"

A soft groan came from Croygen's lips, his lids fluttering.

"Croygen!" I gripped his face tighter, turning it toward me. "Wake up."

His mouth moved, but I couldn't understand what he said.

"What?" I leaned down closer to his ear.

"I liked it better when I woke up to your face in my crotch," he whispered, his voice weak and gravelly. "And if you wanted me chained up, all you had to do was ask."

Relief flooded my eyes, forcing me to blink. "Well, I'm sure I can find a whip or two in here as well." I tried to joke, but my throat caught on held-back tears.

"You know how I like it." His eyes stayed closed, but his mouth formed a smile. "But let's leave the monkey out of it this time."

"Only you." I snickered, straightening. "Tortured and barely coherent, but you still think with your dick."

"That's where his brain is." Sprig held up his fingers. "A very, very tiny one."

"Have you ever had barbequed monkey? I have... tasty." Croygen's eyes opened, his gaze dull and unfocused. I didn't want to think of how much they tortured and tested him. He groaned as he tried to sit up, but the handcuffs dropped him back to the bed.

"We have to get you out of here." I looked over at Sprig.

"Sprig, can you get his handcuffs off? They contain goblin metal."

We were back where everything had been coated with goblin metal, but Sprig was so low on the magic list, it only seemed to affect him when he got straight injections of the malicious metal. It was worth a shot.

"I can try... but do you really want to, *Bhean*? I mean, really take your time and think about this. If we let him go, aren't we only hurting society instead of helping it?"

"Sprig?" I lifted one eyebrow.

"I think you need to take more time."

"Now, Sprig!" My patience was thin. We didn't have much time.

"All right. But this is on you!" He moved to one of Croygen's cuffed wrists.

Croygen snarled at Sprig, but he turned back to me. "Have you found Lexie? Is she all right? Are you all right?" His piercing dark eyes roved over me.

"No. We haven't found her. Ryker went down another corridor looking." I bit my lip. "We'll find them."

"Them?"

My heart sank. I didn't want to believe Annabeth was here, but my gut told me so. If she was, I would find her. "When did you last see Lexie?"

"Yesterday." The corner of his eyes flinched, his voice going soft. "It's not going to be long."

I nodded. "I know." We had so much to tell Croygen later, but right now all I could say was, "Thank you, Croygen, for going with her. What you did... the sacrifice you made... I don't know how I can ever repay you."

"Hey." His arm strained against the bracelet Sprig was working on, trying to touch me.

Snap. The restraint broke open, freeing his right arm.

321

"Good job, rodent." Croygen shook out his hand, nodding at the little sprite with admiration. "Impressed."

"Funny, that's not what the ladies say about you." Sprig squeaked as Croygen swiped for him. With a chattering giggle he ran down to one of Croygen's manacled ankles.

"Little shit." He rolled his eyes, but I could see the caring in his slightly pained smile.

We really were a twisted family.

"So, after you free me, what's your plan, love?" He leaned back on his pillow, his eyelids drifting closed for a moment. "I was a gentleman and escorted your dear little sister here. I'm done... thinking about taking a nap now."

Croygen was good at making me smile, even in the worst conditions. He had been the one who sat next to me, holding me, when I had to mutilate Ryker. He gave me strength. In that moment to have Croygen here meant the world to me. It had bonded us for life. No matter what front he put up, he would be part of my family. He had pulled me out of darkest depths and stood me back on my feet again.

"Taking a nap without pillaging and seducing all the women in town?" I lifted my brow. "Losing your touch, but not really surprised after that humiliating loss with the nurse. I think you should hang it up now."

"Not. Funny." One lid opened.

I was about to respond when I heard metal releasing near the end of the bed.

"Supersprite!" Sprig held up his arms in victory and hopped over to his other leg, working on the cuff. "You know..."

"All the honey you want. Once we are out of here," I responded, already knowing where his trail of thought was going.

"All the honey?" His eyes widened, and he stopped what he was doing, staring at me.

"Well, until you pass out."

"I can work with that."

A loud echo tore down the hallway, like a door slamming, making all of us jump.

"Hey, gerbil. Get back to work." Croygen nodded at his leg. "Or no honey packets."

"How ab—" Sprig opened his mouth.

"Or Izel's pancakes, churros, mango chips, granola bars, honey sticks, or nuts... of any kind."

Sprig gasped.

"Not messing around, hamster. Get me out of these now."

"No wondered no one likes you. No honey nuts or sticks," Sprig muttered, turning his focus back to the cuff.

Croygen tore his gaze from Sprig back up to me, cupping one hand around my cheek. I stared at him.

"Responding to your earlier statement. You never have to repay me. You know there is nothing I won't do for you. Or for Lexie."

I tried to swallow over the tightness in my throat. Tears flooded my eyes. "Why?" My head shook, almost afraid to hear his answer.

He tipped his head.

"Croygen... I..."

"You're afraid I'm going to say I'm in love with you, aren't you?"

My mouth opened and shut.

"Sorry, I love myself too much to ever really love anyone else. But I have to admit, you are the closest I've probably been." His fingers brushed lightly over my lips. "Deep down, I knew I never really loved Amara. It was more like an obsession." His eyes drifted back up to mine and once again I forgot to breathe. "Love is fickle with me anyway.

With you it's more... you are more..." He cleared his throat. "You've become..."

"Family," I filled in.

His lips lifted slightly, his gaze going back to my arm. "Like a damn tree with roots."

"I feel the same," I said. "And you know what?"

He peeked at me.

"You are my family, Croygen. You are a part of me, of my life. And certainly part of Lexie's. We've been through too much to be anything less." He looked away. "I'm going to be around a lot longer now—well, if we live through this— but you will never be able to get rid of me. If I have a home, you have a home. You will always belong with me, with us."

He stared at the ground, then shook his head and chuckled. "Damn, that was some sentimental crap."

"Completely. And unfortunately entirely true."

He laughed and turned to me, cupping my head he pulled my face down to his. He tipped my forehead toward him and kissed it. "Man, you are a pain in the ass."

"I was born this way."

Another clink of metal sounded through the room, and Croygen looked to his legs. "Damn, that feels good." He kicked out his feet.

"Sprig," I squeaked, rubbing his soft head as he moved up to the last cuff on Croygen's left wrist. "You are amazing."

"Why don't we trade this ass bandit in for *Leanbh*?"

"Shut up, banana lover."

"Wha-at? How dare you say such a thing?" Sprig sat back on his heels. "Say you're sorry or I will leave you here, gnawing on your arm like every poor girl who got drunk and woke up next to you."

I lifted one eyebrow at Croygen.

His eyes widened like I was insane. "No. No way."

I lifted both my eyebrows.

He huffed, looking away. "Sorry, fuzzbutt," he mumbled like a pouting schoolboy.

"I need to get paid for this shit," I told the ceiling.

Ping. The last cuff broke away from Croygen's hand. He let out a yip and sat up, rubbing Sprig's head as he tried to stand up. He fell back on the bed, making it skid a few feet.

"Croygen, you need to take it easy." I reached for him.

"We don't have time." He threw his arm around my shoulder, letting me help him stand. He was right, we didn't. Every minute here we risked another moment in which someone I loved could be hurt. Sprig sprang for Croygen's free shoulder, since mine were being used as a crutch.

Neither one said a word. Awww... all my boys secretly loved each other.

"Okay, we need to find Ryker." I walked us slowly for the door.

"Is Amara with him?" Croygen's head turned to me.

"Uh... no..."

"That purple wicked witch turned them over to Vadik," Sprig exclaimed, throwing his arms out. "I swear if I ever see that pop tart, I'm going to poop in her hair and shoes."

Croygen's lips thinned at my nod that, yes, once again she had betrayed us.

"She better be long gone, or I will do worse to her." He gritted his teeth, every step painful for him, but his weight became lighter on my arm.

Sprig nodded at Croygen's statement. At least they had hating Amara in common.

"Okay, let's go get that bastard." Croygen sucked air through his teeth and stood up fully on his own.

"Rapava?"

"No. Your man."

325

TWENTY-FIVE

"Do I get a weapon?" Croygen grunted, his torso swathed in deep green, yellow, blue, and black bruises. His skin was punctured from so many needles he looked like a voodoo doll.

I struggled to keep him upright and also hold my gun ready to fire as we snuck down the hallway. The place felt like a graveyard on this level. It made me extremely nervous.

"I think you having a weapon would be detrimental to yourself."

"Please." He rolled his eyes.

"Then it would be bad for me." I kept my voice low. We moved back down the passage toward where Ryker and I parted ways.

"You act like this is the first time I've been drugged and woken up chained to a bed." His black hair hung in greasy pieces, brushing his shoulder. He looked like he hadn't seen a shower in a while.

"Dare I ask what they did to you?"

"No," he stated. His jaw twitched, his gaze went distant, and a chilly mood descended on him. Then he jerked his head, a smile curling his mouth, pushing away the darkness. "Nothing a couple bottles of Jack and a razor blade can't handle."

"Croygen," I growled.

"Just kidding. Not about the Jack, but just throw in a couple hookers instead."

"Only way you can get them. Purchased." Sprig snorted.

"At least they're real." Croygen glared at Sprig. "Maybe for your birthday I can take you to the petting zoo, full of real-life goats."

"Okay. Shut up." I cringed.

"Pam is real!" Sprig reached around for his backpack, patting the top of her head. "Don't listen to the assbuckler, baby."

I held my finger up to my lips giving them both a warning look and continued down the hall. Croygen took more of his weight the longer we moved. When we reached the intersection, I propped him against the wall and peered around the corner. The hall stood empty.

Damn it. Where did he go? And where was everyone else?

We ventured down the new corridor moving past rooms, but none of them had display windows.

Then the sounds of talking, deep, anxious voices along with the vibrations of boots against the floor caught my ear. Fear gripped my chest, the voices nearing us, about to curve around the corner. I wildly looked around. There was nothing but closed, locked doors.

"Sprig?" I nodded toward the handle, but I knew we didn't have enough time.

"How about that weapon now?" Croygen said. We had no choice but to stand our ground. To fight our way out. I tugged one of my extra knives set against my hip and handed it over to him.

"How many?"

"More than us."

"That's what I figured." Croygen gripped the blade, trying to steady himself on his feet.

I lifted the gun, turning the way of the commotion. Nerves bounced with electric static inside my muscles.

A door opened behind me, and a hand slid over my mouth. I yelped as my body sailed back in the room. Terror turned me into a stiff block.

Croygen jumped on my captor. Sprig made a squeaky sound, grabbing on to Croygen's neck.

"Get in here now," Ryker hissed behind me.

"Fuck, man." Croygen bolted into the room, shutting the door. "I think I just pissed myself."

"Definitely not the first time." Ryker dropped his hand from my mouth, but his arm stayed around me. I was thankful because I felt a little woozy from the shot of adrenaline to my heart.

"Or the last," Croygen mumbled, voices speaking over him.

"This way." A man's familiar voice echoed down the hall. "I heard something." Peter.

"*Bhean*, look." Sprig pointed.

My head swung to the far bed in the corner. My heart leaped from my chest.

"Lexie!" I cried, moving toward her.

Ryker's hand slipped over my mouth, pulling me the opposite way of my sister. Instinct caused my arms to fight his hold, to reach her no matter what.

"Zoey, stop," he said into my ear. "She's alive. You need to stay that way too."

"Check on the girl," Peter ordered. "They'll be searching for her."

There was nowhere to hide in the room. The moment the door opened, we would be discovered.

"Sprig." I pointed to Lexie. "Go!" The thought of him getting hurt again... No. I couldn't take it. The best place was for him to curl up and hide with Lexie.

He sprang from Croygen's shoulder and scrambled to Lexie, just making it when the outside door jingled.

Ryker released me and pulled out his knife. Croygen copied his action. I bounced on the balls of my feet, watching the door swing open, my heart thumping in my chest.

The blond, six-foot, ex-special-ops figure stepped into the room. Matt, his seer partner, and two military men rushed in the room behind him. For the briefest moment they stopped, their eyes landing on us.

Then everything ignited with a tornado of movement and voices yelling. A blur of bodies ran for each other. Ryker slammed into Peter, both men sliding across the room into the wall. The two military men went for Croygen while Matt lunged for me.

Seer vs. seer.

Packing or not, he should have known better. I always won with him. I swung for his face. He threw his arm up, blocking my strike. Peter had trained him by the book. Daniel liked the rules, but he had not been afraid to show me how you really won a fight. Plus, my experience in the ring taught me how dirty I could play.

In the background I could feel people wrestling around me, but I kept locked on Matt. *Don't lose focus on the fight in front of you.* Daniel's lessons weren't always fun, but they came with a reason, and he made sure I learned them.

Matt reached out to grab my arm. I knew the move, he wanted to pull me in, get a hold of me. I twisted the opposite way. Pain erupted from my eye as Matt's fist collided, his knuckles plowing deep. I tipped back, already feeling the pounding of blood circling it.

His arm went to his side grabbing for his gun. *Shit.*

My knees hit the floor with bruising force, my fist knocking into Matt's kidney, bending him over. I sprang up, my elbow ramming down on his gun arm, breaking his hold. The gun listed forward, clattering to the floor. He staggered to the side as I struck the soft part of his throat. He grabbed the injured area, bowing over, struggling to breathe. My knee slammed into his face, the cartilage in his nose shattered, and he screamed in pain. Somewhere down the road I might feel bad for beating Matt to a pulp, but my motto was kill or be killed. And there was no room for sympathy. It only caused hesitation. Hesitation got you killed.

The final two blows dropped him to his knees before my boot cracked into his temple, knocking him out. He would need hospital care, but he would live. Reaching down I snatched Matt's gun from the floor and whirled around to take in the scene.

The room was a jumbled mess of men. One of the soldiers struggled to get his gun out of Croygen's grip, the barrel facing the pirate. Croygen remained nowhere near his full strength, sweat shining off his features as he nudged the man back. The gun went off, echoing in the small room like a bomb. Blood soaked into Croygen's sleeve.

"No!" I screamed, rising from the ground, my finger wrapping around the weapon. Fae bullets killed.

Peter flew across the room, stopping my progression, his head bouncing off the floor. Ryker roared and turned for Croygen.

It was like watching a scene on fast forward. Peter shoved himself up, grabbed his gun, and directed it straight at the Wanderer's back. The click of the trigger resonated in my ears as his finger clenched down.

My brain shut off, only reacting on primal instinct.

330

Killed or be killed. My hand strangled Matt's gun. A raw wail thundered from me as my finger yanked back.

BOOM. BOOM. BOOM.

Bullets zinged in the room, fear gripping my heart, not knowing if it came from my gun or Peter's.

My ears rang. My arms were frozen in dread.

Peter fell back against the wall, his body slumping to the side, smearing blood across the eggshell paint.

My eyes darted back to Ryker. His gaze caught mine, full of astonishment and appreciation. Relief flooded me. He was all right. He turned back around, grabbing one of the guards by the throat, and twisted the man's neck. Between Ryker and Croygen, they quickly dispatched the last guy.

I struggled to move, my gaze back on the form before me. I just killed Peter, Daniel's old friend and one of my fellow hunters. We didn't always get along, but I had not felt one ounce of hesitation to kill him. I stared at his body, watching blood leak from the holes in his neck and side. A crimson-drenched bubble formed out of the gap, and he gave one final shudder.

Holy shit. He was still alive.

My eyes lifted from the puncture up to his face. His lids were narrowed on me. He swallowed, causing more blood to gush from the wound.

"Yo-you chose them." He briefly closed his eyes before trying again. "One. Of. Them... dis-gusting. F-filthy whore."

Boom.

A gunshot tore through the room, and I cried out as Peter's brain burst onto the floor.

My heart and breath slammed in my chest, and I stared at Ryker. He stood with a gun in one hand, glaring down at the body. "Fucking asshole."

"Remind me not to call you a filthy whore," Croygen quipped, motioning to me.

"Croygen." I shoved the pistol in my pants and went over to him, reaching for his arm. "Are you okay?"

"Yeah, it just grazed me." He looked down at it. "Hurts like a bitch though. And it's gonna make me feel like utter crap soon. Like I don't already."

I inspected his wound, making sure it wasn't deadly before letting myself exhale.

"We need to get Lexie and get out of here." Ryker bent over, claiming the weapons on the ground. "But I'm not leaving this time till I find my axe. Hate these things." He shoved a gun into the back of his pants.

"Especially if you shoot your own ass off." Croygen took the other one Ryker offered and turned for Lexie, stumbling to the side.

"Whoa." I grabbed him. He had been unsteady before, but now he had enough goblin metal pumping in his system to make him sick.

"I'm fine."

"No, you aren't." I steadied him. "All I need you to do is hang in long enough to get yourself and Lexie out of here."

"You're not coming?"

"No. I need to end this." I glanced over at my sister. A tip of a fuzzy tail could be seen from underneath her curly hair. Knowing Sprig, he was probably fast asleep. "You know that."

"Yeah, but I thought…" Croygen trailed off.

"That I would forget or let it go?" I jerked my head back and forth. "No, I'm not leaving till I face Rapava."

"Luke, I am your father," Croygen spouted.

It was sickly appropriate. Rapava was my creator. He and Dr. Holt had given me life. They were my mother and father. "No saving him from the dark side. He can't be left alive. That's why I need you to take Lexie and run. Please,

Croygen. I know how much you have already done for her, for me, but I beg you to do this last thing. Then you can get far away from this mess. From us."

"Zoey, I told you. I'm not going anywhere. And you never have to ask me to protect her." He nodded to Lexie. My arms flew around him, and he hissed as I hit his bullet wound.

"Sorry." I stepped back.

"Just warning you. You are going to have to get her out of here through the elevator where death, mayhem, and destruction are at every turn." Ryker smacked his good shoulder.

Croygen shrugged. "I've been in far worse predicaments, but it was usually getting away from a jealous husband. There was a benefit in it for me."

"Okay, just imagine this being like that," I replied. "Except without the chance of getting laid before or after."

"And no alcohol, opium, or treasure." Ryker smirked.

"Yeah, you guys are really selling this."

"You will have my undying gratitude." I winked.

He lifted his lip in a snarl, but I knew it was all for show.

"Can I exchange that for a geisha?"

"No, but I'm sure *some* girl will take pity on you. Someday," I teased. It was a complete joke because Croygen could have women lining up just to be near him.

"*You* could always kiss me *again*." Croygen smiled coyly with a wink.

Ryker's head jerked. "Again?"

"Oh, wow, we really need to get going."

"What does he mean *again*?"

"What, Lexie?" I backed up to the bed. "I think she's waking up."

Croygen chuckled as he passed, and I punched him lightly in the stomach. He only laughed harder.

Damn pirates.

"Okay, so who's ready to get stabbed, shot, and possibly tortured? No different from some of my nights out in the Orient." Croygen clapped his hands, staring down at Lexie's sleeping form. "You with me, little shark?"

TWENTY-SIX

"*Bhean?*" Sprig tugged my earlobe. "Have we passed the cafeteria? They have those honey packets there, right?"

"Zip it, furball," Ryker whispered harshly at my shoulder. Sprig had actually been awake when I went over to Lexie. I found him cuddling his backpack, Pam's head poking out, and stroking his tail soothingly. Loud noises, especially gunfire, really scared him.

"But it gives me superpowers! Without it, Supersprite is far less super," he whined. "And my tummy is SUPER cranky."

"I'm about to stuff that tail in your mouth and thread it through your ass if you don't shut up," Croygen snarled.

With Lexie wrapped tightly in Croygen's arms, I was having serious *déjà vu* of when we escaped here the first time. Part of me felt like maybe I had never gotten out and life above ground had all been a dream. Maybe I remained locked up in the room, my arms strapped behind me as I rocked in the corner, so deep in my mind I couldn't tell reality from the world I created.

If that were true, I'd pick the dream. As long as I could actually feel Ryker, I was happy.

"Okay, you go as far as you can. At least get to level two. There are stairs leading out near the elevator. You lie, steal, cheat, or kill, but you get her out of here. We will follow." At least I would be sure Ryker and Sprig did.

Croygen nodded. The elevator dinged and the doors opened. I leaned in and swiped the card to access the lower levels. Croygen held Lexie's sleeping body close as he stepped in, a gun in one of his hands.

"Croygen?" I was at a loss for words. "Thank you."

"Oh jeez, just say you love me. Make it really dramatic." The doors started to close.

I grinned. "I love you."

"Wow! That lacked finesse." He frowned.

"Stay safe, asshole," Ryker snarled.

"Kiss my honey muncher," Sprig added.

"See, now those had flare. I believed them."

The doors shut.

Please, please, let them get to safety.

Shouts came from down the hallway where I found Croygen. There had to be other ways in and out of these levels, but they were well hidden. I knew we wouldn't find obvious exit signs or pictures of stairs. Rapava probably only showed those who needed to know how to get out of here. I had never been on that list.

Ryker grabbed my arm, pulling me back the way we came. The building had been designed with an elevator on either end. Our feet quietly treaded over the tile. Ryker fell behind, guarding our backs, while I weaved through the maze. Sprig held tight, deep in my hair. I paused at a corner, peering down the corridor for trouble, and spotted the elevator at the far end.

"Do you know where he'd be?" Ryker whispered behind me. I craned my neck to see him.

"My gut tells me to go down."

Ryker's eyebrows lifted.

"Seriously?" I couldn't fight a small chuckle.

"I'm completely for the idea. But maybe now is not a great time."

"Might be your last chance." I meant it as a joke, but his face darkened, his eyes flashing.

"Don't say that," he rumbled. "You are going to live through this, human. I want many years ahead of fucking you senseless."

I almost choked on air. "Well, if anything will keep me fighting, it'll be that."

"And honey," Sprig squeaked in my ear, his backpack hitting my cheek.

Ryker's heat bounced off my body, and it took everything I had to turn around and focus. I examined the bare hallway and slipped around the corner, Ryker right behind me.

My attention was trained so intently on our destination, I missed the flare of warning teasing the back of my neck. I stepped past an open door, when a click of a gun ticked in my ear. Ryker instantly pointed his firearm at the assailant.

"Drop your weapon or she dies." Liam jammed the barrel of his gun into my temple. "I'm not kidding. Whatever you think you can do, I will be quicker." He spoke to Ryker, nodding at his gun.

Ryker's tattoo and eyes flashed. It would be so easy for him to take down Liam, if it wasn't for the fact Liam held a fae gun to my head. There was no question I would die. Ryker growled as he placed the weapon on the ground. He stared at Liam, his expression so determined and full of hate. I felt Liam's hand tremble against my head. Liam walked around, turning my back to the elevator.

"Now you." He dug the weapon into my skin. I bent over, wiggling my shoulder, hoping Sprig would understand my meaning. We had done this last time.

He did.

Sprig dropped down my back, his soft fur brushing a slip of exposed skin, and the elevator key slipped from my back pocket. He inched down and hid behind my boot. I set down the knife and gun I carried.

"Step back," Liam ordered.

Ryker and I stepped away from our weapons. Sprig took the opportunity to slip away.

Please don't see him. Please don't see him.

My glamour wasn't really working, and it certainly wouldn't work down here, but I still sent out the thought with everything I had.

Thankfully Liam was too focused on me to notice. He moved with me, keeping the gun glued to my head, kicking the other weapons a little farther away from us.

He reached for a walkie-talkie on his belt, putting it near his mouth. "I have the targets. Send down a team to the fifth floor," Liam spoke into the device, keeping us in his sight the entire time. Someone responded on the other end. Liam hooked the walkie-talkie back on his belt, licking his lips nervously as Ryker growled again.

"All fluff and no bite. Not sure if I want to laugh or throw up. A fae in love with a human. But I guess you're not really human anymore, are you? You two are perfect for each other. I hated Daniel, but at least he was human. This is just foul."

"Shut up, Liam," I snarled. I didn't care to explain to him I was now full fae. It would probably disgust him more.

"Poor little Zoey." A smug smile twitched at his mouth. "Did you know most of us were on the inside the whole time? Only you and Daniel weren't. What does that say? Rapava knew even then not to trust you. Looks like he was right. Both you and Holt became traitors."

Many confusing moments of my past made sense now. Like the night of the storm when Rapava had me locked up down in a level I didn't know. The rest of them knew about it. There were so many other things to think about then, so my brain didn't fix on it. But now I realized all the Collectors had been down in the lower levels when I had been a prisoner. Only Daniel and I had never been brought in. Daniel knew more than he let on. Even keeping it from me. It also explained why Sera and Liam always had that smug *I'm better and smarter than you* vibe. They were in the cool kid's club while Daniel and I were blackballed.

"Rapava has been secretly planning this. Training an army to fight. You and your little group are going to die. All this is for nothing. We've been waiting for this day for a very long time."

I wanted to tell him our so-called "little group" included the Unseelie King's private guards. But of course, I couldn't.

"You don't think we weren't prepared for an attack from fae?" Liam snarled, keeping his weapon directed at my head. "I just never imagined *you* would be the one leading it." His gaze rolled over me, his lips hitched up in repulsion. "I'm not sure why I'm surprised. I always sensed there was something *wrong* about you."

Fury pushed my shoulders back, and my nails sliced into my closed fists. I would not give him the satisfaction of retaliating. That was what Liam lived for. To get a rise out of me. Or Daniel when he had been alive.

"My eyes have been opened and now I see the truth." I turned to face him, letting the barrel of the gun hit the middle of my forehead. "You want to hide, little boy, in your closed, sad mind?" I pushed against the gun, letting it dig into my skin. "Even Sera saw the truth at the end. If you really loved her, you would not be able to handle what Rapava did to her."

"Shut up," Liam said, his jaw straining. Oh yeah, I picked at a nerve.

"Zoey…" Ryker mumbled my name, but I ignored him.

"You sat there while he tested her and let her die a slow, painful death. Alone. All for research. What kind of man does that make you?"

"Shut. Up!" Liam bellowed, waving his gun around. It was a fine line between him shooting me and him breaking down.

I glanced at Ryker. Without a word spoken, I sensed he picked up on my meaning.

"I held her in my arms when she died, as blood leaked from her eyes and mouth…" I sensed in my gut this would be the last words he'd let me say. "You let her die. And weren't even man enough to be there for her in the end."

I watched his finger twitch, pulling the trigger back. In that split second, I dropped down.

Bang!

The bullet raced over the top of my head. Ryker drove into Liam, both men colliding hard into the wall. Ryker immediately went for the weapon in Liam's hand, but Liam was not a small man or untrained. He wouldn't go down easy.

I went for my own firearm and knife when the sound of feet and shouting thundered down the hall.

Shit!

The elevator door behind me dinged. Sprig sat on the railing next to it, stabbing at the button repeatedly, and the doors rolled open. "Come on, *Bhean!*"

"Zoey, go!" Ryker screamed back at me as he struggled with Liam.

A handful of men dressed in fatigues and holding rifles came around the corner, running toward us.

"Go! Now!" Ryker bellowed.

I bobbed on my feet. Hesitating. How could I leave him? Pain sliced my heart. I didn't want to part from him, leave him here by himself. But I made a promise to a little girl. And a promise to Daniel.

And promises in my world now were not something you could break.

I could feel the seconds between me getting away and being taken by the throng of men coming at us whittling away. I bit down on my lip. With a strangled cry I pivoted away from the man I loved and ran for the elevator.

"*Bhean*, hurry!" Sprig's face appeared around the elevator door. As they started to shut, someone yelled behind me. Then gunshots began to ring out. The sound of swishing near my head told me they were shooting at me. Moving targets were not as easy to hit, but with so many coming my way, one of them would find their target.

"*Bhean*, come on!" Sprig chattered as my exit narrowed. I kicked my legs faster and fell onto the floor. It was a trick Daniel had taught me. Like a baseball player sliding into base, I twisted to my side, using the meatier part of my thigh and butt and skidded across the slick tile. The gun and knife dug into my skin as this final burst of speed slid me over the elevator entrance. I felt the pressure of the doors closing in. I whipped my head to the side, the doors nearly snapping shut on my ponytail.

Holy shit.

"Turtle droppings!" Sprig looked down at me from his perch on the railing around the small space. "That was like from a movie." The elevator jerked, heading down again.

"Doesn't feel like it looks in the movies." I groaned and sat up. No doubt a massive bruise would form along my hip and back. "Damn, that hurt."

"Still, it was like double-0-eight."

341

"Don't you mean double-0-seven?"

"If you want to go down a score."

"This is going to be like aye-matey thing, huh?" I stood, rubbing where the gun bruised my bone.

"I still don't know who this Matty is with the one eye, but I really need to meet him someday."

"Sure," I responded, but my mind was already back with Ryker. I tipped my head forward, hitting the metal doors, squeezing my lids closed. *Please let him be okay. Please...* The elevator dinged, jolting my eyes open again. Eighth floor. *Okay, focus, Zoey. This is it.*

I pushed thoughts of Ryker out of my head and set my shoulders back. I could feel it in my bones—the time was here. Either I succeeded and fulfilled my promises... or I failed, which meant I wouldn't be walking out of here. None of us would.

Gripping the Glock firmer, I hid in the corner of the elevator, the buttons digging into my back. Sprig jumped on my shoulder. The doors released, sliding open to a level that held an abundance of horrors, nightmares, and secrets. From my time down here, I knew the lay of the land well. But that locked door at the end of the hallway remained a mystery to me. If this floor was exactly like all the floors above, that meant half of it was still undiscovered.

Rapava was here. I could feel it in my gut, as if there were some Jedi force pulling me to him. I gulped, setting a foot outside the elevator. No one was at their desks, but I didn't think anyone would be with the building under attack. Did any of his faithful followers realize he wasn't fighting next to them but hid in the depths below, with the things he loved the most—the creatures and experiments from his twisted mind?

Sprig's claws dug into my neck as I inched us farther

away from safety. The fluorescent lights reflected brightly off the tile, my boots lightly squeaking. Instinct made me want to crouch and become as invisible as possible. But there were no shadows to hide in.

And I was done hiding... from love, life, fears... and certainly from Boris Rapava. We both knew this had been coming for a long time. He waited for me.

I kept my weapon raised, cautiously stepping down the corridor. Without thinking, my body drew me toward the room where I had been forced to torture Ryker. As I got close to the room, I noticed the door stood ajar.

"Crapple," Sprig whispered hoarsely in my ear.

"Crapple?" I couldn't help but ask.

"It's crap and apple together."

"Do I dare ask?"

"Apples make you crap... so crapple."

"Yeah," I breathed, reaching for the door. "Double crapple."

I pulled out the door with one hand, my other on the trigger. Darkness encased the outer room, but the glow from the inner one pulled my attention. The blinds were drawn, but I could sense life behind it. It was like the day Rapava brought me here, showing me Ryker, bound and helpless, like some sick peep show.

Why did I feel as if it were happening all over again? My teeth ground together, my gut rolling and bucking, but my steps continued into the room. Sprig dug in tighter to my neck as fear played with us like props in a haunted house.

"Zoey." My name rang through the intercom, halting me. "Or should I call you by your real name? Project B-06."

Pricks of warning ran down my arms. He stayed behind the curtain, but I knew the glass was bulletproof. He really couldn't have set this up better. Sweat coated my palms, and

I tightened my grip on the gun. "Project B? What happened to A?"

"Project A's specimens all died. You were the second batch." As though creating babies in a dish was no more than making cookies.

"Why are you hiding behind the curtain? Come out and actually face me." I licked my lips, stepping a foot closer to the glass. At least I knew he couldn't shoot me from there either. "Come on, dear old Dad. Don't you want to see how well your offspring has turned out? How much we love you?" I taunted. If he wanted to claim he gave me life, and that he was my sire, then I would let him see firsthand how I felt about my architect.

"Oh, Zoey. You could have been great. We could have been magnificent together. But like Daniel, your true weakness is your righteous need to be good. To be loved. Sentimentality causes you to be soft. Family and friends only hold you back. Limit you. I learned that lesson a long time ago. Soon you will too."

A buzz filled the air as the curtains rose and flooded the outer room with light. Rapava stood on the other side of the glass, almost exactly where Ryker had stood. He wore his white lab coat, his silver hair and blue eyes reflecting the lights from above, his arms loosely hooked behind his back.

"Do you want to see how friends and those you care about only hinder you?" His mouth curved into a smug grin.

I lowered my gun, my lids narrowing on him. Sprig stirred under my loose ponytail, keeping out of sight.

Rapava took my lack of response as a yes and stepped to the side, nodding down toward the back wall.

I gasped but quickly swallowed back my true emotions.

Against the wall sat Kate and Delaney. Their hands were

bound in front of them as they sat on the floor, fear deep in their eyes.

The two people who had secretly been on my side and helped me escape were now his hostages. Bait. And he had me reeled in.

"Let them go," I ground out, straining my neck muscles.

Rapava smirked and turned for the table beside him, reaching for something. "I caught them trying to steal these." Rapava picked up a yellow-and-green folder stuffed full of documents, notes, and information. My gut dropped to my knees. Daniel's files. The ones I lost the day we jumped to Peru when Ryker and I were being attacked by my own people.

"I always knew one day Kathryn would step out of line. Her sympathy for fae…" He trailed off, looking back at her. "Even having a fae lover."

Kate's eyes widened as Rapava revealed he knew about her and Dunn.

"There is nothing I don't know," Rapava spat. "I, too, have spies out there. You were never one up on me."

Kate's throat bobbed as she swallowed nervously, keeping her eyes on Rapava and her mouth shut.

Through the glass, his cool blue eyes darted back to mine. "I will always be smarter and one step ahead of everyone here." He pulled out a gun from his coat pocket.

"No. Don't." My feet rushed to the glass, fear taking over my limbs. Seeing Rapava with a gun felt wrong. It didn't fit the image of the studious scientist I had seen him as for so many years.

Almost as if he were reading my thoughts, he glanced down at the pistol in his hand. "I always preferred science over violence. Brains over mindless weapons. It takes no intelligence or wit to kill a person." He licked his bottom lip and stared back at me. "But I'll bet you didn't know that I trained as a soldier? To get away from my father I joined the army. The government swiftly realized they were wasting my talents as a mindless fighter. I worked my way quickly into intelligence, working as a spy. It was where I discovered the classified files on fae. It was also how I escaped to the United States, using one of my missions to defect. I knew so much about Russia's plans and secrets about fae that even the Americans were unaware of, they couldn't disregard me. The US government brought me in. I became invaluable to them, and from there they allowed me to continue my studies and start my own work."

He reached over and touched the top green folder. "The government knows only what they want to know. They don't understand the true threat of fae. But I have enough supporters that these files would have been useless to you. They like being in the dark. As long as I keep protecting them, allowing them to think they are safe, tucked in their beds each night with their milk and cookies, they don't care how far I have to go. Ignorance is bliss to the stupid."

Every time Rapava let me see inside his head, the more frightened I became. His god complex ran deep. He thought himself above everyone, even the highest tiers of the government.

"So, Kathryn." Boris turned toward his work colleague. "If you thought you were hiding the truth about your daughter's parentage from me, you sorely underestimated me. Like I told you, there isn't anything I don't know, or that I am at least steps ahead on."

Kate's body jerked as she slumped back harder into the wall, fear and horror contorting her features. Her eyes watered as she pushed herself to her feet. At her movement Rapava gripped the gun, pulling it up slightly.

"Please, Boris. I beg you. Please don't hurt her." Kate's bottom lip shook, but she kept her gaze locked on him.

"Your daughter is more human than fae and holds very little magic. She is of no use or threat to me," Rapava replied, making it clear he had already tested her. "But oddly enough, your *granddaughter* has strong fae magic in her."

It was in that moment everything changed. The shift in Kate's expression went from scared to fierce. It was like watching a movie, an outsider to what was about to happen. Everything went so fast, but so slow at the same time.

Words burned in my throat, but before I could get them out, Kate with her arms still tied, bulldozed toward the doctor, a screech tore from her lips. Rage converted her face into a feral animal.

Rapava's eyes widened, his arm with the gun lifting, his finger pushing back on the trigger.

"Nooooo!" A cry broke through the room. Delaney stood up and hurtled toward the doctor.

Boom. The room shook with the rebounding sound.

I flinched back with a cry. Sprig shrieked as blood sprayed the window in front of us, coating it with dripping, red liquid. Delaney's eyes went wide, blinked, then she fell to the ground. My hand went to my mouth, bile burning my esophagus.

"No," Kate screamed, her knees hitting the ground as she wiggled closer to Delaney. Delaney gulped, her eyes wide with terror, her body twitching and moving. The hole in her stomach painted her scrubs a deep maroon color, the floor puddling with blood. "You're going to be all right. Stay with

347

me." Kate leaned over, getting closer to the girl, and set her tied hands over the wound. "You hear me? You're going to be all right." Kate's voice broke, sobs fizzing up.

Delaney nodded at Kate, lifting her tied hands to Kate's face and wiped tears away from her eyes. A wordless exchange passed between them, a closeness, a bond only they shared. Kate leaned over and kissed her on the forehead. Then Delaney closed her eyes, her body going limp. Dead. Another casualty of Dr. Boris Rapava.

Kate took another moment, then sat back on her heels, her head slowly twisting to Rapava. "You are a murderer," she seethed.

"Don't be naïve, Kathryn. So are you. You are no different."

Her lips went up as she got to her feet. "I am nothing like you."

"You admit fae lives don't count then? The murders you committed aren't the same?" Rapava's eyebrow lifted.

Kate's shoulders rose, taking in a deep breath.

"How many have you tested and let die while you tried to build evidence against me?" Anger darted from the doctor's gaze. "We are the same. Even if we wanted different things, you let fae die for your cause as well. A few sacrificed for the masses because you also had the bigger picture in sight."

Kate's breath came out shaky. I could see ire building behind her eyes. It was like watching two fighters provoking each other until one couldn't take it anymore and reacted.

I had to stop her. Otherwise she would be the one lying on the floor next to Delaney. I moved slowly to the door.

"What are you doing, *Bhean*?" Sprig whimpered softly in my ear. It wasn't really a question, but more a hope he was wrong in what he thought I was doing.

"Go. Now." I kept my eyes locked on the two people in the room. "I'm in this all the way, but get out of here. Please."

"No way, *Bhean*. If you're here, I'm here. I will never leave you."

His words made my heart swell with love but also pump with fear. Everyone I loved got hurt. I couldn't take it if anything happened to him.

"Sprig..."

"Don't bother. I'm sticking to you like a monkey on your back." He snickered softly. "Get it?"

This wasn't the time for jokes, but a smile still fluttered over my mouth. "Just so you know," I whispered. "You're my best friend. I love you, buddy."

"Same, *Bhean*. And I love you... *almost* as much as honey." He nuzzled my ear. "Okay, maybe you're equal, but only because you have an enchanted bra with magically delicious tits."

"It's always about boobs with you boys."

"Only when they pop out honey like a toaster."

I got to the door and reached up to the code box. I was going to have to be fast. Really fast. I took a deep breath, gripping the gun with my left hand as I typed with my right. The eleven-digit code pinged as I hit every number. The release echoed in my ears along with my breath. I just needed to get Kate out safely. That was the only goal I had in that moment. I flung the door open, my gun pointed up, ready to shoot. Hope fell around my boots, sticking them to the floor.

Kate leaped for Rapava, using my entrance to attack, her eyes set on the gun.

"No!" I shrieked.

"You monster!" Kate wailed.

Rapava twisted back around to Kate just as she plowed into him. He stumbled back, his arm rose in the air and came down with a crack, the handle of the gun striking the crown of her head like a drum.

I felt a scream bubble up in me as Kate fell to the floor with a thud. There was a stunned moment before I shuffled to her. "Kate!"

"Stop right there, Ms. Daniels." Rapava whirled around, the gun pointed between my brows.

I skidded to a stop, adrenaline pumping in my ears. I kept my head facing the doctor, but my gaze drifted to the newest body on the floor. Blood trailed from the wound down her forehead, slipping over her nose and dripping to the ground like raindrops. Her chest still rose in shallow movements. *She's alive.* Relief exhaled from my lungs. She was knocked out and had one hell of a lump on her head, but she was alive.

I lifted my weapon back to Rapava, both of us staring at each other in a standoff.

"You're not going to shoot me." He smiled.

"Don't underestimate my hatred for you," I growled, edging closer.

"Oh, I don't doubt you hate me, but your drive for knowledge, where you came from, what I'm doing behind those doors is much *more* powerful than hate."

My throat closed around the wrath I held in, filling the gaps with disgust and revulsion at myself because he was right. The burning need to see the truth behind the curtain, to know more about my origins, my parents, the sperm donors, overwhelmed me. But I didn't want him to know that.

"I've lived this long without knowing." I took a step closer, the barrel pinpointed at his chest.

"You mean you're not curious about the little blonde girl who has been screaming your name, hoping you will come rescue her?"

Annabeth. Emotions I couldn't even name wove inside my throat, choking me. "What have you done to her?"

"You keep putting me in the role of the bad guy. Why can't any of you see I am doing all this for you, for humans?"

"I don't even think *you* believe that lie anymore."

Rapava tilted his head, watching me carefully. "Put the gun down. It's up to you if you want to see your friend again or not."

"You're going to take me to her?"

"I am going to do better. I am going to show you what I've accomplished." A strange glint hinted in his eyes like an excited boy about to reveal his favorite toy at show-and-tell. "You have been a big part of it. Both you and Sera." The way he said it caused an icy sensation to tingle the back of my neck. My finger twitched on the trigger. "I know Daniel trained you well, but I promise you, with my background, I could shoot that thing off your shoulder and drive a bullet through your brain before you could even blink."

I had never seen the ruthless soldier in Boris Rapava. He had always been the scientist, the doctor. Now I caught a glimpse of his military training, the cold disregard for human life. He only kept me alive before because he needed me. Something had changed, and I could feel it in my soul. He no longer needed me. I had understood when we were planning this I had little chance of walking out alive. But I needed to try for Annabeth.

I set my gun on top of the files. I could still hear Daniel's words in my head: *Don't let DMG get hold of these.* But I failed. I failed him in so many ways. *I am so sorry, Daniel.*

Rapava grabbed the extra weapon and pushed me back out of the room. I gave one last glance to the bodies on the floor. One would never get up again. Delaney had known the risks, the danger of working here, but she stayed, willing to fight for her beliefs. This should not have been her end. It wasn't fair. But life was anything but fair, and I knew that too well. Kate would have a hell of a headache, but at least she would wake up. I hoped it would be soon after we left. *Run, Kate. Run fast.*

Sprig held tight to my shoulder as we moved awkwardly out the main door into the hallway. My gut screamed to run as we stopped in front of the large doors. I wasn't sure I was ready to see what lay on the other side. Truth doesn't always set you free. Sometimes it's the precise thing that drags you down into the darkness to the place from where you can never return.

I was terrified because I felt certain of one thing—I was not coming back. I needed to make sure Annabeth, Sprig, and Kate escaped. But for me and the stone in my pocket, this was our last stop. The Unseelie King could dig it out of the rubble, next to my dead body. And Rapava's.

Ryker was unaware I took it back. When he stayed behind in the room at Vadik's warehouse, I took the opportunity to pinch it out of Sprig's bag, giving him a honey packet to distract him. It might have started out as Ryker's burden, but it was *mine* now. The stone and I had a connection he never had. Maybe I seemed weaker, but for some reason the stone picked me. Whatever the purpose, it remained my obligation. I could feel it in my soul. The stone had dug deep into me and would not let me go so easily, a realization almost scarier than the demons behind the wall. I wasn't sure I wanted it to let me go.

All you have is to say yes, Zoey. And all this could be over now, the stone whispered into my head. *Just say the word and I am yours. Just give me the power to end this.*

I will. I swallowed. *You have my word.*

I felt it vibrating against my thigh, sensing the genuineness in my statement. The magic emanating from my hip could flatten this place in seconds.

But not yet. Not until the people I cared about were out.

TWENTY-SEVEN

The double doors beeped, one sliding behind the other. Rapava escorted us through, keeping his gun on me.

This level had been set up differently. Where the upper floor was a maze of corridors and rooms, this was void of either. A huge main room gave way to one hallway on the far back wall, leading to who knew where.

My attention locked on the hundreds of cylinders circling the large room, each full of a clear liquid. The cases looked to be made of glass and metal, about seven feet tall and three feet wide. Each and every one of them contained a figure.

A person.

I wanted to throw up, horror binding around my throat like weeds.

"Most were dying of some disease or addiction." Rapava pushed me to walk forward. "Their lives won't end fruitlessly. They are doing something for their country, for the greater good."

Did he think if he kept saying it out loud, I would start to believe it too? All I saw were unwilling victims. The nearer I got, the more details became clear. Faces looked back at me. Some with no arms, others with no legs. Every one of them missing a body part.

My eyes stopped on one, and like a nightmare, I felt my feet move, unable to stop my forward progress.

"No." My chest heaved in and out, taking in the girl behind the glass. Her long brown hair flowed freely around in the liquid, her eyes were closed as if she were sleeping, but I knew better.

A flash of her wearing a red cape came into my head. A cape that I had seen in a closet down the hall. It was the girl I fought when I had jumped back to Seattle and been caught by Maria. The girl who no longer wanted to fight. I had seen it in her eyes. She had lost hope. Given up.

The shock at seeing her wasn't what pulled my shoulders down. It was the truth I had known a long time ago but didn't want to admit when I saw the super girl tattoo on an ankle.

She had no legs. Because those legs were attached to my kid sister.

My neck turned, and saliva gathered in my mouth when I caught a glance of a familiar dark-skinned woman across the way. She was missing an arm and leg. Tears burned behind my lids. Jada.

Girls are disappearing. Annabeth's voice came into my head. Vadik was selling them to Rapava when they grew too sickly and were no longer useful.

Sprig tucked tighter into me, hiding his face against my neck. It had to be tearing his soul into pieces, just like when we saw the monkey parts. I touched him softly, wishing I had forced him to stay back. He shouldn't see this, be a part of this truth. His heart was too big. He couldn't handle the darkness like I could.

Rapava had been dissecting what he claimed he wanted to protect. This was not about protecting human life or even revenge. It was all about proving his supremacy over everyone—fae and human alike. He wanted to be the smartest, the cleverest, the one who surpassed everyone.

I tried to swallow. "Where's Annabeth?" Fear chilled me to the bone.

Rapava tilted his head toward the hallway. "See for yourself."

I wished I could go back to being ignorant and retreat to the bliss of not knowing what true horrors awaited me in the dark recess of the building—deep in the tarred hole of Dr. Boris Rapava's soul.

Because if I knew how far he would truly go, I would never have followed him.

We walked down the short corridor to another room. This area appeared to be smaller but filled with even more tanks and cylinders.

Sprig squeaked softly in my ear and dug into my neck. My knees hit the ground with a bang, but I felt nothing.

"Oh my god," I whispered. Acid rose up my throat, sizzling holes in my esophagus. My eyes locked on the chambers.

A hundred or more incubators filled with what appeared to be a thick syrup lined every free space on the walls, some ten high like cages in a pet store. Only a dozen were in use; the others looked to be waiting for occupancy. A dozen too many.

Inside the jelly-filled containers were babies. But these weren't normal human babies. They were of various sizes, from a few inches to a few feet. Air tubes went into each tiny body, keeping them alive as they grew, a horrifying version of a womb. My fist knotted against my abdomen.

At long last I gazed at my "mother." This was how they created me, how I was brought into this world.

"Let me introduce you to Project D." Rapava walked to my side, motioning to the containers. He no longer pointed the gun at me, but he kept it firm in his grip, watching me carefully. "Sadly, Project C did not do well. But thanks to you and Sera, this bunch is thriving."

I slowly rose, and my chest heaved in and out as my feet took me closer to the fetuses.

"*Bhean...*" Sprig whined, clearly seeing what I saw.

They were all horribly deformed.

"What is wrong with them?" A voice spoke, and it took me a moment to realize it was from me.

"Nothing. They are perfect. No faults in their DNA, unlike your group." Rapava stepped up to me, touching the glass to one of the experiments. "With your group, I thought too small, creating top-of-the-line seers. But being a seer alone will not help win the fight against fae. This group has extra abilities like fae."

My head jerked to him. "What?"

"They are hybrids like you."

My stomach somersaulted. This seemed all wrong. Not natural. Half-human, half-fae babies were common enough, but this was something else altogether.

The one in front of me had a tail. It curled up, and triangle-shaped ridges grew out of it like shark's teeth. Its face looked twisted and distorted.

This was more chilling than I could have ever imagined.

Another one of the experiments stirred in a larger vessel close to me. It appeared to be the size of a toddler. A dark-haired boy on the outside, but it opened its mouth enough for me to see the razor-sharp teeth. Hundreds of them filled its mouth like needles.

"That one is combined with a strighoul," Rapava replied proudly. "The first human-strighoul hybrid ever. But this one will be on our side."

I had hunted strighoul before. They were the lowest, most evil scum in the fae world. They actually preferred to attack their own. There was no bottom they wouldn't sink to. People liked to associate them with vampires, but they didn't just suck your blood, they ate you. Like, for dinner. They consumed every part of you, taking your energy and essence that way. They took on the powers or traits of whomever they ingested until it passed through their digestion.

"What's wrong, Zoey?" Rapava's voice sounded even, his eyes watching me expectedly. "Are you not proud of your own children?"

My head whipped to him. "Wh-what?"

"These are yours. Yours and Sera's. They are your children, Ms. Daniels, your offspring."

The world tipped on its axis, and I grabbed on to the wall to keep myself upright.

"What are you talking about?"

"During those two weeks you were out, you were ovulating, a perfect time to harvest your eggs. Sera as well. I wanted them all to have the seer gene. You and Sera were some of the strongest seers out there." He pointed to the lower group of mutant fetuses. "These are yours. I wanted to see if you having fae genetic material now would influence them. How would it affect them? Would they live longer? Be more powerful? As you can see, yours are growing at a more rapid rate. They have double the magic and strength."

My hand unconsciously went to my abdomen, which suddenly ached as if he had shredded my gut with a razor. I couldn't speak as I gazed at the handful of organisms along the wall that were supposedly *mine*. Now I could see some of the experiments had Asian characteristics like Sera. Some had green eyes and brown hair like me.

My head spun, my muscles locking to keep me upright. I didn't feel suddenly connected to them or instinctively protective. I felt disgusted. Angry. Violated. He took a piece of me when I was unconscious and vulnerable, and created monsters, things meant to kill and destroy. Only revulsion and hatred burned in my chest.

I could feel Sprig rubbing my neck softly, and it was then I realized my breath was hitching and twisting around in my chest. *I can't breathe.*

I could no longer look at the grotesque figures and whirled around, trying to gain footing. I bent over my knees and tried to suck in deep breaths. Yet there appeared to be nowhere safe in the room to look. On the other wall, each tank contained one living adult human inside, men and women, ranging in ages, air tubes up their noses. This wasn't the worst of it: beside them, attached by electrodes to the human subject's brain, was a sub-fae.

"You gave me this idea, Zoey. Remember?" Rapava gestured toward them. "Once again, all this is because of you and the underling there." He pointed to Sprig on my shoulder.

Our conversation rushed into my memory.

He knows me, sir. He grew an attachment to me. He listens to me, follows me. At first it bothered me, but now I see it could be useful, I'd said.

Rapava had replied, *I had not thought of that. Both animal and sub-fae seek a master, someone to command them…*

I gave him this idea. The horrors in this whole room existed because of me. My eggs, my ideas.

"I am trying to link their brains, connect them. The human will dominate and control the other with just a thought." Rapava nodded toward the farthest tank in the corner. "That is my newest. She is our first experiment with one of my fae-primates."

I stepped closer, getting a better look. My eyes locked first on the monkey. It looked to be the one I saw with Croygen down the hall. One of the experiments made of the bits and pieces of different types of primates.

My eyes followed the wires linking its brain to the girl's. The earth's axis tilted, smashing my world into thousands of tiny shards. A cry shattered from my lips. I moved without thought, running for the chamber. I hit the glass, crying out for the fragile blonde girl floating weightlessly in the tank. My hands flailed against the glass.

"Annabeth!" A sob broke from my lips. Tears stung my eyes. I should have never left her that night at the warehouse. No matter what, I should have fought and gotten her out.

Annabeth was technically alive, but would she be herself or some monster Rapava created? The burden of so many deaths lay on my shoulders, but Annabeth's felt like a mountain, one that would bury me, especially if Lexie would soon follow.

I pressed my head against the window. "I am so sorry."

Her eyes popped open. I yelped and jumped back from the glass. "What the hell?"

"She has not taken to the drug like the others. She fights it and keeps waking up," Rapava said evenly behind me as if he were talking about the weather.

Annabeth blinked a few times. Her hand lifted and pressed against the glass. I put my hand against hers. Her eyes squinted and bubbles came out of her mouth. She was crying, but her expression looked relieved.

My heart broke. I could not let her down again. I couldn't. My muscles shook, and I had trouble keeping my feet under me. I wanted to curl into a ball and weep, but I would stay standing for the girl on the other side of the glass. I would not quit till she was safe.

The time had come. This had to end. All of it. This lab would be Rapava's tomb.

I gulped and pressed my hand harder into the window and stared deep into her eyes, willing her to understand. *I will get you out of there.*

Terror filled her eyes as she watched me step back, her head shaking. My soul felt skinned and quartered. Turning away from her was unbearable. The sheer panic and fear showed on her face as she thought I was walking away. Giving up on her.

I just wanted Sprig and Annabeth to get out of here safely. I hoped Ryker wouldn't leave them. He and Croygen could take care of the girls and Sprig. They would do it for me.

"Let her go." I strode up to Rapava, my neck straining as I set my chin high. He drew his gun back up to my forehead. "You have me. You have all the experiments you need. Let her go."

"Why would I do that?" Rapava's light blue eyes narrowed. "She is my trial run for this experiment. If this goes how I think it will, the ape will respond to her with just a thought. He will do her bidding, and she will do mine." He stared at me contemptuously, like my stupidity was an insult. "I have the upper hand, Ms. Daniels. I always do. She stays and so do you and the thing sitting on your shoulder."

"Thing?" Sprig spit back with outrage. "I'll show you—"

"Really, *Boris*?" I cut Sprig off and leaned my head to the side, a knowing smirk curling the side of my cheek. "Are you sure you hold all the cards?"

He stirred, his lids constricting farther.

"Because I think I might have something you want." I let a ridiculing smile unfold. "More than you want her, me, or Sprig."

"What?" Rapava's gaze sparked with interest.

"I have what you most desire." I grabbed the barrel of the gun and pushed it down, away from my head. "Why you made me torture Ryker."

I felt Sprig stiffen. "*Bhean?*" he whispered, his voice unsure, slicing with fear.

Ignoring him, I kept my attention locked on the doctor. "What do you most yearn for, *sir*?"

"The stone." Rapava licked his lips. "Do you have it? The Stone of Destiny?"

"You let her free. It is yours."

"*Bhean*, what are you doing?"

I took another step toward Rapava, sliding my hand into my pocket. *You ready?* I pushed the thought toward the object.

You are mine after, like you promised? the stone's voice spoke into my head.

You kill him, you can have me the moment I take you back.

Say it. Say yes, the stone sang in my head, energy vibrated off it, bouncing off my hip.

I took a deep breath and wrapped my fingers around the stone.

Yes.

TWENTY-EIGHT

Magic slammed into my system, and I stumbled to the side, grabbing a table.

"*Bhean!*" Sprig's voice sounded distant, like he was whispering to me from down a long corridor. I gritted my teeth, pushing back the power pumping into me.

Push through, Zoey. Keep going, I instructed myself.

Rapava's head snapped down to my hand, my body shaking violently as I tugged the item from my pants. Power sizzled up my arm into my chest. Muscles flinched and twitched under the intense magic. I took little sips of air, energy so extreme it was blissfully painful.

"*Bhean*, have you seriously gone insane?" Sprig squeaked, bobbing up and down nervously. "What are you doing?"

"Ending this." I swallowed. My legs wobbled under me, dropping me to my knees with a groan. The stone didn't knock me out this time. It tried to hold back the influx of magic pounding into my system, but I still wanted to vomit all over the floor as I curled over.

"That's it?" Rapava pinched his fingers together greedily, moving closer to me, staring at the small mundane-looking rock in my palm.

"Get Annabeth out of there," I demanded, grabbing the table again to keep myself sitting up.

Rapava looked behind me, then back at the stone, his eyes wide and full of life. His tongue ran over his bottom lip, like he was actually salivating. The stone didn't look like much, but anyone with a pulse could feel the energy radiating off it, soaking the air, making you desire more. More power, more money, more supremacy. It made you feel alive, filled you with the urge to follow or do whatever it wanted if it only could give you another hit, while it took from you. Your soul, your essence, your choices.

My head swirled with the idea to use it, to take all I ever wanted. *Do it, Zoey, don't fight anymore*, a voice in my brain said, unnerving me, because I could not decipher if it was me or the stone talking.

The longer I held it, the more I couldn't find the line between us. I still tried to fight, to not let it control me. Another asshole stealing away my soul. But my struggle was waning, on the edge of toppling over.

Rapava reached for it and my hand instinctively wrapped around it, shifting it out of his reach. A snarl filled my mouth.

"*Bhean*, don't do this." Nothing Sprig said mattered in that moment.

Let me have you now, Zoey. We can end him together.

I felt metal tap against the space between my brows. My gaze lifted to a dark hole stretching down the length of the weapon.

"Give it to me now." Rapava's voice was high and scratchy as he stood over me.

"No." The words fell from my mouth without thought. "It's *mine*."

Yes, Zoey, and you are mine.

363

"Give it to me!" Rapava slammed the pistol harder against my skin.

"No." The word came out again. The stone thumped in my hand. My fight gone. It was taking over, but I didn't care. I wanted it. I craved the bliss of its power and the euphoric dream of losing myself in the magic: dissolving, falling, seeping, spinning…

My back slammed onto the floor, snapping my brain out of the coma-like state. A squeal pinged my eardrum as Sprig went flying across the floor, tumbling over, before hitting a table. Rapava pounced on me, his expression wild and vacant.

"It's mine," he screamed, clawing at my hand and arm like a wild animal. The gun banged into my temple.

The point of this was to let Rapava have it, but my hand wouldn't open. The need to hold on to it dominated me, took away all rational thought.

"Ahhh!" Rapava bellowed, his movement growing more frantic. He then stopped, sat back, and clutched the gun. His lips arched up in a snarl. He shoved the end of weapon in my bruised eye socket. "I no longer need you." His finger tugged back on the trigger, and I heard the sound of the metal coil pushing at the bullet.

A cry broke from my lips, my hand flew up to his face, my fist slammed deep into his parted mouth, the stone breaking off his front teeth like crystalized sugar candy. He fell to the side, landing on his back. The moment my fingers left the stone, air bolted into my lungs, logic returned, and I scrambled away from the doctor.

He tugged the stone out of his mouth, ignoring the chunks of teeth crumbling down like falling rock. A smile turned up his face, showing off his jagged, bloody mouth.

"It's mine," he slurred, staring at the stone in his hand with a fevered longing. "All fae will die at my hand, from an object they created." Fear pushed me back into a table, hiding from his crazed laughter, like a mad doctor.

What if the stone had double-crossed me? What if I just handed the most powerful weapon on any planet to the most insane man?

Rapava climbed to his feet, swinging around to me, his arm outstretched, holding the stone. "Finally, the power to end their race is mine. I will be the most feared and respected man in the world. It is all mine," he spat through his missing teeth, sounding like a drunk chipmunk.

I saw him shudder, and I climbed back onto my feet.

"No." I shook my head. "It is all the stone's power. You still have none without the fae."

Now, I shouted in my head, hoping the stone could hear me.

His form went rigid, then a scream tore from his mouth, a shrill, horrible wailing as though he was being gutted alive.

"That's for all of those you tortured, tested, and killed," I seethed.

His eyes went wide, his body dropping to the floor, convulsing like a dying fish.

I walked over and looked down on him. "Know this, you will not be remembered, or feared, or worshipped. You did not save the race or lead us in any way. The government will bury you and what happened here so deep in the archives, it will be like you never existed. I will make certain nothing here will survive. You did nothing but fail. Even with me. I only stand before you because of a fae. His power saved me. Not you. You are nothing but a pathetic hack."

His gaze met mine for a moment, clarity and fear boring deep, before his eyes went glassy. A muffled moan rolled from his chest. His skin started to sink and shrivel against his bones, as if a vacuum sucked out his insides. He flopped and wiggled as noises and blood erupted out of his throat. His tall frame seemed to shrink before my eyes. In his right hand he still clung to the stone. I knew it would not let him go until it took every bit of life from him.

Rapava lifted his skeleton-like arm, skin hanging loosely, flapping around. He reached for me and screeched, sending chills down the back of my neck. I jumped back, his fingers clawing at my boots.

The stone sucked him dry, bleeding him of energy and essence. A shrill moan came from him as he tried to drag his body to me.

"I'm only doing what you did, doctor. Killing one to save the masses."

Then a burst of heat shot from his mouth, his eyeballs melting into gooey puddles on the floor, leaving his sockets bare. The stench of burned flesh and hair filled my nose, making me heave. A strangled cry ruptured from my throat as his head fell forward and landed on my shoe. I kicked away from him; the spot my boot hit crumbled into a lump.

He was dead. Really dead.

Only the shell of the man remained, burned and shriveled beyond recognition like a thousand-year-old mummy, with the bones of his right hand still clasping the stone.

"Oh. My. God." One hand went to my mouth, the other to my stomach. This was what the stone was truly capable of. What it would have done eventually to me.

"Wow. He looks like charred troll nuts," Sprig exclaimed. I looked over at Sprig. He stood on the table, staring at Rapava, his face scrunched up in disgust. "Or barbequed bat."

"I thought sprites were vegetarian?"

"We don't talk about that winter." He shook his head. "Did you know pretty much anything tastes good with honey?"

I turned my head back to Rapava. "Not everything."

"Dicks and assholes only work with honey when—"

"Sprig," I cut him off, clutching my stomach harder. Where he was going with that I didn't want to know, but it wasn't what made me feel ill.

The stone summoned me over. My feet moved back to the crispy body.

I did what you asked of me, Zoey. Now it is your turn to fulfill your promise. The stone's words curled around, pulling me to it. *Take me. The moment I am with you we can show this world what you are capable of. All those who hurt you... all those who thought you'd amount to nothing.*

I squatted next to Rapava's clutched hand, my attention locked on the gray object.

Zoey...

My hand quaked as I reached for it. *No, Zoey, it will destroy you!* But I didn't stop.

A tiny body came into my view and slapped my hand.

"*Bhean*, stop!"

Ignore the sub-fae. He is nothing. You and I will create greatness. Go beyond anything you ever imagined. It will be all yours. The money, the recognition, the power.

My fingers reached out again.

"*Bhean*," Sprig's voice pleaded. He crawled up on my outreached hand, getting into my eyeline. "Don't listen to it. You are stronger than a piece of rock. Don't let it take you away from me. Don't leave me, *Bhean*... please." His huge, wide eyes, full of desperation and love, were like a rope around my heart.

"Sprig," I whispered. "I can't fight it."

"Yes, you can! Do it for the Viking, *Leanbh*, the new fair lady *Bebinn*, me, even the dumb-ass pirate."

You promised! You are fae now. You cannot back out on

an oath. The stone sizzled, pressure slid into my head, and pulsed angrily against my temples.

I never prom—said any oath, I replied.

Yes, you did! You said you'd be mine. If I killed this human, it would be us. You said yes.

I said yes, that you can have me the moment I take you back. I tried to roll my hand into a fist, but my muscles ignored me. *If I don't touch you, there is nothing you can do.*

Silence followed my statement, but I could feel anger rippling off the stone's surface like heat. Then a slam of power shot inside me and I gasped. *Stop fighting me, Zoey. You and I are meant to be.*

"Noooo," I hissed, struggling the overwhelming need to touch the stone, to hold it in my hand, to cradle it.

"*Bhean,* fight it!" Sprig jumped down, moving in front of Rapava's hand.

I shut my lids, my teeth sawing into my lip as nausea rolled from my stomach up my esophagus. My will was strong, but the stone pushed against me. Once again, I felt myself slipping. I was going to lose.

A knock sounded across the room, jolting my eyes open. I glanced over my shoulder. Annabeth's hand was plastered against the glass, her eyes wide and full of hope. Her stare bore into me. This teenage girl, her brain latched to a patchwork ape, trapped in a tank, looked so strong. She showed no sadness or fear... just a belief. In me.

I looked back at Sprig, his wide eyes full of the same confidence in me. I reached deep, grappling for every bit of strength I had.

NO! I screamed in my head, forcing my hand back. I curled it around my waist. *You will not have me. Ever.*

I released a deep anguished cry and pushed against the stone's power till I felt it crackle. Then it snapped, throwing me back on my butt. There was a moment of silence. Every ounce of magic dissipated from the room. Was that it? Did I actually beat it at its own game?

Of course, deep down, I knew better. The quiet before the storm.

A rumble started shaking the ground beneath our feet. Fury spiked the air, stabbing into me like a million pins. Magic filled back into the room, claiming ownership of the air. The hair on my arms stood up as energy drilled into the space, streaming down to a certain spot, like the rock was pulling life to it. The sound of glass tubes clattered on the table, the floor rattling harder. The lights swung, and my ears popped with pressure. My lungs ached from lack of air. My insides wanted to explode under the density.

You think you can betray me, little girl? I am more powerful than you can possibly imagine. I own you. I always will. Every time you look at your hand it will be a reminder. I will always be there, the stone seethed.

Pain slashed over my palm, burning so hot it felt like it was set on fire. A shrill, guttural scream ripped from my throat as lines began to form under the pooling blood. Agony shredded my throat as I wailed. Holding my hand in horror, I watched the cuts connect and create some kind of symbol. Magic curled inside the wounds, scorching the skin to heal around the cuts. Tears and sweat dripped down my face, acid slick in my throat. Red liquid filled my palm, disguising what it was. Right then it didn't matter. The stone had marked me, entrenching into my skin and making me connected to it. Forever.

I could have given you everything, Zoey. Now I will take it! Including your friends. Say goodbye to your little sub-fae mutant.

My mouth opened to scream for Sprig when a sonic explosion blasted through the room, like an atomic bomb.

BOOM!

My body went up in the air.

369

A scream. Shattering glass. Metal ripping.

Bones crunched as I slammed into the wall and dropped. I went into shock, not able to contain any more pain, and let myself go. Where I felt nothing. Saw nothing. Heard nothing.

TWENTY-NINE

My lids opened to murkiness. Only the soft glow from the exit signs lit the room. Hissing and crackling popped around the dark space. Debris covered my body. Stabs of pain fizzed through my nerves, my bones cracking as I tried to move from under the wreckage.

"Sprig?" I pushed off the fragments and ignored the throbbing covering every inch of my body, especially my hand, which pulsated and beat with the rhythm of my accelerated heart. I pushed aside the unbearable agony in my worry for my friend. "Sprig?" Panic gurgled in my throat as I stood up searching blindly for him.

A spark sizzled above my head; a chunk of the ceiling fell to the floor with a crash. *Shit.* This place was crumbling. If we didn't get out of here soon, we would be buried with it, eight stories below.

"Sprig, where are you, buddy? Please be okay, please be okay," I chanted as I climbed over rubble, stinging my hand. I found a cloth and knotted it around the wound, guarding it a little from being directly touched.

Liquid hissed out of the cracks in the tanks, cascading onto the floor. A quick glance showed me a few of the incubators had broken, letting the specimens slip out.

I felt a touch of sadness. It wasn't their fault they were

monsters, but still, they were. Their creator's dreams would die along with them.

Seeing a few still trapped in their chamber, I realized their end would come fast. The explosion cut off the electrical power.

No electricity. No air.

Holy shit.

"Annabeth!" I stumbled, heading for the blonde girl in the tank. Through the darkness I could see her eyes wide, her fingers tearing at the window. The monkey bobbed lifelessly up and down in the liquid next to her.

There was only a slight cut across her window leaking water out slowly. She would die way before the water would drain. With a strangled cry, I banged my fist against the cylinder, to no avail. I searched around for anything I could use to break the plastic. The ceiling sprinkled down chunks on my head that grew larger and larger. I picked up a broken plastic office chair, throwing it against the barrier. The chair bounced off, only cracking the split farther across the window.

Shit! I got this far and she was going to drown.

A groan of metal came from overhead only upping my panic. Annabeth's fingers stopped clawing at the window as her lids flickered.

"No! Stay with me," I screamed. I picked up the chair again, and using the wheels, I bashed the glass over and over.

Crack! Swoosh!

Water pounded into me, shoving me backward as the glass split. Her limp frame drifted on the current, sliding her out of the prison along with her companion. The force separated them and ripped the electrodes from her temple.

"Annabeth!" I pushed my way to her, diving to my knees.

No air came in or out of her lungs.

"No!" I cried, pumping at her chest.

One. Two. Three.

Three breaths.

One. Two. Three.

Three breaths.

I continued to repeat the cycle, feeling only an empty shell below me.

"Come on, Annabeth!" The pain in my chest stole the air from my lungs. My hand thrust harder against her ribs. I could feel hot tears spilling down my face. A bit of the ceiling crashed next to us, stirring a tormented cry from me. "I can't lose you now. *Please*."

One. Two. Three.

She remained lifeless.

"No! I won't allow you to die!" Shaking her, her body flopped around like a doll. A zap of electricity struck overhead, raining down sparks. "No. Nononononono... don't leave me." I leaned my head on her chest, anguish strangling my throat.

She was gone.

Dead.

Sounds of the room fell down around me and echoed as they smashed, the hiss of voltage in the wiring. Water from the ceiling and tanks inched up my legs. Despair struck me so harshly I couldn't control the sobs storming in my heart.

I had tried so hard and still failed her. Her life was not supposed to be like this. Anger at myself for not protecting her, for not saving her roared up my spine like a bear.

The room glowed with another spark, blazing close to my head. I sat back, my head falling back, fury raging, I let out a bellow. Guttural, raw pain thundered from me. My fists came down in primal anger, hitting Annabeth's chest.

Her eyes burst open, water heaved from her lungs, and sprayed out of her mouth in a violent surge onto the floor.

"Oh my god! Annabeth!" I screamed, grabbing for her, rotating her on her side.

More water hurled from her mouth, her body curled as she convulsed and coughed up the liquid in her chest. A whimper of happiness raced over my tongue, my hand drumming on her back, getting the last of the water out. Coughing meant air was getting to her lungs. My heart thumped in my chest with emotion. *She's alive.* My hand continued to rub and pat her until the shuddering and vomiting stopped.

Finally, after her body relaxed and her breathing took on a more regular pattern, she turned up to look at me, her voice weak. "You came for me."

"Of course I did. I promised you. I wouldn't leave you." Tears rolled down my face.

Her finely boned hand set on top of mine. "Thank you." Her eyes drifted closed.

Another spark flamed along the darkened ceiling. Drops of water hit my head. Electricity and water were an exceptionally bad combo. Of course. Nothing could be easy. The pipes in the ceiling above had burst. The water would only weaken the already fragile structure.

"Hey." I nudged her. "You're going to have to be strong a little longer. We have to get out of here."

Annabeth nodded and sat up, her face wrinkling as another set of coughs caused her lungs to spasm.

"Sprig?" I called out while helping Annabeth to her feet. *Please be okay. I can't handle him being hurt... or worse.* She put her arm around my shoulders, stumbling, trying to keep up as I wound through the room. Water was already a few inches deep as a continuous stream poured from the tanks and ceiling.

If I could only jump.

"Sprig!" I bellowed, tripping over medical equipment and fixtures. I moved closer to where I had fought Dr. Rapava. Through the dim security lights, I could make out a furry figure wearing a honey-pot backpack curled on a piece of broken furniture. In his hand he held the stone.

"Oh my god." I leaned Annabeth against a table and raced to him, my knees slicing as I crawled over a twisted chunk of metal. Careful not to touch the stone, I snatched up my friend in my arms, cuddling him.

The anger off the stone thumped into my skin. I could feel the power and fury bashing around the tiny thing. It was powerful, but it still had its limits. It couldn't win against a human/fae hybrid.

"Sprig, buddy, please wake up." I stroked his head. Nothing. "Please. I can't be without you."

He didn't respond.

"Sprig, please wake up." Tears burned down my face, my fingers shaking as I tried to feel for his heartbeat. "Don't leave me. You aren't allowed to leave me." My hand pressed against his chest, and I felt it lift slightly. A thankful cry discharged from my mouth.

His eyes stayed shut, but a frown pulled down his lips.

"Sprig?" I chirped excitedly.

"I think it's pretty clear I'm not talking to you right now." He blinked a lid open. "Neither is Pam. She is really pissed."

"Oh thank gods." A relieved chuckle exploded from me.

He poked my bra. "If any of the gods are listening, tell them to fill that holder with endless packets of sweet nectar."

Annabeth came to my side, her eyes huge. I forgot she had yet to meet my crazy, narcoleptic, talking sprite-monkey.

"Did he just talk?"

375

"Why does everyone think I'm stupid?" He picked up his head, staring at Annabeth. "Yes. Sprite. Talks."

The floor above moaned and dropped more portions down on us. "Sorry, your introduction is going to have to wait." I stared up, taking a step toward the exit.

"Turtle taco shells." Sprig wormed out of my tight hold. "We gotta go, *Bhean*." I nodded in compliance.

"Sprig, grab the stone and put it in my pocket, please."

"No, *Bhean*. The Viking asked me to hold it." Sprig waggled his head. "Plus, he said if I carried it, he'd take me back to Izel's. And he added churros and Inca soda for dessert."

"No wonder you didn't tell me." I laughed. "Bribery at its finest."

"And for post-dessert he said I could watch my soap and have honey-covered mangos."

"Damn him... always making me the mean one," I grumbled with a smile, then nodded at Sprig to grab it.

I knew he could handle it without problem. There was no way I would touch it. I had no doubt it would probably kill me, even more cruelly than it had the doctor. I betrayed it, outsmarted it. It would never let that go. But I had an obligation to Lars, and by fae law I had to fulfill it.

Sprig chirped and jumped down, picking up the rock and tugging his backpack around to his front. I could see Pam tucked inside as he stuffed the stone beside her, under his "cape." My lids briefly closed as I felt the stone's emotions brush against my mind. Torture. Hate. Death. Treachery. It promised me all. My body shook, the temptation still too close for comfort.

"*Bhean!*"

"Zoey."

Both Sprig and Annabeth shouted, my eyes popping

open. A large square of drywall smashed on the table beside us, breaking into tiny pieces.

"Come on!" With the room crumbling around us, we darted for the exit, leaving the body of Dr. Boris Rapava and his experiments behind.

The door to the main area stood ajar from the quake the stone caused. It was heavy, but with my adrenaline still pumping through me, I slid it open enough for us to get through. The shocks from the blast spread throughout the entire floor and above. Water leaked through, crashing down on the computers and lab rooms.

I kept hold of Annabeth, who stumbled on weak legs. Sprig sat on my shoulder. "Stay here," I ordered, stepping away from her.

"Where are you going?" Annabeth reached for me. "Don't leave me."

"I will be back." I squeezed her arm with my good hand. "I have to get Kate. Sprig, stay here with her. Keep her safe."

"Eye-Eye Matty." Sprig leaped to Annabeth's shoulder.

If we weren't in a life-and-death moment, I probably would have laughed at Annabeth's *what the shit* expression when Sprig patted her cheek.

Then the ground shivered under my feet, the building swaying and buckling. I swore under my breath and darted into the room. Every area down here held horrors beyond my imagination, but this one would always be the most painful. What I did to Ryker, how far I was willing to go…

You better be alive, I said to him in my head. Leaving him to fight a dozen well-trained soldiers with fae weapons felt like I handed over my heart to a shredding machine. *Please be all right.*

"Kate?" I stumbled through the dark room, the green emergency light giving a ghastly glow to the room. The testing devices, lab equipment, and chains could qualify this space for a haunted house. But nothing here was fake or set up for a movie. It was real. And so was the water from above. A buzz sounded from the exit lights, flickering and sparking. Water, embers, and flammable lab equipment sizzled around us, making this entire building a bomb waiting to go off.

The door to the inner room still stood open, and I saw the outlines of two figures on the floor. "Kate," I called her name, rushing to her side. I kneeled down, rolling her over to her back, my fingers finding their way to her neck, feeling for a pulse. Water and debris covered her. Her heartbeat thumped under my index finger.

"Hey." I tapped at her face, shaking her a little. "Wake up." A groan came from her throat. I wiped the wet hair clinging from my face.

She stirred, her lids blinking open. "Zoey?"

"Yes. Come on." I sat her up. She hissed, her hand going to her head. "We don't have time. We need to get out of here now. The place is going to collapse."

She gazed at me confused, then looked around, staring up at the oozing water. A square panel fell from the ceiling, breaking a line of beakers laying on the table, sending glass flying through the space.

"Now!"

She reacted like I slapped her face. She jolted, her eyes clearing as though really understanding the danger we were in. She tugged on my arm, trying to stand, her body stiff and slow.

The emergency light above the door sparkled, sending a

ray of flickers through the air landing on the table of broken beakers. *Whoosh.* A deep blue hue ignited across the table, and heat instantly seared my face and an acidic smell scorched up my nose.

"Get out!" Kate yelled, her eyes wide. Whatever chemical burned across the table sent fear into her. "Go!"

I grabbed her arm and pulled her toward the door. She let out a heartbreaking noise, and I glanced over my shoulder to see her hand on her heart as she stared at Delaney.

"I'm sorry, my sweet girl. You deserved better than this. I should have never brought you in." Kate's pain rippled over her expression.

The flames crackled and popped like a bowl of Rice Krispies, shattering the glass vials as they devoured everything in their path and drinking the toxic liquid like it was a piña colada.

"Kate."

Kate took a breath then turned her head, running with me. "Wait!" She pulled from my grip, leaning back for the table.

Crack!

A large flask ruptured, sending slivers of glass at us like a machine gun. I ducked, tucking my face into my arm, but razor-sharp slices cut my arms and forehead.

I lifted my head to the sound of hissing. The flames leaped over to a burner.

"Oh. Fuck."

Kate swiped the files off the table, tucked them into the back of her pants, and whipped around.

We both bolted. We hit the outer door and rounded the corner. "Run!" I screamed at Annabeth and Sprig.

We had only taken three steps down the hallway when I heard it, the inner room exploding. The blast rattled through my bones. My ears echoed with its thunder.

Then there was a moment of backdraft before I soared through the air. I flew down the hallway across the tile floor. Kate hit my legs, while Annabeth's featherlight body sailed farther down the corridor, taking Sprig with her.

I lay there in shock, trying to grasp which way was up.

"Annabeth?" I lifted my head. "Sprig?"

"Double dingleberry nuggets." I heard Sprig down the dark hallway.

"Yeah. I'm okay," Annabeth responded. "I think."

I sat up and reached for Kate.

"Damn, my old body can't take this kind of activity." Kate struggled to push herself up. "Why I never joined a gym."

"Yeah, because this is exactly the routine I do at the gym." I rose and helped her to her feet. Smoke and fire billowed out of the room behind us. It wouldn't be long before we were incapacitated by smoke inhalation. I quickly helped Annabeth up and tossed Sprig on my shoulder.

"Pam? You okay back there?" He looked over his shoulder. "She better be all right, *Bhean*, or I will seriously think about maybe not talking to you."

Annabeth was soaked from the tank and still wearing the hospital gown. "Annabeth, use your gown to breathe through. The moisture will help filter the smoke." She nodded, pulling up the bottom and covering her mouth, her arms trembling with weakness. Kate and I used our T-shirts, while Sprig used my sleeve.

It wasn't until my eyes landed on the elevator did I realize our problem.

"Shit!" No electricity. No elevator. And in the building's brittle state, I didn't really trust we could get to the top. We had no other choice since we were approximately eight stories down. "What do we do?" We couldn't climb through the vents. Each floor was separate. Plus, Rapava had made sure to block all paths leading outside.

Another blast shook the ground, and a loud whine of metal ripped across the building.

"I know another way." Kate grabbed my arm.

"Another way?"

"Rapava always had an additional escape route for himself." She waved us to follow her down another hallway. "He may be insane, but he's not stupid. He trusted only a few with this information."

"You?" I couldn't help the surprise in my voice.

"Oh gosh no." She curved around another corner, Annabeth and me on her tail. "He never trusted me. But he wasn't the only one who was sneaky and deceptive."

Another boom in the distance shifted the ground, dropping us all to the floor. The paneling above came raining down, burying us in debris. Sprig curled under me, my hands on the back of my neck as I protected both of us from the fragments. Warm liquid trickled from the back of my head to my neck and matted my hair. All I wanted to do was shut my eyes and fall asleep. Let all the pain go away.

I suddenly had images of the night the big fae storm brought Seattle to its knees. Even though he hated me then, Ryker had instinctively covered my body with his, taking the brunt. He had not known about the powers yet. He just reacted. And I was doing the same for Sprig. If I could have tucked Annabeth and Kate underneath me, I would have.

Even though I disliked him just as much at that time, that moment of protection had stuck with me. He had always been there for me. Protected me. These thoughts made me more frightened. What if I never made it out? What if he didn't?

No! Get up, Zoey! Find him. I gritted my teeth and sat up, letting the rubble fall off me.

"Sprig, you okay?"

"Define okay."

I kissed the top of his head and stood.

"Zoey." Annabeth's arm rose in the air only feet away from me. Wounds sliced across her face, legs, and arms, but she pushed up to her feet.

"Kate?"

The building continued to groan and grumble. We had little time left.

"Oh no." I saw white hair and an arm peeking through the remnants. "Kate?" I dug her out of the debris. Blood covered her face. "You can't die on me. None of you can. We are getting out of here. Absolutely no excuses," I barked, feeling emotion stabbing the back of my lids.

"Anyone tell you that you are *extremely persistent*?" she tried to joke, wiping the blood from her eyes.

"Yes," both Sprig and Annabeth answered.

"You can tell me what a bitch I am when we get out of here." I tugged her arm.

"Oh, child, I never said bitch."

"Can I?" Sprig raised his hand.

"I don't care what you call me." It took a couple of tries to get Kate back on her feet. "But only if we get out of here."

"Damn, these files came in handy." Kate readjusted them against her, securing them. "Only place I don't have any cuts."

Flickers of flames and smoke scorched the air from down the hall, as though the building was having a coughing fit, the walls heaving in on us as it rumbled. We all limped forward until Kate came to a stop.

"Here." She pushed at a partition.

"Here?" It looked like an ordinary wall.

"He wanted to be sure it remained a secret, but I followed him one day and watched him. He used it sometimes so he could get to other floors undetected. He definitely was a consequence of the Cold War with its secrecies, espionage, paranoia, and distrust."

"How do you open it?" I pressed my hands against the flat surface, trying to find a button or trigger.

"That I don't know."

My gut tightened. The twisting of metal braces screeched in my ears as the building vocalized its pain.

Kate's hands shook as she kept touching and pushing at the door.

"What about this?" Annabeth poked a bare toe at a small translucent button at the bottom edge. It was high enough no one would accidently kick it walking by and blended into the wall so you wouldn't notice if you weren't looking. She hit it with her big toe, and the door swung open to a narrow spiral staircase heading straight up.

"Holy honey turnips and banging biscuits. That was awesome, *Bebinn*." Sprig held out his hand to Annabeth. It took her a moment but then she slowly smiled and lifted her hand, high-fiving him back. Sprig, no matter how odd, was hard to resist. He crawled inside your heart and plastered himself there like he rolled in glue. Or honey...

I ushered Annabeth and Kate in, their feet hitting the metal, pinging underfoot as they circled their way up. I gazed up, the staircase disappearing into the darkness.

I took a step.

And crumpled.

Sprig clung to my neck as I crashed onto the steps.

"Zoey, what's wrong?" Kate stopped, her hand on her chest, peering down at me. I could barely see her, but the level had an emergency light, giving a dim awareness of space.

"The stairs," I choked, struggling to breathe or talk. "Goblin. Metal."

"Of course." Kate's lids fluttered and her head nodded. "That bastard would cover his ass."

I understood right away. Rapava would want to escape, but by chance fae had escaped, he would not want them to be able to follow him. They would be trapped and die, just how he preferred them.

My body felt like it was being torn apart and drained of blood. The stairs were more potent than anything I had felt before. I couldn't move. My eyes were slamming shut.

"Get up, Zoey!" Kate demanded, skirting Annabeth and coming for me. "You are not giving up now."

"I can't." No one but another fae could truly understand what goblin metal did to us. Sprig's head curled forward, falling into my lap, out cold. It was so potent it even took him out without touching it.

"Yes, you can. You are the strongest person I know." She came down, putting her shoulder under my arm. "Daniel used to tell me how in awe he was of you. I knew then he was crazy about you." I lifted my eyes to hers as she tried to get me on my feet.

"Really?"

"Yes, Zoey. He was deeply in love with you. I always told him he needed to get his head out of his ass and act on it, but he never did. Stupid man." She grunted trying to get me up. "He missed his chance. But I've seen your face when you talk about this Wanderer. He came here for you, got captured and tortured. He didn't let fear hold him back from loving you. He is the one you need to get up for, along with your sister, Sprig, Annabeth... me. We all need you. You are stronger than this. Now get up!"

"Talk... about... persistent," I forced out through my gritted jaw, grasping to pull myself up. It felt like standing with a mattress on my back.

A soft smile inched across Kate's. She turned to Annabeth. "Take Sprig."

Annabeth rushed down a few steps, taking Sprig from my arms, tucking him in safely against her. She turned back and started up the steps.

"I won't lie to you, Zoey. This is going to be horrible and painful. You have hundreds and hundreds of steps ahead of you. But we have no choice. I am old; Annabeth is weak. I need you to dig down and find the place in you that keeps you moving."

I nodded. I wanted to hold on to the rail to help pull myself up, but as soon as I touched it my legs caved, forcing me to crawl on my hands and knees. The agony felt excruciating. Even worse was I could feel the stone calling for me again. One touch and all of my pain and struggle would be gone. The metal and the stone yanked at my energy.

No. The word tore from my gut as I pulled myself up another step. *You will never have me. You lost, stone.*

I never lose. And I have never been deceived.

First time for everything. My words were strong, but I wasn't. The magnetic pulse drew me to it, and my will bent under the goblin metal. Then Ryker's voice echoed in my head, his image standing strong at the forefront of my mind, like the guardian keeping the stone at bay. I clung to him, his strength pushing me up the stairs.

Sweat poured down my face, my lip bloody from biting it. I cried and collapsed every other step, but I kept pushing. The thoughts of Lexie, Croygen, Annabeth, Kate, and Sprig all helped, but there was one face driving my legs, forcing me to take another step.

Ryker stood over me on the steps, staring down. *Get up. Push harder, human. You do not give up. You are a survivor.*

Oh hell. I was hallucinating now. And Ryker was channeling a boot-camp instructor.

"I'm trying…" I whimpered. My soul felt like it was being torn into pieces. I could barely push my knees up the steps.

Try harder. I will not let you give up. Do it for your sister. For Annabeth. Sprig… even the fucking pirate needs you. I need you. A pained expression came over his face. *No matter what happens. I'm always with you.*

"What are you talking about?" Cold dread plummeted into my stomach as my skin tingled with heat.

You know I will fight to the ends of the earth to get to you if I can…

My gut sensed the goodbye in his tone. The unsaid words. "Don't you dare say goodbye! You want me to fight? You fight too! Find me, Viking. Don't you dare leave me."

The image of Ryker faded away. *I love you, human. Always have. Even when I didn't know it.*

"Ryker!" I screamed.

"Zoey? Honey, stay with us." Kate's face was in front of mine, bending over me on the stairs. Ryker was gone. "You can do it. We're almost there."

She helped me continue up the narrow steps. Red faced and sweaty with blood still flowing from her head, she barely kept upright herself. My gaze wandered to Annabeth. She looked like a skeleton, so pale and sickly, her steps faltering, but she kept Sprig close to her chest.

I thought I was hallucinating again when Kate said, "We made it."

"What?"

"Come on, a few more steps." She grunted, stuffing her shoulder under me, trying to get me on my feet. We took the last steps together, pushing through a door, moving off the metal to concrete.

Relief flooded my body, and I almost burst into tears with happiness. I bent over, sucking in deeply. Several moments passed before I noticed the surroundings. We were in an underground corridor. I knew exactly where I was, having used this tunnel to escape DMG last time.

Annabeth stumbled toward me; her arms wrapped around the tiny furball.

"Hey, buddy." I scooped him up. He was awake, but I could see the metal had also drained his energy. His limbs hung limply. He nuzzled deeper into my arms.

Part of me was about to hand him back to Annabeth. The treasure he carried in his honey pack hummed against my skin. My teeth clenched, fighting back the siren song.

Annabeth's head fell forward on my shoulder. "I still can't believe you came for me."

"Of course I would." I rubbed her arm. It was so skinny and feeble, like the rest of her.

"Why?" She leaned back to see my face. "You barely know me."

"For one, I never break promises." Especially now. "Second, we may not have spent a lot of time together, but from the moment I met you, I knew you were family. And I fight for my family."

"And you're mine." Tears wiggled from her eyes, her irises gleaming with love. I kissed her forehead.

"Thank you, Zoey." Kate stepped up to us, her face contorted, like she struggled with her words. "I'm not sure I deserve it, but thank you for saving my life. For coming back for me."

"Of course you deserve it."

"I've done so much bad in my past. Lost my way."

"You found it again. Dunn told me everything. I know why you did it. And I am so grateful for the help you gave me here even when your daughter and granddaughter were at risk."

Kate's hand came up to my face. "They are my blood, but I always thought of you and Daniel like that too. He would have wanted me to protect you. And there was no way I wasn't going to do everything in my power to help you. He'd be so proud of you, Zoey."

A soft smile curved my mouth. "Daniel would be proud of both of us." I gave her a hug, trying not to squeeze Sprig, but clearly not doing a good job because he grunted and climbed underneath my tangled, bloodstained hair, hugging my neck. The stone thumped like a heartbeat against my ear, fury knocking into my skin. *Stay strong, Zoey.*

"Thank you, both of you." I wrapped my arms around Annabeth and Kate in a group hug, so happy we all survived and for everything they did down there. "We can talk later. I need to see if everyone else is all right."

Battle worn, the three of us hobbled for the exit to the street level. When I opened the door to the glow of morning light, a few tears escaped. The warm rays felt like a rebirth. A new beginning.

I did it. I ended Rapava. He was dead.

No. *We* all did it.

The thought of my loved ones moved me quicker out onto the street than I thought myself capable.

I expected to see fire engines and police cars, but there was nothing like that. A dusting of dead bodies scattered down the lane and around the building. The fight was over up here also, and the bodies on the ground declared the fae were the winners.

With the gunshots and screaming you'd think someone nearby would have heard and called the cops. But I could only hear the chirping of birds waking up and the groans of hurt people mulling around the space. Groups of fae dressed in gray scrubs along with some of Lars's men clumped around, healing themselves. There were a few men in lab coats sprawled dead on the ground, but not as many as I feared. I had expected a lot more mayhem with blood running into the gutters. It was probably painting the walls and floors inside, hidden behind the doors of the building. Those lives could be thought of later, my mind was on the people I cared about.

"Ryker? Croygen? Lexie?" I bellowed, scanning the crowd. Kate walked with Annabeth as I rushed forward.

"Ms. Daniels," a deep voice said, his voice a mix of velvet and death. My stomach locked, and I whirled around to face the Unseelie King. Sprig mumbled under his breath, inching deeper into my knotted hair.

Decked out in his suit, he appeared pristine and unbelievably handsome. Goran walked behind him as usual. His clothes and hair were at least rumpled as if he had been fighting. Lars probably sat in his car having a drink as he watched the battle like it was a TV show.

"You look like you've been through hell." Lars's yellow-green eyes drifted over me.

"You could say that."

"I am pleased you survived."

Most likely, he was only glad because of the stone.

"I believe you have something of mine?"

Goran took a step, a box in his hand. He lifted the lid, sticking it out.

"Sprig?" I nudged the figure strapped in fear to my neck. He took tentative steps out of my dirty, matted mane and crawled down my arm. He took off the backpack and opened the top, dumping it out over the box.

Pam and my underwear fell out along with the rock into the chest. Sprig squeaked, reaching back for Pam and the cape.

Goran quickly snapped the lid closed and drew it back.

"No!" Sprig cried, then turned to me, his eyes wide and full of sadness. "B-but... Pam? I just got her back."

Lars took a step forward, his face showing nothing, then looked at the box. He lifted the lid slowly, and his long fingers dipped into the case. They brushed the stone and his eyes turned black, his face sharpening. I felt a punch of power to my chest, my hand pulsing like a Bat-Signal.

The stone slammed pressure into my head, bending me over, flashing image after image of a bloodstained field. A battle. Earth burning. Crumbling. The walls between the Otherworld and Earth disintegrating. A beautiful woman with bright red hair and a cruel smile. A gorgeous, dark-haired girl with different-colored eyes. A tiny, pretty brunette holding a sword. Death, blood, screaming.

Holy shit.

Lars grunted, shoving his power back at it. My brain felt like it might pop. I cried out as another wave of magic collided against the other. Then it burst, like fireworks in my brain, splintering down my arm to my palm. The pressure and images seeped out of me like a bucket with a hole. I drew my hand to my chest, my gaze darting up to the King.

"It's angry with you." Lars licked his lips, his features returning to normal. "Very angry."

I continued to huff as if I had run a marathon, the vibrant images fading from memory.

"What?" He tilted his head.

"I-I... saw..." My mouth wouldn't work.

390

"What did you see?" His gaze intense, his voice almost demanding.

I tried several times before I waggled my head. "I don't know. War. I think." I straightened.

Lars watched me, his stare drilling into me before it drifted to the stuffed animal between his fingers. He lifted Pam slowly from the container with one hand. His eyebrow hitched as he picked up the underwear with the other hand. Damn. The King of the Dark was holding my underwear.

"I think this is yours." He placed Pam and the cape delicately in Sprig's hands, acting as if the strange moment with the stone never happened. "She is a lucky girl."

My jaw fell open. The Unseelie King just politely returned a stuffed goat and my undergarments to my sprite-monkey and acted like it was normal, treating Pam like she was real. *What. The. Hell?*

"Thank you." Sprig hugged his arms around Pam, looping the undies around his neck before running up to my shoulder.

Lars's intense gaze landed back on me. "I thank you, Zoey. You are an unbelievable young lady. Maybe our paths will cross again."

"Sorry, no offense, but I hope the fuck not." Stupid Zoey, why did I always have to open my mouth?

However, he just tipped his head back and started to laugh, which made me even more nervous. He shook his head. "You two really would get along. Be the undoing of every male who crossed your paths."

"Get along with who?"

He just smiled, giving Goran a nod. The man reacted instantly and moved to the car, the box in his hand. The farther the stone moved away, the more my legs itched to follow it. But I held my ground, letting its beckoning slide over my skin.

We are not done, it hissed in my head.

Yes, we are, I sent back, but my gut felt the doubt in my declaration. I pushed back the uncertainty and lifted my head. I could feel an easing in my chest the farther the stone went from me. *Go. Go... far away.*

Lars stood watching me intensely, like he saw and heard more than he let on. He cleared his throat. "I want to forewarn you."

"Warn me about what?"

His lips pinched. "There *is* a war coming. It's not fae against human, but it will be fae against fae. Light against the Dark."

"Why are you telling me this?"

"Because I admire you. You are strong, and I want you to be prepared. It is not if, but when, and nowhere will be safe."

"Then what can I do?"

"Be ready." He started to turn. "You think this was a fight. What's coming will make this seem like child's play."

I swallowed. *Hell.*

"The moment I leave, so will the glamour. I have a cleanup crew for the dead fae, but the human authority will get wind of this soon. I would get far away."

Ah. Lars was the reason no one had yet called the police. No outside human could see or hear anything out of the ordinary. Yet.

I peered down at Sprig, rubbing his head. When I looked up the King was gone, as was the bond he'd put on me. My soul felt fifty pounds lighter. "Fuck, he scares me."

"Like crapple."

"Yes, he definitely makes me crapple." I sucked in air.

And what really terrified me was I just handed one of the most powerful objects to the King of Darkness. A demon. Did

I doom the worlds, both the Otherworld and Earth? Was that what the stone was showing me? Would it be wise for anyone, especially someone as powerful as him, to hold a relic he could use to destroy and dominate everything in its path?

I swallowed back the sour taste in my mouth and shrugged to myself. *There's nothing I can do about it now.* I had to believe he had become King because he was smart, and that such a man would be too powerful to be controlled by a tiny rock.

"Zoey?"

I swung around.

Happiness exploded through my chest and I rushed instinctively toward the speaker, the Unseelie King all but forgotten.

"Croygen!" I almost knocked Sprig off my shoulder as I ran into his arms. He crushed me against his frame, a sigh bursting from his chest.

"You're all right." He breathed out in relief, kissing the top of my head.

"Ugh, you didn't get shanghaied or something?" Sprig exclaimed, making a face.

"You didn't fall into a rat trap?" Croygen squeezed me again then took a step back.

"Lexie?" I dropped my arms.

He nodded behind him, and I saw Kate hovering over Lexie's blanket-wrapped body. Annabeth stood close to both.

I was at Lexie's side before I could even blink, hugging her. Sprig leaped down next to her, cuddling close.

"Zoey." She reached for me.

A burst of happiness erupted from me in garbled words and tears.

"I think *Leanbh* needs some honey. She'll feel better then. It always helps me."

393

She smiled weakly and nuzzled into him, then her lids drifted closed. After all the battles we had fought, my little sister was *still* dying. Those legs were poisoning her system.

Kate grabbed my hand. "We will handle this. I know a surgeon who doesn't ask questions."

"Then do it. Whatever it takes." Lexie's only hope for survival was to remove the legs and probably a blood transfusion. The chance of her dying on the table was too high for me to think about, but her chance of dying without an operation was a hundred percent.

Kate nodded. "I will contact Dunn. He will get us there quickly."

I placed my hand on top of Kate's. "Thank you." I couldn't fix or fight for Lexie anymore; Kate was my only hope.

"You sure you're all right?" Croygen twisted me to face him, his attention going to my wrapped hand. "What happened?"

Before I could get a word out or pull my arms away, he unwrapped the cloth. The cool air stinging the tender wounds.

"Holy shit." He sucked through his teeth and took a step back, his eyes glued on my hand.

"What?" Trepidation strung like lights running across my shoulders.

"How did you get these?" His black eyes were wide as he looked at me.

I swallowed nervously. "The stone. It got really pissed at me."

"Do you know what they mean?"

I shook my head, my gaze going to the two etchings in my palm. The first one, still crusted by blood, reminded me of the symbol pi but the vertical lines were more like Js each facing out, the bar across lower and thicker with curved edges. The second looked like a lowercase cursive R with a curled end. I knew whatever they were, it was permanent. The scars too deep. The magic in it strong.

Croygen cupped my hand again, pointing at the top one. "This one is the symbol for remembrance, and the strength of stones." He moved to the one below. "This one means hatred or vengeance. Not good, Zoey. Especially together."

I bit down on my lip, pulling my hand back and covering it up again. "Well, there is nothing I can do about it now." My voice sounded clipped, pushing away this news. "Have you seen Ryker?"

It took Croygen a beat to pull his attention from my hand. "What? No. He was with you."

Dread tumbled into my stomach like an avalanche. "You haven't seen him? He hasn't come up?"

"No." He shook his head, worry flickering in his eyes. Despite their petty arguments and bickering, I knew if Ryker was really in trouble Croygen would be the first one to go after him. Okay, the second. He'd have to get past me first.

I moved before I could think, screaming his name. Then I remembered the vision of Ryker on the stairs. It hadn't been real, had it? My body felt weak with terror. If he were here, he would have found us already. He would have found *me*. Fear quickly rolled into terror, and I could barely breathe.

"Zoey, I've been watching, waiting for either one of you to come out." Croygen didn't have to say more. Ryker had never reached the surface.

"Did Liam come out?"

"No." Croygen replied. "If he had, I would have killed him myself. And any one of those hunters."

I couldn't stop searching or calling his name.

"He's not here, Zoey."

Nonononono. My brain and heart cried, propelling me toward the entrance of DMG. *I have to find him.*

395

"Zoey, stop!" Croygen yelled, clutching my arm. "You can't go back in there. It's too dangerous."

"I don't care! He's still in there, Croygen." I ripped from his hold, darting for the alleyway.

"Zoey..." Croygen's words were trampled by a boom so loud, my hands went to my ears, covering them. The explosions kept going off, like a cannon. The ground vibrated underfoot and knocked us to the ground.

I felt frozen, my gaze locked on the trembling structure in front of me.

"Zoey!" Croygen screamed.

The building crumpled, like a child kicking down blocks. Slabs of concrete tumbled and smashed into the street.

Arms came around me, pulling me back as the ground gave way. Dust billowed around the base, as if the DMG was built on clouds, pushing debris, smoke, and dirt in a wave over us. Then in a whoosh it slipped below the surface. Gone. The ground devoured it in a gulp. Croygen pressed me to the ground beneath him. The dust cloud rained pieces of the building down on us, clogging my lungs.

It was probably only seconds, but it felt like eternity. Then everything went silent.

Croygen lifted off me, and I sat up, staring at the empty lot through the haze.

"Nooooooooo!" I wailed, getting to my feet. Croygen didn't stop me as I ran, stumbling, and then falling to my knees close to the edge of the crater. A block-long hole sank deep into the earth, showing nothing remained. Another guttural scream tore out of me and shredded my throat.

Ryker had been five stories below. His axe was eight. He was hard to kill, but even he couldn't live through that explosion.

Croygen wordlessly came to my side, wrapping me in

his arms. If Ryker was in there, he would be staying there. My brain was blank of words, filled instead with a rushing agony, white-hot sound and pain like a million tiny buzzing insects trying to tear their way out of my chest and throat.

He rocked me back and forth, my body limp. My head spun, and I felt overcome with a fatigue so powerful I almost begged it to come, to take me away. I didn't even realize I had stopped crying or moving. I hunkered over my knees, making noises that didn't sound human.

Breathe in. Breathe out.

That even seemed like too much. I'd have to be strong for my two sisters. But in that moment I just wanted to join Ryker. I could not live without him.

"Please, Croygen," I whispered. "Tell me he isn't dead."

He held me tighter. "I'm sorry."

My throat burned as I screamed up at the morning sky. The sun mocked me. I needed night to swallow me up, carry me away forever. I collapsed forward over my knees.

Time was irrelevant, but I knew it was ticking by. Another moment I lived without him.

My mind latched on to his memory, feeling his touch, seeing his face. I could even hear him call for me. After a few seconds I heard my name again. My eyes opened. Did I imagine that?

"*Zoey?*" a distant voice screamed through the dense air.

My head popped up, looking over my shoulder.

I wasn't even sure if his voice existed only in my head, but I scrambled to my feet.

"Ryker?" My heart pounded in my chest, air struggling to move out of my lungs. "Ryker?" My throat was scraped raw by anguish. I circled around, scanning every inch of space.

From the burning ashes a hazy outline of a man appeared. Like a Norse god he strode out of the smoke, a glistening axe strapped to his back. His hair hung loose and covered one side of his face. His shirt and pants were shredded and his body, his gorgeous, chiseled physique was covered in red burn marks, weeping cuts, and flowering bruises. He locked on me and all at once I felt alive again.

"Ryker!" I ran. My boots hit the pavement as my heart soared. I flew into him, leaping into his arms. He crushed me in his embrace, a guttural sound rumbling from his chest.

"You're alive," he whispered, his voice breaking. He held me so tight I almost couldn't breathe, but I didn't care. He buried his head into my neck, his voice cracking. "You're all right. I-I thought I lost you."

I couldn't speak.

Hearing his voice, the legendary Wanderer, the feared Viking, terrified over losing me, my heart wanted to explode with emotion—with the love I felt for him.

He gripped my chin, his gaze searching my face with so much love. I didn't even know I was crying until his thumbs brushed the tears from underneath my eyes. A grin hooked the side of his mouth.

"Human."

"Viking."

Sirens wailed in the background, but I ignored them as I pulled his mouth to mine, telling him with my kiss everything I couldn't say in words.

He breathed me in, his hands tugging through my hair, bringing me closer. His mouth moved over mine intensely. Full of passion, love, and happiness.

I knew we would still have a lot of obstacles ahead of us. But with this man by my side, I could handle them all. There was nothing we wouldn't fight or challenge. We could barrel through anything, even if we had to lie, cheat, and steal. There wasn't anything I wouldn't do for him or my family.

This was the life I had always yearned for. This was the love I wanted.

A Viking, a monkey-sprite, a pirate, two teenage girls, and a kooky aunt.

Nope, Disney had nothing on me.

EPILOGUE
(5 Years Later)

The uneven planks of the porch slid beneath my bare feet, my steps lazy and heavy. I sighed deeply, inhaling the thick air. You could feel a touch of chilliness as the season shifted to fall. Suddenly, I missed Seattle. The knowledge that I could be there any time to check on things eased the homesickness as the leaves turned.

The sun dipped halfway behind the mountain and ignited the hills and rooftops in unbelievable reds, purples, and deep blues. This was home too.

I split my time between the Pacific Northwest and Peru, sometimes in the same day. For practical reasons to be close to the children's shelter, we lived close to Lima in a pretty village called Barranco. I also jumped to Machu Picchu to hike quite often. That place would always hold a special place in my heart.

I rubbed my arms, feeling the scarred symbols rub against my skin on my arm. The stone's mark. Everyone knew how I got them, but no one knew sometimes I still felt them throb. It was as if the stone was taunting me, telling me I would never be too far from its reach. The scars it left on me went more than skin deep. My hands trembled from time to time, the restless feeling itching my soul, reminding me of the days of being an addict were never far behind me. The weeks after handing it over to Lars had been tough. Withdrawal had been even worse than death. Lots of late nights with Ryker holding me in the shower as I vomited and cried. I never wanted to go back to that again. But deep down, I felt it. It owned me and someday it would come for me. Seeking its revenge.

"Zoey?" My name rang out from inside the two-story villa, causing me to jump.

"I'm outside," I called back.

Movement followed my words. "We're back from the beach." Lexie stuck her head out of the open sliding glass door.

I swiveled around to see my eighteen-year-old sister standing before me. Her wavy black hair had grown down her back. She wore a bikini top and white, flowing cotton pants. She had matured into an extremely smart and stunning woman.

"You girls heading over to Casa de la Miel?"

Lexie took a step out, walking smoothly over to me. It had taken a few years after the operation that removed her false legs for her to heal, but she had been on her prosthetic legs for more than two years now and was adapting well to them. We almost lost her on the operating table, but the girl was a fighter. She made it through.

"Yeah, Annabeth is just grabbing us something to eat. We're going to change and then head there."

The moment the words left Lexie's mouth, Annabeth yelled from the kitchen. "Sprig, get out of there! And stop double-dipping. Licking your fingers doesn't count as them being clean."

"He will never learn." Lexie chuckled.

"Oh, he knows. He just gives us those eyes, and we let it go."

"Yeah, not hard to see who rules this house." Lexie nudged me, throwing her arm around my shoulder. She had grown taller than me, especially with her prosthetics. She goaded me about it every chance she got.

"Zoey?" Annabeth came to the door. "Sprig is now curled up in the honey peanut butter jar. Asleep."

I snorted.

"I'm not eating that." Annabeth's nose scrunched up. "Full of monkey hair now."

"There's another one in the pantry," I told Annabeth. She nodded and disappeared back into the house. Her colorful swimsuit cover flittered after her.

After the battle with DMG, Annabeth chose to come live with us instead of her maternal grandparents. I forced her to at least contact them and let them know she was alive and all right. They didn't try to fight for custody rights, and I was grateful.

Annabeth and Lexie bonded immediately. You couldn't separate the two. They looked nothing alike but identified as sisters, through and through. The first couple years after Rapava's fall, we lived in Seattle during the school year and in Peru the rest of the time. Travel was easy enough.

Annabeth had graduated and wanted to stay in Peru more. She woke up many nights with either nightmares of being trapped underwater, drowning, or being held down by a faceless figure. At fourteen her innocence had been ripped from her in the most disgusting way when she was forced to do things no one should ever have to. It became mandatory for her to see a counselor. But because of what happened to her, Annabeth liked to stay close to us.

"I'll go get Sprig." Lexie leaned over and kissed my head. "You want a sandwich?"

I wrinkled my nose. "No. I'm good."

402

"Come on, it could be tasty," she teased, stepping back across the porch. "You know he farts in his sleep."

"Ah, come on. Like I'm not nauseated enough," I yelled after her.

She giggled evilly all the way back in the house.

I twisted back around with a smile, watching the last bit of the sun dip below the horizon. Magic danced in the air, thick and unnaturally bright over the forested mountains.

Lars's warning had come true.

Two years earlier the realm between Earth and the Otherworld collapsed, forcing the two worlds to mix. A lot of things did not survive. Human technology and Earth's infrastructure were pretty much destroyed, but rebuilding with new materials got better every day. It was like we were back in the Industrial Age again, building and exploring new ideas. This time we were starting fresh and more environmentally healthy.

Dr. Rapava had always been afraid of a war between humans and fae. In a way his fear came true. But like the Unseelie King had warned me, it had been a fight between Light and Dark fae. Humans got caught in the middle, but the casualties were as devastating as Rapava had predicted. The Seelie Queen broke the barrier between the worlds. Now the deep secret of the fae became known to all. And the human world still wasn't handling it well. The new Seelie Queen, the first Druid to ever reign, was doing her best with the help of Lars, trying to put our worlds back and bring our two species together. But centuries of tradition and fear would not go away overnight. If ever.

"Sprig! Get down off the fan, or I'll turn it on. You threw up last time, remember?" Lexie's voice sailed out to me on the deck. I smiled.

Then I felt a change in the atmosphere. Energy sparking. Someone came up behind me.

"That smile better be for me," a deep voice growled in my ear.

"No." I whirled around, throwing my arms around the man behind me. "But you could make it be."

It had been six months before both of our jumping abilities even partially returned and about a year before we could completely control them again. Never a day went by that I wasn't thankful for being fae, for having these powers, and for this man in my life.

Ryker's hand slid up along my jawbone, tilting my head to his. His mouth pressed to mine, his lips devouring mine. I opened my mouth to deepen the kiss. His fingers dug into my hips as he lifted me up, my legs wrapping around his torso. One arm skimmed my back, the other crushed my head into his.

After five years, he still set fire to my veins. I never seemed to get enough of him.

His kiss turned hungrier. Our breaths caught.

"The girls are in the kitchen," I mumbled against his mouth. "But the moment they walk out that door...?" I lifted my eyebrows.

"We lock a monkey-sprite in the bathroom?"

"Exactly." I smiled.

"The hammock or the Chevelle in the garage?"

"Both." I grinned mischievously.

For my last birthday he surprised me with a Chevy Chevelle. To everyone else it looked like an old classic car, to me it represented our union, changed by the night we both confessed we were in love with each other. Not surprising, we spent more time on the hood or in the back than we did driving it.

"I like the way you think." He kissed me again, his tongue slipping past my lips. I groaned and squeezed my legs tighter around him, desire invigorating my skin.

"If you don't stop, everyone in this house is about to get an incredibly kinky view of my ass." He brushed his lips over my ear and nipped.

"Like that would be a first." I pulled his mouth back to mine. He crushed his hand into the back of my head, inhaling me. I was past caring who was around. But he pulled away, setting me back down on my feet.

"Did you get the stuff?" I sighed.

He tilted his head in a *what do you think?* expression. "I already distributed it around to the clinics and left some for us at Casa de la Miel."

"Thank you. Wish I could have gone with you."

"No. Way too dangerous."

I pouted, but I knew he was right. At least for now. I had to admit I started counting down the days till I could join him again.

Ryker and I would never be nine-to-fivers or be typical in any way. Some might think it wrong, but robbing from the corrupt drug cartel to give back to the clinics, orphanages, and less fortunate felt right. We were thieves. And we were damn good at it.

Since the collapse of Earth and the opening of the Otherworld, a lot of fae got in on drug trafficking. Illegal drugs would never go away, and people took advantage of the weak state of the world. Ryker and I took from those.

That was just one of our businesses. The other was in Seattle. Lars helped Kate and me establish a new form of DMG, what DMG first started out to be. He bankrolled it and offered his ideas on what he wanted us to accomplish, but otherwise left it to Kate and me to run. She was the lead scientist with a ton of researchers under her. I was more the face of it, and the ideas person. I jumped to Seattle all the time to collaborate on new research projects. We were still trying to help find a cure for cancer and a variety of disabilities, but without the killing, kidnapping, and torture.

When not with Kate or pilfering with Ryker, I tried to create a new format for orphanages and foster care. There was an even greater need for help with children whose parents died in the fae war. Hence Casa de la Miel—Honey House. Wild guess on who named it. It was still new, but Lima became my test case, a place for orphaned kids with and without special requirements who needed homes. We wanted to get them a better education and medical coverage while providing a place where they felt loved and wanted. This was all funded by the money Daniel left me. It was exactly how he would want me to use it. I hoped someday my new format would take off and start moving around the world.

"Why is the bottle of rum empty?" a man's voice bellowed from the doorway, his footsteps on the deck treading on the wood.

I glanced past Ryker.

A tall, dark, sexy pirate stood there with an empty bottle in his hand, waving it around.

"Because you finished it last night and just don't remember." I raised an eyebrow.

"Oh. Right." Croygen nodded. "Never mind. Is there another one somewhere?"

"There's beer in the fridge," Ryker mumbled, though he kept his hands cupped to my face, lightly kissing my jawline.

Croygen snarled. "Beer?"

"Yes." Ryker straightened and glanced over his shoulder. "You will have to suffer unless you want to get your lazy ass in the jeep and go get more. How about you do that and take it back to your own house?"

"I don't have a house."

"I know." Ryker sighed, turning back to me.

"I have a ship."

"Which you're never on."

"The bed is comfier here," Croygen grumbled, then made his signature cocky smile. "I'm starting to think you don't want me to live here anymore. Nah, that can't be true. I know you love having me here."

Ryker growled, while I grinned. Croygen was right. I did want him here. The house was big enough, and I loved it filled with people. Not just people, my family. I sometimes would tear up when heading down the stairs in the morning, hearing them laugh, bicker, and talk together. Truly a dream come true.

"Here you go." Lexie popped around Croygen, holding a sandwich on a paper plate for him. She had changed out of her bathing suit to a tank top, pants, and zip-up hoodie.

"Thanks, little shark." He took it, smiling at her.

"I'm not *little* anymore."

His gaze roamed over her striking features. "Don't I know it," he mumbled and turned his attention to the sandwich.

A soft blush covered her cheeks before she turned to Ryker. "You want one? Annabeth is making a whole bunch to take down to the shelter."

"I'm good. Thanks," Ryker said to her, but his eyes were on Croygen. She disappeared back in the house.

Croygen's gaze followed her.

"No." I shook my head. "Absolutely not."

"What?" Croygen's head snapped back to me.

"You know what," Ryker growled. "If you even think about touching her, I will kill you."

"Me too." I nodded.

Croygen's eyes widened. "Oh come on, give me more credit than that. She's a kid."

407

But she wasn't anymore, and he had noticed. We all had. Lexie's crush on him had grown over the years, even though he always treated her like a little sister. Lately that seemed to be shifting, his gaze lingering a little longer, his teasing a little flirtier. He almost seemed nervous around her. If I hadn't witnessed it, I would have thought it a tall tale, but Croygen seemed smitten. In her presence he was kind, sweet, patient. His eyes focused only on her when she spoke. And Lexie was growing stronger, more relaxed, and confident in herself. I could see their connection. They laughed a lot, and in my gut, I felt it was inevitable. There seemed to be something between them you couldn't explain.

Croygen had changed. He helped Ryker and me with our "business" and took side jobs every once in a while, but mostly he hung out with us, living in the house. He wasn't a saint, but he no longer seduced every woman who walked by.

"*Bhean!*" Sprig tore around Croygen, a black pair of underwear trailing behind. He clambered up my leg to my shoulder, adjusting his "cape." "*Bebinn* is not letting me have any more honey."

"You've had half a bottle." A head of long, wavy blonde hair stuck out the door, defending herself. Her beauty was almost unearthly. She could easily be mistaken for a fairy. We'd celebrated Annabeth's twentieth birthday the month before. She helped me at Casa de la Miel full-time. She had found her calling helping displaced children. Annabeth wanted nothing more than to stay at Honey House with me, while Lexie had a restless spirit. She was ready to go out into the world and explore it.

"Sprig, you know you can only have one," I chided him.

He huffed, folding his arms.

"Such a tight ass, huh?" Ryker said to Sprig, patting my behind.

"Seriously." They high-fived each other behind my back. "Especially lately."

"Don't encourage him. You know what happens when he overdoses." My lids narrowed on the Viking. "I'm always going to be the bad parent, aren't I?"

"Yep." Ryker winked and chuckled.

"Zoey?" Lexie joined the group on the porch, with our Border collie, Matty, following her out. Yes, Sprig named him too. "Kate just sent a message marked urgent." Phones and computers were victims of the collapse. The Unseelie King had started a new system for both, much higher tech.

"Urgent?"

"Yes... very urgent." A smile broke over Lexie's mouth. "She wants to know what date you decided on for the shower."

I groaned, my hands automatically going to my tiny protruding belly. "I told her I didn't want one."

"You know how well she listens." Lexie grinned playfully, giving Matty the crust of her sandwich. He gobbled it up in one bite, his eyes on her till he realized she didn't have anything else, then he wandered over to me. I rubbed his head and behind his ears. He was a family dog, but Matty mostly followed me around. He must have sensed the change within me because in the last few months he rarely left my side.

"I'm barely four months and she wants to start planning all these things." I leaned my head into Ryker's arm. "Why couldn't that have been one of the customs that disappeared?"

"Sucks to be you." He wrapped one arm around me, kissing the top of my head. One hand rubbed my belly.

"I don't care. Tell her she can pick one." I shrugged.

"Okay." Lexie turned to head back in, motioning to Annabeth. "We're going to take off. Be back after the kids go to sleep."

Annabeth waved to us. "See you later. Love you." She never left the house without telling us that.

"Love you too," I said back. "Check the stock Ryker just left, will you?"

"Sure thing." She waved and disappeared into the house.

"I'll go with you guys." Croygen abruptly rounded after the girls. "I have to head into town anyway."

"Rum?" Lexie glanced over her shoulder at him, a playful smile etching her mouth.

He nodded.

"You're such a cliché," she teased.

"Cliché?"

"A pirate drinking rum? Come on." They walked deeper into the house.

"Tradesman! I am a tradesman," Croygen's voice exclaimed.

"Sure, Hook," Lexie replied. The front door slammed.

"Is there any way we can stop that?" Ryker turned to me.

"I don't think so." I pressed my body into Ryker's. "The more you try to keep people apart, the more determined they are to be together."

He grinned, bending over to kiss me.

"You know what I was just thinking?" Sprig piped up from my shoulder.

"No," Ryker replied, his mouth still on mine.

Sprig ignored him. "When the mini *Bhean* gets here, it will get to taste your honey tits."

"Sprig," I warned.

"Sweet nectar boobs."

"Please, stop." Ryker cringed.

"Honey udders!"

"Go. Now." I grabbed him from my shoulder and placed him on the ground.

"Come on, Matty!" He clambered up on the dog's back. "Let's storm the castle." He patted the dog's head. Matty knew this game and liked it since it usually resulted in treats. "Castle" meant the pantry. "But first let's go pick up Pam. She'll be pissed if I forget her in our adventure."

Matty barked, taking off for inside the house. "Eye-Eye Matty!" Sprig grabbed his collar, bounding off, underwear cape billowing behind him.

I lived in a circus.

And I loved it.

Sprig was just out of sight before Ryker's mouth came down on mine, his hands in my hair, tugging me into him.

I pulled his shirt over his head, exposing his unbelievable torso. He followed suit and ripped my tank top over my head. He went down on his knees, his lips brushing my bare stomach. His hands caressed the slight bump. The love I saw in his face for his unborn child was mindboggling. I knew how much this meant to him.

He gave my belly another kiss before he glanced up with a mischievous smile. "I guess while I'm down here..." His fingers wrapped around the sides of my pants and underwear, slowly tugging them off. The evening air hit my skin at the same time as his warm mouth did and my knees began to buckle. He pushed me against the deck railing, giving me something to lean against.

I moaned, arching my back. The sky was now dotted with a few stars, the deep purples bathing us in a hazy glow. My nails dug into the wood as Ryker nipped my thigh. I ran my fingers through his soft hair, pulling him closer. I felt so lucky.

He was mine. This house was mine and the people in it. I had a family. A growing one. And I fulfilled Daniel's wish. I brought DMG down and rebuilt it. I think he would be happy for me.

411

Everything I dreamed of came true.

The journey had been messy, heartbreaking, bloody, and scary. But it also had been magical, wonderful, and exciting. Wasn't that what life was about? Finding your place in the world wasn't always going to be easy. But once you found it, you fought for it, with everything you had.

My place was always meant to be here. With Ryker.

I had once been a seer, a Collector, a hunter.

That girl died the night of the fae storm.

And from burning ashes, I rose again.

A fighter. A thief. A human. A fae. A survivor.

But I only needed one definition.

Zoey.

A girl who found home.

Want to find out about my next book? Sign up on my website and keep updated on the latest news.
www.staceymariebrown.com

THE DARKNESS AND COLLECTOR SERIES DON'T STOP HERE!

THE SAGA CONTINUES ON IN THE LIGHTNESS SERIES!!

Kennedy and Lars are up next!
They will tell their tales next before all three series collide!

The Crown of Light
Lightness Series #1

A war is brewing.

Kennedy is one of the last known Druids. Wanted dead by the Seelie Queen and as a coveted asset to defeat this cruel ruler, Kennedy has become a mark. Especially by a sexy, merciless Dark Dweller, Lorcan Dragen.

Kidnapped and taken prisoner, Kennedy's life takes a dramatic turn, down a path she never imagined. Spending time with a man who killed her best friend's mother and her friend, she knows he is not someone she should care about. But the longer she spends with her enemy, the more her feelings blur the line between what is right and wrong, what is true and what is not.

As her magic grows, so does the shy, nerdy girl, and she soon realizes nothing on a list or in a book will prepare her for what is ahead.

Even her own feelings.

ACKNOWLEDGMENTS

I am so lucky for the people I have helping me stay strapped in on this crazy rollercoaster!

A special thanks to:

Rachel at Mark My Words P.R., I have no idea how I ever did without you! Thank you for everything you do. Especially when I'm being that crazy neurotic writer!

Jordan, your developmental help and editing are crucial to me. You constantly push me to be a better writer while giving me such encouraging positive notes. Thank you. http://jordanrosenfeld.net/

Hollie "the editor", thank you for your endless support and love. So glad I can call you my friend! http://www.hollietheeditor.com/.

Judi at http://www.formatting4u.com/ As usual you have made the anxiety of getting my books out on time so much easier.

As always to Mom. There'd be no books without you!

To all the readers who have supported me. My gratitude is for all you do and how much you help indie authors out of the pure love of reading.

To all the indie/hybrid authors out there who inspire, challenge, support, and push me to be better. I love you!

And to anyone who has picked up an indie book and given an unknown author a chance. THANK YOU!

ABOUT THE AUTHOR

Stacey Marie Brown works by day as an Interior/Set Designer and by night a writer of paranormal fantasy, adventure, and literary fiction. She grew up in Northern California, where she ran around on her family's farm raising animals, riding horses, playing flashlight tag, and turning hay bales into cool forts.

Even before she could write, she was creating stories and making up intricate fantasies. Writing came as easy as breathing. She later turned that passion into acting, living and traveling abroad, and designing.

Though she had never stopped writing, moving back to San Francisco seemed to have brought it back to the forefront and this time it would not be ignored.

When she's not writing, she's out hiking, spending time with friends, traveling, listening to music, or designing.

To learn more about Stacey or her books, visit her at:

Author website & Newsletter:
www.staceymariebrown.com

Facebook Author page:
www.facebook.com/SMBauthorpage

Pinterest: www.pinterest.com/s.mariebrown

Instagram: www.instagram.com/staceymariebrown/

TikTok: www.tiktok.com/@staceymariebrown

Amazon page:
www.amazon.com/Stacey-Marie-Brown/e/B00BFWHB9U

Goodreads:
www.goodreads.com/author/show/6938728.Stacey_Marie_
Brown

Her Facebook group:
www.facebook.com/groups/1648368945376239/

Bookbub:
www.bookbub.com/authors/stacey-marie-brown

CPSIA information can be obtained
at www.ICGtesting.com
Printed in the USA
BVHW090537030123
655382BV00013B/750